THE
LYING
MAN

ALSO BY ANDY MASLEN

Other Fiction:

Blood Loss – A Vampire Story

Purity Kills

You're Always With Me

Green-Eyed Mobster

THE LYING MAN

A DETECTIVE KAT BALLANTYNE THRILLER

ANDY MASLEN

Text copyright © 2025 by Andy Maslen
All rights reserved.

Published by Thomas & Mercer, Seattle

www.apub.com

Amazon, the Amazon logo, and Thomas & Mercer are trademarks of Amazon.com, Inc., or its affiliates.

EU Product Safety contact:
Amazon Publishing, Amazon Media EU S.à r.l.
38, avenue John F. Kennedy, L-1855 Luxembourg
amazonpublishing-gpsr@amazon.com

ISBN-13: 9781662530623
eISBN: 9781662530630

Cover photography and design by Dominic Forbes

Printed in the United States of America

This one is for Merlin.

'The more laws, the less justice.'

Marcus Tullius Cicero

Welcome to Middlehampton for the tenth annual *Criminal Herts* crime-writing festival. 'Where writing crime is murder.'

Dear Crime Fiction Fan,

Once again, Middlehampton plays host to this fabulous community of writers, readers and publishers of crime fiction. Criminal Herts *is always a special time, but this year we have something extra-special to celebrate.*

This is our tenth consecutive year (barring a certain worldwide event in 2020 we won't mention, ever!) of celebrating all that is brilliant, bloody, perplexing, intriguing, terrifying, chilling and, yes, funny in the best of contemporary crime-writing.

Whether you love to cuddle up with a cosy mystery or scare yourself silly with a serial-killer chiller, you'll find plenty to keep you entertained as we enjoy another fantastic weekend of discussion, debate, readings, panels and social events, from meet-the-author lunches to our perennial favourite, Killer Karaoke. And to round things off on Saturday night, come and dance the night away with our celebrity-author band, Blunt Force Trauma, fronted by the doyenne of darkness, Viv McDonald.

As always, we have convened a stellar line-up of crime-writing talent, from dazzling debut authors like M. J. Grahame to blood-soaked superstars like Mark Swift.

So polish your magnifying glass, strap on your tac-vest, fire up the Quattro and let's do this!

My very best,

Maria Sheriff, Festival Director

DAY ONE – FRIDAY

Chapter One

Kat Ballantyne's stomach clutched as she thought, for the hundredth time that morning, of her comatose bagman's pale face. Eyes closed, mouth slack.

She'd been visiting him in hospital almost daily since they'd both been attacked by a murder suspect. An attack engineered by her corrupt boss, DI Stuart 'Carve-up' Carver. With each trip to Tom's bedside, her hatred of Carver burned deeper, along with her determination to bring him down.

Ivan, her husband, was worried about her. With good reason, she knew. With no active cases occupying her, he'd persuaded Kat, on her precious day off – a Friday at that – to come to an event at Middlehampton's annual crime-writing festival, *Criminal Herts*. 'It'll take your mind off everything, love,' he'd said.

She'd agreed, even though it was Van who loved crime fiction. Her first choice would have been a spa day with a couple of girlfriends from netball. Or maybe a lie-in and a long lunch in a nice country pub.

They were sitting in the ballroom of the Guildhall, a rambling Tudor building on the edge of the Old Town. Contributing their own body heat to the already humid atmosphere this sweltering July day were several hundred other people. All waiting to see celebrity author Mark Swift interviewed live onstage.

To Kat's left a woman was fingering a miniature bloodstained carving knife that dangled from her earlobe. She leaned over and murmured to Kat, 'Mark's just amazing, isn't he? I mean, how he dreams up all those disgusting ways of killing people – well, it makes your blood run cold, doesn't it?'

Kat smiled thinly. 'My husband's the fan. I don't really like reading about murder.'

The woman nodded sagely. 'Well, it's not for everyone, is it, dear? You need a strong stomach.' She leaned around Kat – so that Kat's left elbow was sandwiched between her ribs and the woman's bust – and addressed Ivan. 'Which is your favourite of Mark's books?'

Van's eyes lit up. 'Easy! *The Guillotine Man*. I've brought a copy for him to sign.'

Kat had to lean right back in her chair as the two fans swapped notes on the famous author's elaborate MOs. At least it took some of the pressure off her belly. She was feeling a bit fat this week, same as every month. Normally she'd wear a looser pair of jeans, but these were her best ones and she liked how they showed off her bum. As always, Van had noticed, and she'd wondered whether they could fit in a nice little afternoon shag before Riley got home from school. It would be a welcome distraction from everything else going on in her life, like a reset switch, even just for an hour or so.

Her phone buzzed. She checked the screen. Liv. She declined the call. She'd call her bestie back later.

Onstage, the interviewer, a culture critic from Radio 4, looked over the audience's heads towards the back of the hall. Kat craned her neck, as far as her neighbour's insistent pressure would allow, but could see nothing bar an abundance of expectant faces, or the tops of heads as their owners checked phones or the event programme.

Behind her, a woman muttered into her neighbour's ear, 'Bloody man! If it was *me* up there, talking about *my* latest book? I'd have the decency to show up on time.'

'Yeah, but you're just plain old D.A. Cartwright, aren't you?' the other woman said, rolling her eyes. 'He's the great Mark Swift. Wanker.'

The first woman snorted. 'I heard he ripped off the plot for his last book from an old episode of *Columbo*.'

'Really? It was so clunky, I wondered whether he'd used ChatGPT to write it.'

'No way. It would have been much better if he'd used AI.'

'It's just so annoying how much money he makes when his books are so bloody bad.'

'Maybe he's had a heart attack.'

'We can always hope,' her friend responded, earning a salty laugh.

The woman next to Kat turned in her seat and shushed them loudly. If looks could kill, Kat thought, she'd be investigating two murders.

Kat checked her watch – 10.56 a.m. The interview was billed for an 11.00 a.m. start. Surely Swift should be onstage by now? As it was, the battered green leather club chair remained empty.

'Mark always likes to make an entrance,' her neighbour confided. 'I saw him at Harrogate last year. Five minutes late and carrying an actual chainsaw. Not going, obviously. I'm sure there are health and safety rules about that sort of thing. But anyway, you can imagine the scene. *Quite* the furore.'

Kat nodded, starting to regret acceding to Van's wishes. Still, the interview would be over by midday and then maybe they could get that pub lunch in.

The interviewer looked offstage and tapped his watch, eyebrows raised.

At the back of the room, a door banged loudly as it was thrown open.

The woman next to Kat sighed contentedly. 'Here we go.'

Heads swivelled. A few people gasped. Kat twisted round in her chair.

Standing at the back, her face pale, a woman in her early twenties held aloft her bloody arm, her index finger extended.

Her voice, high-pitched, tremulous, pierced the expectant buzz. 'He's dead! Mark Swift is dead!'

Chapter Two

The first laugh came after a brief silence.

'Typical Swift,' a man brayed, to approving chuckles.

Others joined in. Soon, the ballroom was ringing with laughter and applause as if Swift had pulled off the comedy stunt of the century.

Kat looked at the interviewer, wondering whether she should do something. But he seemed completely relaxed. He leaned back in his chair and put his hands behind his head, joining in with a gruff laugh picked up clearly by his lapel mic.

Kat's neighbour nodded approvingly. 'Didn't I tell you? He'll probably stagger in from the wings covered in fake blood – just you wait and see.'

But Kat's cop whiskers were twitching. The young woman at the back wasn't laughing. She wasn't even grinning. Her face was a mask of horror, lips drawn back from her teeth as if someone had just tasered her. Her arm remained outflung as if she were a scarecrow.

Kat got to her feet. She bent down and whispered to Van, 'Something's up. I'll be right back.'

He nodded tightly as she crab-walked along the row then hurried down the central aisle to the back of the hall.

Worst case, she was making a fool of herself and the famous author would duly appear – probably as she was trying to seal off the scene – patting the air for silence and smiling good-naturedly. She'd have to apologise as she shuffled back along row F to rejoin Van.

Best case?

Except, 'best' didn't really cut it, then, did it? Because 'best' meant the man genuinely was dead.

Kat reached the back of the room seconds later. The young woman turned to her and lowered her arm. Blood was dripping from a long, shallow cut on the underside of her forearm. Messy, but nowhere near life-threatening. It looked a lot like a defensive wound. Kat leaned over to an elderly man with a white handkerchief in his breast pocket.

'Excuse me, could I borrow that, please? This young lady's got a nasty cut on her arm.'

He plucked the snowy square free and handed it to Kat. She shook it out, folded it into a narrow strip and wound it round the woman's upper arm.

At five foot five, Kat wasn't tall, but the young woman trembling in front of her made her feel like a giant. Even in her thick-soled white sneakers, she couldn't have been more than five foot one or two. Her diminutive stature coupled with her make-up-free face gave her a childlike appearance.

'Can you keep pressure on that for me, lovely? Now, tell me again. What's happened? Is this a publicity stunt?'

Wide-eyed, the young woman shook her head so violently that a biro poked into the messy bun at the back of her head flew free.

'No! Why won't you believe me? H-he . . . He's dead! I told you. I just told you!'

She was close to panic, hyperventilating and trembling so violently Kat was afraid she might faint. If this *was* an act, it seemed she'd gone straight down a very deep rabbit hole.

'OK, let's slow it down. What's your name?'

'It's Bella. Bella Gabbard. I'm a volunteer. I'm only supposed to liaise with the authors.'

'Right, Bella. I'm Kat. I'm a detective with Middlehampton Police. Let's get this sorted, and then they can get on with the event.'

'But they can't, can they? Because he's *dead.* You're not *listening* to me. Nobody *ever* listens to me.'

Kat looked around. Some audience members were standing, filming the whole thing on their phones. Others were deep in conversation, heads bowed towards their neighbours. A few faces betrayed what looked to Kat like genuine concern. She needed to nip this in the bud quickly, or at the very least they might have some sort of public order issue.

'I am listening, Bella,' she said. 'I promise. Can you start at the beginning and tell me exactly what happened?'

Bella took a deep, shuddering breath. Kat was pleased to see her shaking had quieted, even if her chest hitched every couple of seconds.

'I was checking where Mark Swift was, because Maria said he ought to be onstage by now, and when I went to the green room, the door was locked. I don't have a key and I couldn't find the caretaker, so I went out through the kitchens and round the back. There's a window that looks out on to a passage down the side of the building. I stood on an old flowerpot. It was empty so I turned it upside down. And that's when I saw him.'

'Mark Swift?'

'Yes.'

'Describe what you saw for me.'

Bella nodded. 'He was lying on his back. Not moving. I smashed the window and climbed in to check. And you know, he was dead. Then I rushed back here.'

'Did you climb back out the window? Is that how you cut your arm?'

'Yes.'

Kat's cop brain kicked into high gear. She was too experienced to take a member of the public's word for it that someone was dead. But she had at the very least a medical emergency on her hands.

The noise level in the ballroom had grown steadily during her brief conversation with Bella. Nobody was laughing anymore. On their faces were a mixture of expressions, from worry to irritation. Kat's stomach clenched as she realised what she needed to do.

She ran down the aisle and leapt up on to the stage. Bending close to the BBC journalist, who was shifting in his chair and gesturing at someone in the wings, she pointed to his lapel mic.

'I need to use that.'

He unclipped it and stood as she turned away from him.

'Wait! The cable's threaded down my shirt.'

He fiddled with his shirt buttons, eventually disentangling himself from the snaking black wire. As he did so, Kat found Van in the crowd. He was looking at her and mouthing, 'You OK?'

She gave him a quick nod. Wished it were true, given the sudden appearance of roughly a million butterflies in her stomach. Kat brought the little foam-covered mic up to her lips.

'Ladies and gentlemen, can I have your attention please? Please take your seats.'

The room stilled. Those standing, sat. Those sitting ceased their conversations. Five hundred pairs of eyes were trained on her. Her stomach flittered and squirmed, and she felt light-headed.

'I am Detective Sergeant Kathryn Ballantyne. I'm afraid Mark Swift has been taken ill in the green room and I'm going to check on him. Please remain seated and be patient. Thank you.'

A swell of muttering and a couple of shouted heckles rippled around the room. Behind her the culture critic tapped her on the shoulder. She turned.

'Tell them I'll take some questions about my show. It's called *Reserved Seats*.'

Kat nodded then turned back to the audience.

'Ladies and gentlemen. I've just been told by—'

Her phone buzzed against her hip, distracting her. Her mind went blank. She couldn't remember the guy's name, even though Van had been going on about his show before the ruckus began.

'Dev Sridhar,' he murmured, just loud enough for Kat to hear.

'Yes, Dev Sridhar is going to take questions for you about his show, *Reserved Seats*, and the amazing guests he's interviewed.'

She handed the mic back. 'Thanks, you're a star. I have to go.'

As Dev stumbled through an introduction, Kat ran the length of the aisle, drawing curious stares. She reached Bella, who was clutching the bloody handkerchief to her arm and looking paler than before.

'Show me,' Kat said. 'And are you going to be all right? Not feeling faint?'

'I'm fine. It's this way.'

Waving away a lanyard-wearing steward, Kat followed Bella out of the ballroom. A plate of chocolate cookies sat atop the reception desk, which was draped in a sheet daubed with crimson handprints. Kat grabbed one and handed it to Bella.

'Here. Try and eat this. It'll give your blood sugar a boost.'

Relieved that the young volunteer, at least, wasn't going to die on her, Kat ran after her. Out of the Guildhall via ornate double doors, down a flight of steps and around the corner of the building.

A vast white canvas marquee dominated the landscaped back garden. Beneath its tented roof, a couple of hundred people were chatting at top volume, holding glasses or takeaway cups. Many carried tote bags stuffed with books. Bella wove through the milling crowd.

She turned to Kat. 'Down here.'

Then she ran down a narrow path of herringbone-patterned bricks, leaving the hubbub of the crowd behind her.

Thankfully, the side of the Guildhall where Bella had led Kat was behind the kitchen. Devoid of interest to festival-goers and the general public alike, it was deserted. A large horse chestnut tree shaded the path here, casting the narrow passageway in deep shadow. Weeds and rounded tufts of moss grew between the old bricks.

A large terracotta flowerpot sat upturned beneath a window. Saw-toothed shards of glass stuck up from the sill like shark's teeth.

Bella pointed upwards.

'He's in there.'

Chapter Three

Kat mounted the upturned flowerpot and peered through the window into the green room.

Just as Bella had said, a middle-aged man Kat assumed was Mark Swift lay supine on a richly patterned Turkish carpet in the centre of the room. Behind him, she could see an armchair and a little table with a champagne bucket on it. Nothing in the room seemed out of place. There were no obvious signs of a struggle.

She called out. 'Hello! Hi! Can you hear me?'

Behind her, Bella huffed impatiently. 'He's dead. I told you!'

Kat twisted round, balancing precariously on the narrow base of the flowerpot. 'I'm just taking things one step at a time, Bella.'

'Are you going in then? To check for yourself?'

'Hand me that rock, would you?' Kat said, pointing to a large flint in the flowerbed.

Taking the stone from Bella, she scraped it left and right, dislodging, breaking and grinding down the glass until the window frame was clear. She took off her jacket, laid it across the sill and climbed in. Three strides and she was at Mark Swift's side. She knelt and pushed her fingers against the pulse point under his jaw. The skin was cold. She closed her eyes. *He's dead, Kat*, her internal pathologist whispered. No pulse. Even when she adjusted her fingertips and probed further.

She lifted his left eyelid. The brown iris stared off into the middle distance, or perhaps wherever Mark Swift's soul had travelled. She gently touched the cornea. The invasive manoeuvre elicited no response.

She sat back on her heels. Jack Beale, the *actual* pathologist, would have to confirm it for legal purposes. But as far as Kat was concerned, this was a corpse.

Just a corpse? her internal voice whispered. *Or a murder victim?*

It was too soon to say. But maybe she could get closer by following a few simple steps.

She looked at the body. His face – handsome, even in death – bore no bruises or wounds of any kind. No traces of vomit. She leaned down and sniffed around his mouth and nose. No trace of alcohol. She looked around. Beer bottles sat on a table topped with a blue paper tablecloth, and then there was the champagne she'd seen through the window, the foil partially removed. So he'd died before opening it.

Checking Mark Swift's hands, she found what she'd expected: soft-looking skin, neatly trimmed nails under which she could see no evidence of blood or tissue. Knuckles bearing none of the characteristic damage caused by a fist fight. No lacerations or cuts that might be defensive wounds. His clothing – a navy linen jacket, tan chinos, and scuffed but still expensive-looking brown lace-up brogues – wasn't disarrayed, marked or damaged in any way.

Kat peered at his scalp, at the dark hair streaked here and there with silver. No blood – fresh, dried or clotted. No depressed wounds. No blood pooling beneath the occipital bone at the back of his skull. Hair still damp from his morning shower.

All in all, it appeared that Mark Swift had suffered some sort of sudden physical trauma and simply died where he stood, collapsing to the floor on his back.

Various options presented themselves. Natural first. A heart attack. Or a seizure of some kind. Even an aneurysm, although she wasn't sure how these would change a body upon death. She could rule out anaphylaxis. His face and neck bore none of the trademark swellings that Kat had become intimately acquainted with on a case the previous year. Now *that* had been a bizarre MO.

If his death was not by natural causes, then could it have been suicide? It was an odd time and place to choose, but then, Kat reflected sadly, nobody could know the depths of pain and despair that would lead someone to take their own life. Perhaps this just happened to have been the time and place for Mark Swift.

Not hanging, though. No ligature in evidence, and no marking on his neck. None of the artefacts that strangulation produced, either, from the horribly protruding tongue and blackened face to the voided bladder and bowels.

Pills, then? She scanned the carpet, the furniture, and a large glazed pot containing a droopy ficus plant. No empty medication bottles or blister packs. He could have taken them first then locked himself in. She wrinkled her nose. Why, though? If he'd wanted to kill himself that way, why not do what most people *in extremis* did? Take the tablets at home, in a favourite armchair or in bed. Or even, as she'd once seen, in a garden beside the river in which the victim had fished daily until his wife's untimely death in a car accident.

Natural and suicide ruled, if not out, then at least not in, Kat considered the third option. The one she believed she'd been put on this earth to remedy.

Had Mark Swift been murdered?

But how? In the absence of any defensive wounds, gross trauma to the body, bloodstained clothing, pooling or spatter, stabbing was out of the question.

She sniffed the air. Didn't detect even the faintest trace of burnt propellant, which would surely have lingered inside. Crossed shooting off the list.

The obvious causes were diminishing. How else did people murder one another? Iron bars, hammers and bats weren't uncommon, but his skull looked intact. No way had he been beaten to death.

Poison, then? Had someone given him a deadly agent, slow-acting enough for him to have continued with his preparations for his interview? Presumably he'd locked the door himself before expiring.

Except he looked so peaceful. Kat had seen deaths from poisoning. They did not leave a pretty corpse.

However it had happened, Mark Swift was dead. If it *was* murder, they'd need photographs. No way could she justify the cost of hauling a member of the forensics team out here. Not yet. But she had her phone, and its camera was more than up to the task of producing high-quality images.

Kat pulled out her phone. More missed calls from Liv. In all the chaos, she'd stopped noticing its vibrations. She took twenty or so shots of the room and everything in it, from multiple angles. She squatted and took several photos of the face, hands and then the entire body.

Finally, she was satisfied. Time to leave and get things moving. She crossed to the door before remembering it was locked. But as she looked closer she saw the key.

Yes, the door *was* locked.

From the inside.

That argued for suicide. He'd wanted privacy for his final act.

She took a picture of the key. But as she stood there, trying to imagine his last few moments alive, she frowned.

If the green room in Middlehampton's five-hundred-year-old Guildhall was the scene of a murder, then it was one of the most unusual Kat had ever encountered. Mark's attacker had killed him without leaving any visible sign, then escaped without unlocking the door or breaking the window.

How the hell had it been done?

But she was getting ahead of herself. First things first. She called an ambulance and gave quick, efficient information on the location. Then she called Jack Beale.

'Murder?' he asked.

'Honestly? I have no idea. At the moment all I have is a dead author with no signs of violence. No point calling out the troops if you're going to tell me he had a fatal heart attack, is there?'

'I suppose not. Give me fifteen minutes.'

Calls made, she reached for the key. Then stopped. Guided by instinct, she put on a pair of gloves she always carried and unlocked the door. On its other side someone had taped an A4 sheet labelled *Green Room – Mark Swift Only (Friday)*. She relocked the door. In her right jacket pocket she found an unused dog poo bag; she had spares in most of her trousers and jackets. She dropped the key inside and knotted the bag shut.

She'd been straight with Jack. This wasn't a murder investigation. She just happened to be on the scene. But this thought was followed immediately by another. One that had her feeling a pang of guilt.

If Mark Swift had been murdered, she could take the case and focus on her work full-time. It would be a relief not to be worrying about the troublesome problems that had led her to accept Van's invitation to the crime festival in the first place. Not just Tom and their despicable boss, but her murdered half-sister Jo and, sitting at the heart of it all, her dodgy property developer father.

Chapter Four

Reaching the front steps, Kat sidestepped a knot of white-haired ladies enthusiastically discussing knife wounds and collided with a tall, striking-looking woman coming in the opposite direction. She had a wide mouth, drawn into a taut line so that her lips had all but disappeared. A laminated badge on a red-and-black lanyard bounced against the front of her short denim jacket. A stubby walkie-talkie at her side squawked and buzzed erratically.

The woman cried out and stepped back hurriedly. Kat recognised her from the photo at the front of the festival brochure.

'You're Maria Sheriff, is that right?'

'Yes. Sorry, I don't have time to chat,' she said distractedly. 'I'm looking for our speaker. He's late.'

Kat dragged her warrant card out of her jeans and showed it to Maria. 'I'm Detective Sergeant Ballantyne, with Middlehampton Police. I'm afraid Mark Swift is dead.'

Maria clapped her hand to her mouth, which had formed into an 'O'. Her hand dropped away.

'Dead? How?'

'It looks like he suffered some kind of medical emergency,' Kat said, keeping her suspicions to herself for the moment.

Kat frowned. Having a star guest at your festival die would be shocking enough, but there was something in Maria's expression that Kat recognised. 'Were you and Mark close?' she asked.

Maria flapped the hand not holding the walkie-talkie.

'Close?' She laughed once, a rough-edged crow-caw that contained precisely zero humour. 'Well, I suppose we were once. I'm his second wife.'

And then she pulled out a tissue from a pocket in her dress and sobbed into it.

Kat was torn. On the one hand, she knew how awful it would be for Maria Sheriff to learn of the death of her ex-husband from a detective. On the other, she was a murder detective. And she had questions.

'Listen, Maria. When I got there, the green room was locked from the inside. Can you shed any light on that for me?'

Maria nodded vigorously. 'Mark insists on locking himself in. He hates anyone, as he calls it, "bursting in" on him. It means I have to find a second room for the other authors. He won't even share it with the interviewer.'

'I'm going to need a spare key for the green room,' Kat said, thinking that the one in her pocket might be needed for evidence if a crime had been committed.

'You need to speak to Ernie. The caretaker. Although I think he likes to be called "custodian". I don't know . . . that sounds a little American, don't you think?' Perhaps realising she was babbling, Maria clamped a hand across her mouth for the second time. Above it, her eyes were wide.

'Where can we find him?' Kat asked.

'He has a little room. Beside the kitchen. I can take you there if you want.'

'Yes, please.'

It took two minutes to round the rose-festooned building and negotiate the crowds at the front before they could get inside. Clustered at the foot of a wide staircase where the ornately carved handrail swooped around in a spiral, tables stood heaped with books.

Behind one table, a young woman in a festival polo shirt and lanyard the same colour as Maria's was rearranging a pile of books.

She looked up and smiled. 'Oh, hi, Maria. Everything OK?'

'Not really, Rosa,' she said tightly. 'Have you seen Ernie around? It's rather urgent we find him.'

'He was here about ten minutes ago. He was going for, in his own words, "a nice little brew". I guess that means that little cubbyhole where he squirrels himself away when he doesn't want to be found.'

Nodding, Maria moved on, past the tables of books. 'This way,' she called over her shoulder.

Kat hurried to catch up, wishing she had Maria Sheriff's impressively long legs.

At the end of the corridor – which was panelled, as much of the interior was, in dark wood – Maria stopped in front of a door. No sign. She knocked once, sharply, and went straight in.

Kat followed her and found herself squashed into the corner of a little room. Every square inch was occupied. A half-desk. A wooden filing cabinet with polished brass fittings on which stood an electric kettle, recently boiled to judge from the wisps of water vapour escaping its limescaled spout.

Occupying a worn swivel chair with brass-nailed upholstery was a man in his late sixties. Grey hair – what was left of it – ringed a bald pate flecked with dark brown liver spots and blackish scabs; the curse of balding men who worked among low doorways and tight spaces.

He had paused in the act of raising a royal jubilee mug featuring a faded image of the late queen. Now he placed it on the little desk. Gave a little sigh.

'Something in your expression, Maria, tells me my tea break's over before it's begun.' He consulted his watch, a nice gold number. Not flashy, like Carve-up would wear. 'It's not something to do with that kerfuffle I heard from inside the ballroom, is it?'

His voice was pure Middlehampton. He sounded like some of Kat's old schoolfriends' dads. Hints of East London still audible despite one or two generations who'd made the town their home. Something about his face was ringing a faint bell of recognition, but Kat couldn't place him.

'This is DS Ballantyne,' Maria said. 'She'll tell you.'

'Mark Swift is dead,' Kat said. No point in sugar-coating it. 'The green room was locked from the inside. Do you have a spare key?'

'Bloody hell! Of course. Give me a second. Knees aren't what they were.'

He got to his feet, emitting little groans as his joints popped and his spine cracked. He pulled a bunch of keys from his pocket, selected a small brass one and unlocked a dark wooden cabinet on the wall. Inside, more keys were arranged, in ascending order of size, on a row of brass hooks. He took down a long black one that looked as though it might open a cell at the Tower of London and held it out to her. 'This is the official spare. I've got one in my drawer, too, but that's strictly for my use. People sometimes forget to bring that one back.'

'Has anyone borrowed it from you in the last twenty-four hours?' Kat asked.

'No. And I always lock my little office when I leave for the day.'

'What time is that?'

'Four sharp every afternoon. I leave early to look after my daughter. I'm her carer.'

Thinking that she might need to get into the green room again when he was at home with his daughter, Kat asked if she could borrow the spare key. He agreed and she thanked him before leaving with Maria in her wake.

They reached the front steps side by side. Maria was clutching her walkie-talkie like a talisman. Her face was drawn, that generous mouth stretched into a grimace.

'Is there any chance it was, you know' – she dropped her voice – 'murder?'

Kat's antennae twitched. 'Is there any reason you think it might have been?'

'Oh. No. I mean, of course not. But, you know, look where we are.' Maria threw her arm out in a wide arc encompassing the milling crime fiction fans. She laughed brokenly. 'How fitting!' Then she began crying again.

'It's too early to say. It *is* sudden and unexplained' – which was putting it mildly, she thought – 'so I will be investigating. I can't rule anything out, but we'll know more when the pathologist has conducted the—'

Kat hesitated. Ex-wife or not, Maria Sheriff had just lost someone close. When talking to relatives and friends of victims, Kat made it a rule to avoid using the cold clinical terms of officialdom that surrounded the dead. 'Post-mortem' chief among them, conjuring up the most unwelcome kind of images.

'The post-mortem,' Maria said, breaking through Kat's train of thought. 'It's all right, Detective Sergeant, I'm a crime writer too, although in a much smaller way than Mark. But I'm familiar with that world, if you know what I mean.'

'Tell me, did Mark have any health conditions that might have led to his death? Heart failure, a history of seizures? I'm sorry to have to ask you such personal questions, but it might help us establish what happened.'

Maria nodded. 'I understand. It's just such a shock, and right before his appearance too. And in answer to your question: no. Mark was always fit and healthy. Never smoked, drank moderately – for the most part – no drugs, played tennis every Saturday, or he did when we were married. He lived well, but nothing to excess. His parents are both still alive and they're in their nineties.' Her eyes widened and her hand fluttered up to cover her mouth. 'Oh, no. Miriam and Geoff, they'll be devastated. The shock if police turn up at their door could kill them. Please don't.'

'They will need to be informed. And soon. Even when the person isn't famous, news spreads fast nowadays.'

Maria nodded decisively, a quick sharp bob of the head. 'I'll do it. They live in the area. Always have. They were so proud that a local boy – that's what they always called Mark, a "local boy" – had made it big. I'll get my car and then, and then . . .'

Without warning she burst into more tears. Her face crumpled and her choking sobs drew curious stares from passing punters who then turned away, as if embarrassed to have witnessed genuine emotion at a festival dedicated to fiction.

Kat fished out the packet of tissues she routinely carried and offered them to Maria. After blotting her eyes and blowing her nose, she held them out to Kat.

'Keep them.'

'Look, this is going to sound cold, but I need to know. Can I keep the doors open?'

'Sorry, Maria, I don't understand . . . You mean the doors to the green room?'

'No, to the whole thing. Can I keep the festival open? We close on Sunday and I really need to see it through. I've booked lots of other authors for the next two days – I can't let them down. We're not in great shape financially since we lost our main sponsor thanks to those bloody activists, and we need all the revenue we can raise.'

Making a mental note to check on the 'bloody activists', Kat nodded.

'It's fine, for now. The post-mortem probably won't be until next week. Just maybe reassure your audience that Mark has had a medical emergency and has been taken to Middlehampton General. It's true, even if it isn't the whole story.'

'Thank you . . . Kat, wasn't it?'

'Kat, yes.'

'You don't know what this means to me. I know the police get a bad press a lot of the time, but I for one am grateful for what you do. I hope if you ever read one of my books, you'll see that respect coming through.'

Kat felt a flicker of distaste. Was the dead man's ex really trying to push her books at Kat *now*? She gave a mental shrug. After all, she was the one half hoping she'd just caught a murder as a distraction from her own personal problems.

'Thank you. If you'll excuse me, I have some things to take care of.'

'Of course. I do, too. Will you keep me informed, though. About Mark?'

'Of course. Oh, one more thing.'

'Yes?'

'I want you to seal off the green room. Lock it and get Ernie to board up the window. I don't want anyone going in or out until I give the OK.'

'But when will that be? We have other authors we need to accommodate, and the temporary green room isn't really suitable.'

'Maria, a man just died in there. At this stage I'm not treating it as suspicious, but it is a potential crime scene. I need it securing until I can be sure nothing untoward happened.'

'Of course, I'm sorry. It's all just, you know . . .'

'A shock. But you'll do it?'

'Of course.'

Maria hurried off, already issuing instructions into her walkie-talkie.

Reflecting that at the very least she'd have an interesting story to share with the team on Monday, Kat made her way to the ambulance. A small crowd had gathered but the festival security team were doing a good job of keeping them back.

Kat texted Van:

Swift gone. See you as soon as I can. x

His reply popped up straight away.

no probs thought as much when u didn't come back

do what you need to im going to stay here grab a pint xx

Van had mastered the fine art of streamlined texting, she thought, thanks to Riley's tutelage. Their son was deep into the teenage tunnel at age fourteen, but occasionally emerged long enough to help his poor benighted parents try to stay current.

She'd just put her phone back in her pocket when it vibrated. She pulled it free again and glanced at the screen. Liv.

This time, Kat answered.

Chapter Five

Funny how your best friend could come back from the dead – not the final victim of a serial killer after all – and you could still feel a shiver of anxiety every time you spoke to her. But then, Kat had helped Liv stay hidden to prevent the entire case against Stefan Pulford from blowing up.

But now Stefan was in prison on a whole-life order, and Liv was living happily on a commune in rural South Wales.

'Thelma! What the hell?' Liv asked, practically shouting.

Kat was Thelma and Liv was Louise. They'd bonded over the film back when they were at school together.

'What the hell what, Louise?'

'Mark Swift, that's what. He's been murdered!'

Kat's mind reeled. 'How did you even hear about that? He's dead, but it's not murder. Not officially, anyway. And it only just happened.'

Kat's stomach sank as she realised exactly how Liv knew: a certain mutual acquaintance.

'Mutt-calf just livestreamed himself at the scene,' Liv said. 'Says it's some kind of weird locked-room mystery that'll have the cops baffled. Dickhead.'

Perfect. Mutt-calf was Ethan Metcalfe, once a socially awkward boy at school with the hots for Kat. Now the host of a bafflingly successful true crime podcast called *Home Counties Homicide*. Of course he'd be at *Criminal Herts*.

'Look, Liv. I can't say anything yet. Certainly not on an open line, but we're seeing you on Sunday. We'll talk then.'

'OK, cool. And I might have a little mystery of my own to share with you.'

'What do you mean?'

'Tell you Sunday. Laters!'

The line died.

The familiar *whoop-whoop* of the ambo's siren broke into Kat's thoughts.

Jack Beale had also arrived, looking tanned and, Kat hated to admit it, handsome in a crisp white shirt with the collar unbuttoned. He was about as far as it was possible to get from his predecessor's rather more traditional garb of tweed or pinstriped suit, tie and waistcoat, whatever the weather. But Dr Feldman was happily retired now, and his successor was striding towards her.

'Morning,' he said, his leather doctor's bag swinging from his right hand.

'Morning. Come with me.'

He frowned. 'Everything all right?'

'Yes. Kind of. I'm not sure. It depends on what you find.'

He shrugged. 'I'd better get on with it, then, hadn't I?'

Kat led him to the green room and unlocked the door with the spare key. Jack entered first, rolling up his shirtsleeves. Kat looked at his toned and tanned forearms, and experienced one of those infuriating little pangs of physical desire that had plagued her ever since the first time they'd met.

Mentally chiding herself, she stared down at the waxen face of the dead author as Jack crouched beside the body.

After a minute, he looked up at her. 'Well, he's definitely dead. Which means *The Guillotine Man* was his final book. Shame, really – they were quite good.'

She wrinkled her brow. 'I wouldn't have thought you were a fan, Jack.'

He got to his feet, speaking into his phone as he did so. 'Jack Beale pronouncing life extinct at 11.37 a.m. on July 19th, 2024.' He pocketed the phone and turned back to her. 'Nor would I. Think I was a fan, I mean. But for a little light holiday reading by the pool, yes, I love them. Mark Swift had a real talent for the macabre.'

'How did he die, Jack?'

He shrugged, rolling his sleeves down and rebuttoning his shirt cuffs. 'Honestly? I have no idea. And before you say anything, that's not me brandishing my professional scruples. If I had a clue, I'd tell you.' He pointed at the body. 'What do *you* think? You've seen your fair share of corpses, murdered and otherwise.'

'I'd have to say natural causes, then. Some kind of medical episode. A heart attack, or a stroke, or an aneurysm.'

'I agree that's what it looks like. His hair's damp so I imagine he showered shortly before coming to the Guildhall.'

'Or he had a bath.' A thought occurred to Kat. 'Can people faint after having a really hot bath? Maybe he had some sort of delayed reaction and fainted. Hit his head and caused a brain bleed?'

Jack smiled. Kat recognised the expression. It carried just a hint of smugness and reminded her why she found herself simultaneously attracted to and repelled by Jack Beale.

'That's quite a stretch, don't you think? I mean, yes, rapid changes in body temperature – in saunas, for example – can cause faintness. Especially if one were to stand up suddenly. Though I've not heard of a delayed reaction. But if it does turn out to be that, I'll buy you lunch. Or dinner.'

There it was again: that flirtatious glint in his eye.

'Fine,' she said shortly. 'Could it be suicide? Or murder?'

He pursed his lips. 'It could be. Poisoning, maybe, or sharp-force trauma. Although I'm not seeing any signs of blood loss or internal bleeding. A bit odd to come here to kill yourself, wouldn't you say?'

'So answer me this. If it *was* murder, how the hell did the killer do it? The room was locked from the inside, and until the girl who found him broke the window there was no other way out.'

Jack finished putting on his jacket. Grabbed his bag and made for the door.

'Sounds like something out of one of his books,' he said with a grin. 'Maybe you should ask around the Guildhall. Plenty of crime fans and authors who'd love to help you solve it.'

She rolled her eyes. 'When can you do the post-mortem?'

'Monday morning, 9.00 a.m. See you there?'

'No sooner?'

He paused, hand on the door handle. 'I have plans. Look, Kat. My best guess? It was natural causes. The guy looks reasonably fit and healthy—'

'Apart from the obvious.'

That twinkle again. 'Indeed. But he's carrying a couple of extra stone, and I spy a bottle of Moët, so he was a drinker. Probably had a heart attack. The simplest answer, etc., etc.'

And with that he was gone, leaving Kat to supervise as two paramedics entered the room and loaded Mark Swift on to a stretcher. Kat followed them outside, then started as a woman's high-pitched shouting silenced the chatter of the onlookers.

'For God's sake, let me through!'

Chapter Six

Two security team members were blocking the way of a woman in a short denim jacket, teal print dress and white sneakers. Her face was streaked with tears.

Kat hurried over to the trio, skirting the paramedics who were sliding Mark Swift's blanket-shrouded body off the gurney and into the back of the ambulance.

'I'll take this,' she told the security guards, holding out her warrant card.

'I need to see him,' the woman said. She was in her late forties, tousled hair swept back from a high, unlined forehead.

'Who are you, please?' Kat asked.

'I'm Saskia Swift. I'm his wife, for God's sake. Someone said he'd had a heart attack.' She looked over Kat's shoulder. 'Oh my God, is that him? Is he dead? Mark!' she wailed, pushing against Kat's outstretched arms.

'Come with me, please, Saskia,' Kat murmured, drawing the older woman away towards the rear of the ambulance. People were holding phones aloft, and among them, Kat saw her third-least favourite man in Middlehampton.

Every time she caught a case, Ethan Metcalfe popped up again, as welcome as a bout of cystitis. The fact he clearly had some sort of sexual fixation on her only added to the sense of dread she experienced whenever she saw his greedy-eyed stare behind the unfashionable gold-rimmed glasses.

Now, he looked straight at her and raised a hand to his ear, waggling outstretched thumb and little finger. 'Call me!' he mouthed.

On balance, Kat thought she'd rather have the UTI. She helped Saskia into the back of the ambulance after getting her contact details – the second woman to be crying grief-sodden tears at Mark Swift's death inside thirty minutes. A well-loved man indeed. Unless Jack Beale told her someone had killed him. But that would all have to wait until Monday morning.

She texted Van again.

Gonna be busy for a while longer. U ok?

He replied at once.

its cool u do u

Bloody hell! Even Riley would be impressed with that one. Shaking her head, Kat turned to go back inside the Guildhall, wondering whether she ought to risk calling out a full team. The big boss, DCI (Crime) Linda Ockenden, would do her nut if Kat wasted any of her precious budget. Then a familiar face appeared in front of her. Immaculate make-up, hair in a sophisticated up-do. And an expression at once friendly and as cold as ice.

'Hello, Kathryn. I wouldn't have pegged you for a literary type, what with you having abandoned your degree.'

Kat eyeballed her older sister. 'Hi, Diana. And there was me thinking the only kind of books you were interested in were the ones with two sets of accounts. How silly of me.'

There it was. A lifetime's relationship compressed into a waspish exchange. Diana's disdain for her university dropout sister clashed with Kat's suspicions that she was whitewashing crooked companies' business dealings.

'We're doing well enough to be a silver sponsor for this little show,' Diana said, waving an arm expansively around the sun-drenched gardens. 'And since those idiots from Books Not Bombs forced Savile Harvey to defend their sponsorship, it's given us a little more of the limelight, too. Anyway, what can you tell me about poor Mark Swift? I assume it was you who dealt with his heart attack?'

'Did you know him, Di? As a sponsor, I mean?'

Her sister's elegantly curved eyebrows curved still further. 'Know him? I was talking to him earlier this morning. Quite the charmer, even if his opinions about certain people here would curl your hair.'

Kat's inquisitiveness kicked up a notch. 'What time was this?'

Diana checked her watch, a pretty silver piece studded with green stones Kat knew had to be emeralds.

'It was 10.25 a.m. The festival director introduced us. What with me being a sponsor I suppose she felt it was the least she could do.'

'Where was this?'

Diana's plum-coloured lips curved into a sly smile. 'Are you interrogating me, Kathryn?'

'I just need to ask, Di.'

'Well, since you "just need to ask", it was in the green room. Mark was sitting in an armchair – very much playing the king of crime-writing accepting visits from his subjects. I had to sit on a silly little side chair.'

'How was he? I mean, how did he seem?'

Diana cocked a single eyebrow. '*Seem?* Well, since you ask, he seemed like a complete arsehole. Apart from looking me up and down like I was a streetwalker, he could hardly wait to get rid of me. I was out five minutes later.'

'But not depressed or anything?'

'Not that I'm a psychiatrist, but no. If I had to choose a word I'd say "smug".'

'Did you see anyone else around that part of the Guildhall?'

'No. Just me. Why?'

'Because he's dead, Di. And' – Kat knew she shouldn't feel this way, but she was savouring her next sentence – 'it sounds like you were the last person to see him alive.'

'But he had a heart attack! That's what I heard. You make it sound like I killed him or something.'

'Did you?'

The words were out before Kat could weigh them. Diana's reaction took a few seconds to coalesce around a single theme. Her eyebrows shot up and her eyes widened, whites showing all the way round her irises. Her mouth worked but no sound emerged.

Then she jabbed a deep red nail towards Kat. 'I'm going to assume – charitably, I might add – that you're suffering from work-induced stress, and ignore that question. If you have any more off-colour insinuations to make, let me know and I'll bring my lawyer. Now, if you'll excuse me, I have people I need to meet.'

Diana departed, her heels clicking on the Guildhall's stone-flagged floor, in a cloud of disdain and Chanel No.5.

Kat was aghast at her clumsy question. Diana couldn't be a murderer, could she? Of course not. The idea was ridiculous. The last person to see Mark Swift alive she may have been, but his killer? No.

No!

Jack had said the most likely explanation was natural causes. And after the weekend, she'd know one way or the other.

She went back to the green room and stood in front of the door. Had it been for Mark Swift only, as the sign indicated? Or had someone else found a way to get inside?

Chapter Seven

That evening, over heaped bowls of Van's signature spaghetti Bolognese (mince, garlic, onion, red wine, Tesco Italian seasoning, tinned tomatoes, and no slow-cooked shin of beef or fresh herbs in sight), Riley raised his head from his food. His chin had broken out in another crop of whiteheads, one of which he'd clearly picked right before tea, judging by the bead of dark blood glistening on his oily skin.

'So did he die, or what?'

Kat held back a sigh. Riley's adolescent voice had settled into a growly baritone, and it had taken his moods down with it. The current monosyllabic thundercloud was one of several he rotated. Others included – as christened by his parents – 'the Grumble', 'Ultimate Disdain' and, most feared, 'the Rage'. This last was an apocalyptic triple-threat of soaring testosterone, weapons-grade swearing and a hair-trigger temper.

'If you're talking about Mark Swift, then, yes, I'm afraid he did. How did you hear about it?'

'Er, hello? There's this new thing called social media. I don't know if you've heard of it?'

'Riley, watch your lip,' Van said.

'Well, it's no great loss, is it?'

His callousness shocked Kat. 'Riley Ballantyne! He was a human being. He had a wife who was distraught when I met her. Please try to have some compassion. If it's not too uncool,' she added unwisely.

'Uncool? Do you want to know what's *uncool*, Mum? Swift was an arsehole. I've seen his tweets. He was anti-trans, racist, a climate change denier.' He turned to Van. 'Why do you even read his stuff, Dad?'

'Well, I know he has a certain reputation' – Riley snorted in exasperation, but Van refused to be goaded – 'but even if an artist holds unpalatable opinions, we can still appreciate their art. That's what I feel about Mark Swift. The books are great; the man, maybe not so much.'

Kat shot Van a quick, appreciative glance. It had become an art form, holding their tempers while Riley was forever losing his. She thought Van had just achieved a new level of fluency. Clearly, Riley disagreed.

'Oh, right. And you probably think Hitler was OK because he painted shit watercolours. Or J.K. Rowling—'

Van held up a hand.

'All I'm saying is things aren't always black and white.'

'Yes they are! Swift was an arsehole. Right this morning he was spreading lies about Books Not Bombs. I'm glad he's dead.'

The mum in her wanted to argue with her son – to try to reach that sweet boy she knew was in there somewhere. But the cop part of her had battened on to a name she'd heard once today already. From Diana.

She ignored Van's warning look, which was as plain on his face as Riley's pimples were on his.

Instead, she ploughed on. 'What about Books Not Bombs? What exactly did he say?'

'Oh, like you care.'

'Just tell me, Riley. Now!' she barked.

The sudden edge to her tone shocked him into acquiescence. 'He said they were just, quote-unquote, "performative trust-fund revolutionaries who ought to grow up and stop starving authors and publishers of the means to communicate". Which is a total laugh given the crap most of those books are full of.'

He swung round and addressed Van, who was concentrating on mopping up the last of his spaghetti sauce. 'I looked at that one you're reading, Dad. A bloke cutting women up with a homemade guillotine. Misogynistic, much? I mean, why don't you just go out and start raping women if that's your thing?'

Van's head snapped round. 'That's enough. Go—'

'—to my room, yeah, yeah. Don't worry, I've heard it all before. I'm going.'

Riley shoved his chair back, taking care to produce a wince-inducing squawk from the legs, and stomped out of the kitchen. Neither Kat nor Van said a word while, eyes locked in a sort of parental mind-meld, they waited.

Five, four . . . a newly muscular teenaged boy's angry tramping up the stairs . . . *three, two* . . . down the hallway . . . *one* . . . and . . .

The light fitting tinkled cheerily over their heads and a hairline crack in the ceiling lengthened by another couple of millimetres. In his basket in the corner, one of several scattered around the house, Smokey, Kat's cairn terrier, raised his head. His right eye, droopy since a puppyhood seizure, widened fractionally as he looked up at Kat. *What's up, boss? Did the young master have another one of his moments?*

She sighed. Smokey wouldn't understand. He lived in a world comprising equal parts food, sleep, stroking and walks, which she sometimes thought all signified pretty much the same thing to him. Love. He was also the only living thing in the house on whom Riley bestowed uncomplicated affection.

'How does he produce that amount of force?' Van asked.

But for once, the joke about their son's brutal mistreatment of his bedroom door failed to raise a smile. Kat was thinking about her run-in with Diana earlier that day. They weren't Colin Morton's only daughters, but two of three: Diana, Kat and – the sister who Kat had never really known until her death – Jo.

'What is it?' Van asked, the distant Scottish burr still evident in his voice when, as now, he dropped it to a concerned murmur.

'It's Jo. Why she bullied that girl to the point of suicide and then changed overnight into this paragon of virtue. It's been really bugging me, Van. And the way her parents died in that plane crash.'

'Don't let it get to you, love,' Van said, laying a hand softly over hers. 'Look, I know it came as a bloody great shock, but think about it – you had no real connection to Jo beyond your dad's . . . well, you know, his affair with her mum. And I know you always say nobody deserves to die' – he held his other hand up like a traffic officer performing a stop – 'and before you jump down my throat I agree with you. But maybe it would be best to let this one lie, eh? Yes, you and Jo were related by blood, but by that standard you ought to be tracking down every third cousin, twice removed, and distant great-auntie.'

From nowhere, tears spilled down Kat's cheeks. For a lovely man, Van could sometimes have all the emotional sensitivity of a lump hammer.

'She was my *sister*, Van! Don't you get it?'

He drew in a deep breath then puffed out his cheeks as he exhaled. 'Look, I'm sorry. Maybe I don't understand, being an only child. But talking of your dad . . . what about the money? Have you had any more thoughts about what you're going to do?'

It was a transparent attempt to distract her. But all Van was doing, in his lovably clumsy way, was reminding her that her own father, apart from cheating on her mum, had conspired with

Carve-up to fit Kat up on a corruption charge via an anonymous fifty-K bank transfer. And if she hadn't been stacked out with cases over the preceding month, she'd have done something about it. But maybe now, while she waited for Mark Swift's post-mortem on Monday, she could start digging – and find some evidence, even a shred, that would expose both men.

She knew exactly where to start. In a drunken outburst at a family dinner – Kat shuddered at the memory – her mum had let slip that her dad's long-standing and dog-loyal PA Suzy Watkins 'handles all the banking, not him'. Maybe Suzy had arranged the whole thing to protect her employer.

While Van loaded the dishwasher – in his own, distinctive style Kat had learned to ignore – Kat moved to the sitting room and called a friend.

'Hi, Iris,' she said when the forensic accountant answered after the usual four rings.

'Hi, Kat. Thank you so much for taking me to see *ABBA Voyage*. It was truly the best night of my life. So realistic. Although obviously they were holograms.'

Kat had to smile at Iris's slightly off-kilter way of seeing the world.

'I wish I could have taken you every night for a week. You saved my life, Iris, truly you did.'

'That's a metaphor, I know that. Your life wasn't really in danger. And anyway, it would be a waste of money to go seven times. Was there something you wanted to ask me, Kat?'

'Since you ask, and I'm sorry to keep asking for favours, but if I gave you a name, could you see if you could link this person to the money my dad sent me?'

'Of course. Now we have the key we can use it to unlock the door again.' A beat. 'That's another metaphor.'

'It's great, Iris.'

'Really?' Iris sounded pleased.

'Really. So, her name is Suzanne Watkins. She might go by Suzy.'

'Leave it with me.'

Kat nodded with satisfaction. Feeling that the odds of her besting her father had just shifted in her favour, her thoughts drifted back to the green room. Everything pointed to Mark Swift having died of natural causes. But her gut wasn't having it.

Nothing for it.

She grabbed her car keys and headed back into town.

Chapter Eight

Light poured out from the front of the Guildhall. Festival punters were coming and going, standing in the square enjoying the warmth of the evening. Kat let herself into the green room using the spare key she'd borrowed from Ernie.

Inside, she compared the pictures she'd taken on her phone earlier in the day to the layout of the furniture and smaller items in the room. Everything checked out, right down to the placement of the beer bottles on the tablecloth.

Yet, as she stood there, a niggling sense that she was missing something kept intruding. It was telling her this *was* a crime scene. But not *why*.

She moved to a corner, between the now boarded-up window and a wall bearing a vast and ugly oil painting. Some white-whiskered general on a horse, resplendent in red-and-white tunic with a sabre resting nonchalantly on one shoulder.

'I'll just have to figure it out, then, won't I?' she told him. 'So, what am I missing?'

She surveyed the room, looking at the ceiling, all four walls, and the floor in turn. No more doors or windows. No hatches. She tapped each wooden wall panel. All sounded perfectly solid. If there *was* a hidden door, its fabricator had done a bloody good job.

It ought to have been a natural death. Jack had as much as confirmed it. But something wasn't right about the scene she was inspecting. She moved from the corner to stand behind the armchair where Mark Swift had presumably spent his last few moments alive. About to place her palms on its smooth wooden frame, she stopped. From her pocket she fished out a pair of nitrile gloves. She leaned on the chair back and stared down at the seat. Conducted an imaginary dialogue with Mark Swift.

—*You were sitting here, where Di left you?*

—*Yes.*

—*You started to feel poorly.*

—*Very.*

—*Had you taken something, Mark? Were you trying to end your own life?*

—*Why would I? I was rich, successful, famous. Beautiful wife, as you've seen.*

—*OK, so then what?*

—*I stood up, clutched my left arm, which was hurting like a bastard, then the big one hit and I fell down, dead as a dodo, right there where you found me.*

But as she stared at the spot in the centre of the carpet where ghost-Mark had been pointing, she saw the problem. Pushed up against the front of the brass-nailed chair was the delicate little side table with the champagne bucket and flute on it.

—*How did you get from the chair to the floor without knocking the table over?*

—*Uh, maybe I got that bit wrong. Maybe I died in the chair.*

—*Then who moved your body on to the carpet?*

—*No. Sorry. I mean I* did *die on the carpet.*

—*And you're telling me that, as you died, you found the energy and time to push the table back against the chair without knocking over the glass or the bucket? Why?*

—How should I know? I'm dead.

Kat shook her head. This made no sense. If Mark had died of natural causes, he'd either have been found dead in the armchair or among the debris as he fell on to the little side table. The same if he'd committed suicide. That only left one option. Someone had murdered him and then moved the table themselves before fleeing.

'Elementary, my dear Tomski,' she said aloud, then sighed.

Every time she visited Tom, she asked the doctors the same question: 'Any change?'

And every time they gave her the same answer. 'I'm sorry, no. But don't give up hope.'

She tried not to. But with each passing week, she felt a little more despair crowding out her optimism. On two separate occasions, both late at night, she'd thought he was waking up. His eyelids had fluttered and his right index finger had twitched. She'd yanked the crash button, but by the time the medics and nurses had arrived, Tom was as still as a statue, his EEG trace a subdued green line barely broken by the once-a-second peak that rose and fell as if even it found the effort too much.

She dragged her thoughts back to the murder case, as she'd started thinking of it. Walked to the centre of the room and looked down at the spot where Mark had been lying.

'But then how the hell did they kill you? And how did they get away?' she protested. 'It doesn't make any sense.'

She called Jack Beale.

'Kat! Nice to hear your voice out of office hours. What can I do for you?'

Jazz was playing in the background. Some sort of squealing she thought might have been a saxophone. Horrible racket. Jack notched down a tick in her estimation.

'Mark Swift was murdered. I need you to bring the post-mortem forward. Tomorrow if possible.'

Loud rustling had her holding the phone away from her ear. Cautiously she replaced it.

'—going to be difficult, Kat. I'm not in Middlehampton.'

'Are you close, though? Can you get back?'

'Not by tomorrow. We're in Bruges at a jazz festival. I was on my way to the airport when you called me. Almost missed my flight. Why are you suddenly so sure it was murder?'

She explained. Waited. Heard the doubt crystallising among all those miles of fibre-optic cable, copper wire and satellite beams.

'I don't know, Kat, that's quite the leap, don't you think?' he said eventually. 'Maybe he just stood up and moved the table so he had room to pace up and down. Maybe he was nervous and needed space to do some yoga. He could have had OCD and liked to arrange things in some specific pattern that would allay his anxiety. Or he could have—'

'OK, Jack, I get it,' Kat snapped. Then immediately regretted it. 'Sorry. Not your fault. Maybe I am reaching, after all. I'll see you on Monday. Enjoy the music.'

With Jack gone, she fought down a wicked little twinge of curiosity. No, she had to be honest, it was a kind of jealousy. Jack had said 'we're in Bruges'. Who was 'we'?

That was another little detecting job that was going to have to take a ticket and wait to be called.

Right now, she had a murder to solve. And the beginnings of a timeline.

Assuming Kat's sister, Diana, wasn't the murderer, Mark Swift had been alive at 10.30 a.m. Bella Gabbard had announced his death to the audience in the ballroom just after 10.56 a.m.

So Mark Swift had been killed in the twenty-six-minute period between those two points.

DAY TWO – SATURDAY

Chapter Nine

The next morning, after Smokey's morning walk, Kat made a quick call to the big boss. Not Carve-up, he could wait. Linda Ockenden, however, could not. Kat wanted her to know of her suspicions regarding Mark Swift's death.

'Morning, Kat. Is this about Mark Swift?'

'Morning, Ma-Linda,' Kat began. The DCI's informal nickname – caused by Kat's hesitating between addressing her as Ma'am or Linda on their first meeting – had stuck, becoming something of an affectionate in-joke. 'Still got proper cop smarts despite that big desk of yours. Yes, it is about him. You heard, then?'

'*Everybody's* heard! Steve's five-a-side WhatsApp group chat's full of it. They've all got a theory. As, I'm guessing, do you. And thanks for the compliment. Anyway, speak. I have a golf game in an hour and I'm still in my dressing gown.'

'I think he was murdered.'

'Why?'

Kat hesitated. Just for a second. Was she, as Jack had suggested last night, grasping at straws? Was she spinning a natural death into a murder so she'd have another case to solve?

'The crime scene was staged.'

'"Crime scene". Not getting ahead of ourselves, are we, Kat? Did you get Jack Beale up there?'

'Yes.'

'And?'

'He said in all likelihood it was natural causes. But likelihood isn't certainty,' she added.

'No, it isn't. But despite the sudden, and may I say welcome, influx of cash from the Home Office, budgets aren't bottomless wells. So, what are you saying?'

'Just that I want you to know of my concerns.'

As she said this, Kat saw the inner truth that had motivated the call. Carve-up would round on her at the Monday morning briefing, belittling her in front of the whole team for another episode of what he liked to call her 'grandstanding'. Bastard. If only she were a DI, she could tell him where to stick his pathetic putdowns.

'Duly noted,' Linda said. 'Now, you'll have to excuse me, Kat, but I need to get my game face on. I'm playing in a ladies' four with the Chief Con, and I do not intend to let Ingrid "How-does-she-look-so" Young take another fifty quid off me.'

Feeling she'd done all she could with Linda, Kat checked social media for news on Mark Swift. An author on X – which Kat still thought of as Twitter – had speculated that Swift couldn't have picked a better way to go than inside a locked room. *Kudos*, she'd tweeted. Plus book, dagger and sad-face emojis. An editor had opined that the publishing world had lost a 'controversial but talented' voice. That was interesting. Riley had mentioned Swift's anti-woke views in his rant at the dinner table.

Motive, Kat's inner voice whispered.

Riley entered the kitchen. Actually, Kat didn't feel that was quite right. The days of Riley simply entering a room were in the past. These days he might invade, storm or, rarely, bounce into a room. But an everyday entrance was beyond him.

'Morning. What's for breakfast?'

Kat nodded towards the fridge, then the bread bin. 'Whatever's in there, you can have.'

'But can you cook something for me?'

'Me?'

'Yeah.'

'You want *me* to make *you* a cooked breakfast?'

He pooched his mouth out with two fists pressed against his cheeks. Batted his eyelashes. 'Please and thank you?'

She smiled. 'I worry about you, Riley Ballantyne. Your amnesia seems to be getting worse.'

'What?'

'Last night? You were very rude to me. And Dad, actually.'

'Oh, that. I'm sorry. But he really was a douche, you know. Swift, I mean, not Dad.'

'You said he was really unpleasant on social media. Do you think he could have made enemies there?'

'Like enough for someone to want to kill him? Sure, why not?'

'But what sort of things was he saying. Specifically, I mean?'

'Well, there was this woman. An author, like him. She said it was a shame he didn't put as much energy into fighting injustice as he did into fighting trolls. And he just basically called her a clicktivist. That's someone who signs online petitions and writes blog posts but doesn't actually do anything offline, you know?'

'I had heard, but thanks for the clarification,' Kat said with a quick smile.

'Yeah, well, there's tons of it. He was like, I've got all the money and all the followers, so I get to say whatever I want. It's all free speech and you can basically do one if you don't like it. Like he's this wannabe edge-lord. He called this one person a sex-starved cat lady, and when she went after him he basically said she had no sense of humour. I screen-grabbed it. Hold on. Yes, here,' he said after a few seconds' scrolling. 'He goes, "So I make jokes that are maybe too sharp-edged for some people, a) that's their problem not mine and b) fascist? Really? What is this, 1986? It's called free speech, people. Deal with it."'

'Charming.'

'Like I said, a total douche. Anyway' – he flashed his best charm-the-grandmother smile – 'about my breakfast . . .'

'How about bacon and eggs and hash browns?'

'Any sausages?'

She grinned. 'And sausages.'

'Also toast and tomatoes. And if there's any mushrooms, them too.'

She shook her head. 'Where do you put it all? I heard you making toast last night as well.'

'Maybe I've got a tapeworm. That's what Mr Osgood says.'

'Well, your games teacher could be right. I should get Jack Beale to take a look at you.'

'It's fine. Feed the monster,' he growled, before slumping into a chair and pulling out his phone.

Kat started assembling the ingredients for the fry-up, wondering whether Carve-up had ever had to juggle being a cop, a parent, a friend and a husband. Of course he hadn't. The twat was divorced, for one thing. Sensible woman, his ex-wife.

As the smell of frying sausages filled the air and made her tummy rumble, Riley groaned.

'Oh, man, he's at it again.'

'Who is?' Kat said, adding rashers of bacon to the pan and then smiling as Van arrived, kissing the back of her neck.

'Morning, sexy pants.'

'Gross, parents! Get a room,' Riley moaned.

'We already did,' Van said with a grin, filling the coffee machine.

'Double-gross. Stop, please, this is child abuse!'

'Yes, Van, please stop. Riley, who's at what again?'

'Your stalker. Ethan Metcalfe. Middlehampton's own podcast nerd and all-round incel is doing an investigation into Mark Swift's death.'

The smell of the frying meat suddenly lost its savour. That was all Kat needed. Mutt-calf sticking his greasy nose into things that didn't concern him.

Except, she was forced to admit, they did.

He'd ridden the perfect storm of citizen journalism, true crime podcasts and his own obsessive personality, and created an actual business. A *successful* one, with tens of thousands of listeners – including, if he was to be believed, half the brass at Jubilee Place.

She shoved the thought down. She had enough to deal with without worrying about Mutt-calf.

'I'm going up to see Tom. I'll be back for lunch,' she said, plating up the breakfast.

'How is he?' Van asked.

She shook her head. Tried not to give in to the feelings of hopelessness that swamped her every time she thought of her comatose bagman.

'Same as always. The doctors say he could wake up at any time, but realistically the longer it goes on the worse his chances get.'

'Could he – you know – die, Mum?'

She smiled down at Riley, who was looking up at her, his fork poised midway to his mouth. 'I hope not, darling. But yes, he might.'

'Oh, well, I hope he doesn't. I know you like him. And, Mum?'

'Yes, darling?'

'I'm sorry about last night, really. I just, I mean, it's not an excuse, but my emotions get the better of me sometimes. You too, Dad. Sorry.'

Van reached across and ruffled his son's hair. 'Thanks, mate. Forgiven and forgotten, eh?'

Kat risked placing a quick kiss on the top of Riley's head before grabbing her car keys.

'I love you, boys. See you later.'

Twenty minutes later she entered the calm, ordered space of Middlehampton General's Acute Medical Unit.

Hoping for the best, fearing the worst.

Chapter Ten

Sister Ellie, as everyone called her, was a petite Filipina, quick to smile but with an icy glare she deployed to great effect when dealing with entitled male consultants.

When Kat asked about Tom, she shook her head sadly. 'I'm sorry, Kat, but there's no change. One of the night staff said she thought he might have twitched, but she wasn't sure when I spoke to her. She'd been on for twelve hours by then so maybe she was just tired, isn't it?'

'Thanks, Ellie. I'll go and sit with him for bit anyway.'

'You're an angel, Kat. Somewhere in there he knows you're there. Believe that, OK, my love?'

Kat entered the side room. Tom lay on his back, arms by his sides. Tubes and wires snaked under the bedclothes as the life support systems around him bleeped and hissed.

She reached for his hand, careful not to dislodge the pulse oximeter clipped to his index finger, and squeezed gently.

'Hey, Tomski,' she said, looking down at his face, as immobile as a marble statue's. 'It's me. Your big, bad boss. The university dropout with a chip on her shoulder. You need to come back to me so I can start ragging you about all that there book larnin'.' She went for a comedy old-timey American accent like her bagman used to do, but it caught in her throat and she choked up.

'Carve-up's going to pay for what he did to you, Tomski. One day, when you're better, we're going to take him down together. All above board, all by the rules. But we're going to do it, OK?'

She stroked his left cheek with her knuckles. Sniffed back the welling tears. Something flickered in the corner of Kat's eye, distracting her. A bright green light flashing on and off rapidly.

Kat looked over at the EEG trace on the bedside monitor. The green trace was spiking and jumping about, a rapid series of peaks and troughs completely different to the odd irregularities she'd seen before. Was the machine malfunctioning? She didn't want to cause trouble like she had before, summoning a crash team for nothing more than 'a transient paracerebral event', as the yawning junior doctor had said.

She looked back at Tom. And sighed. Nothing had changed. He looked like one of the full-sized mannequins they used for first-aid training. Her phone buzzed on her hip. She pulled it out to check, but it was only an alert for her to come up to MGH.

She looked back at Tom. And gasped.

His right eyelid twitched. Fluttered. Then, slowly, like a blind being pulled up from a darkened window, his eye opened wide. And he looked up at her.

'Oh my God! Tomski!'

She crouched beside the bed and brought her face closer to Tom's. 'Tomski! Can you hear me? Oh, Jesus, Tomski. Are you back? Are you awake?'

His left eye opened. For a second his eyes moved in different directions, a disconcerting effect. Then they locked on to hers. Her heart was tripping and tumbling along like the green trace on the EEG. She broke out into a huge smile, so full of elation it wiped away all thoughts of Mark Swift's death, even Carve-up's murderous actions. Tomski was back.

She twisted round, not letting go of his hand. 'Sister! Staff! Tom's awake!'

Within a few seconds, the door flew open and a blue-uniformed staff nurse arrived, followed by Sister Ellie, then a junior doctor. More medics followed, plus green-uniformed carers.

'He's awake!' Kat said, unable to keep the excitement out of her voice. She pointed down at Tom, whose eyes were still open and following her as she moved away from him to allow the clinical staff to get closer.

'Right, my love,' Ellie said briskly, 'we need you to leave so we can help Tom, isn't it?'

'Sure, sure.' Kat craned around the doctor bending over Tom, shining a penlight into his eyes. 'I'll be right here, Tomski. Right here!'

Grinning from ear to ear, she left the side room and, unable to sit still, ran the length of the ward, jumping up and punching the air. Everything was going to be OK. She came back to Tom's room and hovered in the doorway.

The nurses not attending to Tom beamed at her, and each other. She guessed his recovery was more of a rarity than she'd been prepared to admit to herself.

Without warning, her knees buckled and she staggered over to the nurses' station.

'Hold on, Kat, I'll get you a chair,' one of the nurses said.

Kat gratefully flopped down into the visitor chair when it arrived.

'Are you all right?' the nurse asked.

'Just got a bit giddy, that's all. It's so fantastic he's back.'

'He's a fighter, that one. I'm praying he will make it.'

Kat didn't find her words reassuring.

'But he's back! You saw him. He's better.'

'Just try not to get your hopes up too high, Kat. With coma patients, sometimes they can come round but then, you know' – she dipped her gaze – 'maybe it will only be temporary. We have to wait for the doctors to finish.'

The nurse left her, to attend a bleep from a nearby room. Kat tried to stay positive and not give in to the doubts the nurse's well-meant but terrifying words had engendered. With nothing to do for now, Kat called Leah, the other DC on her immediate team. Leah promised to get over as soon as she could. Next, Linda. Her phone went straight to voicemail. Kat left what she hoped was a halfway coherent message.

Half an hour passed, during which Kat walked the length of the hospital and back again, returning to her seat only to jump up again and peer into Tom's room until Ellie shooed her away.

Just when Kat thought she might throw up from anxiety, the consultant neurologist emerged. She was smiling, though the dark bags under her eyes spoke of long-term fatigue. It was a look Kat had grown used to on her daily visits.

'He's actually staging something of a miraculous recovery. We need to run a lot more tests, obviously, but he's fully conscious, taking a little water through a straw, and he can make himself understood.'

'So he's going to be all right? I mean, he's going to be back like he was. To normal?'

The doctor frowned. 'It's too early to say. This is the thing with comas, they're basically brain injuries. It's not just like waking up after a long sleep. There can be—' She stopped. Smiled tiredly. 'All of which you don't need to hear right now. Yes, it's fantastically good news. I've seen lots of patients leave a comatose state and Tom is already among the top two or three in terms of initial responses. You can be hopeful. It's good news. Truly.'

Time entered a peculiarly stretched form Kat had only experienced on surveillance duty until her daily visits to Tom's bedside when she'd talk to him, play his favourite music and update him on her cases and Jubilee Place gossip – each time she looked at the big station clock mounted on the wall above a set of computers on wheeled trolleys, the red sweep second hand seemed to freeze for a moment before resuming its treacly progress around the white dial.

Fifteen minutes passed. Kat called Van to let him know the good news.

Another five passed.

Then ten.

Then the door buzzer bleeped. Kat heard the visitor give their name.

'Leah Hooper, I work with Tom Gray.'

Kat rose to her feet and greeted Leah as she emerged from the little dog-leg into the ward proper.

'He's really awake?' Leah asked.

'They're checking him over, but yes. He's back.'

Kat's mind was spinning. So many things clamouring for space, from her lost half-sister to the Mark Swift case. But now Tom was awake, she felt like there was a little bit of headroom that had been missing for weeks. And, in that space, one problem began shouting louder than all the others. Her dad. His money. The plot with Carve-up to kick her off the force.

'Listen, I need to do something,' Kat said. 'Could you stay here? Try and talk to him as soon as they'll let you.'

'Of course. I was only putting a wash on. Emily never does it.'

Kat rolled her eyes. 'Neither does Van. He shrank one of my lovely jumpers once. I think he did it deliberately, just to get out of it.'

59

Leah suddenly hugged Kat fiercely before releasing her. She was beaming.

'This is so epic! I can't wait to have him back. I've missed the posh little sod.'

Kat laughed delightedly. 'Me too! I'll be back soon.'

Leaving Leah to go and sit with Tom, Kat raced out to the car park. It was time to confront her father about the money.

Chapter Eleven

Outside the mock-Tudor house that her mother insisted on referring to as the 'Morton residence' when answering the phone, Kat pulled up, scuffing the gravel beneath her car's tyres.

A gaudy gold replica of the Piccadilly Circus Eros aimed his arrow straight at her from the centre of a goldfish pond.

'Just try it,' she said, looking the statue right in the eye. 'I'll stick it straight up your gold-plated arse.'

She stabbed the doorbell.

After a few seconds, the door swung inwards. As soon as the gap was wide enough, a ginger-and-white bundle of needle-sharp teeth, bug eyes and unbridled aggression flew at her. She bent down to its level and shouted, 'Sod off!' into its pop-eyed little face. With a startled yelp, the creature fled for the safety of its owner's expensively clad calves.

Kat's mother, Sarah Morton, reached down and scooped up the little dog, which was growling loudly now it was safe.

'Darling, how nice to see you. And without having to chase you, either. What a treat. Come in.' She stroked the top of her dog's head. 'Although if you could manage to stop swearing at poor little Sidney, that would be wonderful.'

Her mum's words might have passed a threshold labelled 'borderline polite', but the ice in her voice was thick enough to skate on.

Kat followed her into a large sitting room, dominated by a grand piano. Her father was sitting in a saddle-brown leather recliner, his velvet-slippered feet up on a matching stool.

'Darling, look who's paid us an unscheduled visit,' Sarah said, depositing Sidney on the carpet.

Retreating beneath the piano, the little dog assumed a combative stance towards Kat, hackles up, forepaws planted, that made her laugh despite the tightness in her chest.

'Morning, Kitty-Kat,' Colin Morton said as he rose from the recliner and bestowed a brief peck on her cheek. She had trouble accepting this greeting, so fierce was the urge to hit him. But she'd resolved on the drive over to use guile rather than gut feelings. She stuck to the plan.

'I wanted to apologise for my outburst at dinner last time,' she said. 'I would have come over sooner, but work has been absolutely manic.'

Her father looked genuinely taken aback. Beside him, Sarah regarded her younger daughter with a look that was equal parts suspicion and satisfaction. Kat knew how her mum's mind worked, and the opportunity to play the dignified lady would be irresistible.

'Well, that's very gracious of you, Kathryn,' she said. 'We'd all had a little too much to drink, and I suppose you were entitled to be a little peeved about that money.'

'I was wondering when you'd turn up here to ask me about it,' her dad said.

Unlike her mum, her father's psychology was hard to read. He was adept at masking his true feelings. She never quite knew what was going on behind that affable exterior. Except that it would always be at least two separate and possibly conflicting strands of thought. Always, though, with a unified aim: to achieve whatever Colin Morton felt was in his best interests at that time.

She shrugged as she took an armchair. 'Like I said, work's been busy.'

'Well, now you're here, perhaps we can clear the air.' He looked over at Kat's mum. 'Darling, could we have some tea, please?'

Sarah nodded and swept from the room, leaving father and daughter staring at each other across a few metres of antique Persian rug on which camels trudged in an endless caravan around the perimeter.

Kat was enjoying the moment. It would be interesting from a professional standpoint to see how inventive her dad could be in explaining away the fifty thousand.

She eyeballed her dad. 'So?'

'Well, Diana and Eamonn are obviously doing very well for themselves these days. And I thought if I made a discreet transfer of funds, it might help you and Ivan out. He always bats me back when I offer him a stake in one of our new ventures.'

She gave his lie three out of ten.

'Why anonymously?'

'Well, isn't it obvious, darling? If I told you it came from me, you'd hand it straight back. However many times I assure you my business dealings are all above board, you do persist with this wild notion of yours that there's something dodgy going on at Morton Land.'

Two out of ten for plausibility. Although ten for sheer brass neck.

She asked the literal $64,000 question. 'What on earth made you think I could cheerfully accept that much anonymous cash and not wonder where it came from, Dad? Do I *look* like an idiot? And before you try and concoct an answer, how come Stuart Carver knew about it before I did? Tell him during one of your golf games, did you? "Just doing my little girl a solid", was it?'

'I have no idea how Stuart found out. But I can assure you it wasn't from me.'

'Let's say I believe you. How could you possibly think I'd accept the cash? Working in Major Crimes, it would be a huge red flag. I'd be duty-bound to report it.'

He held his hands wide, then looked over Kat's shoulder. 'Ah, tea. Just in time. Thanks, darling,' he said, accepting a bone china cup and saucer from Sarah's manicured fingers. 'I was just explaining to Kitty-Kat about the money. Why *did* I send it anonymously, when that would cause her problems?'

Sarah Morton handed Kat a cup and then slid her yoga-toned bottom on to the arm of her husband's recliner.

'You thought she'd just assume it was a bequest from a distant relative, darling, don't you remember?'

He looked at Kat.

'Your mother's right.'

What her mother was, Kat thought, was *in it*. Right up to her Diane von Furstenberg-clad elbows. They'd been rehearsing the confrontation between them. Probably after discussing it with Suzy. Fine. She didn't need to win this battle. Her aim was to win the war.

'Well, that must be it, then, mustn't it?'

Kat stood, placing her undrunk tea on the coffee table. 'I'm heading back to the hospital. Tom came out of his coma this morning.'

Her dad straightened in his chair. 'That's great news. Really, I mean it.'

Did he really? Kat wondered. After all, if her dad was able to corrupt a DI, a newly minted DC would be little more than a pawn to be moved around the board and sacrificed as needed. She fought down a scowl.

'I have to go. I'll see myself out.'

From his lair beneath the piano, Sidney growled. Kat hissed back and left without a backward look.

Case or no case, money or no money, she wanted to see Tom again.

Chapter Twelve

Leah was making a cup of coffee when Kat arrived in the Acute Medical Unit.

'How is he?' Kat asked.

'He's good. Amazingly good, considering. Look, would it be OK if I left now, only Em and I had plans?'

'Of course! We'll all be back together soon, so go. Do your thing. Send Em my love.'

Kat hurried over to Tom's room. He was sitting up in bed reading a magazine. Something with a bright pink masthead and lots of pictures of grinning, orange celebrities.

Kat broke into a wide smile, feeling the happiest she'd felt for weeks. 'You're up!'

She bent over the bed and hugged him as fiercely as she dared before kissing his cheek. He was clean-shaven. Had a nurse done it? She pulled up a chair and sat close enough to hold his hand.

He smiled, and she was delighted to see it was symmetrical. No lopsidedness. Or was that from strokes, not comas?

'Hey, Kat,' he said in a voice that sounded like a long-neglected door creaking open.

'Oh, Tomski, I'm just so glad you're back. Did you shave? Sorry, don't answer that. I'm a bit overwhelmed, that's all.'

'I'm a bit overwhelmed myself,' he husked. 'Sorry about the serial killer voice. It'll be better soon.'

She squeezed his hand. 'I don't care if you sound like Jeffrey Dahmer with laryngitis.'

'What happened, Kat? My memory's a bit hazy. I remember I was saying the arrest script, and then there was a fight. After that, it's a blur.'

Kat filled him in on the details. The violent scuffle. Tom falling backwards through a glass coffee table. The arrest. And that nightmare ride to the hospital.

'But we got him?'

'Yes, we did. But he died before he went to trial. The official version is suicide. But I think Frank Strutt had him killed for what he did to Alana and Callum.'

Tom nodded thoughtfully. 'I know you say nobody deserves to be murdered—' he rasped.

'I know, I know. If anybody did, he did. Look, let's not talk about him. The most important thing is, you're awake. How are you feeling? Can you move your hands? Oh, of course you can, you were reading that magazine. How's your memory? Have they done tests? When can you go home?'

Tom smiled. 'Wow. Might need to brush up on your interview technique, boss. They say a few more days. I really want to come back to work.'

'Oh, God, Tomski, and I really want to *have* you back. We all do. But best do things by the book. I don't want you keeling over halfway through an interview.'

'What are you working on now?' he asked.

'It's weird. This famous author, Mark Swift—'

Tom nodded. '*The Guillotine Man*. I read it earlier this year. I can remember that, at least.'

Kat pulled a face. 'Am I the *only* person in town not to know who he was? Anyway, he was supposed to be onstage at *Criminal Herts*, but he was lying dead in the green room. Van and I were in the audience.'

'Why weird?' Tom asked, pulling himself more upright against the pillows.

'Because the room was locked from the inside and he was alone when we found him.'

'That *is* weird. And sort of classic.'

'Please – not you, too.'

'And it's definitely murder, not suicide or natural causes?'

'The PM's tomorrow, but there are a few inconsistencies that make me think someone killed him.'

She explained about the positioning of the side table and the undisturbed champagne bucket and flute.

'Maybe you should borrow some Agatha Christies from the library,' Tom said with a crooked smile. 'Get some ideas.'

'Have *you* got any ideas?'

He screwed up his face. 'My brain feels a bit like someone used it for a game of five-a-side football. But I have this really cool mentor. Admittedly she isn't a graduate, you know, couldn't hack the pace. But she's a pretty good jack all the same. And what *she* always says is, find out how the victim lived and you'll find out how they died.'

Kat grinned. 'Funny. But you're right. So, we have a very successful man with a wife who was distraught when she heard he was dead, and an ex who seemed genuinely to care about him. But against that, Riley said apparently he was a bit of an arsehole on social media. Although for Riley's generation, that takes in roughly ninety-eight per cent of the adult population. So, you know . . .'

'Tainted testimony?'

'Yep. Plus hostile witness. And snarky into the bargain.'

'Fourteen, isn't he?'

'Mm-hmm.'

'I remember when I was his age. I drove my mum and dad crazy.'

'Yeah, me too.' Kat sighed. 'He'll grow out of it, that's what Van keeps telling me.'

Behind her, the door opened. Ellie stood there.

'I don't want you tiring Tom out, isn't it?'

'Oh, of course.' Kat leaned over Tom. 'Rest, yes? Eat your greens. Do what Sister Ellie tells you and get better. Love you, Tomski. Call me.'

'I love you too, boss,' he said, but his eyes were already drooping.

Half an hour later she was home, a glass of Pinot Grigio in her hand. Van was talking but she was miles away, pondering how Mark Swift's murderer had done it.

Van was looking at her expectantly.

'Well?'

'Sorry, love . . . Well, what?'

'What did your dad say?'

'Oh, he spun me this ridiculous line about how he wanted to support us because Di's doing so well.'

Van snorted. 'Probably because I keep knocking him back whenever he tries to get me to invest in one of his developments.'

'Yes! He actually said that!'

Kat explained how her dad had put forward a flimsy reason for not owning up to the money. It had Van rolling his eyes in a fashion Riley would have approved of.

'Well, either way, I hope it won't spoil tomorrow for you. Riley's really looking forward to seeing the farm. I think he and Liv have been texting. There's been talk of quad bikes.'

Kat shook her head. 'No, of course it won't spoil tomorrow.' Then she noticed the way Van was staring off into space.

'Everything all right, love?' she asked.

'Yeah, fine. Why?'

'I don't know. You look a bit' – she shrugged – 'distant.'

'It's nothing.'

'Come on, Van. Don't "it's nothing" me. I know you, remember.' She had a flash of insight. Van had been off about Liv recently, making the odd disparaging comment when her name cropped up in conversation. 'Are *you* looking forward to tomorrow?'

'Yeah. I mean, work's a bit hectic, but sure. I probably could use the break.'

'And that's all?'

It wasn't, she knew.

'That's all.'

Kat felt torn. Maybe Van was wary of her spending time with Liv, but Riley wasn't the only one looking forward to relaxing far from Middlehampton and its murderous occupants. Yet the Mark Swift case and the peculiar mystery of how he was actually killed was acting on her like a magnet on an iron key.

Maybe she could find some private time with Liv and ask her for her take on Mark's death. Strictly unprofessional, but then, Liv didn't really exist anymore. As far as the outside world was concerned, she'd died in 2008. Nothing wrong with consulting one murder victim about another, was there?

DAY THREE – SUNDAY

Chapter Thirteen

Kat had to hurry to keep up with Liv, who picked her way along the stony streambed like a mountain goat. Or a river goat, anyway. But at least out here in the Welsh countryside they were free of the oppressive heat smothering Middlehampton like a heavy wool coat.

Somewhere to their right, on the grassy hillside, Smokey was playing with Duffel, the farm's ageing border collie. The latter had rediscovered puppyhood as they raced around, yelping excitedly whenever they flushed out a ground-nesting bird.

'For a dead woman, you don't half walk fast,' Kat said.

Liv cackled. 'Farm life, Thelma. Builds muscles you never knew you had.'

'Oh, Louise, you big show-off,' Kat said in a passable American accent.

'Break? I brought coffee and flapjacks.'

They sat on a wide flat rock. Liv poured two coffees and handed Kat one of the sticky treats.

'Riley's grown, hasn't he?'

'Half my pay goes on shoes,' Kat said ruefully.

'He was proper pleased to be going out shooting with Rhys, wasn't he?'

Kat rolled her eyes. 'You think? He was only expecting quad bikes. But having the farm manager hand him a shotgun? Hopefully I'll rack up some cool points. I could do with them.'

Liv nibbled her own flapjack. She looked nervous all of a sudden. Was this to do with the 'mystery' she'd teased Kat with on the phone? She wasn't going to say she'd decided to come back to Middlehampton, was she? Kat decided to let her friend get to it in her own time. She'd never been amenable to pressure.

'Van looked pleased, too,' Liv continued. 'Dafydd gave him his second-best rod. He's caught some lovely fat trout with it.'

'If Van catches anything bigger than a minnow, we'll never hear the last of it. It'll be all, "When Dafydd and I went fishing." I think he's a bit in awe of him, actually.'

Liv bit her lip. Frowned.

'I've got something to tell you, Thelma.'

'Well, don't keep me in suspense, Louise,' Kat drawled, fighting down a sudden wave of anxiety. 'I could surely die!'

'Don't be sad, but – well, I'm not moving back to Middlehampton after all. I'm going to sell Mum's house and put the money into the farm.'

'Oh, Liv, is that it? Is that why you're not eating this frankly delicious flapjack?'

Liv nodded. 'My whole life is in Summerleaze. In fact . . .' – she paused; took a quick gulp of her coffee – 'Dafydd has asked me to marry him and I know it's sudden and we're going to have the wedding right here at Bryn Glas and I really, really hope you're pleased for me.'

Kat jumped up and threw her arms around her friend.

'Oh my God, this is fantastic! I *am* pleased for you, Liv. It's such good news. First Tomski comes back, and now this.'

Liv pulled away a little. Stared deep into Kat's eyes.

'Thelma.'

'Louise,' Kat answered, still smiling.

'Will you be my matron of honour?'

'Of course I will! I'd be honoured. Hang on a minute, though.' Kat took Liv's left hand in hers. 'Where's the ring?'

Liv grinned as she reached up to her neck and unclasped a thin leather thong. She took a silver ring off and drew it down over her finger.

'I didn't want you to see it before I was ready to tell you.' She held her ring finger out so the diamond sparkled in the sunlight. 'What do you think?'

'It's beautiful.'

'It is, isn't it? And guess what? There's more good news.'

'Jesus! More? I don't think I can cope with more.'

'No, you'll love this. I'm taking Dafydd's name. I'll be Olivia Jones. There's bloody thousands of us in Wales alone, so I'll be properly anonymous. No worries when I come to visit you now. And who knows,' she said, blushing a little, 'if I get pregnant, I'll swell up and be so fat nobody would ever recognise me in a million years.'

Kat felt a huge weight slide off her shoulders. Liv, aided and abetted by Rhys, had perverted the course of justice by faking her own death. Ever since she'd found out, Kat had been worried sick their shared secret could overturn the conviction of the serial killer Stefan Pulford. Now those fears just melted away. The name-change would only leave the faintest of trails, and Liv was staying in Wales, virtually off the grid. It was a win.

Relief flooded her heart, making her shiver with a kind of giddy excitement.

'Oh, Liv, you're a bloody star, do you know that?'

Her appetite returned, Liv scoffed the rest of her flapjack in three enormous bites. She washed it down with coffee then shared the remainder equally between the two plastic mugs.

'I've been following this Mark Swift thing.'

'What do you think? Could it be murder?' Kat asked, anxious suddenly that Liv would disagree with her.

'Hundred per cent. I guarantee it.'

Kat exhaled quietly. Thank God for that.

'Because . . . ?'

'It has to be! A rich, powerful middle-aged man like Swift? He was bound to have enemies.'

'Enough to want him dead, you think?'

'Mutt-calf thinks so.'

Kat groaned. Liv had bestowed the nickname on Ethan Metcalfe back when they were all at school together at Queen Anne's comprehensive, for the way he'd 'slobbered after' Kat. Now Liv listened to his podcasts as a way of feeding intel back to her.

'Go on, then. I'll bite. What's he been saying?'

'Nothing specific yet. And guess what, he's already throwing shade on you. Said he'd be relieved when Middlehampton Police, in the person of DS Ballantyne, finally decide to take the sudden death of a celebrity seriously.'

Anger surged through Kat. If Mutt-calf had been here with them right now, she'd have cheerfully pushed him headlong into the stream and held his head under.

'What about you, though, Liv? What's your take on it?'

'I had a bit of a rummage around in Swift's social media. The guy was a complete prick.'

Kat's pulse quickened. Liv was echoing Riley's judgement, almost word for word.

'Loads of people are, though. On social media, I mean.'

Liv shrugged. 'Yeah. But he was a prick online and now he's a dead prick in real life. Go figure.'

Kat stared down at the tumbling stream. Figuring it out was exactly what she intended to do. And maybe having a twisty case to focus on might help her sideline everything else going on in her life.

They walked back to the farm, Kat asking Liv all about her fiancée.

How long had they been going out? A year.

When had he arrived at the farm? Seven years ago, but they'd only been friends until a drunken party after the last harvest but one.

What was he like? Kind. Brilliant with animals. And kids.

During a long barbecue lunch, Riley regaled Kat and Van with tales of shotgun shooting. Van happily reported his haul of 'a decent-sized trout', all the while sharing fist bumps with Dafydd. Kat and Liv exchanged a knowing glance across the table.

Too soon, it was time to leave for the drive back to Middlehampton.

Kat pulled Liv into a tight hug.

'Congratulations again, lovely. Let me know when the wedding plans are coming together. Anything I can do to help, I will.'

'Thanks, mate. We'll always be there for each other, whatever happens.'

Kat smiled against Liv's neck. 'Always and for ever.'

She climbed into the car and started the engine. Behind her, Riley settled his headphones over his ears and gazed out the window, giving Rhys a thumbs-up. As the lunch party waved back, Kat turned the Golf round in the farmyard and drove out of the gate.

She buzzed the window down and inhaled the summery smell from the fields. After a couple of miles of silence, she flicked a glance at Van.

'You all right, love?'

'Yeah. Good. Just hoping that trout makes it home before it starts to smell.'

'Dafydd packed it in plenty of ice. I'm sure it'll be fine.'

'Yeah.'

She frowned. Another mile went by in silence.

'Radio?' she asked.

'No.'

'You want to tell me how you caught your trout again?'

'Leave it, Kat, yes? Just drive.'

'What? No! What's going on, Van? One minute you're giving everybody your best Old Man and the Sea impression, and now you're snapping at me like I've done something wrong.'

'It's Liv, OK? Liv. Like it always bloody is. Just when we've got some distance, she gets you to be her matron of honour. Now you'll be in and out of each other's places, with her making demands on you all over again.'

'Hold on a minute. Liv didn't "get" me to be her matron of honour. She *asked* me. And I was glad to accept. It'll be fun. It'll be lovely. She even hinted they might be trying for a baby. And if she asks me to be the godmother? I'll say yes like *that*.' She snapped her fingers hard. 'And as for making demands, I literally don't know what you're talking about.'

Van twisted round in his seat. 'You really want to know? It's great she wasn't murdered by a serial killer. And I'm pleased you two seem to have patched it up since she did her Lazarus bit on North Street. But when I met you, Kat, you were in bits. She faked her own death and you had to leave uni after a breakdown. I just don't want her to hurt you again.'

Kat exhaled. So she *had* been right. Van was being overprotective. But it was coming from a good place. She could rescue this.

'Look, if you're worried about my mental health, don't be. I'm fine. I was eighteen when it happened. I'm thirty-four now. God, that makes me feel so old! Anyway, I've moved on. And so has Liv. You heard what she said over lunch. They're staying in Summerleaze. And she's changing her name, too. Life just happens, Van. We can't stop it, and when it comes to me and Liv, I don't want to. So' – she reached over and patted his thigh – 'are *we* OK? Are *we* cool? Are *we* going to have trout and chips for tea?'

He grunted. The sound of a husband allowing himself to be won over.

'I'm stuffed with so much lamb I doubt I'll want to eat before Wednesday.'

'We'll freeze it, then.'

'No! Dafydd said you have to eat them fresh. It's the only way.'

'Oh, *Dafydd* said that, did he? Maybe *you* should marry him instead of Liv, seeing as how you *love* him so much.' She put on a sing-song voice. 'Ooh, Dafydd, remember how that cast of mine put the fly right over its nose?'

He flicked her ear. 'Shut up and drive, stinky.'

So she did. Back to Middlehampton and her doubts over Mark Swift's death. Was Liv right? Did all rich, powerful men have mortal enemies?

It was her job to find out.

DAY FOUR –
MONDAY

Chapter Fourteen

Carve-up waited at the front of the big meeting room to begin the regular Monday morning briefing.

His suit today, one of a growing collection of Italian designer brands, shimmered silver and grey as he moved beneath the fluorescent tubes overhead. An image swam into Kat's head. One of those lean, torpedo-shaped predatory fish that darted out of the shadows and took a bite out of you.

He cleared his throat. Waited for his customary three-count. Unnecessary, since the room had immediately fallen silent.

'Nice to be back, people. I tell you, a month's rotation shadowing a Met DCI is not to be undertaken lightly. Still, what I learned in the Smoke will be invaluable in boosting our clearance rates and other KPIs.' He made a 'silly me' face, mouth bunched to one side, eyes rolling. 'Sorry. Key Performance Indicators. Must've picked it up from my oppo.'

As Kat glared at him, she wished it had been him taking a shard of toughened glass to the femoral artery instead of Tom. He must have picked up on the hostility, which was coming off her in waves, because he turned and looked right at her.

'DS Ballantyne, anything to report? Any suicidal authors you're going to try and talk up to murder?'

So he'd heard. Of course he'd heard! He might be the world's most useless detective but he made sure he knew what was happening in his department. You never knew when a juicy bit of intel might come in handy for your paymaster.

She ignored the taunt. Carve-up's attempts to belittle her in front of the team had long ago lost their sting. Instead she turned away from him to address the room.

'Stu's half-right,' she began, using the nickname she knew he hated as much as she hated Kitty-Kat.

'Better than usual, then,' someone muttered, just loud enough for his neighbours to hear. A snicker rippled outwards.

Fighting down a grin, Kat continued. 'Mark Swift, a world-famous crime author, was found dead last Friday morning in the green room at the Guildhall.'

'Yes, we all have social media, DS Ballantyne,' Carve-up interrupted. 'Locked from the inside, blah blah blah. So far, so Twitter. What else?'

Part of her wanted to back away from the confrontation. The sensible, the *risk-averse*, thing to do would be to wait until after that morning's post-mortem. After all, there was still a chance, probably a *good* chance, that Jack would slice and dice, measure and weigh, sniff and probe, and then pronounce cause of death as natural.

But the other part of her, the part she felt made her a decent detective, wanted to get Mark's murder on the sheet so resources could be allocated, a team assigned, a case file opened. And, sooner rather than later, a suspect identified and arrested.

'There are aspects to the scene of Mark Swift's death that militate against it being suicide or' – she shot Carve-up a warning glance before he could interrupt her a second time – 'natural causes.'

'*Militate*,' he echoed with a smirk, his eyes roving the room, looking for an ally. 'Been reading the dictionary over the weekend, DS Ballantyne?'

She inhaled. Held for a count of three. Let it out.

'We can discount suicide. I found no ligature at the scene, so he didn't hang himself. No pills, either. Are we to believe he took an overdose, then climbed into his car and drove to town, parked, made his way to the Guildhall, made small talk with the festival director and one of the sponsors, then locked himself in and died?' Carve-up started to open his mouth. She held up a hand. 'It was rhetorical, Stu. You'll find it in the dictionary. So, is that what happened? I don't think so. As to natural causes, to me the scene looked staged. The furniture was undisturbed, yet he ended up on the floor like the cover of one of those true crime magazines we all claim never to look at in WHSmith.'

Over the year she'd been working in Major Crimes, Kat had grown in confidence. And she'd found a way to use humour to get her point across. A few of the other detectives chuckled at this remark.

Craig Elders, another DS, chipped in. 'I know the Guildhall. At the College, we had the use of a couple of rooms as our sixth-form centre. It was common knowledge there was a secret passageway.' He addressed the room at large. 'Apparently, Henry the Eighth had the Guildhall built for when he was doing his royal progress. He put in this tunnel so he could visit his mistress without anyone noticing.'

'Look, people!' Carve-up protested. 'The history lesson is all very interesting, but really? Secret passageways so Henry the Eighth could sneak off for an extramarital shag? This is MCU, not the Friday Murder Club.'

'It's Thursday,' Leah said, winking at Kat on Carve-up's blind side.

'It's actually Monday, DC Hooper,' Carve-up snapped, 'but maybe you're as tired and confused as DS Ballantyne obviously is.'

'No, Stuart,' Craig said, 'Leah means it's the *Thursday Murder Club*. The book. I wouldn't have had you down as a fan, to be honest.'

This time there was open laughter.

Carve-up's face darkened. The barracuda bared its teeth. 'Thursday, Friday, it doesn't matter. What does matter is that I am trying to run a major crimes team and deliver on the metrics that this entire department gets judged on by the brass over in Welwyn Garden City. So unless you've got *concrete* evidence that a murder was committed, DS Ballantyne?' He stared at her. She stayed silent. 'No? Didn't think so. So all we've got, and obviously it's sad and all the usual, is a dead middle-aged bloke who probably carked it from a coronary because he didn't look after himself. You know what those authors are like. If it wasn't booze and big lunches that did him in, it was probably an industrial-grade coke habit.'

'Which the post-mortem will tell us,' Kat said. 'It's in half an hour. Excuse me, everyone, I need to go or I'll be late.'

Kat left the room, the barracuda gaping after her, his teeth visible but, for once, unable to do any damage.

Next stop, the forensic autopsy suite at Middlehampton General and the truth about how Mark Swift's killer had managed to commit such a perplexing crime. As she drove, she told herself she didn't need to wish another murder case into being. She had enough on her plate at work without adding to it, let alone her tangled personal life.

But still she pressed on, feeling the overwhelming need to do something as simple as pulling on a thread attached to a dead body, until the murderer came into view attached to the other end. Van had caught a trout at the weekend. Maybe she could hook a murderer.

Chapter Fifteen

Mark Swift's corpse lay on the gleaming dissection table.

Grey hairs curled on his chest and he had a definite paunch – probably the result of good living, if not quite on the scale suggested by Carve-up in the briefing. But despite that, even naked and dead, the author was in reasonable shape.

Kat looked at his genitals. She'd seen the bodies of men murdered by jealous spouses. A degree of injury to the offending parts wasn't unusual. Swift's appeared unmarked.

'Happy for me to begin, Kat?' Jack asked.

She looked up. Was he grinning behind that mask? It was impossible to tell. But there was definitely something in his voice. A knowingness she would have preferred not to be there.

'Dive in, Doc,' she said. 'He's all yours.'

Jack began with a visual examination of the body.

'Apart from the beginnings of livor mortis on the forehead and chest, nothing on the front. Ashleigh, how about the fingers?'

His assistant lifted the right hand, then the left, examining the fingertips.

'No debris beneath the nails. No abrasions on the knuckles. No signs of struggle or defensive wounds,' she said.

'Thank you. Could you help turn him over, please?'

'Certainly, Dr Beale.'

Jack sighed. 'I've told you before, Ashleigh. It's Jack. Dr Beale is my father.'

Together, Jack and Ashleigh pushed, rolled and lifted the body until it lay face down on the stainless-steel table. Larger dull red patches were present on Swift's shoulders, upper arms, buttocks and thighs, where blood had pooled beneath the skin.

'Livor mortis more developed on the posterior surface, specifically over the deltoids, triceps, gluteus maximus and biceps femoris.'

Jack parted the hair at the centre of the scalp and peered at the exposed skin.

'This is interesting. Tell me what you see there, Ashleigh, please?'

Jack stepped back. Ashleigh bent over the head and used her own fingers to probe the area Jack had indicated.

'There's a contusion, oedema and some broken blood vessels,' she said.

'Which you interpret as what?' Jack asked.

'It looks like either he fell and hit his head, or someone smacked him with something hard but smooth.'

'Like what?'

'A bat? A rolling pin?'

'We'll leave that to our colleagues in MCU,' Jack said, nodding to Kat, 'but yes, I agree. Blunt force trauma to the parietal bone roughly halfway along the midline.'

'Would it have been enough to knock him out?' Kat asked.

'Judging by the size of the swelling and the extent of the bruising, I'd say yes. Easily. When we examine the brain we may find evidence of contrecoup injury. Which is what, Ashleigh?'

'Oh, right. When the brain executes a . . . er . . .'

'Plain English is fine,' Jack said encouragingly.

'It's when someone gets a blow to the head and the brain sort of sloshes away from the site of the injury and smashes into the other side of the skull. You find broken blood vessels and tissue damage on the opposite side of the brain from the point of impact.'

'Excellent. Couldn't have put it better myself.'

Kat nodded with satisfaction. She'd been right all along. Mark had been murdered.

After another five minutes, they rolled the corpse over again.

'Let's have a look under the bonnet, shall we?' Jack said.

Without being asked, Ashleigh handed him a large-bladed scalpel.

With the torso opened and the flaps of skin folded back, Jack took a smaller scalpel and started an incision in the throat.

'We'll check his airway and gullet, shall we? Who knows, we might find a few wheat grains, eh, Kat?'

She grimaced inside her mask. Jack was referring to Stefan Pulford's MO.

'Hmm, what's this?' Jack murmured. 'Artery forceps, please, Ashleigh.'

He poked the long slender instrument into the corpse's throat. He closed them and pulled them clear. Clamped between their jaws was a fragment of blue and silver paper that glinted in the overhead light. He tapped it into the waiting debris pot, on to which Ashleigh screwed a red plastic top before labelling it with a Sharpie and setting it to one side.

The tone of Jack's voice changed as he cut into the trachea.

'That's odd. Ashleigh, can you find me the suction pump aspirator, please?'

'What is it, Jack?' Kat asked, as everybody leaned closer.

'There's liquid at the fork where the trachea divides into the bronchi.'

'What kind of liquid?'

'That's what we're going to find out.'

Ashleigh returned to Jack's side holding a bright yellow plastic device that resembled a weedkiller sprayer. Jack inserted the clear plastic tube into the exposed windpipe, pushing it down into the right lung. He pumped the handle a few times and a thin stream of clear fluid flowed into the collection bottle.

'What is that?' Kat asked. 'Vodka?'

Jack unscrewed the bottle from the tube and sniffed the contents. He wrinkled his nose and sniffed again.

'I'll have to test it, but I think it's just water.'

He screwed the bottle back in place and repeated the process with the left lung, this time pushing it deeper and pumping for longer. Jack withdrew the pipe and held up the half-full bottle where everybody could see it.

'Well, this is odd,' he said. 'It looks like Mr Swift drowned.'

Chapter Sixteen

When the post-mortem was finished, Kat hurried back to the car park and climbed into her Golf. The murderer had knocked Mark out with a blow to the head using a weapon of some kind. Finding it was a priority. It might have fingerprints, epithelials or hairs. All of which could link a suspect to the murder.

Having rendered him unconscious, they'd drowned him by either piping water into his throat or holding his face underwater. It explained the wet hair, at least. But where had the water come from? She couldn't remember seeing a sink or empty receptacle of any kind. A champagne bucket, sure, but it had been full of ice, not water.

And, the most perplexing thing of all, exactly *how* had the killer managed to escape from the green room? Was there a secret passageway, as Craig had suggested at the morning briefing? A central heating duct on the ceiling? Some funny business with magnets?

There was only one way to find out. She called Leah: 'Meet me at the Guildhall. We've got a murder to solve.'

Then Darcy: 'Hey, Darce. It's confirmed. Mark Swift was murdered. Can you bring a team to the Guildhall?'

With the troops assembling, Kat drove out of the hospital, scrupulously observing the 20-mph limit. On gaining the freedom of the B road that led back into town she floored the throttle, enjoying the eager roar of the Golf's engine and the shove in the small of her back. Carve-up's red Alfa Romeo convertible it might not be, but she loved her trusty little VW. It would be taking her where she needed to go long after Carve-up's penis substitute was rusting in a scrapyard somewhere.

It was just a shame his career couldn't deteriorate along with it. But then again, she had no intention of letting him serve out his thirty.

Fifteen minutes later, she parked outside the Guildhall, slapping a laminated homemade sign on the dash. *On Police Business*. No legal force, but she knew most of the traffic wardens in town and they usually cut her some slack.

Leah was standing on the steps holding two takeaway cups and a paper bag.

'Thought you mightn't have had breakfast, what with the PM,' she said, holding up the bag. 'Americano and a bacon sarnie with brown sauce.'

Kat grinned as she put her murder bag down. 'You're a star. Any sign of Darcy and the CSIs?'

'Nope. Traffic was terrible getting here, though. They've put a contraflow in on Roseveare Way again.'

Kat took a bite of the bacon sandwich and washed it down with the coffee. 'God, that's good. Thanks, mate. Right, let's go in and find the caretaker. I want to give him a heads-up.'

They found Ernie in his cubbyhole, reading the *Daily Express* and drinking tea from his royal jubilee mug.

'Hi, Ernie,' Kat said, wiping her fingers on a paper napkin before shaking hands. 'We need to have a look inside the green room again. It's officially a crime scene now. There'll be quite a bit of coming and going, I'm afraid.'

'Don't remember me, do you?' he said, winking at Leah.

'Of course I do. It was only Saturday,' Kat replied.

'Not then. Cast your mind back. You were fresh out of Hendon, wandering around Jubilee Place like Dorothy in the Land of Oz.'

Kat stared at him, trying to see past the ageing effects of the last twelve years. She closed her eyes. Took a quick virtual walk around Jubilee Place. What had she done in those first few, nerve-racking days? Toured the station in a small group of new recruits, of course. The squad room. The locker room. CID. MCU. The custody suite. The data centre. The—

Her eyes snapped open.

'You were the night custody sergeant! Oh my God, it's you, Skip. I can't believe I didn't recognise you.'

'It was a long time ago.' He patted his belly. 'And I've put on a few pounds since then. Lost my hair too. I retired a couple of weeks after you arrived.'

'So you must have known Barrie Price?'

Ernie smiled. 'Baz? We play bowls together. You know him?'

'We see each other on dog walks. He's my sounding board when cases get sticky.'

'Like this one's about to?'

'What do you mean?'

'People don't see me, Kat. These brown overalls are better than Harry Potter's invisibility cloak. Especially when I'm pushing a broom around. But I see them. And I listen too. Old habits.'

'What have you heard?'

'Well.' He dropped his voice to a conspiratorial murmur. 'Couple of publishing types on Sunday, last day of the festival, right? Women. They were drinking Pimm's in the garden. Quite a lot, to judge from the state of them. One of them said, "I hope he *is* dead. Good riddance." And the other said, "I'd like to give whoever did it a medal." Sounds like Swift had a few enemies.'

Kat thought back to the two female novelists who'd been badmouthing Mark Swift while they were waiting for his interview to start. Maybe he had more than a few.

'It does. Thanks, Ernie. I don't suppose you got a name for either of these women?'

He grinned crookedly. 'You can take the man out of the job, Kat . . . One of them was an author whose books I used to like. Amy Swales. She's got a website. The other one I didn't know, but Amy called her Cheryl. Find Amy, you'll find the other easily enough, I'd have thought.'

Kat grinned at Leah. 'Blimey! First my bagwoman buys me a bacon sarnie, then the caretaker turns out to be Rebus.'

He nodded his acceptance of the compliment. 'If you ever fancy a brew, my door is always open.'

She nodded from the doorway. 'I will.'

It was time to get to work.

Chapter Seventeen

'What are we looking for?' Leah asked as she and Kat entered the green room in full protective gear.

'Mark Swift was whacked on the head with something smooth and heavy. And, get this, he was drowned. So a bucket of water or a hosepipe leading to a hidden tap would be peachy.'

'How about a fairy holding a sign saying, "This way to the murderer's DNA"?'

Kat smiled behind her mask, hot and already sweaty in the Noddy suit as the temperature outside climbed into the high twenties again.

'Also nice,' she replied. 'You take the left side, I'll do the right.'

At first glance, the room was devoid of anything big enough to fit Mark Swift's head. The ice bucket, now holding a few inches of lukewarm water, briefly presented a candidate. But up close, and after a three-second dip-and-dunk experiment, Kat dismissed it. Her own head simply wouldn't fit. Even if the murderer had somehow managed to squash Mark's head down far enough to drown him, the sharp metal rim would have cut across the bridge of his nose, and probably severed his ears into the bargain.

The bottle of champagne was a different story. Kat shone her iPhone torch on to the dark green glass, hoping to pick up a fingerprint. The CSIs would dust it, fume it and use their alternative light sources on it, but she had an impatient streak that had characterised her time as a cop.

Nothing. Didn't matter. Darcy would probably roll her lovely blue eyes and mutter about 'detectives playing at science'.

Alone with her thoughts, Kat walked a grid pattern over the carpet. Different detectives favoured different approaches. Some swore by the spiral approach; others, the strip. When blood spatter was present, the elevation zone was the best approach. Looking up as well as down to locate cast-off spatter as well as jetted droplets.

'I know this sounds silly, Leah,' she said without turning away, 'but try tapping the walls. If Craig's memory is right, there could be a secret passageway. I did it before, but you might have more luck.'

Leah snickered from inside her own paper mask. 'Sounds a bit Famous Five, don't you think?'

Shaking her head, Kat continued pacing across the carpet. Nothing stood out. As crime scenes went it was extremely well ordered – no tipped-over furniture, no broken pictures or domestic items. Nothing out of place at all, bar the smashed window and, when it had been here, the dead body.

A large, dark wooden chest sat in one corner. Atop its richly carved lid stood a glass vase full of deep pink peonies. For a second, Kat's heart lifted. Here was the water source. But as she looked closer, what she'd taken for water was actually glass beads. The flowers, though extremely realistic, were artificial, some soft-to-the-touch plastic.

She lifted the vase off the chest and set it on the floor. The chest was six feet by three and about two feet high. Easily big enough for an adult to hide in. But when she tried to open the lid, it resisted her as if carved from a solid block. She knelt in front of it. Hidden between two curling carved eels – long a symbol of the town's prosperity – was a small brass keyhole. She jerked the lid again just in case it was merely stuck shut from warping, or perhaps centuries of varnish. But it held firm.

Someone knocked loudly, making her jump back. But it was the door to the green room. She smiled guiltily at her reaction. She unlocked it to find Darcy Clements standing there with two CSIs, already suited up. Darcy was carrying a DSLR camera with a ring flash.

'Morning,' she said with a wry smile. 'I see you've already got your grubby fingers all over my crime scene.'

Kat held up her blue-gloved hands and waggled them, jazz-style.

'I'm wearing gloves!'

'Where'd you get them? Off the front of *Women's Weekly?*'

Grinning, Kat yanked her mask off. 'God, I'm boiling in this.'

'Wait till you get outside. My car said it was twenty-nine.'

'More like thirty-nine in here.'

Darcy gestured over her shoulder at the waiting CSIs. 'May we?'

'Sorry, Darce. Have at it.'

While the three forensics officers began their work, Kat and Leah headed outside to grab what Kat hopefully called 'some fresh air'.

She was disappointed. Middlehampton had turned muggy and the sun beating down out of a cloudless sky felt ominous rather than cheering. Images of charred meat and decomposing corpses flooded Kat's mind.

'What next, boss?' Leah said as she crouched beside her murder bag and stuffed the last of her gear into it.

'Can you start tracking down the two women Ernie mentioned? Amy . . . what was it? Swales?'

'Yes.'

'And Cheryl whatever-her-name-is. I want to know more about their views of Mark Swift. Sounds like they didn't think much of him.'

'Where are you going?'

Kat sighed. She had to let Carve-up know they were definitely investigating a murder. There were processes to be started, and – as he would delight in telling her, as patronisingly as possible – 'protocols' to be observed. Not to mention the dreaded 'metrics', to be invoked like some gimcrack deity at whose feet the Armani-clad DI worshipped.

No. She decided not to let Carve-up spoil her morning just yet. Policework first. Dealing with her misogynistic boss second.

'I'm going to talk to Maria Sheriff. She was one of the last people to see Mark alive, along with my sister, ironically.'

Leah raised her eyebrows in mute enquiry.

'I really hope not, mate,' Kat said, picking up Leah's unspoken question. 'Because if Princess Di's a person of interest, I will never hear the end of it. My mum will probably disown me. No, Di's a sponsor. Maria introduced her to Mark a few minutes before he died.'

'Wow. I see what you mean. Your mum would storm Jubilee Place like Hyacinth Bucket on PCP.'

Kat snorted. She'd shared her mum's put-on airs with Leah over wines in the pub. Saying 'one' instead of 'I'. Calling the loo the 'little girls' room'. And, whenever she was reasonably sure of the translation, using French instead of English. '*Entrez*' instead of 'come in'. '*Chez nous*' instead of 'at ours'. And her favourite, when the stress of dealing with her younger daughter's amusement became too much: '*merde*'. The fact she pronounced it *murd* added a certain *je ne sais quoi* for Kat, conjuring up as it did images of dead bodies.

'Let's hope it doesn't come to that. I don't think we've got enough riot gear.'

Agreeing to meet for a debrief before lunchtime, the two detectives went their separate ways.

Before leaving to interview Maria Sheriff, Kat went to find Ernie. She found him polishing the brass door plates in the ballroom.

He turned as she approached and stuck his cloth in a pocket of his overalls. 'What's up, Kat?'

'Two things. One, is there a key for that big wooden chest in the green room?'

He shook his head. 'Not that I know of. I've got all the keys here and none of them open it. It was one of the first things I tried when I took this job. I'm not even sure it's original to the Guildhall. Looks Jacobean to me. What was the second thing?'

'A bit of a history lesson. Is it true that Henry the Eighth had the Guildhall built?'

'It is,' he said, his eyes twinkling. Like he already knew where she was going.

'It's just my oppo used to hang out here as a sixth-former. And he said there was a . . .' God, it sounded so silly to say it. She hesitated. Would Ernie roll his eyes and laugh at this newly promoted DS?

'A . . . ?' Ernie prompted, clearly enjoying himself.

'A secret passageway. So he could sneak off to shag his mistress.'

Ernie frowned. Put his finger to his chin. Looked up at the ornate plasterwork ceiling then back at Kat. 'A secret passageway? With flaming torches stuck in metal wall brackets, you mean? Masses of spiderwebs? Maybe arrows shooting out of holes in the stones?'

She punched him lightly in the arm, setting him cackling gleefully.

'That's Indiana Jones! Come on, Ernie, I feel embarrassed even asking.'

He shook his head and sighed. 'If I had a quid for every time I've been asked about the' – he made air quotes – '"secret passageway", I'd be a bloody millionaire. And to answer your question: no, there isn't. I'm a bit of a local history buff. Always was, even before I landed up here. I've seen the original blueprints for this place, drawn up by one Thomas Pomeroy in July 1531. Let me tell you, Kat, I've been over them with a magnifying glass, literally. No secret passageway.'

Now she was here, Kat found she couldn't let go of the idea, however fanciful, without at least another push.

'But surely if it was secret, it wouldn't have been on the plans? Perhaps he had it dug after the house was built.'

'He might have. Which is why I've also been over the Guildhall like a rat in the walls. There *could* be a tunnel, but if there is, I haven't found it and I've had twelve years of looking.'

That seemed to settle it. The murderer had found a different way to make his escape from the green room, without the help of Henry VIII's scattergun libido. She thanked Ernie and headed back to the front doors. She pushed through, into the humidity and heat, to find a young woman with facial piercings and a spiderweb tattoo on her throat shoving an iPhone into her face.

'DS Ballantyne! Ten seconds of your time for my *Swiftly Killed* podcast? Actually it's for my TikTok? A listener magnet? Anyway, people are saying Mark Swift was murdered by a reader who was angry that he'd used AI to faux-create his latest book? What's your view on that?'

Kat froze, bamboozled by the young woman's rapid-fire, jargon-laden questions.

'What?'

'Or, my hot take, Mark Swift faked his own death to avoid paying tax on his vast royalty income?'

Kat dodged round the podcaster – anxious, even in her confusion, not to lay a hand on her, which would lead to a long session in front of a PC filling in a use-of-force form.

With the young woman's increasingly strident questions coming after her like a cloud of angry wasps, Kat practically sprinted for her car, her mind reeling. This was getting out of hand. AI? Faked deaths? What next? Russian assassins? Aliens?

Relaxing as the air con chilled her sweating forehead, she aimed the Golf towards Mortimer Grove. Maybe Maria Sheriff would be able to shed a little more light on Mark Swift's final moments.

Chapter Eighteen

Mortimer Grove was one of Kat's favourite parts of Middlehampton. Not least because if you strolled along Mortimer Street on Windrush Day, you could buy the best jerk chicken you'd ever tasted, while bass-driven grooves rattled the windows and thrummed inside your chest.

Maria's neat red-brick terrace house was situated halfway down Jamaica Road, half-hidden from the street by an enormous spreading-branched sycamore tree.

The Maria who opened the door looked very different from the chic festival director Kat had met earlier. Her blonde hair was gathered up in a messy bun through which a yellow pencil was poked. Tortoiseshell-effect glasses dangled against her chest on a leather thong. Her lanky frame was draped in a floaty paisley-patterned maxi-dress. White sneaker toecaps peeped from under the hem. In her head Kat dubbed the look 'author goes to Glastonbury'.

'Come in,' Maria said brightly. 'I was just making tea. I'm taking a break from writing. My latest book has hit the tricky second act. Let me pour the tea and we can drink it in the garden.'

'How are you coping, Maria?' Kat asked when they'd taken cups of tea outside and were seated beneath a wide cotton parasol. The tiny green space was bursting with loud, tropical flowers and shiny, waxy-leaved plants, as if to remind its owner of the place the road was named for. In the sticky heat, colourful birds singing from the trees, Kat felt she could actually be in Jamaica.

'Well, it was a shock, obviously. Like I told you, Mark and I parted on good terms. And although he'd remarried' – her voice hitched and she took a sip of tea before continuing – 'I still had, well, not exactly feelings, but, you know, I respected him. He was a fantastic storyteller. And he saw me OK in the divorce.'

Kat sipped her own tea. It was delicious. Just a hint of the perfumed flavour of Earl Grey.

'There's no easy way to tell you this, Maria, but we've established that Mark was murdered. I'm sorry.'

Maria stared at Kat. Then, very slowly, she placed her tea on the cast-iron table between them. The cup rattled, once, in the saucer.

'Murdered? I thought it was a heart attack?'

'I'm afraid there's no doubt. I witnessed the post-mortem myself.' She brought out her phone and placed it on the table beside her teacup. 'Is it OK if I record our conversation?'

'Of course.'

'Thank you. So, I wanted to ask you whether you knew if Mark had any enemies. People who might have had a reason to want him dead. Or even just see him badly frightened.'

Maria took a steadying sip of tea. Sniffed. 'Look, Mark wasn't perfect. He was married three times so obviously not the best husband. At least to me and Rachel.'

'Rachel?'

'Rachel Dixon. She was Mark's first wife. They married young.'

'Do you know why they divorced?'

Maria shrugged. 'It's the old story. He became mega-successful and dumped her for a younger model.'

'Which would have been you?'

Maria blushed. 'Oh. I didn't mean that I was prettier than Rachel or anything. Once Mark and I divorced, she and I became friends. She writes, too. Historical fiction, though, not crime. But you know what men are like, Kat. They never really grow up, do they? Rachel was a few years older than Mark, and I think, I mean . . .' She tailed off, still blushing furiously.

'It's fine, Maria,' Kat said. 'I wasn't judging you. I'm just trying to build up a picture of Mark's life. You're friends with Rachel. How would you say she felt about his divorcing her to marry – as you put it – a younger model?'

Maria blinked. The question appeared to catch her by surprise. How could she be that innocent? Had she really thought this was just a cosy chat about her ex while they drank tea in her Caribbean-inspired back garden?

'It's not my place. You ought to talk to her.'

'And I will. But for now I'm asking you, Maria. So? How did she take it?'

'How do you *think* she took it?' Maria snapped, the brittle good humour cracking like a bone china teacup that had been given a sharp tap. 'She was mortified. Angry. Humiliated. Rachel and Mark had been childhood sweethearts. They went to school together right here in Middlehampton. Then his first book goes straight to the top of the charts on both sides of the Atlantic, and two months later the papers are in and Rachel's scrambling to find a lawyer in town Mark hasn't already talked to.'

She stopped suddenly and slurped her tea.

The cup tinkled as she placed it back in its saucer with a visibly shaking hand.

'Do you think she could have held a grudge all this time?' Kat asked. 'Was she the type of woman who could commit murder?'

'You should know this better than me, Kat,' Maria said carefully. 'I'm not trying to incriminate Rachel. But I think, given the right circumstances, anyone could be capable of murder. Even you.'

She was right. But it wasn't relevant.

Kat pressed on. 'Apart from Rachel, can you think of anyone else who might have wished Mark harm?'

'Listen, Kat, I know we crime writers have a certain image as experts on the dark side of the human mind. But do you know how we spend our days? We're not hanging out with drug dealers, serial killers and rapists. Or riding shotgun with armed response units. We sit at our little desks, or our cafe tables, and we peck away on our laptops. Most of the research we do is online. Oh, we might phone the odd copper if we're lucky enough to know one, or email a professor of entomology or a poisons expert, but we're writers. The worst injuries we get are paper cuts. The most frightening people we come into contact with are agents – and they're usually on our side.'

It was a good speech, and Kat wondered whether Maria had given it before. But she had work to do and Maria, though perfectly open, clearly didn't have much more to offer. Kat gave her a card and asked her to call if she thought of anything.

She got to her feet, dread settling in her stomach like a bad takeaway. She couldn't put it off any longer.

It was time to tell Carve-up she was upgrading Mark's death to murder.

Chapter Nineteen

Kat pushed through the doors into MCU.

The room throbbed with noise. Ringing phones, cops discussing cases and, in the background, Radio 2, which someone had presumably thought would 'lighten the mood'. ABBA were singing 'Money, Money, Money', reminding Kat that Iris was tracking down the originator of the bank transfer. Her stomach flipped at the thought. She pushed the anxiety down.

Leah stood up to greet her as she made her way through the press of desks towards Carve-up's office.

'Annie rang. The big boss wants to see you.'

'Thanks, mate. Need to go and brief Carve-up first, though. Might as well get the rubbish job done first.'

Kat paused outside Carve-up's door. Closed, as usual. She checked the fly zip on her jeans. Up. The buttons on her shirt. Not gaping. The soles of her boots. No loo paper. She took a deep breath, knocked and entered, leaving Carve-up's 'Come!' floating redundantly in the aftershave-scented air between them.

'Hold on,' he said, without looking up from his keyboard, over which his fingers hovered, stabbing keys one at a time as if trying to drive them through the board. 'Control, Alt, Save. OK, we're done.' He looked up. The smile vanished as he saw it was Kat. 'DS Ballantyne. What is it now?'

A brief but pleasurable image floated into her head. She was shoving the DI's head down into an ice bucket full of water. Never mind the tight fit. She'd just push harder.

'Mark Swift was murdered. Bashed on the head, then drowned. I'm setting up a case file and a team and just wanted you to know.'

He sighed. Regarded her silently for a few seconds. Adjusted his cuffs, closed today with small golden truncheons. The move revealed a shiny watch on an expandable gold and steel band, its bezel a striking cobalt blue. Somehow, without seeing the logo, she knew it would be a Rolex. She wondered whether her father bought them wholesale.

'Any suspects?' he asked.

'It's only just been confirmed. We're already identifying persons of interest.'

'Was he married?'

'Three times.'

'Check the exes. He probably screwed them over in the divorces.'

'On it.'

'And the current Mrs Swift. Maybe he was screwing around on her, too.'

So many ripostes presented themselves. Wanting to thank him for his piercing investigative insights came top, but what would it achieve? Maybe an oblique approach would be more satisfying.

'Nice watch,' she said, gesturing at his wrist.

He turned it and, as if surprised to find an expensive timepiece there, inspected it, eyebrows raised. It wasn't a bad act.

'It is, isn't it?' he said.

'Rolex?'

'Submariner. It's vintage: 1988. A modern masterpiece.'

Wondering whether a watch could be both vintage *and* modern, she pressed home her advantage, suddenly keen to know the watch's provenance for sure.

'Must have cost you a bit. Emma forgo her maintenance payments for a few months, did she?'

'That's none of your business,' he snarled.

'Or was it a gift? You know, from an admirer. Or a golf buddy. Someone happy to repay a favour.'

He glared at her. But behind the hard eyes, she could see the knowledge they both shared: Carve-up was in her dad's pocket.

'Was there anything else, DS Ballantyne? I've got to leave for a meeting in five. Debriefing the big chief over in Welwyn.'

She leaned across the desk and dropped her voice so he was forced to match her posture or miss what she was saying.

'I'm going to find out who signed off on the money, Stu. And now I'm wondering how you got to know about it. I'd keep that Rolex wound up if I were you. Because time's running out.'

It was a decent parting shot. She left him, wisps of smoke curling from his ears, before he could shoot back a closing insult. It was childish, but she wanted to have the last word.

A quiet 'Fuck you, Kitty-Kat' slipped round the door as it closed.

Shaking her head, she made her way to Linda Ockenden's office.

'She's expecting you. Go straight in,' Annie said with a smile.

'Am I in trouble?' Kat asked, only half-jokingly.

Something about being summoned to Linda's office always reduced her to the status of the snarky teenager who'd knocked around with Liv at Queen Anne's, getting into scrapes on average once a week.

'No. I think you'll be quite pleased, actually. By the way, how's Riley?'

'Fine. Basically. Cross half the time and sullen the other, but we're getting by. How about Ollie?'

'The same,' Annie said with a grin.

Kat crossed in front of Annie's desk, tapped lightly on Linda's open door and went in.

Linda smiled at her.

'Can we have those coffees now, Annie, love?' she called out. Then she motioned for Kat to sit. 'Go on then, ask me.'

'What's the good news, Ma-Linda?'

'The Home Office just got given more money. And some of that has found its way to us.'

'Bloody hell! You don't mean we've actually got more budget?'

Linda's lipsticked mouth widened into a smile. 'I know, right? Harder to believe than a serial killer's alibi, but there you go. And that means I have more money for warm bodies in MCU.'

The door opened behind Kat. She turned in her chair. Annie was carrying a tray bearing three mugs of coffee. And she was not alone.

'Kat, I want you to meet Faisal Mohammed,' Linda said. 'He's joining us from West Midlands Police. Take a pew, Faisal.'

The young, strikingly good-looking man stood there in a beautifully cut charcoal-grey suit, a kingfisher-blue tie, and the sharpest haircut and goatee she'd ever seen.

He offered his hand. Kat shook it. She frowned. His fingers were rough with calluses.

'Sorry,' he said, as he sat. 'I'm a spin bowler. Goes with the territory, I'm afraid.'

'Faisal had a try-out for Warwickshire,' Linda said, sounding like a proud mum rather than DCI. 'And he was playing for the Brummie police team until his transfer.'

'Cricket, right?' Kat asked. 'Sorry, I'm not much of a sports fan. That's more my husband's thing.'

Faisal smiled widely. 'It's OK. Although, if we're going to be working together I might have to educate you.'

Kat turned to Linda. 'He's mine?'

'Would have been anyway, but given Tom's situation, it makes sense. When he's back, you'll have three DCs. But for now you'll just have to manage with two.'

Kat turned to her new DC. 'What were you doing in Birmingham, Faisal?'

'I was based in the intelligence unit out of Lloyd House. That's the HQ there. In Snow Hill?'

'Yeah, I worked with a guy who'd been up there.'

He nodded. 'I mainly ran intel ops but I did some undercover assignments, too. People trafficking, mostly. And grooming gangs.' He paused for a split second. 'Not the white ones, obviously – you may have noticed I have Pakistani heritage.'

Sensing that here was a man she could build a great relationship with – no side and plenty of self-aware humour – Kat warmed to him at once.

'I thought I detected a couple of signs,' she said with a smile.

He grinned. 'Be honest, it was the goatee, wasn't it?'

She cocked her head to one side.

'That or the constant cricket references.'

'What are you working on right now, boss? Should I call you that? Or do you prefer something else?'

'Kat's fine. Boss if you must. Just, please don't call me guv. Makes me feel like a TV copper in his fifties with a brown suit and a beer gut.'

'Kat it is, then. And if it's OK, I like to be called Fez.'

Kat glanced at Linda to include her in the conversation. 'We have a murder. Weird one, actually. This famous author, Mark Swift, was found dead in a locked room in the Guildhall on Friday.

I was there with my husband, so first on scene. The pathologist confirmed earlier today he was knocked out then drowned.'

Faisal's eyes had popped wide open as Kat mentioned Mark by name. 'I read about that over the weekend in the *Echo*. I love his stuff. Although I don't think *The Guillotine Man* was as good as people are making out. For me, *Black Roses in Winter* was a far better book.'

'Looks like we've got a literary man as well as a cricketer,' Linda said with a wink.

'Back in Brum they used to call me Dickens,' Faisal said. 'I don't think they could get their heads round someone who looks like me being a *Guardian* reader and having a library card.'

Kat laughed. 'Oh God, I don't know what you'll think of *my* literary tastes. When I'm on holiday I mostly read chick lit. You know, pink swirly fonts and meet-cutes in seaside sweetshops?'

'My mates mostly used to read the back pages of the *Birmingham Mail*,' Faisal said. 'If it wasn't a story about Warwickshire County Cricket Club, they weren't interested.'

Linda checked her watch. 'Kat, why don't you introduce Faisal to the rest of the team? Keep me posted on the Swift case, yes?'

'Yes, Ma-Linda,' she said. Then, 'I'll explain later,' to Faisal, whose brow had furrowed at the nickname.

As they reached the door, Linda called her back.

'Hang on a tick,' Kat said to Faisal. She went back into Linda's office.

'Close the door, would you, Kat?' Linda said.

'Everything all right, Ma-Linda?' Kat said, unaccountably nervous. Had she said the wrong thing to Faisal?

'Fine. But do you really want to take on this murder? I know your caseload's pretty full already. Why not let Craig handle it?'

'I'm fine, really,' Kat blurted, realising suddenly how badly she wanted the distraction of a fresh case. 'The other cases are all winding down. It's only paperwork and meetings with the CPS. Honestly, Ma-Linda, I can manage.'

Linda observed her for a few seconds. That feeling of being back in the headteacher's office came back twice as strong. Kat held her breath.

'Fine. But don't hang about. You haven't done a celebrity case before, but I have. This town will be like a bloody true-crime convention soon.'

Kat swallowed.

'Thanks. I won't let you down.'

Then she left, feeling her anxiety recede – a little – and the thrill of the chase take its place.

Chapter Twenty

Kat led Faisal into MCU, hoping to introduce him to the team before Carve-up noticed the new kid and inserted himself into the discussion.

The DI was in his office, head bent over his keyboard. Good. She had at least a few minutes.

'Come and meet Leah,' Kat said. 'She used to be my bagwoman.'

'Used to be?'

'I was working with DC Tom Gray. He's on the fast track but . . .' Her throat suddenly thickened and speaking became hard.

'Everything all right?' Faisal asked.

'Yeah, yeah. Sorry. Tom and I were in the middle of an arrest of a violent suspect and Tom got badly hurt. Almost bled to death. He was in a coma.'

'Bloody hell!'

'He's out of the woods now. He woke up on Saturday, but it'll be a while before he's back with us.'

Faisal nodded. 'Can I meet him, though? Just to introduce myself?'

'He's up at MGH, that's Middlehampton General Hospital, but sure. I'll arrange something.'

'Don't suppose he's a cricket fan, is he?'

'I think golf's more his game. You can ask him when you see him.'

Leah came out of the kitchen carrying a mug of coffee. Spotting Kat, she smiled and wove through the press of desks.

'Leah, this is Faisal Mohammed. He's just joined us. He'll be working with us on the Mark Swift murder.'

Kat stood aside as Faisal stuck his hand out. 'Hi, Leah, good to meet you.'

Leah flashed a brief smile at Faisal as she mechanically shook hands.

'Hi.'

That was odd. Normally Leah was super-friendly to newbies. Even Tom, with his posh-boy accent and studiedly casual dress sense she and Kat had christened 'FTM' for Fast-Track Modesty. But unless Kat was mistaken, Leah was radiating exceptionally chilly vibes towards Fez despite the muggy heat in MCU.

'I suppose I'm losing the bagwoman's job for a second time,' she said.

Kat frowned. This really wasn't like Leah at all. Maybe she had something on her mind. She and Emily had recently got a new cat. Maybe it was poorly. She decided to ask later. Leah wasn't one to beat around the bush if she had a gripe about something – or someone.

'Not on my account, I hope,' Faisal said, looking concerned and glancing at Kat for reassurance. 'I'm happy where the boss puts me. I'm not here to rock the boat, Leah. On which subject, what do you want me to do, Kat?'

'Let's give you the tour and sort you out a desk, and then I want you digging into Mark's life. Nobody reaches middle age without rubbing at least one person up the wrong way, so if he had any enemies, I want to find them.'

He nodded and smiled, glancing at Leah, who sipped her coffee, regarding him over the rim of her mug.

'Perfect. That's right up my street. I used to be in intelligence,' he said to Leah. 'Ironic, really. I was a bit thick at school. Too busy with cricket.'

Leah offered another pained smile. 'I need to go. I've got some reports to write. See you later, Kat.'

Kat watched her bagwoman's retreating back, wondering what on earth had got into her. She might as well have held up a sign saying, *I don't like Faisal.*

Obviously, Faisal had seen the placard, too. Not difficult since it was about five feet tall. 'Was it something I said?' he asked, with an anxious half-grin.

'That was totally out of character. I'm sorry, Fez. It's probably nothing. She's been putting in a lot of hours recently. Probably just tired.'

It sounded weak and Kat could see he knew it. But they seemed to have reached a tacit agreement to go with it for now. A niggling little voice piped up in the back of Kat's mind: *You don't think her issue is because he's Muslim, do you?* But it couldn't be. Not Leah. Carve-up, yes, any day of the week. But not Leah. Kat dismissed the thought as unworthy and decided to see how things panned out. It could simply be that Leah was having a bad day.

'Come on, I'll introduce you to Craig. Don't ask him about cricket,' she said in a stage whisper loud enough to have Craig turning his head. 'He's an Eels fanatic. Craig! Meet Faisal Mohammed aka Fez. He's just joined MCU.'

Craig stood, smiling broadly, and offered his hand. Thank God, at least one member of MCU was willing to be friendly to the new boy.

'Nice to meet you, mate. Where've you come from?'

'Birmingham.'

'Snow Hill?'

'Yep. Intelligence and undercover ops.'

'Nice. So what brings you down to our fair town?'

'My wife's work. She's a doctor. Just got a new job at MGH.'

Kat added a little green tick beside Faisal's name. He'd already known what MGH stood for when she'd explained. But, unlike some of the male cops in Jubilee Place, he'd waited to hear it from her rather than interrupting.

'What kind of doctor?'

'Nazima's a max-fax surgeon.'

Craig's brow crinkled into deep furrows.

'A what now?'

'Sorry. We use so much jargon at home. NHS from Naz, cop-speak from me. Max-fax means maxillofacial. She does reconstructive work, after car crashes and the like. But she specialises in kids' cleft palates. Does a month in Africa every year, repairing clefts among village children and teaching the local surgeons the latest techniques.'

Craig nodded his appreciation. 'That's bloody amazing. Kat, if you're busy on the Swift case, why don't you leave Fez with me? I'll sort him out with a desk and a locker. All the usual.'

'Is that OK with you, Fez?' Kat asked.

'Totally. Although there's something you should know about me, Craig.'

'Oh, yeah?'

'Kat's right, I am a WCC fan. But I follow the footie too.'

'Oh, no,' Craig groaned comically. 'Which team?'

'Aston Villa.' A beat, then Faisal started singing, softly and surprisingly tunefully, to the tune of 'Amazing Grace'. 'Three-ee one, three-ee one, three-ee one, three one . . .'

'Oh, do me a favour,' Craig protested.

'Your new striker's got two left feet and neither of them work!' Fez crowed.

Kat grinned. 'I'm going to leave you boys to it. Fez, I'll see you later. Craig, please don't kill my new DC.'

As the good-natured bickering about the worth of the Eels' new player faded, Kat went over to Leah's desk. Her number two was hunched over her keyboard, fingers rapping out a report with a sound like hail on one of the station's glass skylights.

'Leah? I thought we could go and see Maria Sheriff again. And Bella Gabbard, too.'

'The one who found it, drowned it?' Leah deadpanned.

'Well, it wouldn't be the first time the murderer called it in to try and throw us off, would it? Come on, you've got a face like thunder. You need some fresh air and sunshine.'

Leah hauled herself to her feet. 'OK, but have you been outside today? Middlehampton's like a bloody sauna.'

'Come on, misery, we can work on our tans.'

Chapter Twenty-One

On the drive over to Mortimer Grove, Kat tried to find the right way to ask Leah why she'd been so snotty to Faisal. It was so out of character. Nothing sounded right in her head. Maybe she'd just have to say something – anything – and wing it.

Then Faisal's own phrase came to the rescue.

'Was it the goatee?' she asked.

'What?'

Kat indicated right at a roundabout, and waited until she'd straightened up before replying.

'Faisal's goatee. Do you have a thing against men with beards? Is that why you were so off with him? I wouldn't blame you, given Carve-up's got one, too.'

'Me? *I* wasn't off.'

'Leah! You practically told him to do one. You barely even made eye contact.'

'I was fine! It was him. He's got that whole big-city cop thing coming off him in waves. The suit, the sharp haircut. The attitude. "I used to be in intelligence",' Leah droned in a bad imitation of Faisal's Birmingham accent. 'Like us hick-town cops wouldn't be able to find the ladies' without pink stripes stuck to the floor.'

Kat shook her head. This wasn't like Leah. She resolved to dig deeper, try to work out what was going on. The last thing she needed was tension between two of her team. Especially when the third was still recovering from a coma.

'For a start, Middlehampton isn't a "hick town". It's a fine market town with a proud history of commerce, sport and culture,' she intoned, going for a comedy audio-tour vibe. She glanced across at Leah. Nothing. OK. Press on then. 'And Faisal's got about the least attitude of any cop I've ever met. You included. Come on, mate, what's really up?'

'It's nothing. I told you. I just got this superior vibe off him.' Leah pointed through the windscreen. 'Next right.'

Kat signalled. Leah obviously wasn't ready to talk. So she'd leave it for now. But if there was something Leah was hiding, she needed to find out. Maybe the team was three now, rather than two, but Tom was still out of action, even if he was out of his coma. She needed everyone totally focused on solving Mark's murder.

She drowned out her doubts with a cheery, 'Here we are, 31 Jamaica Street. Come on. Maybe Maria'll give us a glass of iced tea.'

Leah harrumphed. 'It'll probably have cyanide in it.'

Ignoring her disgruntled bagwoman, Kat locked the car and strode up to the front door. Time to go beyond the niceties of amicable divorces and find out more about the dead man. Who'd clearly had at least one enemy.

'Kat!' Maria said with a strange expression. Half-smile, half-frown. She looked to Kat's left. 'And . . .'

'Maria, this is my colleague, DC Leah Hooper. Can we come in?'

'Of course, it's boiling out here. I was working in the garden. There's just the hint of a breeze. Would you like a cold drink?'

Kat caught Leah's eye and smiled. Mouthed, 'Iced tea.'

'I was drinking rosé,' Maria said. 'Well, a spritzer. Ice and soda water. Would you ladies like one? It's very weak.'

'It's mega-tempting,' Kat said, 'but it'd better be water. We're on duty.'

'Sorry. You'd think I of all people would know that, wouldn't you?'

Maria filled two tall glasses with water and added ice and wedges of lime, which released a zing of pungent citrus zest into the air as she cut them. Once they were seated, Maria tapped a couple of keys before closing her laptop.

'So, Kat, Leah, what can I do for you? I assume this is about Mark?'

'It is. You told me about your marriage, and also his first wife, Rachel. I met Saskia, which makes number three. So what we're doing now is building up a detailed picture of Mark's life. I'm hoping you can help us with that?'

Maria had been nodding and *mm-hmm*-ing as Kat was speaking. Now she steepled her hands under her chin. 'Victimology. Of course. Well,' she said, 'ask away. Anything I can do to help, I will.'

'Did Mark have any other wives, girlfriends or mistresses you know of?'

'Not that I know of. You've already probably come to the conclusion he was a serial shagger. But he really wasn't. If he was guilty of anything it was of loving women too much, that's all.'

That sounded odd to Kat. Like the lyrics to a really bad nineties pop song.

'Although you said he dumped Rachel for you – specifically a younger model – as soon as he became famous.'

Maria went pink. 'Yes, well, I mean in general that's what happened. You'd have to ask Saskia whether he was faithful to her, but as far as I'm aware he never screwed around during *our* marriage.'

'If not girlfriends, maybe any boyfriends?' Leah asked.

'Again, not as far as I know.'

'Maria, I know Mark was important to you as an ex with whom you had a decent relationship. And he was obviously key to *Criminal Herts*, but I'm just struggling to see how he could have been murdered unless he had some serious enemies,' Kat said. 'You were a bit reticent before. But we're conducting a full-scale murder investigation. I need you to be frank with me. Can you think of *anyone* who might have had it in for Mark?'

Maria sighed and sipped her glass of pink spritzer, the sides of which were beaded with condensation.

'It's all so difficult, Kat,' she said. 'Publishing is a very close-knit world. Very gossipy. I would hate to think that people might know I'd, well, dobbed them in to the police. *Criminal Herts* would be forever tainted. Who'd want to appear at the festival then?'

Kat had to rein in her impatience. Clearly, Maria knew something, and she was apparently more concerned about protecting her reputation, and that of her festival, than helping to catch Mark's killer.

'I understand that but, to remind you, this is a murder investigation. Now' – she hardened her tone a touch – 'I would much rather chat in the garden like last time. But we could equally ask you to attend a voluntary interview under caution at Jubilee Place station. Your call.'

The silence lengthened. An ice cube in Leah's drink cracked. A hoverfly zoomed over the table, stopping directly in Kat's eyeline and regarding her with huge, plum-coloured eyes.

Just as Kat was thinking she needed to turn the ratchet tighter still, Maria sighed heavily. Was this it? The breakthrough she needed? Was Maria about to reveal some dark secret about her ex-husband that could explain who had murdered him and why?

Chapter Twenty-Two

Maria picked at the skin along a fingernail.

'There are one or two people who might not have regarded Mark as fondly as I did. Off the top of my head, you could start with Cheryl Holiday, his first agent. He dumped her, got himself a new agent in New York, and almost immediately signed the deal I told you about with Portico Fiction. She was not a happy bunny. Her fee would have run into the high five figures. You could also talk to Richard Bannister. He and Mark used to be friends. Then Richard accused Mark of stealing his idea for *The Guillotine Man*. Oh, and poor Amy, I suppose.'

'Would this be Amy Swales, by any chance?' Kat asked.

'Yes! She writes, well, wrote, as A.L. Swales. She's self-published,' Maria said slightly sniffily, before brightening. 'But very nice.'

'Why did you call her "poor" Amy?'

'Oh, well, she and Mark had a rather public spat on Twitter about whether self-published authors were "real" authors. Amy took that badly and made some rather ill-judged comments about Mark and Richard's falling-out. So Mark had his lawyer dig into Amy's past. They alleged that her first five books were plagiarised from a Belgian author from the 1930s. Well, *somehow*, that got out, and Amy was cancelled, poor thing. She survives on her dwindling book sales and running writers' retreats in France.'

'Do you know his lawyer's name?' Leah asked.

'I do. It's rather impressive, actually. Sir Anthony Bone. He's a partner at one of those rather swish London firms.'

Kat had been making notes as Maria spoke. She consulted her phone now. 'So, apart from an ex-wife he dumped for you, an agent he cheated out of a big payday, an author who claims he stole a plot for a bestseller, and another author who basically lost her livelihood due to his exposing her, anyone else you can think of who might have had a motive for killing him?'

Beside her, Leah coughed then thumped her chest. 'Went down the wrong way.'

Maria bridled. 'I know how this all sounds, Kat, but honestly, can you really see a writer or even a writer's agent actually committing murder? We type stories for a living. All that gruesome stuff on the page? It's all made up! If you gave them a gun, most crime writers would probably shoot themselves by accident.'

'But Mark wasn't shot, Maria,' Kat said. 'He was drowned.'

Maria's eyes flashbulbed. 'Drowned? How?'

'That's one of the things we're investigating,' Kat said. 'Can you think of anyone else who might have wanted Mark to come to harm?'

Maria shook her head. 'No. Really, nobody springs to mind.'

'Thanks, then. This has been really helpful.'

'And you'll be discreet, won't you?' Maria asked. 'About where you got those names from?'

'Of course. There's nothing to worry about. Your reputation's safe. And the festival's, too,' Kat added.

'Which, I have to tell you, is a massive headache.' Maria enclosed Kat and Leah in a confiding glance. 'I don't know if you can believe it, but running a literary festival is just this massive responsibility. It costs a fortune, and we have so many people we have to keep happy – authors, readers . . . Not to mention all the publishers and so on and so forth. I'm just so grateful we have Bruno bankrolling us.'

Kat's ears pricked up. People often became talkative when they felt the formal interview was over. Had Maria just done the same?

'Bruno would be who?' she asked.

Maria smiled and finished her spritzer, flicking at the hoverfly, which had zoomed to her side of the table.

'Bruno Collins. The managing partner of Savile Harvey. They're an investment firm and our gold sponsor. Have been ever since we launched ten years ago. Despite all the pressure, Bruno's always stood firm.'

'What kind of pressure?' Leah asked.

'Oh, the Books Not Bombs people. You've heard of them, I suppose?'

Kat had, but playing the innocent often yielded more useful information from witnesses.

'Who are they?'

'They sprang up last year and started lobbying literary festivals to drop any sponsors associated with fossil fuels or arms sales. They're lovely people, don't get me wrong. Young, for the most part, and idealistic, which is wonderful. But I worry they're going to kill the thing they claim to love. Festivals can't survive on ticket sales alone. We need sponsors. Some of the big ones have been hit badly but Bruno's made of sterner stuff.'

'Where is Bruno's firm based?' Leah asked.

'London. Mayfair, specifically.'

Kat wondered again about motive. Money was right up there alongside sex. 'Did Mark have any connection to Bruno, or the Books Not Bombs people?' she asked.

Maria sighed again. 'It was not his finest moment.' She picked up her glass, before noticing it was empty and setting it down again with a clink. 'BNB were being very vocal on social media and they put together an open letter signed by a couple of hundred authors. Mid-ranking, mainly, although there were a couple of big names, too.'

Kat saw what was coming. 'But not Mark.'

'Mark wrote to the *London Review of Books* with a rather, shall we say, impassioned diatribe about artistic freedom, free speech, and so on and so forth.' Maria looked off to one side as she continued speaking. 'He called their leader, Venetia Shelby-Hales, an "eco-fascist" and said the only reason they weren't already burning books in the street was because they were worried about the carbon footprint. Books Not Bombs went into overdrive. They tried to get his publishers to drop him, which naturally fell on deaf ears. I mean, Mark's their banker.'

And then, out of nowhere, like rain from the blindingly brilliant sapphire sky, she burst into tears. Great racking sobs that brought snot dripping from her nose. Kat hurriedly offered the little cellophane-wrapped packet of tissues she always carried.

'Are you all right, Maria?' she asked, knowing how redundant her question was, but asking it all the same. Sometimes, people just needed to find a way to block their grief.

'I just used the present tense. But that's wrong. Mark's past-tense now, isn't he?' Maria sobbed.

'We're working hard to find his killer,' Kat said, motioning for Maria to keep the packet of tissues when she offered it back. She stood. 'You've got my card. Call me if you think of anything.'

At the front door, just as Maria was about to close it, Kat turned back.

'Did *you* have a reason to want Mark dead?'

Maria drew her head back. 'Me? I told you – he helped me keep the festival going. I *needed* him.'

Which was half-true. What Maria had needed to keep the festival going was money. And Bruno Collins was supplying it.

Could the two men have fallen out? Over money? Or a woman? Or Mark's controversial tweets? Had they come to blows in the green room? As the main sponsor, Collins would surely have had unfettered access.

This was a lead worth chasing down personally.

Chapter Twenty-Three

After letting Leah out in front of Jubilee Place, Kat noticed a familiar figure standing to the left of the station signboard, under the skin-bleaching glare of a TV light. To her horror, Ethan Metcalfe was talking to what appeared to be a Sky TV reporter. She swore, sharply.

Normally, Ethan would be wearing one of a seemingly endless collection of black T-shirts with band logos on them. Today, however, he sported a surprisingly well-cut grey jacket, with a crisp white shirt underneath.

He'd lost some weight, too. Strike that – he'd lost a *lot* of weight. And he'd done something to his hair. Or maybe it was just a shampoo and cut. She couldn't – could never – call him good-looking. But today he radiated an unusual air of confidence. Chin up, smiling, hands in pockets: all in all, quite the power pose.

Curious, she got out and crossed Union Street, arriving just as Ethan was answering the journalist's latest question. He rotated his head by a few degrees and stared directly at Kat, just for a second. He smiled. My God, had he had his teeth fixed?

'I have the greatest respect for the police, Flora. But here's the thing. Mark Swift was murdered on Friday, virtually in the presence of one of Middlehampton's Major Crimes Unit's detective sergeants. It's now Monday lunchtime, and they have come up with precisely nothing. The clock is ticking and the Golden Hour – as we in the trade call it – has long since turned to rusty steel. My question for Middlehampton Police is a simple one.' His eyes flicked over to Kat, then back at the glamorous Sky reporter. 'Mark Swift was well known for starting feuds with his fellow authors. I've named a couple in my podcast, *Home Counties Homicide*, which reaches a worldwide audience including Jakarta, Tallahassee and Vilnius. Surely it's not beyond the wit of man – or woman – to find out which one he enraged badly enough to want him dead?'

Kat was furious, her heart thrashing in her chest. She stalked back across the road, stopping traffic with an angrily raised hand, and climbed into the scalding interior of her car. Tyres squealing, she pulled out and swung the wheel to take the turn into the station car park.

Mutt-calf couldn't have worked things more to his advantage if he'd murdered Mark Swift himself.

As soon as she reached MCU, she marched straight over to the incident board, snatched up a purple marker pen and scrawled the names Maria had given her on the greasy white surface. She hesitated, then scribbled a sixth name.

Ethan Metcalfe, podcaster. Gaining listeners after MS murder = benefit.

It looked lame. Possibly even spiteful. She wiped it off again. But she resolved to keep an eye on him. She turned to see her sister, Diana, striding along the edge of MCU, accompanied by a tall Black man in a beautiful linen suit, carrying a fat burgundy leather briefcase. She caught Diana's eye and hurried over.

'What's going on, Di?'

'Nothing to worry about, Kathryn,' her sister said, smiling down at her, thanks to the three-inch heels she was wearing. 'I just thought, given I was one of the last people to see Mark alive, I should come and offer a voluntary statement.' She turned and indicated the man standing beside her. 'This is Darcus Ogunsola. My lawyer.'

He held out his hand and Kat shook it. 'How do you do, DS Ballantyne?'

Suave didn't even begin to cover it. In those six softly uttered words, she caught the inflections of money, power, education and class.

'Hi,' she said. 'Was everything OK? In the interview?'

'I wouldn't call it an interview,' he said with a smile. 'Diana was here to offer what assistance she could to your colleagues. We spoke to a new member of your team, I believe. DC Mohammed?'

'Yes. He joined us today.'

'Indeed. It seems he and I share an interest in test cricket. His from childhood, mine from my time at Oxford.'

'Did he – I mean, did you have anything relevant to say, Di?' Kat asked, suddenly nervous, as if she were the one being accompanied by an expensive lawyer, and not her sister.

Diana merely looked at her lawyer.

'My client has already shared everything she could remember of her *brief* – he pushed the last word just slightly – 'encounter with Mark Swift. I'm sure DC Mohammed will be able to enlighten you. Now, if you'll excuse us, we have another appointment.'

Kat could only watch as Di and her Oxford-educated lawyer swept out of MCU, heads bent towards each other, as if they'd been considering buying Jubilee Place before deciding it fell short of their expectations. A lawyer like Ogunsola had to cost a fortune. Di must be doing even better than Kat had imagined. Or was their father paying?

She found Faisal in the kitchen, stirring a mug of coffee and looking doubtfully at its surface.

'It's horrible, but after a while you stop noticing,' she said.

'God, I hope not. That would mean my tastebuds were shot and I wouldn't be able to enjoy a nice home-cooked meal.'

'So Naz finds time to cook as well as being a surgeon?'

He grinned. 'I know what you're thinking. How come I don't do my share, right?'

'No!' She put her hand over her chest. 'I would never think that. I mean, not unless you're telling me you're too busy to cook.'

'*Au contraire*, boss. I'm the cook. Naz could burn boiled rice. Plus she really is the busy one in our family. Although half the time it's M&S ready meals or takeaways.'

Kat really wanted to dig down into the leads they had, but this seemed the perfect opportunity to get to know her new DC a little better. Ignoring the nagging echo of Ethan's jibe about the Golden Hour having tarnished, she leaned back against the kitchen counter.

'Busy with childcare, too?' she asked.

He nodded. 'Good guess. We have a little girl. Leila's three. Quite the handful.'

'So how do you guys manage?' Kat asked, thinking back to when she and Van had had to juggle two jobs and a squally little Riley Ballantyne, who'd regarded the small hours as his ideal 'play with parents' time. Maybe he was being a royal pain in the arse at the moment, but at least he was properly independent now. At least, until he needed a lift to football.

'Naz's younger sister lives in St Albans. Noor's not married yet but she loves being Leila's auntie. She comes over to help. And we have a nanny.'

Kat widened her eyes. 'A nanny? Well, excuse me! It seems we have a new power couple in Middlehampton.'

He smiled. 'It's not like that. But Naz really is incredibly busy, and luckily for us she can afford it. Plus we both drink gallons of coffee and we've learned to do without sleep, so, you know, it's all good.'

Kat offered a sympathetic smile. 'Been there, Fez. It does get easier, I promise.'

'So how old are your kids?'

'Kid, singular. Riley's fourteen. A mass of testosterone and Lynx Africa, but he's a good boy.'

'Sporty?'

'Football. He plays for a school team.'

A third voice broke into their conversation. 'Here he is! DS Ballantyne, I thought you must've been hiding this policing powerhouse from me.'

Carve-up entered the tiny kitchen and stuck out his hand to Fez. A heavy gold signet ring glinted on his middle finger.

'Sorry, I've been in meetings all day. I'm DI Carver. Running this little gang of reprobates is my sacred duty. Only joking, they're a great mob.'

'Pleased to meet you, sir,' Fez said, shaking Carve-up's hand. 'DC Mohammed.'

Carve-up tutted. 'None of that. I may have the office and the inspector's pips, but in here?' He thumped the breast of his suit. 'Where it counts? I'm just a hardworking copper like you. Call me Stuart. So, you got a nickname I can use?'

'Fez.'

Carve-up frowned. His mouth tightened and he glared at Kat. 'What the actual f—? DC Mohammed's been here less than a day and you've already given him a racist nickname? Are you living in the eighties or something, DS Ballantyne?'

'It's nothing like that, sir,' Faisal began. 'Fez is—'

Carve-up held a hand out, palm outwards. 'Hold your horses, son. This is a serious breach of police regulations, not to mention the law. Explain yourself, DS Ballantyne. Why have you given a Muslim officer—' He paused and looked at Faisal. 'You *are* a Muslim, right?'

'Yes, sir, third-generation Pakistani. But I—'

'Exactly.' He jabbed a finger at Kat. 'Why have you given a Muslim officer a nickname based on a bloody hat? An Egyptian hat. It's not even the right country!'

Kat stared at her boss incredulously. It was like he'd bulled his way into the kitchen, and their conversation, specifically to try to fit her up on yet another trumped-up charge. As if he'd thought, *well, the corruption rap didn't stick so we'll have a go at hate speech.* But the shock she felt was tempered by a delicious sense of what was to come. The only question was whether she or Fez would get to deliver the killing blow. She shot her new DC a quick glance, offering the sword.

'It's a family nickname, sir. Everyone calls me Fez, including my wife,' Faisal said. He glanced at Kat. Was that a wink? 'Her name's Naz. They call us FezNaz.'

If Kat had been expecting Carve-up to blush or stutter out some half-hearted apology, she was disappointed. Instead, it was like his previous outburst hadn't even happened.

'Right, right. I get it. Like Brangelina. Or Kimye. Very good, very good.' He checked the Rolex on his wrist, giving both junior officers a good eyeful. 'Right, I have another meeting. Nice to meet you, Fez.'

And he was gone – leaving a strong smell of his aftershave and more than a whiff of hypocrisy in his wake.

'That was the boss,' Kat said unnecessarily.

Fez frowned. 'Is he always like that?'

Kat had to laugh, relieved her new DC seemed to have got the measure of Carve-up already.

'Stuart's . . . well, Stuart's Stuart. You'll get to know how he likes to operate. One thing I should tell you, because you'll hear it soon enough. He also has a nickname. It's Carve-up. Do *not* let him hear you using it.'

'Understood,' he murmured. 'Any particular reason?'

What could Kat say. *Everyone thinks he's on the take? The rumour is he once carved up the haul from a drug bust with a mate and only half went into evidence?* No. How could she? It wasn't fair on Fez.

'He, er . . . When he was in uniform, he took down this nutcase with a bloody great carving knife who was yelling, "I'll carve you up!" I guess it just stuck.'

She felt bad, not telling him the truth. But Fez deserved the chance to make up his own mind.

'Come on,' she said. 'You can come with me to talk to Mark Swift's widow.'

Chapter Twenty-Four

The drive from Middlehampton to the village of Bower Heath, where Mark and Saskia Swift lived, took Kat and Fez through rolling countryside, bounded by the gentle upcurve of the Chiltern hills.

The hot summer had turned the fields from shades of green to gold. As Kat crested a rise, she hit the brakes sharply as a huge green tractor emerged from a gate to her left and lumbered across the road into the neighbouring field.

'Sorry about that,' she said, pulling away again. 'I don't suppose you got many farm vehicles in Birmingham.'

Fez shook his head. 'Not round Snow Hill, anyway.'

Something about the way he ended his answer made her glance to her left. His voice had hitched slightly, as if he had been about to say something, then changed his mind.

'What?' she asked.

'Carve-up never took a knife off some nutter, did he?'

She slowed for a bend and uttered a quick driving-course verbal summary of her actions, buying a little time and wondering at his insight.

'Down to third, check mirror, second, back on the throttle, mirror, up to third, gate to the right, any combines? No. Accelerate . . .'

'Kat?'

Kat spotted a lay-by ahead, little more than a tyre-scuffed patch of gritty verge where cars had pulled in as they squeezed past traffic coming the other way. She put the handbrake on and twisted round in her seat to face Fez.

'Why do you say that?' she asked.

'Because I've seen his type before, that's why. Now, you've probably noticed I like my clothes?'

'I have.'

'Yeah, but this is just Next,' he said, running thumb and forefinger down his lapel. 'Naz adjusts them. She's pretty good with needle and thread.'

'What are you saying, Fez?'

'I'm saying, Carve-up's suit was Tom Ford. That's the thick end of four grand, easily. Maybe more. And his watch? A Rolex Submariner. That's easily another ten. There's the 1993 Alfa Romeo Spider in the car park, too. Twenty-five to thirty. A divorced DI with forty-four K's worth of assets on him on a workday? Nah, our kid. Doesn't stack up.'

'You worked in intelligence, right?' Kat asked, her heart beating fast as she considered Fez's takedown of Carve-up's carefully curated lifestyle.

'I did. But before that I did a stint in anti-corruption. I didn't mention it, because, you know, it's like you're the new boy with the bad case of BO. Nobody wants to talk to you.'

'Fair enough. But it sounds like you've already profiled Stuart.'

'No. I mean, it's only my first day, Kat, isn't it? But you get a sense of these things. I saw plenty of cops back home, especially in the drug squad, who had the same kind of tastes as Carve-up. Amazing how many of them reckoned they'd had wins on the horses. The smart ones, anyway. Harder to trace than lottery tickets or inheritances. Has Carve-up ever mentioned how he can afford his stuff?'

It was such a simple question, yet Kat felt the heat of a blush creeping across her cheeks. It hadn't ever crossed her mind to ask him. 'He hasn't.'

'Sorry, sorry,' Fez said suddenly. 'I've got a bit of a bloody nerve, questioning my guv'nor. I'm just keen to understand my new work environment, that's all.'

Kat regarded him for a second longer. Fez was a sharp one. This wasn't just about wanting to fit in. Was he a potential ally in her quest to see Carve-up face justice?

No need to rush things; she could wait to find out. She put the Golf in gear and pulled away.

Ten minutes later, they were scrunching to a stop on the gravelled drive of a wide-fronted Elizabethan house set back from the road. It had mullioned windows like those at her parents' mock-Tudor home, tall, twisted brick chimneys, and a front swagged with red roses and creamy-yellow honeysuckles.

She pulled the bell handle and waited, enveloped in a cloud of sickly-sweet perfume from the flowers clustered over her head. Sweat trickled over her ribs.

The door swung inward on silent hinges. Somehow Kat had been expecting a loud creak.

Saskia Swift was dressed in grey linen pyjamas, holding a tall glass of something red with ice cubes and slivers of fruit in it. A mocktail? It was a boiling hot day, after all.

'DS Ballantyne. Come in,' Saskia said. She swivelled to take in Fez, slopping her drink down the front of her pyjamas. She brushed at the damp patch and slurred a swear word. 'Put these on clean this morning. Never mind. Doesn't matter anymore, does it?'

Kat revised her thoughts on Saskia's drink.

'I'm DC Mohammed,' Fez said, not missing a beat. 'May we come in, Mrs Swift?'

'Oh, yeah, of course. Sorry.' She spun on her heel, losing her balance and leaning against the wall for support.

Kat exchanged a look with Fez. Both experienced cops in their own way, each understood the other perfectly. *Tread carefully.*

The hallway was painted a uniform dark green and lined with pictures in matching black frames. The covers of Mark Swift's ten bestselling books. A bloody knife, a coil of rope, a pistol wrapped in grease-stained canvas, a huge black beetle, a tattoo of a skull on a disembodied arm . . . Kat recognised the themes, if not the actual titles, from Van's bedside reading.

The kitchen was larger than the entire ground floor of Kat's house. A double-height room filled with light and, after the sweltering heat outside, deliciously cool. The bifold doors that gave on to an apparently boundaryless expanse of parkland were closed.

A slight breeze tickled the back of Kat's neck. She looked up at a square white hatch with slanted louvres. In-built air conditioning. She wondered idly whether she could apply to be Saskia's family liaison officer.

On which subject: 'Mrs Swift, I really am sorry for your loss. How are you coping?'

Kat and Fez took the two chairs adjacent to the one Saskia had just plonked herself on, sighing and taking another long pull on her drink.

'Me?' Her eyes swivelled slowly in their sockets until they were more or less focused on Kat. 'I cry a lot. I go to bed at eight and I wake at three.' She held her drink aloft. 'And I drink a lot of these. Mark invented it. It's called a Bloody Murder.'

Kat readied herself to hand over a fresh cellophane-wrapped packet of tissues. But Saskia's eyes remained dry, if unfocused. Maybe she'd cried herself out. It happened.

'I wanted to come and update you personally on our investigation,' Kat said.

'That's nice,' Saskia said, finishing her drink then gesturing to a jug on the counter behind Fez. 'You couldn't reach that over for me, could you, DC Mc— sorry, *Mo*-hammed?'

Fez leapt up and returned to the table with the jug, carefully filling Saskia's glass to the halfway mark.

She waggled the glass and batted her mascara-clotted lashes at him.

'Don't be stingy,' she said with an off-kilter smile.

Was she flirting with Fez? Drinking to deaden her grief? Or celebrating a problem solved? *Tread* really *carefully, Kat.*

Fez topped up the widow's glass further.

'I didn't want it to get warm too quickly,' he said smoothly, replacing the jug on the counter.

Saskia gulped down a good quarter of the drink, then turned to Kat.

'Who did it then?'

'We're following several leads. It's why I came out here today. I need to ask you some questions, if you feel up to it?'

Saskia's mouth twisted to one side. 'Sure, why not? I haven't got anything else on. Can't even arrange the funeral while the coroner's got the body.'

'Saskia, I know this is going to sound callous, and I apologise in advance . . . but I need to ask you, where were you between 10.30 a.m. and 11.10 a.m. last Friday morning?'

Saskia nodded slowly. Her eyes drooped. Kat wondered whether she was about to pass out.

'Ohhh, of course. Rich man dies, gotta be the wife. Gotta be the wife,' she repeated, winking lopsidedly at Fez.

'It's just routine,' Kat said. 'We need to eliminate you from our enquiries.'

'Of course.' Saskia pulled herself straighter in her chair. Cleared her throat loudly. Shook her head. 'OK, Saskia Swift, alibi report. At 10.30 a.m. on Friday I was in my room, number 19, at the Rangely Hotel. A very nice man called Dieter Hossf – *Hof*stetter – from *Prisma* magazine in Germany was interviewing me for a profile of Mark. He also had a photographer with him. Lina . . . something . . . I didn't catch her last name. Battenberg? Bundt? Something cakey, anyway. They were still with me when I heard about Mark and left the room.' She hiccupped noisily. ''Scuse me. Then I bumped into you by the front of the Guildhall.'

She flopped back against her chair, sighing deeply, and drained her glass.

'Thank you,' Kat said, certain she'd just heard a truthful, and watertight, alibi. She was sure the widow was drinking in sorrow, not celebration. Just another next of kin whose life had been ripped apart, the pieces scattered to the ground.

She would get someone to check with the magazine. The journalists could confirm Saskia's alibi and there would be time-stamped photos, too. But it was time to switch tracks.

'Let's talk about Mark,' Kat said. 'As we've been interviewing witnesses, we've been asking about people who might have wished him harm. Quite a few names have come up: Amy Swales, Richard Bannister, Cheryl Holiday, Rachel Dixon. Can you think of anyone who we could add to our list?'

Saskia surprised Kat as she barked out a short sharp laugh. 'You're joking, right? I loved my husband very much, Detective Sergeant, but I have to tell you, not everyone felt the same way. He gave them good reason not to, as well. Those four would be on the list. But so would Desperate Dan.'

'Sorry, Desperate Dan?'

'Oh. Yeah. Our private joke. Danny Elliott.'

'Who is he?' Kat asked.

'One of your lot. Well, used to be. He runs a consultancy called Blue Lights, Red Pens. It's a bunch of ex-cops who charge themselves out to authors and screenwriters so they get the details right.'

'And why would this Danny Elliott have a motive to kill Mark?'

'Because when Danny was setting up his business, he approached Mark and offered him free consultancy in return for endorsements and a video promoting the business.'

Kat could see where the story was going, but she tried not to judge the increasingly unpleasant man now lying in a refrigerated shelf in Jack Beale's library of dead people at MGH.

'Did Mark hold up his end of the bargain?' she asked.

Saskia narrowed her eyes and put her finger to her chin, hitting the target after two attempts. 'Hmm . . . Did Mark hold up his end of the bargain? What do you think?'

'I'm guessing he didn't?'

'Danny was not a happy bunny. He sent polite emails, worried emails, angry emails. Then he got a solicitor who started threatening legal action. But Mark just waited him out. He' – she hiccupped again – 'he told me one evening, "Danny Elliott might be the long arm of the law, but his pockets aren't deep enough."'

'He waited till Danny's funds ran out,' Fez said.

Saskia nodded. 'Danny eventually went away, though not before sending half a dozen more abusive emails.'

'Can we see them?' Kat asked.

'They're on Mark's MacBook, in his study upstairs.' She stretched out a hand towards Fez. 'Can I borrow your pen and a bit of paper, lovey? I'll give you the password.'

He handed the biro over and his notebook and Saskia scribbled for a few seconds. She pushed it over to Kat.

Cr!meDo3sP4y

'Apart from Danny Elliott, is there anyone else you think we should talk to, Mrs Swift?' Fez said.

'Well, Maria, obviously.'

'That would be Maria Sheriff, the director of *Criminal Herts*?' he asked, making a note.

Saskia nodded. 'And the second Mrs Swift.'

'Could you elaborate for us, Saskia, please?' Kat asked, her cop antenna twitching.

Was Maria's divorce from Mark less friendly than she had painted it?

'I know Maria's always put the story out that she and Mark were . . . What's that phrase she uses? Oh yes, "better friends out of wedlock than in it". But according to industry gossip, of which I'm not ashamed to say I pay close attention – you know, goes with the job, what with me being Mark's publicist. Anyway . . .'

Her eyes lost focus for a second and her eyelids drooped. Kat wanted to hear what she had to say before the cocktails she'd been knocking back sent her to sleep.

'What does the gossip say?' Kat prompted.

'Their much-vaunted *amicable* divorce was about as amicable as a couple of those hideous creatures where one eats the other after mating. Which ones are they? Black widows?'

'That's actually a bit of a myth,' Fez said. 'Maybe you're thinking about praying mantises?'

'Could be. I'm impressed by your general knowledge.' She leaned across the table and scrutinised his face. 'And I like your beard. You're very good-looking for a policeman, did you know that?'

'My wife wants me to shave it off.'

Saskia shook her head. 'Keep it. It's very . . . fetching.'

'So why wasn't their divorce amicable,' he asked, returning her frank, appraising stare. 'Any idea?'

'Well, it wasn't because of me, if that's what you're thinking.'

'Nothing of the kind,' he replied, 'just being curious. It goes with *my* job.'

'*Touché*. Oh, well, anyway, she got a generous settlement, didn't she? Mark was always careful with his money. I can't see him giving out a huge slice of it just because he was feeling *amicable*. What's that line they all use? "Follow the money"? Maybe she had something over him? Like how he exposed Amy Swales.'

Kat got to her feet. 'Could we have a look at Mark's study? We'll leave you alone if you can just point us in the right direction.'

'First floor, last door on the left. Key's in the door. I gave you his password. Works on the iMac and the MacBook. Anything else just shout. I'll be in the garden.'

Kat nodded to Fez. They headed upstairs, already pulling on nitrile gloves.

'I liked how you got her talking to you about Maria with that creepy-crawly distraction.'

'You want me to follow that up? Subtly?'

'Yes. Good idea.'

Kat turned the key in the study door. Another locked room. The first had yielded a question. Would this one yield the answer?

Chapter Twenty-Five

To one side of the writing desk, a MacBook stood open on a brushed-steel credenza. On the desk were centred a silver iMac and its keyboard and mouse.

'Why don't you take them,' she said. 'I'll have a poke around.'

Fez nodded and seated himself in the expensive-looking chair, all black mesh, leather and aluminium struts.

'Don't suppose we could seize this, Kat? It's well comfortable.'

'I'll let you take it if you've got an evidence bag big enough.'

'Funny,' he said, bending to the task of entering the password into both computers.

While Fez busied himself at the desk, Kat opened the top drawer of the filing cabinet. She riffled through the paperwork, which was neatly categorised in the suspension files, and paused at 'LEGAL'.

Maria Sheriff had mentioned Mark's lawyer, Sir Anthony Bone. Kat had pictured a cadaverous pinstriped man with a predatory gleam in his eyes, and sharp teeth. A cousin of the well-paid lawyers who occasionally accompanied their clients into interview rooms at Jubilee Place. Clients such as her father, who she'd recently asked to attend a voluntary interview on a different case. He'd brought a local lawyer with him on that occasion, but she could easily imagine him hiring some London bigshot for something he genuinely felt threatened by. *Like a murder investigation,* her mischievous inner voice piped up. *Or a lawsuit from an illegitimate daughter?* She made a mental note to find out if her dad had ever dealt with Sir Anthony. It might come in useful if she ever got the time to look at her half-sister Jo's life.

She pulled out the yellow cardboard folder with Mark's Swift's legal papers in it. It wasn't as fat as she'd been expecting. Just a few pieces of what looked, at first glance, like standard correspondence about publishing contracts or TV deals. No personal stuff, like divorce agreements. She replaced it. Maybe the personal stuff was kept at the lawyer's office. Something told her she would not enjoy attempting to prise information out of *Sir* Anthony Bone.

'Anything interesting?' she asked over her shoulder as she lifted the folder labelled 'Tax' from the drawer.

'I'm not a digital forensics specialist, obvs . . .'

'Obvs.'

'. . . but this is all just book ideas, drafts of novels, character profiles, the odd article he wrote for some writing magazine or other.'

'How about the emails?'

'Haven't got to those yet.'

Kat went back to her reading. An hour later, she slid the final folder back on to the rails in the drawer. If Mark had left a clue for them as to the identity of his murderer, or their motive, he'd hidden it exceptionally well.

'Any joy?' she asked, coming to stand beside Fez and look over his shoulder.

He shook his head. 'He had a virtual PA who handled his fan mail. He forwarded the emails that needed a personal answer.'

'Any stalkers? Obsessive fans?'

'Nope. If Annie Wilkes dropped him a line, she used an alias.'

'Sorry, who's Annie Wilkes? Another author?'

Fez's eyebrows shot up. 'You don't know? Oh my God, Kat, we really need to work on your reading. Annie Wilkes is the antagonist in *Misery* by Stephen King. She's this totally obsessive fan of this writer called Paul Sheldon.'

'Sorry. Not much of a horror fan.'

But Fez wasn't to be put off. 'But you must have seen the film? James Caan? Kathy Bates? It's a classic. The scene where she breaks his ankles . . . ? No . . . ?' He tailed off.

Fez was a deep one all right. Sport she could understand. But the entomology? The reading? Most of the cops at Jubilee Place, if they had interests outside work, were into golf and cars like Carve-up. Craig lived for the Eels. Her mentor, DI Molly Steadman, was a fitness fanatic and had recently completed a half-marathon. But she couldn't think of anyone who seemed to glide so effortlessly between subjects like Fez did.

A thought occurred to her. She smiled.

He furrowed his brow, quirking his mouth to one side. 'What?'

'I bet you were on a pub quiz team in Birmingham, weren't you?'

Fez grinned broadly. 'I was the *captain* of a pub quiz team in Birmingham. Half cops, half CSIs. We were called Guilty as Charged. Everybody hated us, we won that often.'

'Is that why you know all this random stuff about praying mantises and Stephen King?'

'You're mixing up cause and effect, boss. I've always loved reading. Ever since I was a little kid. I begged my mum and dad to get a proper set of encyclopaedias. You know, the old-school kind. Aardvark to Capsaicin, that sort of thing?'

'OK, so put that brain of yours to work on our case. What do we know so far?'

'He had plenty of people we can loosely call enemies. Motives ranging from being cheated out of money to being emotionally hurt. The ex-cop's interesting because he'd be forensically aware and maybe a bit more used to violence.'

Kat tugged her earlobes, a habit from childhood when she was thinking deeply.

'What about the crime itself? The MO, I mean. What does that suggest to you?'

'Do we know what he was hit with yet?'

'I'm going to see Darcy when we get back from this.'

'That's crucial, isn't it? If the murderer took it in with them, like a wrench or a cosh, then it implies premeditation.'

'Whereas if it was something in the room like the champagne bottle then it was impulsive.'

'Unless whoever did it knew there'd be a bottle in there. Then it could still have been premeditated.'

'Well, it was the green room. So pretty much everyone at the festival, if you asked them, would probably guess there'd be something in there they could use. Certainly, our persons of interest would.'

'The drowning's a bit odd, though. I mean, why switch from hitting him over the head to drowning him?'

'Squeamishness?'

'Could be, I suppose,' Fez said. 'Or maybe they didn't want to splash blood and brains all over the place because there'd be more chance of getting the victim's DNA on themselves.'

Kat frowned. 'Sorry, Fez, just to interrupt for a minute – and please don't think I'm being pious – but could we stick to saying "Mark" rather than "the victim"? I hate depersonalising people just because they've been murdered.'

'Oh, of course. Force of habit. Sorry.'

She smiled. 'No probs. Carry on.'

'Why drown him, you mean? Well . . .'

Fez closed his eyes. Kat watched them moving behind the lids. He was visualising the moments leading up to Mark Swift's death. She did the same thing herself at crime scenes.

He opened his eyes again. 'Sorry, boss. I can't think of anything else.'

'How about this? I'm the murderer. You're Mark Swift. Now, Maria said you used to lock yourself in the green room so you could be sure of having it to yourself, right?'

'Right. I'm mega-successful. A bit of an alpha type.'

'Or so you like to think. So, you've locked yourself in, which I would either already have known, or found out when I tried the door. So I knock, maybe I call your name through the door. You know me, so you come to the door and let me in.'

Describing the scene as she imagined it, Kat felt a familiar feeling come over her. She was guessing, but because the events in the green room had that specific, tragic ending, she could predict with some confidence what must have happened.

'Now, at the very least you'd be happy to let me in, otherwise you'd have slammed the door in my face, and I couldn't have killed you. So, it can't have been anyone you were having an open feud with.'

'Maybe a past grudge then?'

'Maybe. Or someone you felt wasn't a threat.'

'Like a woman?'

'Yes, quite possibly. Swift seems to have had a misogynistic side, although Maria told me and Leah he loved women too much. Which, by the way, sounded a bit too rehearsed. So that gives us Amy Swales, Cheryl Holiday, Maria Sheriff and Rachel Dixon. But if you're Swift, it could equally be a man you don't feel threatened by.'

'Maybe because I feel superior to him,' Fez said. 'Like Danny Elliott.'

'Yes, or simply because most murder victims don't wake up in the morning thinking, "Well, I'd better be careful today, I might get murdered".'

'Then what? You're inside the green room with me,' Fez said. 'Do I lock the door again?'

'Or I do. Anyway, we talk. Then we argue,' Kat said.

'Or if you're there to murder me, you wait until my back is turned.'

'Good, yes, because the wound is towards the back of your head and there are no defensive wounds or signs of a fight. So you can't have known the blow was coming.'

Fez nodded. 'You smack me a good one over the head with a cosh or whatever, then you, what? That's the bit I'm struggling with. Where's the water you drown me in?'

Kat took a deep breath. Closed her eyes. But the image of how, precisely, the murderer had found a source of water and a vessel deep enough to drown Mark in remained stubbornly out of focus. Unless . . .

She opened her eyes again.

'What if the murderer was someone you didn't know at all, but had a convincing reason for needing to go into the green room?'

'Like who?'

'Like a member of the catering staff. Am I a waitress or a kitchen porter? I'm carrying a plastic bucket of water.'

'So it *was* premeditated?'

'Maybe. I say, "Oh, excuse me, Mr Swift, I just need to top up the ice bucket for you."'

'With water?' Fez asked, doubtfully.

'OK, it's half ice, half water. Sloshing around. You let me in, I fiddle around with the ice bucket and then, when your back's turned, wham! I hit you with the bottle and then stick your head into the other bucket. The plastic one. You drown, I leave with the plastic bucket.'

'Leave how, though? The door was locked from the inside.'

The flicker of hope that had been kindling inside Kat guttered and died. They were back to square one.

'Crap,' she said with some feeling. 'We need to turn the computers over to digital forensics. Let's get back to Jubilee Place.'

They thanked Saskia and headed outside into the sweltering heat.

They had one new person of interest in Danny Elliott, and exactly zero new clues.

DAY FIVE – TUESDAY

Chapter Twenty-Six

First thing the next morning, Kat grabbed a free meeting room and bundled Fez and Leah inside with her. Carve-up was on the prowl, and she had no interest in becoming the butt of yet another unfunny jibe.

The room was tiny, airless, and lit only by a single overhead neon tube. Probably because it was formerly a cleaning supplies storeroom that someone had commandeered during a reorganisation.

Leah took a chair opposite Fez. Kat's gut twitched unpleasantly. What the hell was going on with Leah? It couldn't be a racist thing, could it? *Oh God, please let it be something I can solve as a friend.*

Kat watched as Fez looked around him. At the scuffed walls spotted with greasy marks where Blu-Tacked posters had been pulled down. At the screw-holes filled with multicoloured Rawlplugs like insect eyes staring out at the occupants. And at the mocked-up 'Wanted' poster with the face of the previous Home Secretary and the legend *£100,000 Reward for capture, dead or alive.*

When he returned his gaze to her, she nodded. 'How do you like the MCU conference room?'

'It's bostin',' he deadpanned. He turned to Leah. 'Brummie slang for "brilliant".'

But Leah was concentrating on her notebook, and if she caught his latest attempt at friendship, she ignored it. Stomach squirming, Kat made another mental note. *Talk to Leah.*

'Leah, what have you got?' Kat asked, anxious to get the meeting on to a professional footing, if not a friendly one.

'While you were looking at people who might have had a reason to hate Mark, I went the other way,' Leah said. 'I've been tracking down everyone who was doing well out of Mark's continuing success. I thought maybe if he was planning to retire or do something to tarnish his reputation, one of them could have killed him to stop it happening.'

'Nice,' Fez said, nodding. 'Like stopping the goose that laid the golden eggs from killing itself.'

'Thanks for the mansplaining,' was all the reply he got.

The alarm bell in Kat's head was clanging louder than ever. *Talk to Leah. URGENT!*

'Who's on your list, Leah?' Kat asked, making direct eye contact with Leah and trying to inject both an enquiry and a plea into her forceful stare. *What's up?* And: *Please lay off Fez. You're making him uncomfortable. And me.*

Leah flipped back a few pages in her notebook.

'First of all, there's his publisher. Sonya Hosseini. She's Iranian. According to the *Bookseller* website, she's just won an award. Publisher of the Year. And she got promoted from editorial director to MD. Then there's his editor. Liz Carter. There were rumours about her and Mark being an item, which would be par for the course given his relationship history. I couldn't find out any more than social media gossip.'

'If they were in a relationship, that would work against her being his killer, surely?' Fez asked.

'It's only a rumour. Anyway, again, according to the *Bookseller*, she was being courted by a couple of big US publishers. I'm guessing all that would fall away if he was revealed as a paedo or something. Finally, this big-shot lawyer, Sir Anthony Bone. He was doing pretty well out of being Mark's legal enforcer.'

Fez frowned. 'I get how they were all doing well out of Mark. But then killing him would put an end to all that, anyway, wouldn't it?'

Leah sighed, as if having to explain something to a small child. 'Yes. But if they never meant to kill him, it would fit what we know. Or they reckoned he'd be worth more to them as a dead legend than a living liability. Especially if he had one last book he'd written. I don't know much about publishing, but I bet a posthumous book by a big-name author would get massive sales.'

Fez opened his mouth to argue, but Kat forestalled his reply. Any more tension between these two and they'd probably come to blows. She didn't think it would be wise to have a second member of MCU assaulting a fellow officer. One was enough. A brief, but satisfying, image of Carve-up nursing the bloody nose she'd given him shortly after joining MCU swam into view.

'We'll look at those three later. But for now I want you to track down Amy Swales, Richard Bannister and Cheryl Holiday. Ask them about their relationship with Mark. Get alibis. Anything strikes you as off, make a note and let me know.'

Ignoring their scowls, she got to her feet, feeling like the mother of two squabbling kids rather than a detective sergeant. While they threw fish fingers at each other, she wanted to know what Darcy Clements had found out.

Chapter Twenty-Seven

Kat walked into Forensics, where she could hear laughter.

Darcy Clements, the forensic coordinator, emerged from a knot of CSIs, shaking her head and wiping her eyes. She saw Kat, and said, 'Hey! You just missed possibly the filthiest joke in human history. Certainly this department's. What can I do for you, Kat?'

'Any news on the Mark Swift crime scene?'

'Let's talk at my desk.' Once they were both seated, Darcy continued. 'First of all, the liquid Jack Beale pumped out of Mark's lungs *was* water. We found calcium carbonate, which is chalk to you.'

'Cheeky mare! I got GCSE chemistry.'

'Did you pass geography, too?'

'Yes, actually.'

'Then perhaps you'd like to tell me what you'd find if you dug down a couple of feet in a Middlehampton back garden?'

'Chalk. The Chilterns are made of it.'

'Exactly. Have a gold star. We also identified magnesium, sodium, and trace amounts of iron, manganese and lead. Plus chlorine and fluorides. Also present, in extremely tiny amounts, were nitrates and nitrites, which probably came from agricultural run-off.'

'In other words, plain old Middlehampton tap?'

Nodding, Darcy showed Kat a blown-up image on her screen.

'This is the fragment of foil Jack extracted from the trachea. We found minute traces of ethyl alcohol and malt soaked into the backing paper. It's from a beer bottle. Judging from the colour and a tiny element of the design, we've identified the brand as Peroni.'

'So what was he doing? Picking the label off a bottle and eating it?'

'Seems unlikely – unless he had some sort of mental health issue. Did he?'

'Don't know. Haven't got his medical records yet.'

Why would Mark have ingested a fragment of label off a beer bottle? There'd been several beers lined up on the table in the green room. They were all in evidence now.

'Maybe he didn't eat it,' Darcy said, breaking into Kat's thoughts. 'Maybe his killer stuffed a bottle into his mouth to try and choke him, then some caught on his teeth, which he swallowed. Sorry, Kat,' she said at once. 'That sounds a bit fanciful.'

Kat shook her head. 'It's fine, Darce. We're just brainstorming. But Jack didn't find any injuries to the mouth or throat, which I'm pretty sure would happen in that scenario. But you've given me an idea. What if Mark didn't eat the label? What if he drank it? Suppose the beer was in whatever the killer used to drown him?' Kat flashed on the outdoor Sunday lunch at Bryn Glas farm. 'You must've been at parties or barbecues where there's loads of beers and whatnot in one of those massive rope-handled plastic trugs full of iced water? There's all kinds of stuff floating around. He could have swallowed the label fragment while he was drowning, and it got lodged in his throat that way.'

Darcy nodded. 'That might work. Except, we didn't find anything like that in the green room. The beers were just lined up on the table.'

Which, now Kat thought about it, was odd. Surely they'd have been in a cooler, like the champagne. It had been a really hot day on Friday.

'Darce, have you got the photos your snapper took at the scene, please?'

Darcy nodded and opened a folder on her computer, tiling all the crime scene photos. 'What am I looking for?'

'Can you find one with the beer bottles lined up on the table?'

Darcy set up a quick slide show and clicked through a dozen or so images before she stopped and tapped the screen.

'There.'

Lit by the photographer's ring flash, a row of ten Peroni bottles sat in a line on a royal blue paper tablecloth, as if waiting for someone to sing a song about them.

'Can you zoom in?' Kat asked, peering at the screen.

Darcy clicked a couple of controls, and the screen was filled with four of the bottles. Kat frowned, took her phone out and paged through the photos she'd taken after discovering Mark's body.

She showed Darcy a particular image. 'Can you get that off here and on to your PC and tile them side by side?'

Her heart was beating just that little bit faster. If her suspicions were correct, she'd identified the murder weapon. Not its location. Not yet. But now she knew what she was looking for.

After a couple of minutes, Darcy handed the phone back to Kat.

'It looks like one of those spot-the-difference puzzles.' she said.

As Kat stared delightedly at the side-by-side images, she felt it stirring. That detective's spider sense that told her she'd made a breakthrough.

'Look at the bottoms of the bottles, Darce. Tell me what you see.'

Darcy stared at the screen silently for a few seconds. Her eyes flicked left and right, left and right. In Kat's photo, each bottle sat in an irregular dark-navy patch of paper tablecloth. Zoomed in, their lower halves were wet. In the CSI's photo, the tablecloth beneath the bottles was a uniform royal blue. And the bottles' sides were dry, though the labels looked a little crinkled.

Darcy smiled, then pushed her chair back and spun round to face Kat.

'You clever little Kat. Those bottles had been in a container of water not long before you found Mark's body in the green room, hadn't they?'

'That's what it looks like. I think the murderer drowned Mark in it. Either before or after, they took the beers out and lined them up on the table. Then they found a way to get out of the room with the container. Probably poured the water away down a drain outside, or a toilet in the loos.'

It was a start. A great start. Now all they needed was to find the container, trace it back on its journey from the green room and, somewhere, hope there was evidence linking it to the murderer.

In the meantime, Kat wanted to know if the literary figures Maria had mentioned had the monopoly on grudges against Mark. And that meant an appointment with the festival sponsor, Bruno Collins. She had to advance to Mayfair.

Chapter Twenty-Eight

Savile Harvey had its offices halfway down Hill Street, a pristine road of Georgian townhouses in the heart of Mayfair. Some had been converted into commercial spaces; others were apparently still residential.

Kat tried to imagine what kind of person could afford to buy a five-storey house here. Images of men in gleaming white robes or expensive designer suits – *Tom Ford* came a whispering echo in Fez's Birmingham accent – and women in head-to-toe Chanel sprang to mind.

On being admitted to Savile Harvey's palatial headquarters, Kat sighed with relief as the chilled air washed over her. Her host, a statuesque twentysomething in heels, with a blonde chignon and an air of ineffable superiority, led her to a waiting area furnished in caramel leather couches with cream piping on their seams.

'Would you like a drink while you're waiting? We have coffee, tea, chai, bubble tea, mineral water?'

Kat shuddered involuntarily as the air-conditioned interior of the building chilled the sweat on her back.

'Coffee, please. Americano?'

'Of course.'

With a cool smile, the young woman moved away, demonstrating a facility for walking in heels Kat marvelled at. Van was always at her to buy a pair of stilettos. She always gave him the same answer. '*You* try walking in the bloody things first and see if *you* like it.'

The woman returned as Kat was studying a copy of the *Financial Times*, wondering at the kind of people who could understand the arcane terminology of its inside pages.

'Checking your investments?' she enquired, placing a bone china cup and saucer in front of Kat.

Kat looked up. Was she taking the piss? But the woman seemed genuine enough. Perhaps in the circles she moved in, everyone had 'investments'. Kat had her police pension and a couple of thousand or so in a deposit-account 'rainy day' fund. Other than that, it was the occasional EuroMillions ticket and a single share in Middlehampton FC, bought at Van's urging so she could vote in the AGM and try to keep the club in decent hands.

'I wish. Not much scope for investments on a police officer's salary.'

'I suppose the job itself must be its own reward, then. Bruno won't be long. He's just with a client.'

Kat had to wait for another fifteen minutes before a door swung open and two men emerged. One, good-looking in a bland, inoffensive way, wore a midnight-blue suit over a white shirt with no tie. He looked like one of those modern male politicians whose outfits seemed designed to say, *Hey, I'm sharp enough to run the country but I'm still a regular guy.* The other, like the men populating her brief fantasy of the street's denizens, was a tall Arab man in a white robe and red-and-white headdress.

'We'll be in touch,' he said, shaking hands and then, after glancing perfunctorily down at Kat, leaving the building, already speaking into his phone.

The first man turned to Kat and smiled warmly. 'DS Ballantyne? I'm Bruno Collins.' He shook her hand. Warm, dry,

161

free of any attempt to break her fingers. She awarded him a tick for this alone. 'Have you been offered refreshments?'

'I have. Your receptionist made me a very nice coffee.'

'Great, great. If you'd like to follow me. I thought we'd talk in the boardroom.'

Once they were seated at a vast polished table, Collins spread his hands.

'How can I help? I follow the news, so I imagine this is about Mark.'

She nodded. Working a celebrity murder case was like operating in a fishbowl. Everybody she met seemed to know in advance about the case.

'I gather that Mark had been arguing online and in the press with a pressure group called Books Not Bombs,' she said. 'What can you tell me about that?'

Collins sighed and ran a hand over his neatly cut black hair.

'I won't bore you with a long lecture, but basically, they think people like me are one step above, or possibly below, Satan. We facilitate genocide, the murder of children, and the wholesale destruction of the planet. Now, that isn't true, but, anyway, among our corporate social responsibility activities we sponsor literary festivals. Couple of the larger ones, but we started with crime ten years ago. It's an underrepresented sector on the wider stage, and we thought we could, in our marketing department's parlance, "own the space", yes?'

Kat nodded her understanding. It wasn't that hard to follow. Even for a town cop with a zero-for-eleven record on the EuroMillions.

'So, Books Not Bombs got wind of our involvement and started making a stink. Chucking fake blood at our office windows, turning up at festivals dressed as police and' – he made air quotes – '"arresting" our people. They want us to pull out, but I told them we wouldn't.'

'How did Mark get involved?'

'Mark and I were at Cambridge together. Always kept in touch. Our wives are friends. I suppose I was griping one night about them and Mark got that look he used to get. A sort of puckish twinkle in his eye. Like, "Right, I'm going to have some fun with this." Then he wrote this pretty hard-hitting article, accusing them of being Nazis who wanted to burn books in the streets.'

'They weren't happy, I'm guessing?'

'Happy?' Collins's eyebrows elevated into two dark black pen strokes. 'Venetia Shelby-Hales – the name says a lot, don't you think? – went bloody ballistic. Anyway, Mark had his lawyer do some digging on her. They put together this dossier. Calculated she'd flown twenty-two thousand miles attending climate conferences in the last five years. They even put a carbon footprint together for her. It was pretty clever, actually, but she had a meltdown on X, saying all kinds of nasty things about poor old Mark.'

'And did this meltdown go anywhere beyond social media?'

'Not as far as I know, but here's something else you should look into. Venetia's got form.'

'For what?' Kat asked.

She imagined that for someone in Venetia Shelby-Hales's line of work, a criminal record was probably a badge of honour. Plenty of public order offences. Maybe some criminal damage. Assaulting a police officer, even. So Collins's answer surprised her.

'She was tried for murder. Her lawyers got her off. Lack of evidence – or, you know, mucked-up evidence. But it comes to the same thing, doesn't it? Her old man's six feet under and Venetia walks, much to the joy of her patchouli-scented supporters.'

Kat had warmed to Bruno Collins on first meeting him. But as he talked, she found she was liking him less and less. Something in his attitude had started to grate on her.

'I just have one more question. Can you account for your whereabouts last Friday morning?'

If he was surprised to be asked for an alibi, he didn't show it.

'I arrived here at 6.30 a.m. Zoomed with colleagues in Osaka then Frankfurt until 9.00 a.m. In-person meetings in this room from then until lunchtime. My secretary can furnish you with the details.' He stood. 'Are we done? Only I have a business to run.'

'Yep, we're done,' she said. 'Thanks for your time.'

Two minutes later, Kat was outside on the pavement, recoiling from the heat that shoved her in the face like a drunken football fan on match day.

She decided to take a detour before returning to Middlehampton.

To meet the woman accused by Mark of being a book-burner, and by the CPS of being a murderer.

Chapter Twenty-Nine

Having established that Venetia was in the office, Kat drove over to Whitechapel.

Emerging from the air-conditioned interior of her car, Kat gasped as the city heat pushed down on her. Books Not Bombs had premises above a bookshop on Brick Lane. She headed north up the narrow road, its pavements jammed with food trucks, the air perfumed and spicy.

Unable to resist, she bought a fish taco laden with fat chunks of white flesh, pink onions, coriander, chillies and tomatoes.

'This is amazing!' she said to the vendor through a mouthful.

He winked. 'Come back soon!'

Buoyed up by the flavours, the heat suddenly seemed more bearable, although she wished policework dictated its female practitioners didn't have to wear trousers, which were clinging to her legs unpleasantly. A good half of the women mingling alongside her in the narrow street looked cool and comfortable in saris, sarongs, floaty maxi dresses and mini skirts. An image popped unbidden into her head. Her, Leah and Ma-Linda rocking thigh-skimming minis. Carve-up would probably have an aneurysm. Maybe she should try, then.

She checked her phone. Three hundred feet to go. Ahead, a tall, red-brick chimney loomed. Painted down its side was the name of the brewer that had originally occupied the site. *TRUMAN*.

She craned her neck, marvelling at the craftsmanship of the Victorian builders who'd constructed the brewery. The white block capitals weren't painted after all: they were bricks, laid with painstaking typographical care to dovetail with the rest of the chimney.

'Watch it, love!'

She started. She'd almost collided with a middle-aged lady in a bright batik headdress and wrapper, her arms laden with half a dozen bulging carrier bags of fruit and vegetables.

'Sorry, sorry,' Kat said, resolving to keep her eyes on the street and stop lollygagging like a tourist.

The bookshop came into view on her right. Echoing the lettering high above it, its fascia read *TRUFAX*. The window showcased books on peace studies and climate change. A hand-lettered sign read, *The World is Burning. Luckily, Ideas are Fireproof.*

Kat pushed the bell to the right of a plain, narrow door set in beside the shop window. The latch clacked without her having to introduce herself. She shrugged mentally and glanced up. The beady glass eye of a CCTV camera observed her from its mount above the door. Clearly her clothes were emitting a cop radiation signature. *Should have worn that maxi after all*, she mused.

Admitted into the hallway, she sighed with relief. It was dark and narrow, but also cool. She climbed the stairs, knocked at the door at the top and entered a cramped space in which two women sat at facing desks.

'You must be Kat,' the older of the two said, stepping round her desk and offering a cool, long-fingered hand. 'I'm Venetia. This is my partner in crime, Gill Cable.'

Kat smiled at the younger woman, and they shook hands.

'Take a seat,' Venetia said, pointing to a folding chair. Kat had the same one at home. IKEA. 'Coffee? Water?'

'Water, please.'

Venetia disappeared through a door Kat hadn't noticed at first and returned with a glass brimming with ice-cold water. Kat took a big gulp, her back teeth screeching in protest as it hit a recent filling.

'You wanted to ask me about Swift,' Venetia said, drawing her long silver hair back and refastening her ponytail.

'Were you aware Mark Swift was murdered last Friday?'

Behind her, Gill snorted and mumbled 'good riddance'.

'I saw it on social media,' Venetia replied.

'Can you describe your relationship with Mark?'

Venetia looked at the ceiling for a second before returning her gaze to Kat. 'I would say our relationship was that of a toxin meeting an antidote.'

'Sorry, you might have to speak a little bit more plainly,' Kat said with what she hoped was a self-deprecating smile.

Venetia sighed. 'Mark Swift was a perfect storm of misogyny, patriarchy and ignorance. He thought because he sold millions of books that gave him the right to pontificate on the issues of the day. Violence against women and girls, climate change, Israel–Palestine, the rise of fascism in Europe.'

'You didn't like him?'

'That's like saying I don't like ricin. You don't have an emotional relationship with toxins. You neutralise them.'

'I see. How did you feel when Mark accused you and your colleagues of being Nazis? Burning books in the street?'

'I thought it was a typical alt-right dog whistle. Gill's Jewish. He knew that. Accusing us of being Nazis is a classic antisemitic trope.'

'He also accused you of being a hypocrite for flying to climate conferences. Is that a dog whistle, too?'

For the first time in the brief interview, Kat detected a shift in Venetia's attitude. The calm, almost playful attitude disappeared. Replacing it was something altogether steelier.

'Shall we just cut the foreplay? You're not warming me up and you're not really my type, either,' Venetia said, earning a snicker from Gill. 'Why don't you ask what you came here to ask? I've got a meeting in ten minutes, and quite frankly the subject we'll be discussing is a lot more important than policework.'

She put such dismissive emphasis on this last word she might as well have said 'toilet cleaning'.

In her younger days, Kat might have struggled to maintain an even temper in the face of Venetia's provocation. Maybe she would have defended her work as vital to the smooth running of society. But over the years, she'd met many variants on the type she always thought of as 'IPYW' – 'I pay your wages'. Whether it was her snotty older sister, bulging-muscled Friday-night drunks, overbearing local bigwigs, or idealistic free-thinkers who wanted to defund the police right up until the day their house got burgled.

Venetia had told her to ask her questions, so she did.

'You just talked about neutralising toxins. Did you "neutralise" Mark Swift?'

'No.' A beat. 'Though I'm very happy someone else did.'

'Can you account for your whereabouts last Friday morning?'

Venetia smiled slyly. Waited for a few seconds before answering. *OK*, Kat thought, *so she's got a solid alibi.*

'I was glued to the window of the head office of Waterstones on Piccadilly. There's quite a lot of video on social media. If you want, we can show it to you?'

'Yes, please.'

Venetia looked momentarily nonplussed. She fiddled with her phone before rotating its screen towards Kat.

A time-stamped video taken near the front of a small crowd of protesters clearly showed Venetia with her left palm splayed over the plate glass window.

Something Venetia had said earlier sparked an association in Kat's mind. Riley's rant about Mark Swift. While she watched the video, Kat asked another question.

'What did you mean about Mark Swift's misogyny? Was it something specific, or just him being a member of the patriarchy?'

Venetia sneered at Kat.

'You think it's funny, don't you? I mean, you're a woman, but you're a cop, too. A cop *first*, I bet you tell people. But you're on the wrong side, Kat. Have you ever asked yourself why the police arrest climate change protesters? Why they protect big business? Why they work with their political paymasters to stifle free speech?'

Kat bridled. She was tiring of the self-righteous lecture she was being forced to sit through. 'We work to uphold the *law*. If people *break* the law, we arrest them. It's really very simple. And right now,' she continued, as Venetia opened her mouth to interrupt, 'I am working to find the person who murdered Mark Swift.'

Venetia had been shaking her head during Kat's impassioned defence of her job.

'And what if the law's unjust, Kat? Do you *still* uphold it? Do you still enforce it? What if they bring in a law that forbids people like me from speaking out about climate change? What if they dictate that people like Gill have to register with a special government department? Wear a special insignia? Are you going to be there with your Taser and your baton, making sure they join the queue?'

Kat's heart was racing. Being a murder detective hadn't prepared her for discussing philosophy in the middle of an investigation.

But she felt she had to respond somehow. 'Honestly, Venetia? I . . .'

Her thoughts whirled. What about her own suspicions regarding the police? Or at least certain officers within its ranks? How hard would she argue to defend Carve-up's conduct, for example?

'Conscience pricking you?' Venetia asked softly.

Damn. It was like she could read Kat's mind.

'I don't know, OK?' Kat blurted out. 'I joined the police because I thought . . . I mean because my best friend was murdered. I always wanted to work in Major Crimes. To solve murders and bring some kind of peace for the victims and their families. I get what you're talking about – and honestly? I don't know. I hope I'd fight against that kind of thing. And if you think I'm the "I was just obeying orders" type, you don't know me at all.'

Venetia tipped her head on one side and smiled. 'Bravo. You're courageous, articulate, and not afraid to admit you don't have all the answers. Pity you're sitting there and not here. We need women like you, Kat.'

'Well, you'll have to do without me for the moment. I have a murderer to catch. You still haven't answered my question, by the way. Why did you call Mark a misogynist?'

'Because I recognise the type, that's why. He reminds me of my ex-husband. Who, I'm sure you already know, I was accused of murdering.'

'*Did* you murder him?'

'I killed him. I didn't murder him. It was justifiable homicide, although the CPS did their best to portray me as a cross between Aileen Wuornos and Lizzie Borden. The case was thrown out because they, and their allies in the police, broke disclosure rules to try and get me convicted.'

'Self-defence?'

'He used to rape me. My ex. Regular as clockwork. Every Saturday night. In the end I'd had enough. That last time, I waited until he was asleep, snoring like the pig he was. I crept downstairs. Fetched a carving knife out of the block in the kitchen, went back to the bedroom and stabbed him.'

'Venetia, I'm sorry to persist with this line of questioning, but did Mark Swift ever sexually assault you?'

'No. And he'd have died a lot sooner than last Friday if he'd tried.'

'Or any of your staff?' Kat asked, glancing at Gill, who was listening intently.

'Gill's not my "staff", she's my co-founder.'

'The answer's no, anyway,' Gill said.

Kat sighed. She had nothing. The whole trip had been a bust. Venetia had an alibi. The Books Not Bombs angle was a sideshow. She thanked Venetia and Gill for their time and minutes later was walking through the oppressive London heat, back to her car.

As she started the engine, she mulled over Venetia's accusations about Mark. The trouble was that's all they were. Accusations. They could just be the venting of a woman bruised by an encounter with the author. She wouldn't be the first to have felt aggrieved by his behaviour.

Kat frowned. *She wouldn't be the first.* Was this a lead pointing to motive? Was there a pattern? Ahead, traffic lights were turning from green to amber. Maybe the trip hadn't been a waste of time after all.

She put her foot down.

Chapter Thirty

Driving back to Middlehampton, Kat's thoughts wouldn't settle on the case, however much she tried to force herself to focus on who'd murdered Mark.

She knew why. She'd almost blurted out the truth about Liv to Venetia. That she'd only *thought* Liv had been murdered. And now her best friend was engaged. Talking about babies. It all seemed so sudden.

OK, they didn't talk every day, or even every week, but Kat was sure she hadn't heard Dafydd's name before Sunday. She hoped Liv wasn't rushing into things. Oh God, was she only settling down so Kat wouldn't have to worry about her coming back to Middlehampton? And she'd said she was giving her inheritance to the farm? Was that wise?

She'd call Liv later. Just for a chat. Maybe they could talk about the case, too. Liv had always been good at getting out of scrapes. Maybe she could figure out how Mark's killer had apparently vanished into thin air.

Back in Middlehampton, Kat called Fez and Leah over to the murder board.

'What have we got? Leah?'

'I finally managed to talk to Rachel Dixon, wife number one. She says she's been in Edinburgh all summer. I've asked the locals to help with CCTV and requested her credit card receipts. I also talked to Richard Bannister in person. Bloody hell, he's tall. It was like talking to a giraffe. I got a crick in my neck. Anyway, he said he was in the beer tent all day apart from the odd trip to the loo or to catch a session. Not much of an alibi. Just, "everyone was mingling in the tent".'

Fez had been nodding as Leah spoke. 'Same for me, Kat. I talked to Cheryl Holiday. She was' – he flipped back through his notebook – 'yeah, here we go, "chatting to old friends on the lawn. It's where we all congregate."'

'Did you get anywhere with Maria?'

'I gave her a call. Got her talking, asked about the divorce. Honestly? She sounded genuinely cut up about Mark being dead.'

'Any CCTV?'

Leah shook her head. 'The Guildhall's a Grade I listed building. They've never applied for permission to put cameras up.'

'There must be pics, though,' Kat said. 'And video. When I was there with Van, everyone was taking selfies. There was even a police line-up booth with heights marked. Van insisted we get ours taken holding up boards reading "guilty of reading crime novels". Hilarious.'

Fez smiled. 'I'm with Van. I love 'em. Can't get enough. Naz thinks I'm mad, what with the job and all. But I tell her, "Well, you read surgery manuals in bed, bab, so it's a bit pot and kettle."'

Beside him, just out of his eyeline, Leah rolled her eyes.

'It'd be a hell of a job trying to get all the photos and videos off people's phones at the festival,' she said. 'You've got hundreds of people, maybe thousands. Over three days. They've come from all over the country. And I bet the organisers wouldn't give up their contact details without a fight. GDPR and all that.'

Kat nodded. Leah was right. She'd hold off on that avenue for a while longer.

'While you were rubbing shoulders with the world of literature, I spent a very hot morning in London,' Kat said. 'I spoke to Venetia Shelby-Hales, co-founder of Books Not Bombs. You remember Mark got into it with them about their protest strategy? Venetia, among some fairly direct criticism of the police, insinuated he was some kind of sexual predator. I'm wondering if that might offer a motive.'

'Did she offer any proof, boss?' Fez asked. 'Any evidence?'

Leah rounded on him, eyes flashing. 'That's right, immediately question the woman. Jesus, this is 2024. Do you not get it?'

Fez stepped back, but paradoxically he also stood his ground. 'Hang on a minute, Leah. I get you've got some sort of problem with me, though I'm buggered if I know what it is, but it's a reasonable question to ask. Evidence? Proof? That's what our job's all about, isn't it? Or do they do things differently down south?'

Before Leah could respond, or maybe 'react' was the better word, Kat held her hands up, feeling like a boxing referee stopping a fight. Because Fez was right. And Leah's behaviour around him was getting stranger and stranger.

'Hold on, Leah. This *is* about evidence. Fez is perfectly right to ask. And the answer's no. She didn't give me anything concrete. Just said he was a misogynist. She claimed he reminded her of her ex-husband – well, *late* husband's more accurate. She stabbed him to death because he was raping her.'

Fez's eyes widened. 'Bloody hell! Was she convicted?'

'Nope. Judge threw the case out. Apparently, the CPS broke disclosure rules.'

A thick silence descended on them at that point. Kat could see unvoiced thoughts spinning in the air above them. All on a similar theme. *Good for her. Murder's murder. Not if it's self-defence. He got what he deserved.* Personally, she thought no victim of crime, up to and including murder, 'got what they deserved', and she'd heard too many abusive husbands and boyfriends claim that as some sort of justification for their crimes.

'So we've *no* evidence he was a sexual predator, then?' Fez asked again. He eyeballed Leah. 'Just for clarification.'

'No,' Kat said. 'But I'm adding it as a line of enquiry. Anything else you two dug up?'

'You might want to speak to Amy Swales,' Fez said. 'I couldn't get hold of her, but I was looking at her books on Amazon. There's one called *Blood's Thicker Than Murder* where this bloke is found dead inside a locked bedroom. He's wearing a black bondage suit. You know, one of those full-body latex jobs. Anyway, he's zipped up inside it with his lungs full of water.'

'Oh, come on,' Leah said. 'You're not seriously suggesting she murdered Swift because you found a reference to drowning in one of her books? I thought you were all about the evidence?'

Fez ignored her. Looked at Kat. 'If you were going to interview her anyway, you could ask her, couldn't you?'

Kat nodded. 'I'll see if I can find her this afternoon. Where does she live again, Fez?'

'Camden in North London. Her address is on file.'

'Right. I'll pay her a visit.'

Kat ended the huddle but called Leah back as she headed for her desk.

'Ladies'. Now.'

Inside the bright white tiled space, when she was sure they had it to themselves, Kat turned to face her bagwoman.

'Right. What the hell is going on with you? You've been treating Fez like he's a leper with BO from the moment he arrived.'

Leah put her hands on her hips.

'Nothing's "going on". I told you, he's giving off these superior big-city cop vibes. I just don't like it.'

'Oh, come on, Leah. Please. I wasn't born yesterday. That's not it at all, is it?'

Leah held her hands wide. The standard 'What, me, guv? I never done nuffin'' gesture for every guilty-as-sin nominal since coppers started arresting them.

'I don't know what you want me to say, Kat. Can't I just not like a bloke?'

'If he's a weapons-grade arsehole like Carve-up, yes, absolutely. Have at it, I'll hold your coat. But a new guy turns up and you're giving him evils within sixty seconds? No. Look, Leah, I hate to even have to say this to you, but as of now I'm being your friend and asking you to sort this. But if this is something else, something' – she hesitated – 'to do with his identity . . . then I stop being your friend and I become your manager. And that will take us into territory where neither of us wants to go. But I will take you there, mate. If you make me.'

Kat felt awful saying this. Coming down hard on her friend. But there was no room on her team for any antagonism, and especially not if it had a racist core. Her heart was bumping uncomfortably in her throat and she felt sick while she waited for Leah to respond. She simply couldn't believe this was Leah standing in front of her.

Leah sighed. And she relaxed, her arms hanging limply by her sides.

'I'm not a racist, Kat. How can I be when I love Craig? He's like an uncle to me. But, yes, I had some trouble at my last station with a Muslim cop. With his attitude. Can I just leave it at that, Kat, please?'

'What kind of trouble?'

'About being gay. Please, Kat. Don't make me go into the details. I promise I'll make an effort with Fez.'

Kat thought for a while. Leah's explanation sounded halfway plausible. But it still left her feeling conflicted. Like the old 'I'm not a racist, but . . .' line trotted out by saloon-bar bores. 'OK. But I'm taking you both out for a drink after work tonight. See if you can't sort it out with Fez, yes?'

Leah bridled. Her eyes flashing. 'Why should I, though, Kat? I'm not the one with the outdated attitudes.'

'And neither is Fez,' Kat protested. 'You haven't even given him a chance.'

Leah sighed. 'OK, fine. Just don't expect me to be best buddies with him, that's all I'm saying.'

'Good. Thank you. Come on, let's get back to work. There's a dead author's murder to solve.'

Kat pulled open the door to find Fez standing there, his eyes flashing dangerously.

Chapter Thirty-One

Kat took a half-step back.

'Fez. Everything all right?'

'Everything all right, boss? No. Far from it, as a matter of fact.' His breath coming in gasps, he stabbed a finger towards Leah. 'I think you've got a bad attitude. In fact, you know what? You've got a racist attitude. From the moment I arrived, you've been treating me like I shat in your locker. Accusing me of mansplaining, rolling your eyes when you think I can't see you. You give me all that shit in the briefing just now then you two disappear off into the ladies' for what? Another let's-hate-on-the-Muslim session?'

Kat's pulse was racing. This had just escalated wildly. She needed Leah to get her act together and stop this before it turned into something none of them would be able to control.

'Leah. Tell him. Everything.'

Leah looked at Fez, then back at Kat.

'OK, Fez. You want to hear the truth – fine.' And the details Leah hadn't wanted to share just a moment ago came out in a rush that had Kat reeling. 'Before I transferred to Middlehampton, I worked in Bradford. My partner, a DS, was this older guy. Fiftyish. Muslim. I quite liked him, to be honest. I had no problem with him. But he had one with me. He found out I was gay. I wasn't out then, but a couple of my mates knew. Anyway, he went off on one. Quoting the Qur'an at me, saying I was unnatural. This one time, on a stake-out, about three in the morning? He leans over and he says, "What you need, lezzie girl, is a good hard seeing to from a real man. That will cure you of your immorality." I just froze. Then I got out of the car and walked home. I got signed off with stress for a couple of weeks, and when I got back, I applied for my transfer. Then you turn up and I heard you quite clearly, that first afternoon. You were talking to Craig and you said, "Dykes're a waste of space." I *heard* you!'

Fez's jaw dropped. '*That's* what this is about? We were talking about Kim *Dykstra*, you idiot. He just signed for the Eels as a forward. From Royal Antwerp. He's a Belgian, not a lesbian. Ask Craig. He'll tell you.'

Silence.

Kat watched as Leah tried to make sense of what Fez had just said. Her brows knitted together. Her lips parted, but no sound emerged.

Fez was shaking his head. Scrubbing his fingers through his hair. He didn't look angry anymore, but there was a wariness behind his eyes. Kat knew why. He'd come to a new town, a new station, a new team, and within hours had faced prejudice. The fact that the trigger was almost comical – a misheard footballer's name – couldn't have done much to soothe the hurt he had to be feeling.

'What that dickhead in Bradford said to you? That was beyond wrong,' Fez said, his voice low, looking directly into Leah's eyes. 'But you need to know this about me. I don't think *anything* about, as you put it, people like you. I take people as I find them. Now, if you were talking about my parents, or maybe my grandparents, OK, fair play, they're very conservative. You could even say bigoted, I wouldn't argue. But that's them. Not me. Yes, I'm Muslim. I'm also a dad, a husband, a copper and, possibly more important than all of those, a proud supporter of Warwickshire County Cricket

Club.' He stepped back, breathing heavily. 'Look, Leah, I genuinely want us to be friends. I've got gay mates – not many, but some. And Naz works for the NHS, which I'm glad to say is a super-diverse workplace. So do me a favour, bab, and don't judge me until you've got to know me.'

Kat glanced at her bagwoman. Leah's cheeks, normally pale, had pinked. She looked completely shamefaced. Her eyes were glistening. But she had the decency to meet Fez's gaze.

'No, Fez. This is on me. Look, I'm sorry, OK? Really sorry. I was totally out of order. God knows what you must think of me. And you're right. I should never have judged you.' She stuck her hand out. 'Can we maybe start again? With me not being such a racist dick?'

'Fine by me,' he said, shaking it. 'Although if I ever hear you've been cheering those Yorkshire bastards on, that's it, we're done.'

Leah nodded, turned on her heel and headed back to MCU. Fez made to follow her, but Kat laid a hand on his shoulder.

'Hold on a sec, Fez.'

He turned, frowning. 'What is it?'

'You don't have to let that go, you know. Whatever Leah's backstory, whatever she thought she heard you saying to Craig, that was racism, pure and simple. If you want to make a formal complaint about Leah's behaviour, I'll support you. I don't play favourites.'

He sighed. 'That's decent of you, our kid. But let me tell you something. Short of announcing you've joined Anti-Corruption, making a complaint about another officer's racism is the fastest way to put a target on your back. You're a troublemaker. Too thin-skinned to cope with banter. You can sense people pulling away, giving you a wide berth. It's like your team membership got secretly cancelled and nobody informed you.'

'But I would never let that happen,' Kat protested. 'It's my team. I'd come down hard on anyone who even hinted at those things.'

Fez nodded. 'I know you would, boss, and I respect you for it. But what Leah did? I can cope. I've seen, and heard, worse. My mum always said pick your battles, right? When the BNP were marching through Small Heath, me and my mates got down there and we drove them out. And I don't mean with the power of our rhetoric, either. But a colleague making some bad assumptions about Muslims because of one bigoted wanker?' He wrinkled his nose. 'That's not a hill I'm willing to die on.'

Kat looked deep into his eyes. 'I think you're a good man, Fez, as well as a great cop. And I know you can fight your own battles. But I've got your back, OK? Every day you're in Middlehampton. And if you change your mind . . .'

He nodded. 'I know.'

Chapter Thirty-Two

Still concerned about the impact of Leah's behaviour on Fez, but parking it for now, Kat headed back into London, and Camden, where Amy Swales lived. An hour later she drew up outside Amy's house, a four-storey building of red and gold brick.

Kat climbed the short flight of steps to the front door and rang Amy's bell, one of six set into a dull grey intercom box.

What would Amy have to say about Mark Swift? And would she deny being at the festival?

Kat heard Amy before she saw her. Heels on hard floor tiles followed by an exasperated shout.

'Yes, yes, yes, I'm coming! Christ! It better be for me this time.'

The door swung inwards. Kat held up her warrant card.

Amy's eyes widened. Her expression slid from amused self-deprecation to something altogether shiftier.

'Good afternoon. I'm DS Ballantyne, Hertfordshire Police,' Kat said. 'I'm investigating the murder of Mark Swift. Can I come in, please?'

Amy glanced over Kat's shoulder and murmured, 'Of course.'

Amy's flat had a small kitchen facing a long narrow garden. French doors were pushed wide open, held in place by bricks slanted against their lower edges.

'Inside or outside?' Amy asked.

'Perhaps inside? It's so hot today, don't you think?'

Amy's shoulders dropped. The smile this time looked genuine. Perhaps she was one of those people for whom a visit from the police was only ever a cause for anxiety. *Which would be all of them,* Kat thought, *apart from the villains. And even they get twitchy.*

'So, how can I help?' Amy said brightly, once they were seated. Then her chin trembled. 'Poor Mark. How awful.'

It looked like the worst-ever amateur-dramatic workshop rendition of 'grief held at bay' Kat had ever seen. And she'd seen plenty.

'Can you tell me where you were between 10.00 a.m. and 11.15 a.m. last Friday?'

'You know I was at *Criminal Herts* I assume?'

Kat said nothing.

'I was in the beer tent. Meeting friends, chatting, catching up, you know what it's like when you're at an event. Police conferences are probably the same, aren't they? Although, do you actually have conferences, or is that only a thing on the telly? You know, the one where they all boo the Home Secretary. Quite funny really.'

Amy was wittering from nerves. Kat had seen this reaction before. But her own nerves had been frayed by the second drive into London in a day, not to mention the oppressive heat.

'Did you visit the green room at any point?' she asked, getting to the point.

Amy rolled her eyes. 'I wish! You know there was a time when that could have been a possibility. But then Mark got me cancelled and that was that.'

Interesting. The grief act hadn't lasted long. Time for a gentle prompt. 'That must have been hard.'

'Hard? I was making a good living. I had a house in Belsize Park,' Amy said, nodding towards a corner of the room Kat assumed pointed towards the chi-chi neighbourhood she was talking about.

'Big mortgage, obviously, but I could afford it. Then Mark set his attack dog on me with those baseless accusations, and now look. A rented flat in Frognal. Oh, we all call it Belsize North, but that's just to preserve property values. Not that that matters to me anymore.'

'A man was drowned in one of your books, is that right?' Kat asked.

Amy looked puzzled. Perhaps she'd thought they'd spend a pleasant few minutes airing her grievances at Mark's treatment of her. Not to worry. Kat would be returning to the subject soon enough.

'Oh, well, yes. *Blood's Thicker Than Murder.*' She smiled. 'It's actually my favourite. Such a clever mechanic.'

Kat crinkled her forehead a bit. Amy wasn't the only one who could do amateur dramatics.

'Sorry, Amy . . . Mechanic?'

'Term of art. How you work up the details of the MO. A way of disposing of the murder weapon or fudging your alibi, getting a killer out of a locked room – which was actually the core of *Blood's Thicker Than Murder.*'

Kat leaned forwards, smiling. 'How *did* you do it?'

'It was so clever! The victim, Alan Williams, is into extreme bondage. Gimp suits, ball gags, all that. Really weird period of my search history. Anyway, so he likes to zip himself into this full-body black latex suit. He's rigged the head mask up to a vacuum pump. He turns a valve on a pump, and it starts to suck the air out. Just as he's passing out from suffocation he, well, you know, *finishes*, and then he turns off the pump. I mean, this stuff is all out there. People really do it. And my idea was by no means the strangest. You wouldn't believe the apparatus people rig up in their spare bedrooms just to get their jollies.'

Kat felt it was Amy who'd be the doubter. She'd seen pictures of crime scenes that really did defy belief. A suburban lounge rigged out with ceiling-mounted pulleys, ropes and a paddling pool had been one particular highlight of her probationary period. She offered another encouraging smile, although now she'd started, Amy seemed to have forgotten she was talking to a detective and not a fan.

'Go on. This is fascinating.'

'I know, right. Well, the murderer, who's actually Alan's . . . No, I won't tell you in case you ever decide to read it. Anyway, the murderer sneaks into Alan's flat and attaches a water reservoir to the pump and then rewires it to push instead of suck. When the body's finally discovered, zipped into the suit, there's no pump and the victim's lungs are full of water. Just for an extra thrill, I made it salt water!'

She sat back, her eyes wide and glittering. Her expression was clear. *Aren't I a clever girl?*

'Mark was drowned,' Kat said. 'Although there was no gimp suit, but no water source either, just like in your book. Did you kill him, Amy?'

Amy reared back. 'Me? No! Why would you even ask that?'

'I'd like to invite you to attend a voluntary interview under caution in Middlehampton. You would be entitled to have legal representation and—'

'—yes, yes, I know the script. I used to write crime novels for a living. I wouldn't be under arrest, and I'd be free to leave at any time, blah blah blah.' She folded her arms. 'That's right, isn't it?'

Kat had withstood all kinds of slings and arrows in her years as a cop, some of them literal. But since working under Carve-up, one thing in particular had started getting under her skin. Being cut off by someone with a point to make. Usually it was Carve-up belittling her. But her dad did it; Frank Strutt, a local crime boss, did it; and now Amy Swales was doing it.

'Yes, Ms Swales, that *is* right.'

'In that case, no. I'm not going anywhere. I've got a new retreat I'm planning, so unless you're going to arrest me, which I highly doubt, I'm afraid I'll have to ask you to leave.'

To emphasise her point, Amy stood and gestured towards the door.

Sighing, Kat got to her feet.

'Amy Swales, I am arresting you on suspicion of the murder of Mark Swift. You do not have to say anything—'

Amy leapt up, arms out in front of her, palms facing Kat.

'Wait! What? No. Stop! I'll come voluntarily. God! Don't arrest me, please. That would really finish me off. Just let me grab some shoes.'

Pleased not to be facing all the arrest paperwork, and with her own ability to persuade an uncooperative witness into the station without cuffs, Kat allowed herself a small smile.

When Amy returned, Kat led her out to the car and ushered her into the back seat.

Chapter Thirty-Three

Amy had handed her phone over without a word of protest. But she'd also insisted on a solicitor.

The wait took two hours, during which Kat asked Fez to run through Amy Swales's social media posts from the time of her feud with Mark Swift. She also texted Van to let him know she'd be late home. Riley had football practice but that was covered. His friend Bishal's dad was taking them both.

Van's reply was short, but made her feel good.

progress?

Yep

coolio x

The duty solicitor eventually arrived. Kat had met him before. Young, tired-looking. But at least his shirt was ironed properly. Last time it had still had the creases from the packaging showing.

Once the preliminaries were out of the way, Kat started with the simplest question of all.

'Amy, did you kill Mark Swift?'

'Of course I didn't kill him.'

'Why "of course"? You had good reason, I'd have thought. He had his lawyer, Sir Anthony Bone, who you referred to as Mark's "attack dog", dig into your past. The upshot was you were cancelled. You lost your publishing revenue. How do you support yourself now?'

'Is that relevant, Detective?' the solicitor asked.

'If Ms Swales suffered a large drop in income, that would have increased her resentment towards Mr Swift and his tactics.'

'It's fine,' Amy said. 'I run writers' retreats. The Dordogne mostly. And before you ask, I make a decent living.'

Kat consulted her notebook. 'But when we spoke at your flat in Frognal, you compared it unfavourably to the house you used to own in Belsize Park.'

'I love my flat. It's easy to manage and I spend most of my time abroad now anyway.'

'Fair enough. Let's talk about *Criminal Herts*. When did you arrive in Middlehampton?'

'Thursday evening. I was staying at the Premier Inn.'

'London's only an hour's drive away. Why didn't you commute?'

'I like to enjoy myself, have a few glasses of wine. It's a long day and I didn't want to drink and drive. I obey the law,' she added pointedly.

'What time did you get to the Guildhall on Friday morning?'

'Nine? A little after?'

'So you would have had time to enter the green room and arrange your – what did you call it?' Kat consulted her notebook again. Needlessly. She knew the word. But it sometimes helped to keep suspects waiting. 'Here we are. Your "mechanic"?'

'I would have done. But I didn't. I went straight to the beer tent, got myself a coffee. Shortly afterwards I would have met a friend and then it was just chatting all day.'

'I see. So if I consult CCTV, I won't find you creeping around inside the Guildhall with a water pump?'

'Could we avoid prejudicial words like "creeping", please?' the solicitor said.

Kat smiled briefly at him. He'd improved. 'I'm sorry. Will I find CCTV footage of you, Amy, entering the green room?'

'I doubt it. As you ought to know, the Guildhall's a listed building. There are very strict limits on what you can screw to the walls.'

'So you'd researched the venue? You knew there were no cameras?'

Amy rolled her eyes. '*Everybody* knows there's no CCTV. Every year, someone will go on about how if we wanted to murder someone – an uncommunicative agent, for example, or a slow-paying publisher – inside the hall would be the ideal place.'

There was a knock at the door. Fez entered and handed a couple of stapled sheets of paper to Kat. He offered the faintest of nods. She glanced at the paper, and Fez's handwritten notes, with a thrill of anticipation. Smiled. *Good lad.*

'Let's talk about your feud with Mark Swift,' she said.

'I wouldn't call it a feud.'

'Oh? What would you call it, then?'

'I don't know,' Amy said breezily. 'A spat, perhaps? Social media makes everything look ten times worse, doesn't it?'

Kat thought anything that involved you losing your principal source of income would rate a higher-value word than 'spat'.

'You tweeted that if there was any justice in the world, Mark Swift would drown in his own self-importance. Failing that, a nice deep bath. Any comment on that?'

Amy looked Kat straight in the eye. 'I never said that.'

'No? I won't find that among your tweets?'

'Nope. Because I never said it.'

'I see. For the recording, I am showing Ms Swales a printout of a blog post by a Janis Armitage, a book blogger, posting under the name *GirlReadsCrime*.'

Kat passed over Fez's printout.

Amy blanched. She glanced left at her solicitor, then leaned over and whispered into his ear. Looking upwards, he nodded, then spoke to her behind his hand.

Kat continued. 'The blog post is a rundown of the feud – sorry, "spat" – between Amy Swales and Mark Swift. It includes a screengrab of two tweets making up a thread posted by Ms Swales, but, as Ms Armitage points out, "hurriedly deleted after Mark's pit bull lawyer Sir Anthony Bone sent a cease-and-desist letter". I'll ask you again, Amy – and remind you that you're under an official police caution – did you write that?'

Amy stared at her.

'It was just a joke. Heat of the moment. Obviously, I didn't really want Mark to drown. Look, this is ridiculous. It wasn't me. Fine, you want the truth? I thought Mark Swift was an arsehole. He was all sweetness and light whenever his adoring fans were queuing for autographs, and the younger and prettier they were, the sweeter he became. But you know what? He did me a favour. I was burning out, writing my books. I love my life now. I coach writers in these beautiful settings, I get to share my wisdom, and I don't have to worry about plots and characters anymore.'

'But I thought that's what writers live for. Surely Mark took that all away from you?'

Amy shrugged. 'I'm a Buddhist. Well, I try to follow Buddhist teachings. The wisdom traditions generally. I let all that go. I live the life I have, not the life I wish I had. It's very freeing.'

To Kat, possibly made cynical by a decade or more of dealing with the very worst people and their victims, that sounded like freshly delivered bullshit. But Amy's caustic remark about Mark's fans struck a chord and she filed it away for later.

But what to do with Amy? Maybe one more push would yield a slip.

'Let's go back to your whereabouts when Mark was murdered.'

Amy sighed dramatically. 'As I already told you, I was in the beer tent.'

'For the entire period I mentioned?'

'Yes.'

'Can you prove it?'

'I've got selfies. Yes, selfies. I was with, er, Helena, Victoria, Sam, David – oh, hundreds of people.'

'The beer tent is about twenty-five feet from the green room, Amy. You could easily have slipped away.'

'Check my phone. I bet there's a bunch of photos from the exact time he was being killed.'

'We're doing that right now.'

Amy shrugged. 'Fine. I'll wait, then.'

Kat was getting all kinds of confusing signals off Amy. She'd initially lied about her tweets about Mark drowning. But maybe that was because she was still nervous about legal trouble from Sir Anthony Bone. She was stroppy and self-righteous one minute, then openly encouraging Kat to check her phone the next. Was she not a suspect after all, and merely a witness?

The selfies on her phone probably held the key. Kat suspended the interview and asked Amy to wait.

She went down to Forensics. Maybe Darcy would have the answer.

Chapter Thirty-Four

Darcy was red-faced and sweating when Kat approached her desk.

She looked up and smiled, blowing out her cheeks. 'Hey, you. I tell you, do not spend three hours in a Tyvek suit outdoors if you can possibly avoid it. It's murder. Pun intended.'

'I was hoping you'd have news for me on Amy Swales's phone, Darce. Any joy?'

Darcy nodded and swivelled her chair round.

'Cam, have you got the data from Amy Swales's phone?'

A young man with a bleached-blond crop got up from his chair to bring a printout across to them.

Kat thanked him and ran her finger down the list of timestamped selfies. Amy had been busy. She'd taken pictures at 10.15 a.m., 10.23 a.m., 10.41 a.m., 11.04 a.m., 11.10 a.m. and 11.20 a.m. They bracketed the time of Mark's murder neatly. The largest gap – twenty-two minutes – covered the period when he'd been drowning inside the locked green room.

The trouble was, Kat could imagine Amy getting *into* the green room and murdering Mark. But she couldn't for the life of her see her getting *out* again.

This kept happening. It didn't matter how many suspects she arrested, she'd never solve this murder unless she could figure out how the mechanic – to use Amy's word – worked.

With every day that passed, more true crime podcasters were flooding into Middlehampton, more articles were appearing in the *Echo*, and worst of all, Carve-up was jabbing Kat with the shitty end of the metrics stick. Her worries about Liv's upcoming marriage and that bloody money from her dad's Swiss bank account were sucking valuable energy she knew she should be devoting to the case.

'You OK, Kat?' Darcy asked gently. 'I thought we'd lost you there.'

Kat opened her eyes. 'Every time I speculate on what happened I run up against that bloody locked door.'

Darcy's mouth turned down. 'I'm afraid I've got more disappointing news for you. We just finished running all the fingerprint tests. You know you said the champagne bottle looked like the best candidate for the weapon the killer used on Mark?'

Kat's heart sank. She felt it as a physical lurch in her chest accompanied by a leaden feeling. 'Go on,' she said resignedly. 'It's only got one set of prints and they're Mark's.'

Darcy shook her head. 'No. It hasn't got any prints on it at all. No epithelials, hair or blood either, before you ask.'

Kat took a couple of seconds to digest this. The foil around the neck had been partially stripped away, ready for someone to untwist the wire cage before popping out the cork. So somebody had to have been handling the bottle. Either in the green room or, less likely, the kitchen.

'So it was wiped.'

'That would be my assumption, yes.'

'The only reason why a bottle of champagne *wouldn't* be covered in prints would be if someone didn't want theirs showing up on it.'

Darcy nodded. 'Otherwise there'd be a minimum of one set.'

'Whoever put it in the ice bucket and began opening it.'

'Again, yes.'

'So we can conclude that the murderer used the champagne bottle to knock Mark out before they drowned him.'

'Again, I'd assume so. If they'd brought a weapon to the green room with them, the bottle wouldn't have been wiped.'

Kat frowned as she fitted this new information into the puzzle she'd been working on for the last three days. The murderer had used what they'd found inside the green room. Which argued against it being a premeditated murder.

'Thanks, Darce,' she said. 'That's really helpful.'

Darcy raised an eyebrow. 'Really?'

Kat grinned guiltily. 'OK, it's infuriating, but at least we have one of the two weapons the murderer used. That has to be good, right?'

It was good. It just wasn't enough. But without sufficient evidence for an arrest, Kat had no option but to release Amy.

Was she a flight risk? Only in the sense that she'd told Kat she was planning another writers' retreat. But as Kat didn't like her for the murder, she decided that the risk of flight was one worth taking.

Chapter Thirty-Five

As MCU emptied at the end of shift, Kat checked her watch. She was about to invite Leah and Fez to the pub when a thought occurred to her. Fez had asked if he could meet Tom.

Her two DCs were at their desks. Deep into paperwork in Leah's case, and database searching in Fez's.

'Hey, you two,' she called out. 'Fancy a drink? The One That Got Away in thirty minutes?'

Fifteen minutes later she was sitting with Tom in a small garden in the hospital grounds. Waving grasses with droopy seed-heads grew profusely through a patch of shingle.

'Fancy a lime and soda, Tomski? I'm taking Leah and Fez out for a drink. Thought you might like to escape for an hour or so.'

'I'd love that. I'm going stir-crazy here.'

'Do you have to get signed out or something?'

'I'm in a rehab ward now. They're pretty flexible. I'll just text the sister and tell her where I'll be.'

Tom texted on the move and the reply pinged back as he was putting his seat belt on. 'Good to go,' he said.

Kat drove carefully around the hospital's internal road system before leaving the grounds and pointing the Golf's nose towards town.

'Have they said when you can go home?' Kat asked.

'All being well, tomorrow, actually. They've done all the tests, some of them twice. My consultant's really pleased. She said all things considered I got off pretty lightly.'

'Apart from being in a coma.'

'Apart from that.'

'Is there any permanent damage? I mean, do you have all your movement back? Or wait, is that after a stroke? Sorry, Tomski, I'm babbling. It's just so good to have you back in the la—'

She clapped her jaws closed before she could complete the sentence.

He laughed. A joyous sound that had Kat smiling out of relief as much as good humour.

'The land of the living? Is that what you were going to say?' Tom feigned outrage. 'God, boss, I can't believe you could be so insensitive. I might have to write you up.'

'You wouldn't dare! You were probably just faking it to get out of all the paperwork I had to do after arresting Paxton.'

They both fell silent.

Kat turned on to the London Road.

'Well that was a buzzkill,' she said.

'Tell me again what happened. I was so groggy before I don't think it really sank in.'

'We went to arrest him and you noticed the firearms team's van wasn't behind us. We went in anyway, and— Oh, God, Tomski, I am sorry I did that. Anyway, he attacked you. Pushed you through a glass coffee table. That's how your leg got cut. He went for me with a golf club but I tripped him. Then I put his lights out with one of his own golf trophies.' She leaned closer. 'Carve-up called off the firearms lads. I checked. He denies it, but there's no doubt in my mind, Tomski. He wanted us dead.'

Tom's eyes widened. 'Why?'

'I'm not sure. But believe me, mate, I'm going to find out. And when I do, I'm going to take him down.'

Tom was silent for a while after that.

'I know what you say, Kat, about how nobody deserves to die . . . but can you really say you're sorry Paxton's dead?'

Kat didn't answer straight away, focusing on negotiating the chicane that signalled the start of a contra-flow. As she nosed the Golf between the two ridiculously closely spaced rows of traffic cones, she tried to formulate a truthful answer to Tom's question.

'I'm sorry he didn't get to serve out his life sentence,' she said finally.

'That's not really an answer.'

'Well, how about you, Tomski? You were Mr Do-It-By-The-Book. You don't really think he deserved it, do you? Being murdered in prison?'

'Honestly? Just between you, me and the coma ward? Yes. I think the world's a better place without Will Paxton in it.'

Kat had no response. She wasn't shocked, not exactly. Tom was only voicing an opinion thousands of cops shared. There were certain types of offenders – paedophiles, rapists, men who tortured and murdered for kicks – that most people wouldn't lose any sleep over if they learned they'd died in prison.

It was just . . . She'd always tried to keep her emotions out of her work. Their job was to arrest the bad guys, charge them, maybe appear for the prosecution in court and then go to work on the next case.

But the Paxton case had affected her personally. Not just because she'd also been battling to clear her name at the time, or because of his violent attack on her and her bagman. But because it went deeper, to a place she wasn't ready to explore yet. A place where what was right collided head-on with what was legal.

Men like Paxton wouldn't attend a men's group and talk about their behaviour before reaching an epiphany. Well, they might attend, if court-mandated. But they'd merely utter the required platitudes before returning to the marital home, where they would continue to beat their wife. The marital routine where, one day, because she hadn't cooked their tea 'properly' or had gone out for a drink with someone they disapproved of, they'd force her to stand in a corner for hours on end. And the marital bed, where they would continue to rape her.

Or maybe the wife might have the temerity to answer 'no' over some trivial request, and finally, they would kill her.

So, yes, she tried to live a moral life, an uncorrupted life, either by money or bad-faith actions. But it was hard. When she did her best to uphold the law and saw how little change that actually effected, God, it was hard.

'Green light, boss,' Tom said beside her.

She blinked. The traffic light was just changing to amber. She accelerated hard away from the lights, leaving the driver behind her blasting their horn.

Five minutes later, they reached The One That Got Away, a riverside pub on the edge of Gade Gardens, a big, landscaped park with tennis courts, a playpark and cycle paths. Fez and Leah had snagged a table down by the water and they joined them – Kat beside Leah, and Tom joining Fez opposite.

'Who needs a drink?' Kat asked brightly.

'White wine for me, please,' Leah said.

'Lime and soda, please,' Fez said.

'Same for you, Tomski?' Kat asked.

He shook his head. 'Pint of Ridgeway bitter, please.'

She frowned. Tom didn't drink. Never had in all the time she'd known him. He'd told her and Leah why: a fight in a Durham pub when he was a student had left an aggressive biker dead of a brain haemorrhage. Not Tom's fault – he'd been defending himself, and his then-girlfriend – but traumatising all the same.

'Sure?'

'Can't a man enjoy a pint on a summer evening? I'm assuming you're going to drive me back to the hospital, so what's the problem?'

Kat caught Leah's frown. Shared a look with her. It wasn't so much Tom's words, though him drinking alcohol was a surprise. It was more his tone. Borderline hostile.

'Of course, it's just . . . nothing. Pint of Ridgeway, a white wine, and a lime and soda. Talk among yourselves.'

She headed inside to buy the drinks, but her mind was still in the garden. People changed their minds about drinking all the time. She'd done a couple of Dry Januaries and hadn't drunk at all during her pregnancy. But Tom had seemed so determined on his path of sobriety she was genuinely worried.

When she returned with the drinks, Fez was grilling Tom about life at Jubilee Place. Kat put the four glasses down. They chinked rims and sipped their drinks, except Tom, who sank half his pint in a single pull. He wiped his mouth.

'God, I've missed this.'

'Looking at you, bab, I'm glad I never started,' Fez said with a smile. 'For the first time I'm starting to think I might be missing out on something! Lucky I'm a good Muslim, I suppose.'

Slowly, then all at once, the three younger DCs bonded while the evening sun slanted across the park, making them squint.

Leah fetched another round.

'So has Eleanor been up to see you, Tomski?' she asked on her return.

Kat looked anxiously at Tom. He'd only been seeing the receptionist from the leisure centre for a few weeks when he'd gone into a coma. It wouldn't be fair, it wouldn't be nice, but it also wouldn't be unheard of for a budding relationship to wither and

199

die in the face of that kind of obstacle. Was that why he'd started drinking again?

'She came up this morning, yeah,' Tom said with a smile. 'She came in as often as she could while I was under. Must be mad, poor girl.'

'Oh, she's a keeper, then,' Leah said.

Inevitably, the conversation turned to work, and specifically Mark Swift's murder.

'I'd like to help, Kat,' Tom said. 'If they discharge me tomorrow, I could come straight into work.'

Kat was torn. Part of her wanted to welcome him back with open arms. Lord knew she could do with all the warm bodies she could get. But there'd be all kinds of hoops he'd have to jump through, from HR to occie health.

'Maybe go home and change first, eh, Tomski? I don't think hospital jim-jams are a great look for a fast-track DC, do you? And check with your neurologist, yes? I can't see her signing you fit for active duty.'

She knew as soon as the words had left her lips that she'd said the wrong thing. Tom's brows drew together and his mouth twisted.

'That's the trouble, though, isn't it? They're bound to desk me and then how am I going to show what I can do?'

Fez leaned towards Tom. 'You can do a lot of good from behind a desk. In Birmingham, when I worked intelligence, pretty much all I did was use my computer. We smashed people-trafficking gangs, money-laundering rings, organised crime.'

'Good for you! But I didn't sign up so I could spend my working life staring at a screen.'

Kat intervened before the good mood was broken completely. 'Which nobody has said you will be, Tomski. One step at a time, yes? In fact, you can take the first one right now and tell me what you think was going on with Mark Swift.'

He took a pull on his pint and stared off into space.

'He was famous. Famous people make enemies.'

'Lots, in Mark's case,' Leah added.

'Right. And whoever this enemy was, they planned on getting away with it. I mean, it wasn't some mugging in the street or a smack in the face in a pub car park, was it?'

'No. But it was also committed using weapons that were to hand inside the green room,' Kat said. 'What does that tell us?'

'Either it wasn't premeditated, or the killer knew what they'd find inside,' Fez said.

Kat noticed Leah staring upwards into the cloudless evening sky. She knew that expression.

'How about you, Leah? What's your take on it?'

'What if it wasn't an enemy *or* a friend?' Leah asked. She leaned forwards and fixed each of her teammates with a quick, searching glance. 'What if it was a stranger?'

'What kind of stranger?' Kat asked.

'Say I'm a waitress. I'm young, I'm attractive. I take in the champagne. Swift makes some sort of inappropriate sexual remark or maybe he actually grabs me. I fend him off, but he comes back at me. I grab the bottle and swing it at him. He collapses and I . . . Bugger! Why do I drown him? Why don't I just call the police?'

'Yeah, but would they believe you?' Fez asked. 'As it stands, there's an unconscious man with a head injury. We know he's got a powerful lawyer. They'd make mincemeat of you. You'd probably end up being charged with assault yourself.'

'But how would drowning him make that better?' Leah asked. 'Now I'm in the frame for murder.'

'I can see someone lashing out in self-defence,' Tom said. 'But drowning? That's like another level. It's not a spur-of-the-moment thing, is it?'

Kat leaned across the table. 'Let's just back up a bit, because Leah's just touched on something that's been bothering me about this case almost from the beginning. According to Riley—'

'Who's he? Another DC?' Fez asked.

Kat smiled. 'My son. He said Mark was misogynistic, or at least his last book was. Riley's a fourteen-year-old schoolboy. If he's saying it, others will be as well. Then, we've got Venetia Shelby-Hales's witness testimony.'

Fez nodded eagerly. 'She said Mark reminded her of her ex, who raped her.'

'Which fails to clear any kind of evidentiary hurdle, but it's interesting all the same. And Amy Swales told me that the younger and prettier the fan Mark was signing a book for, the sweeter he became,' Kat said, feeling the glimmering of an idea. 'Now, leaving aside rules of evidence and just sketching in an idea, how about this? Mark Swift was a wealthy, successful author with a thing for pretty young women. We know he divorced his first wife more or less for that reason. Venetia Shelby-Hales got a vibe off him that I'm going to give weight to, as she was a victim of sexual violence. At some point last Friday morning between 10.30 a.m. and 10.56 a.m., he was attacked and murdered because he said or did something sexually inappropriate. It may not even have been an assault. It could just have been read that way.'

'And the woman who killed him knew enough about the layout of the Guildhall and the lack of CCTV to decide on the spur of the moment to try and get away with it, rather than confessing,' Leah said.

Tom had been nodding as Leah was speaking. 'Yes, and maybe they'd read enough crime novels to see a way to throw us off the scent with all the locked room business.'

Kat felt a swell of pride in her team. For the first time since the case had begun, they were making progress. And they were working together. Properly. They still had no evidence, but at last they had a working hypothesis.

Pleading the need to walk Smokey, she left the three DCs at the table, with Fez having promised to drive Tom back to the hospital and Leah, at last, looking relaxed in the new boy's company.

DAY SIX – WEDNESDAY

Chapter Thirty-Six

The next day, Kat woke at 5.00 a.m. She rolled over and kissed Van. He mumbled something and pushed himself against her. He was hard. She rolled her eyes. Did men come with an off-switch? If they did, Van's was obviously broken.

'Maybe later,' she murmured into his ear, then nibbled the lobe.

After walking Smokey, she headed into work to find Leah and Fez hunched over their keyboards. She called them over.

'Can you do a deep dive into Danny Elliott for me? He's ex-job. I want evidence of his feud with Mark. In fact, throw the net wider. Anything in his background that points to a propensity for violence.'

At 8.58 a.m., her phone rang. It was Annie, telling her Linda had arrived. Kat hurried to catch her SIO before she got mired in paperwork and meetings.

'Morning, Ma-Linda,' she said, after knocking and entering the boss's office.

'You're here to update me on the Mark Swift murder,' Linda said. 'Any progress?'

'Only the kind where I keep eliminating people.'

'No suspects, then?'

'None.'

'What about the wives? He had three, didn't he?'

'The first one lives in Edinburgh. When Leah spoke to her she said she hadn't left the city for months. We've asked colleagues at Police Scotland for help, but I'm fairly sure we're going to get credit card receipts and CCTV confirming her story,' she said. 'The second one divorced amicably with a decent financial settlement and she kept putting him on to speak at the festival. And the current Mrs Swift is clearly grief-stricken, and it looks genuine to me.'

'Murderers can be great actors, Kat, you know that.'

Kat certainly did. The image of a smartly dressed elderly man in handcuffs after he'd finally confessed to hacking his wife's head off with an axe swam, unpleasantly, up from her memory. Gordon Phelps had had half the team believing he was mute from grief before a sly question from Kat had triggered a violent outburst that sent his solicitor reeling.

'I know, but her alibi is rock solid. She was being interviewed for a German magazine when Mark was murdered.'

'Anyone else in the frame?'

'We're still tracking down a couple of people who could have borne grudges.'

'Which all adds up to not very much, Kat. Meanwhile, we've got true crime podcasters infesting the town like a plague of locusts.'

'Which is why' – Kat swallowed, feeling suddenly nauseous – 'and I never thought I'd be saying this, but I want to call a press conference.'

Linda arched one immaculately shaped eyebrow. 'You feeling all right, Kat?'

Kat managed a queasy half-smile. 'I know, I know, wild horses, etc. But I need to get out in front of this one. It's just, I can't figure out how to ask for the help I need without laying us open to accusations we're tarnishing a murder victim's reputation.'

Linda frowned. 'Because?'

'I'm working on the theory that Mark Swift might have made inappropriate sexual advances to a woman while he was in the green room,' Kat said – knowing, even as she said it, how thin it sounded. She ploughed on. 'I think it's possible this woman may have killed him and then tried to cover it up.'

Apparently Linda thought this theory lacked weight, too.

'He made "inappropriate sexual advances"? You mean he grabbed her? Tried to kiss her? Rape her? What?'

'I'm not sure.'

'So, she fought him off or pushed him away or whatever, and then . . . what?'

'Then she grabbed the champagne bottle out of the ice bucket and hit him hard enough to knock him out. She forced his head down into a beer cooler full of water and drowned him, then wiped down the bottle and fled with the container.'

'Any CCTV to back up this theory?'

'No. The Guildhall doesn't have any cameras.'

'Any DNA at the scene?'

'No.'

'Anyone come forward to say Mark made inappropriate remarks to them?'

'No.'

'Then, and forgive me, Kat, but why are you pursuing this line of enquiry? Didn't I read in your policy book – which I appreciate you keeping up to date, by the way – that he had all kinds of enemies with other reasons to want him dead?'

'Honestly? I keep hitting brick walls. Everyone we've talked to has some kind of alibi. And while they're not all perfect, they're enough to stop me pursuing those lines any further. I mean, yes, Mark made enemies like other people make sandwiches, but I can't definitively place any of them at the scene at the right time.'

Linda had picked up a slim gold ballpoint pen and was making notes in a red notebook as Kat spoke. She clicked it off and looked straight at Kat.

'What do you want to ask? And don't worry about politically correct, or even legally correct language. Just tell me.'

'I want to ask any women who Mark Swift sexually assaulted to come forward.'

'Why?'

Kat was about to answer *because it might lead to a victim with revenge on their mind* when she saw what Linda was driving at. The only women likely to answer her call would be those innocent of his murder. The one woman they wanted to reveal herself would stay silent.

'Crap.'

'Not necessarily,' Linda said thoughtfully. 'What I'm thinking is, the murderer might have been a woman Mark assaulted. Now, if that's true, we can assume she won't come forward. Agreed?'

'Agreed. But someone who knew about the assault might. Or maybe the woman who killed him wasn't the victim herself. Maybe she was taking revenge on him for an assault he carried out on someone close to her.'

Linda held her hands up. 'Wait a moment, Kat. At this point, this is so far beyond the realms of evidence it doesn't even count as brainstorming. It's more like wishful thinking.'

'But that's all I've *got*, Ma-Linda,' Kat said.

'Then break it down. You have a hypothesis that whoever killed Mark Swift did it because he was a sexual predator, correct?'

'Correct.'

'And their motive was either self-defence if it was in the moment, or revenge if it was a past attack, on them or someone else, yes?'

Kat's stomach clenched. Her half-sister Jo had been murdered in revenge for her bullying of a classmate. Truly a dish best eaten cold. She swallowed the lump in her throat down.

'Yes.'

'Right. You say we're vigorously pursuing a number of lines of enquiry. Among them is the suggestion from a witness that the motive may have been sexual. We are asking anyone with information about Mark's personal life to come forward in strictest confidence, anonymity guaranteed, and share with us whatever they know.'

'It's a bit vague.'

'Which will keep his lawyer out of our hair. But although it'll look like we're suggesting that Mark's *killer's* motive was sexual, anyone he attacked will hopefully read between the lines and come forward to tell us what *he* did to *them*.'

'But that pretty much guarantees they *won't* be our killer,' Kat said.

'Yes, but it'll confirm your hypothesis that Mark was a sexual predator and give us a way forward. I'm sorry, Kat, it's not much, but we can't risk saying anything that'll have Sir Anthony-bloody-Bone arriving here with a writ.'

'But you can't libel the dead.'

'No, but where there are multimillion-pound estates involved and reputations – along with God knows what intellectual property – you can bet there'll be trouble. Speaking of which, social media's lit up like a fireworks party with speculation about Swift. The world and his wife have got an opinion, and none of them are very savoury. It splits roughly fifty-fifty between Andrew Tate types who say Swift was a hero for defending traditional masculinity and what I'm going to call the progressive community, who basically think he deserved to be murdered. At best. So let's get this sorted, eh? Soon as?'

With butterflies taking flight in her belly at the mere thought of organising a press conference, Kat left Linda's office. She needed Freddie Tippett, the fresh-faced, potty-mouthed MCU media liaison officer.

Freddie suggested they hold the press conference at 10.00 the following morning.

Kat's stomach was still fluttering when she called Fez and Leah over. 'We need to dig deeper into Mark's personal life.'

'What about his work life, Kat?' Fez asked.

Kat turned to Leah, raised her eyebrows. Leah nodded and opened her notebook.

'I finally tracked down his publisher and his editor, Sonya Hosseini and Liz Carter. They were both at *Criminal Herts*, but in back-to-back meetings with other authors all morning at their hotel.'

'How about his agent?' Fez asked.

'An American. Drake Sanderson. He's based in New York and last spoke to Mark a couple of weeks ago. Hasn't been to the UK since May.'

'Did any of them have any thoughts on who might have wanted Mark dead?' Kat asked.

'Sorry, Kat, no,' Leah said. 'I asked about his various feuds and they all pretty much agreed he could be difficult, to put it mildly. But they said it's all par for the course in publishing anyway, and authors mainly like to flame each other on social media. Getting cancelled is about as bad as it gets.'

'OK, thanks, Leah. Keep chasing down leads,' she said. 'Something's got to give. We just need to find the right door to push.'

'Pity there isn't a secret one in the green room,' Fez said.

Kat tipped her head a little. 'If you fancy trying to crack that little mystery, be my guest.'

Fez handed her a folder. 'That's everything Leah and I dug up on Danny Elliott.' He turned and smiled at Leah. 'She found the really good stuff. It's at the front.'

'I've got a mate in the Met's cybercrime team,' Leah said with a dip of her head. 'He helped me out. Although Fez found the reason Danny left the police.'

Kat nodded her gratitude. Maybe they could crack the case after all.

◆ ◆ ◆

With her DCs occupied, Kat read the documents Fez had stapled together inside the folder, then nodded with satisfaction.

She grabbed her keys and drove over to the home of Danny Elliott, the ex-cop who Mark had apparently stiffed out of both his fee and a video endorsement to promote his growing business.

Danny lived in a block of flats on the west side of the town. She parked outside and took another quick look at his website. His outfit, Blue Lights, Red Pens, promised to help writers and TV people avoid 'the kind of rookie errors that have coppers shouting at the screen or hurling your carefully written book against the wall'. Kat smiled. She tried to avoid cop shows, but sometimes Van managed to cajole her into watching one with him. She was allowed one moan per episode.

Danny answered as soon as she buzzed the intercom and the door latch clicked open.

Chapter Thirty-Seven

Danny was six-two or -three, and solidly built, with a barrel chest and thickly muscled arms, revealed by the tight T-shirt he wore. Each bicep was encircled by an indigo tattoo – barbed wire on the left, roses on the right. Kat found it easy to picture those arms holding an unconscious man's head down in a container full of icy water.

'Come in,' he said.

He stood back and beckoned her into a light airy hallway. Jackets and coats hung from a rack of forged-iron hooks, beside a framed photo of Danny and an attractive blonde woman.

'Coffee?' he called as he entered the kitchen before her. 'I mean, it's such a cliché, but you might actually want one. It's good. Beans, not that powdered muck. I could even make it iced if you want?'

'I'd love a cold one. Black, no sugar. Thanks.'

Drinks made, Danny pulled a chair out for Kat then sat opposite her at the table. His face was open, expectant, though he made no move to ask the first question. Copper's instincts, she decided. He probably knew. Why else would a Middlehampton murder cop be knocking on his door?

'You probably know why I'm here,' she said.

'Well, I'm assuming they're not sending detective sergeants out to advise on home security.'

The smile was easy, relaxed. He leaned back, hands in his lap. No tension round the eyes. No nervous glances off to one side. The picture of unconcern.

Trouble was, detectives – current or former – knew all the tricks, didn't they? She resolved to tread carefully.

She reminded herself that Danny wasn't a suspect, just a person of interest. But if he *was* Mark's killer, then he was capable of sudden and extreme violence. She somehow doubted he'd meekly extend his wrists to accept the embrace of a pair of handcuffs.

'I'm investigating the murder of Mark Swift and—'

'—you found out I had an axe to grind because he broke a contract we had to promote my business. So you're here to check my alibi, find out how deep the animosity ran, whether I've got a baseball bat under my bed. How am I doing so far?'

Maybe he thought he was being clever. Showing her he knew the drill and not to try any cop-tricks on him because they wouldn't work. But all he'd done was produce his membership card for the club whose members really, really ticked her off.

'Do you?' she asked innocently. 'Have a baseball bat under your bed?'

'Of course not.' He smirked, and she caught a flash of Carve-up in it. 'Because as you and I both know, that would be an offence. Unless of course I had a ball and a catcher's mitt under there too.'

'Can you account for your whereabouts between 10.00 a.m. and 11.00 a.m. last Friday?'

He nodded immediately. 'Work day. I'd have been at my desk, here, replying to emails, checking in with my team, doing a bit of social media, invoicing, the usual.'

'Can anyone confirm that? Your wife, for example?'

'I'm not married.'

'I'm sorry, I saw the picture in your hallway. I assumed she was your wife.'

He shook his head the way her maths teacher used to when the fifteen-year-old Kathryn Morton gave the wrong answer.

'Never assume, Kat. Don't they teach ABC anymore? Assume nothing. Believe nobody. Confirm everything?'

She smiled back. 'My mistake.'

'She's my girlfriend. Leanne.'

'So who's she married to? If you don't mind me asking.'

For the first time since she'd clapped eyes on him, he betrayed a momentary flicker of concern. Just a minute tightening of the muscles around his eyes and a glance over her shoulder. *Got you!*

'Who said she was married?'

'Nobody. But she's wearing a wedding ring. She's hiding it with her other hand, but you can just see one edge.'

His lips tightened for a second. She watched him force himself to loosen up. He looked relaxed, but she wasn't convinced. He was hiding something.

'Guilty as charged, your honour,' he said. 'Her marriage is basically finished. She's getting a divorce. Happy?'

'Just confirming everything, Danny,' she said sweetly. 'As I was taught. On which subject, can Leanne confirm you were here last Friday morning?'

'No. She doesn't live here, and in any case she was at work. She's a nurse, and yes, I know that's also a cliché.'

Kat shrugged. 'Do you use a desktop PC or a laptop?'

'Laptop. So I could have been working anywhere.'

'If we were to check your phone records, where would that put you?'

'Here. All morning. And yes, I could have left it here and gone out without it.'

'Did you go to the festival any other day?'

'No. Too busy.'

'Really? I'd have thought it was prime hunting ground for a man offering your services.'

'I have more than enough work without touting for it.'

Kat took a sip of her iced coffee. He'd added sugar. Was he just forgetful or trying to needle her?

'Talking of work, tell me about the deal you did with Mark.'

Danny's expression soured. 'When I set up the business, I thought it would be good to have a few celebrity clients. You know, people other writers would have heard of. I contacted a hundred and fifty novelists and screenwriters. I said I'd do a load of free research for them in return for a video testimonial where they'd basically say how great I was to work with and how much better their stories were as a result.'

'What happened with Mark?'

'Oh, he was all over it at first. Told me it was a brilliant idea and how he'd love to help me launch. Said it was just what the market needed. So he gave me a list of dozens of research questions. Some were easy, others I had to really work on. But I delivered. A great, fat file with text, photos, the works.'

'And then?'

'And then he welched on our deal. Said he didn't have time to commit to filming because he had a deadline. Well, I tried to be patient. I mean, this was Mark Swift we were talking about. I figured he'd do it as soon as he sent his book off to his publisher. But there was always something else. In the end I had to threaten him with legal action. Either film the testimonial, although Christ knows what that would have looked like, or pay market rates for the work I'd done.'

'How much would that have come to?'

'Nine thousand, seven hundred and fifty pounds.'

Kat was shocked. She'd had no idea there was that much money to be made from sharing knowledge of the job. But she also scented blood. People had been murdered over much smaller sums. In a case she'd done door-to-doors on as a rookie, the amount had been the princely sum of twenty-seven pounds. And fifty pence.

'That must have been hard to swallow,' she said. 'So did you send a legal letter?'

'Oh, I sent one all right. From a solicitor's in town. And I got one back from this major London law firm. Signed by this pompous prick called Sir Anthony Bone. It was like firing an air pistol and getting both barrels of a sawn-off in return. I don't mind telling you, Kat, it put the fear of God into me.'

'So you backed off?'

'I had to. Even though I was in the right, this Bone character threatened to bankrupt me. Obviously he didn't say that in so many words, but his meaning was clear.'

'You must have been furious with Mark.'

He stared at her. It made her uncomfortable.

'Yes. I was. But to save you the trouble of asking, was I angry enough to kill him? No. I just chalked it down to experience and moved on. Built the business up and had my revenge that way. Anyway, this happened three years ago. Why would I wait until now to kill him if I was that pissed off?'

'I don't know. You tell me.'

He folded his arms, causing his tattooed biceps to bulge. An aggressive move.

'Not my job. Any more questions?'

'Are you familiar with a Telegram channel called CopChat?'

'No. Should I be?'

'Its members are all, or claim to be, ex-coppers. My team searched CopChat looking for mentions of Mark Swift. A user calling themselves PatienceOfJob made a number of specific threats against Mark Swift. Up to and including threats to kill.'

Danny shrugged. No more smiles. A guarded look in his eyes. The fingers of his right hand curled into a fist. Kat tried to keep her pulse steady. Memories of Will Paxton's lightning-fast attack made her catch her breath. If Danny made a move she'd be out the kitchen door before he'd even rounded the table.

'People on those channels say all kinds of crazy shit.'

'Are you PatienceOfJob, Danny?'

'No.'

'No? Only, when I looked at your website, I found your blog. The very first article is headed "Patience of Job". Did you like the pun so much you used it for your Telegram username?'

'I'm not on Telegram, as I think I just said. Was there anything else?'

Struggling to control her breathing and anxious not to reveal how frightening she suddenly found him, she rose to her feet.

'Thanks for your time, Danny.' She got up and headed for the front door. Then turned. Seeing as Danny was so fond of clichés, she thought she'd give him one as a parting gift. 'Oh, one last thing. You left the police when you were only thirty-two. Why was that?'

He didn't answer straight away. He glanced off to one side. Then back at her. Calculating the odds. Did she already know? Or was she bluffing?

Called.

'I didn't like the hours.'

'So you weren't dismissed for gross misconduct after assaulting a prisoner? An assault that resulted in a suspended sentence.'

Folded.

'I think,' he said carefully, getting to his feet, 'that if you have any more questions for me, we'll do it down at your nick. When I'll have my lawyer present.'

'I'll keep that in mind,' she said. 'Thanks for your time.'

Heart racing, Kat backed away from him, keeping a good six feet of space between them. She reached the front door and turned the handle without taking her eyes off him. The memory of Will Paxton was too fresh in her mind to turn her back on Danny, even for the seconds it would take to let herself out of the flat.

She drove straight back to Jubilee Place and circled Danny Elliott's name on the murder board. No alibi. Record of violence – specifically, assault with a baton. And, though it would take a lot more time and money to prove, he was potentially the Telegram user called PatienceOfJob.

He wasn't a suspect. Not yet. But he was close.

Chapter Thirty-Eight

Kat got home after ten that evening. She found Van at the kitchen table, his laptop open before him, a bottle of beer at his elbow.

'Hi,' she said, kissing the back of his neck. 'You're working late.'

He twisted round and returned the kiss.

'So are you. How's the case going?'

'So badly I actually asked Linda if I could hold a press conference tomorrow.'

Van offered a wry smile. 'Blimey, I had no idea it was that bad. You OK?'

'Yeah, yeah, I'm fine.'

'You don't sound fine. What's going on?'

'Part of me is wondering whether Mark Swift was a sexual predator,' she said.

'That sounds like the beginning of a theory about why he was murdered.'

'Yeah, but the other part wonders if I'm just grasping at straws. I mean, we have zero evidence beyond a few ambiguous comments.'

'That doesn't sound like you, love. Usually when there's anything in the news about some senior executive or media figure, you're all for seeing them swinging from the nearest lamp post.'

'Yeah, but that's off-duty me. On-duty me has to follow the rules of evidence.'

'But that type of man works very hard to cover his tracks, doesn't he? They use their power to coerce their victims into keeping quiet. Failing that, there's always the payoff-plus-NDA option.'

Which made Kat think of Sir Anthony Bone. Because if there were any payoffs or non-disclosure agreements flying around, it would be the lawyer who'd handle them on behalf of his celebrity client, wouldn't it?

Maybe now was the time to call Liv. Get her take on the case. She'd always been the more creative one – even if it was coming up with the best ways to shoplift fancy make-up from department stores. But whenever they talked, some of Liv's devil-may-care attitude seemed to transfer to Kat, if only for a little while, and helped her see the world differently.

'I'll let you carry on, with your . . . thing,' she said, lifting her chin towards his laptop. 'Gonna call Liv.'

Liv picked up on the first ring. The first half-ring actually.

'Hey, Thelma! It was so good to see you and the fam on Sunday. Did you enjoy yourself?'

'It was great, Louise, yes. Really great. Listen, this case I'm working. Is there anything you've found that suggests Mark did more than just badmouth women online?'

'What, like he actually attacked women, you mean? Physically? Sexually?'

'It's a line of enquiry, that's all.'

Kat heard a dog barking.

'Quiet, Duffle!' Liv said. 'I'm out with the dog. I haven't read anything that directly says that, although plenty of people are saying he got what was coming to him. But believe me, Kat, I know his type.'

'What do you mean? Specifically?'

'Remember when you were investigating Stefan Pulford? I told you people used to come to Shirley House late at night and collect girls, then bring them back in the morning. They weren't factory workers or dustmen or shop staff. They were rich, middle-aged businessmen. Lawyers. Even senior coppers. All us kids knew what went on. So if you're asking me was Mark Swift a rapist? I don't know. But it wouldn't surprise me. That sort think their money gives them a get-out-of-jail-free card.'

Liv had reinforced Kat's suspicions about Mark Swift. Yes, all she had so far was weak circumstantial evidence. But a picture was beginning to emerge of a man very different from the jokily anti-woke celebrity author, as painted by his ex-wife.

Later, after a glass of wine and a cuddle in front of the TV, Kat led Van upstairs, the memory of his body that morning uppermost in her mind. She needed physical release. But more than that, she needed to forget about the case. Just for a little while. After they made love, she slept in his arms for half an hour or so, then woke with a start as he snored loudly. She rolled him over and climbed out of bed. The blissful feeling of just being totally in the moment evaporated.

Downstairs, with Smokey casting a briefly quizzical eye in her direction before going back to sleep, she made herself a cup of tea and returned to the case.

She wanted to think things through. Calmly, before the morning's press conference. Sexual violence might lead to a motive, and even a suspect, but there were other possibilities involving that ancient and powerful drive. She was too much of an experienced detective to get tunnel vision about her latest theory. Maybe it would come to something. Maybe it would come to nothing.

He might have been having an affair. He had form, after all. He could have ended it and been murdered by his lover. Or Saskia could have discovered it and murdered him.

He could have been the victim of an obsessed fan who'd followed him into the green room. What did the shrinks call it? *Erotomania*, that was it. Plain old stalking, in other words.

Or was it more likely to be another instance of rape-inside-marriage, as suffered by Venetia Shelby-Hales? Saskia could have killed him to stop him.

Staring at her reflection in the darkened kitchen window, Kat wondered whether Saskia would inherit all of Mark's money. Maybe there was a pre-nuptial agreement in place. Could Sir Anthony Bone have drafted one?

She decided to interview Saskia the following day, to see if she was keeping any secrets about her marriage. And to find out about Mark's will.

As drowsiness sent her into a half-sleep with her chin cupped in her hand, her musings on family secrets sent her mind spiralling back to Jo Starling. The desire to know more about her half-sister was becoming acute. Because every time she thought about Jo, she thought about Jo's parents dying in a plane crash. And the fact that Tasha Starling had been in business with their father. The father who'd almost succeeded in getting Kat thrown under the anti-corruption bus.

When would Iris call with news of the signatory on the bank transfer? Kat ached to know the truth, but there was no point trying to gee Iris up. Kat would just have to bide her time and try to focus on the case. Which wasn't exactly hurtling towards a conclusion either.

Maybe the press conference would shake something loose about Mark Swift.

She went back to bed. With her stomach fluttering with butterflies as she pictured herself sweating in front of a room full of journalists, she fell asleep. She managed five hours, during which she woke three times, before finally throwing in the towel at 5.41 a.m.

DAY SEVEN – THURSDAY

Chapter Thirty-Nine

Nausea made Kat swallow, hard. She felt like making an excuse and running for the exit.

The air conditioning in the media room was broken and sweat was trickling unpleasantly from her armpits. The air was overheated already, thanks to the sun beating against the plate glass windows. Add in over fifty journalists and cops and the place compared unfavourably to a sauna.

Journalists? Yes, Dawn Jacobson, the editor of the *Echo*, was sitting in her usual front row seat and offering a sympathetic smile to Kat. And Freddie had pointed out a few crime beat specialists from the nationals, as well as arts correspondents keen to sharpen their teeth on something meatier than the latest play.

But among these card-carrying journos were a fair few podcasters. Including her nemesis, Ethan Metcalfe. Today he sported a surprisingly nice cream linen jacket, cut to emphasise his shoulders. He kept adjusting his press pass on its lanyard so it faced outwards.

'Why did you invite him,' Kat hissed at Freddie as she waited to take her place at the table.

'I had to! I've been monitoring his audience size the last year. Since the Paxton case, it's exploded. He's got a hundred and seventy-five thousand subscribers. And he's a local lad. I know you don't like him, Kat, but we have to play fair.'

Kat bit back the response that it was a shame Mutt-calf never did. Instead, she crossed the stage to the table and took her seat beside Carve-up, who'd insisted on fronting the press conference, despite not being the SIO or actively involved in the case.

Carve-up cleared his throat. The room gradually came to order. When it was silent, apart from the impotent whirring of a small, useless desk fan, Carve-up eyed the room and waited for his customary three-count.

'Good morning, everyone. Thank you for coming. My name is Detective Inspector Stuart Carver. That's Stuart with a "u" for those of you who haven't met me before. I am operating in an overwatch capacity on the investigation into the tragic and senseless murder of author Mark Swift.'

Kat caught Dawn Jacobson's eye. A wealth of unspoken communication flashed between them, its focus Carve-up's insatiable appetite for personal publicity. 'Overwatch capacity'. There was no such role. If anyone was acting in a supervisory role, it was Linda, and she'd been content to let Kat handle the media on her own.

'There will be time for questions at the end,' Carve-up was saying. 'But first, my lead investigator, DS Ballantyne, will update you on the progress she's made on the case.'

Now Kat saw it. Carve-up was merely playing a game, trying to humiliate her in front of the press. Hoping she'd get flustered at having nothing to offer them and then wilt under the fire of their questions.

Dawn put her hand up and shot Kat a blink-and-you'd-miss-it look, then spoke without waiting to be silenced by Carve-up.

'You mentioned an overwatch role, DI Carver. Does that mean you're the SIO?' She twisted round in her chair to address the other journalists. 'For all the literary critics present, that's the senior investigating officer.'

This earned her an approving ripple of laughter from the news and crime reporters.

Carve-up coloured. Kat looked down to cover her smile. His hands were gripped together so tightly the knuckles were white. Kat wasn't the only intelligent career woman he didn't like.

'That would be DCI Ockenden, who is unable to be here this morning,' he said, managing to imply she had better things to do. 'But I am SIO on a number of other murder investigations. And, as I said, I have a general supervisory role.'

Perhaps feeling Dawn would skewer him on that point as well, he turned to Kat. She hated having to rescue him, but this was her press conference and she'd called it for a reason. She leaned a little closer to the mic and delivered the line she'd worked on with Linda.

'First of all, I want to extend my personal condolences, and those of Hertfordshire Police, to the family and friends of Mark Swift. Murders tear apart more than one life, and we are working as hard as we can to bring Mark's killer to justice.

'We are working on the theory that there may have been a sexual component to Mark's murder. I would ask members of the public, and especially people working in the publishing industry, to come forward or call CrimeStoppers if they have any information that might be relevant to that line of enquiry.'

In the centre of the room, a Black woman in her early thirties stood up suddenly. Beside Kat, Carve-up tutted. He switched on his mic and said, 'As I said, there'll be time for questions at the end. If you could just—'

'Dorothy Russell, *Daily Mail*. DS Ballantyne, given that Mark Swift was a known rapist, how do you respond to claims on social media that he deserved to die?'

Kat rocked back in her seat. The room erupted. A forest of hands sprouted, everyone talking then shouting at once. Cameras flashed, leaving her with dancing blue after-images across her retinas.

Freddie Tippett stepped in to restore calm, patting the air for silence while quelling the noise with a stentorian 'Quiet, please!'

Kat's mind was whirling. She had to say something but couldn't think of an answer. Then her own moral compass, whose needle Dorothy Russell's question had jammed, spun to true north once more.

'I can't go into the specifics of my investigation, and I won't comment on unsubstantiated rumours on social media.' Dorothy looked as though she was about to respond, but Kat rode over her. 'But here's what I *can* tell you. I don't believe anybody *deserves* to die. And nor do any of my team. We investigate all murders with the same high levels of professionalism and dedication. That's all. Thank you.'

Ignoring the chorus of shouted questions, and her own conflicted emotions about what rapists *actually* deserved, Kat got to her feet. There was nothing to be salvaged from the conference now. But as she stood, she made eye contact with Dorothy Russell and mouthed, 'Wait.' Dorothy nodded, before leaving with the rest of the media pack.

When the room was empty, Carve-up spun round in his seat.

'Well, that was a shitshow and no mistake. You just invited a journalist to libel a murder victim, DS Ballantyne. And in a police press conference. I hope you're happy.'

Kat got to her feet, her pulse banging in her ears. She pointed down at him.

'No I didn't, Stu. For a start, you can't libel a murder victim because they're dead.'

'His wife could bring an action.'

'No, she couldn't. For a DI you don't know the law very well.'

'Watch it, Kitty-Kat,' he muttered, his nose wrinkling above exposed incisors, like a feral dog trying to stare down a rival. 'You're still just a DS. And you still report directly to me.'

Kat put her hands on her hips. 'Write me up, then. Of course, you'd have to put it in writing that you were wrong about the law of defamation. And what if it's true? It wouldn't be libel then, even if Mark Swift was alive.'

He sneered at her. 'Don't be ridiculous. Jesus, some woke slag from the *Daily Mail* makes a wild accusation, probably to sell more papers, and you swallow it hook, line and sinker. I'd have expected better of you.'

She leaned over and put her hands on each of his chair arms, trapping him. Pushed her face closer to his, so close she could see stray ginger hairs among the darker bristles of his goatee.

'Oh, you'll get more than you expected from me, Stu,' she murmured. 'In the fullness of time you'll get way more than you expected. I guarantee it.'

Then she straightened and marched out, heading for the reception area. Dorothy was waiting for Kat by a large indoor plant. Not quite camouflaged, but doing a good job of blending into the background.

Kat strode over to her. 'Hi. Shall we grab a coffee? Somewhere a little bit more private?'

'Yeah, that would be good.'

For all Kat liked Hatî, the Kurdish-owned coffee shop on North Street, it was becoming increasingly popular with the denizens of Jubilee Place. Instead, Kat led Dorothy to a greasy spoon, bought two cups of coffee and snagged a table at the back.

She took the seat facing the door, and looked Dorothy in the eye, hoping the journalist was going to offer up a piece of evidence that could finally move the case into its closing stages.

Chapter Forty

Kat waited until Dorothy finished stirring sugar into her coffee.

'Look, Dorothy, I'm assuming you asked that question with some sort of purpose. Maybe you could just share it. Do you have any evidence Mark Swift was a rapist?'

Dorothy looked at Kat.

'Do you know who Wayne Couzens is, DS Ballantyne?'

Of course Kat did. The former Met officer had raped and murdered a woman called Sarah Everard.

'I do. And please call me Kat. DI Carver calls me DS Ballantyne and it's really started to grate.'

'How about Couzens's mate, David Carrick?'

'Again, yes.'

Dorothy nodded. 'We have two Metropolitan Police officers convicted of rape – and in Couzens's case, murder. And when we held a vigil for Sarah, what did you lot do? Tried to break it up and arrested us. I'm not saying you're all alike, but trusting the police is something of a crapshoot when it comes to cases of violence against women and girls. Especially if they're women of colour. I need to know if I can trust you.'

'You're the one who accused a murder victim of being a rapist in my media conference. Now I have to prove myself to you? Look, I investigate major crimes. That's what I do. Day in, day out. There are men behind bars for rape because my team and I put them there. But what I said in there holds. I'm not going to go easy on a murder investigation because you say the victim was a rapist. If he was, he should have faced trial, but as it stands, he's been put beyond the reach of justice.'

Dorothy sipped her coffee. Looked at Kat steadily. Put the mug down.

'Fair enough. And I get a vibe off you anyway. A good one, unlike your knuckle-dragging boss. Everything I'm about to tell you is in confidence, yes? You cannot tell anyone else.'

'If it's evidence of a crime, you know I can't do that. I'd be breaching my sworn oath as a police officer.'

'It's personal, private information about a crime,' Dorothy said. 'And as we've already established that the perpetrator is dead, he's been put, to use your phrase, "beyond justice".'

Kat considered this, but not for long.

'I promise. Tell me.'

Dorothy leaned closer and dropped her voice to a low but distinct murmur. 'I was twenty-two years old. It was my birthday. I was a trainee entertainment reporter on *The Sun*. My editor sent me to interview Mark Swift because he'd just had a book made into a film. I was sent to his hotel in Kensington. And' – her breath hitched – 'to cut a long and very unpleasant story short, he raped me.'

'My God! Did you report it?' Kat asked. Her pulse elevated unpleasantly, already knowing the answer to her question.

'No. To my shame I didn't. But men like Swift are very good at working on their victim's sense of shame. He told me he knew my editor, and *her* editor. He said if I reported it, he'd tell them it was consensual, that I'd offered him sex in exchange for a scoop. And that he'd never talk to the paper again unless they fired me. He said he had a real hotshot lawyer and they'd destroy me in court. That

I'd never be able to get another job in journalism. Even back then, I knew the stats on rape convictions. What men like Swift and their lawyers did to women on the witness stand. The police were no better. And I wanted my job so badly. I was the first in my family to make it to uni. One of the first women of colour on the paper's salaried journalistic staff. I had invested so much in my career, so I just sucked it up. Told myself I was bigger than it, bigger than him.'

'Jesus, Dorothy, I'm so sorry you went through that. Truly, I am. Was it because he was murdered? Is that why you've come forward now? Because he's no longer a threat?'

Dorothy nodded, dry-eyed, though the whites were reddened. 'I started a whisper network a few years ago when rumours about Mark Swift being a sexual predator first surfaced. We're all his victims.'

Kat's mind reeled. 'Wait a minute. *All?* How many of you *are* there?'

'I don't keep records. But it runs into dozens. Each woman has a story about how he sexually assaulted her.'

Kat frowned. 'You realise that every member of your network has to be considered a person of interest. You too, Dorothy.'

Dorothy shook her head. 'I didn't kill him. I never wanted him dead. I mean, yes, for a couple of years afterwards I did. But I came to realise that if we were going to fight back, we had to use the system they use to keep us silent to expose them. I wanted him in prison, where he belonged,' she said. 'Anyway, do you really think if I'd killed him, I'd have come to your press conference? Let alone stood up and pointed the finger like that? I'd hardly put myself in the frame if I'd actually done it.'

Privately Kat disagreed. Sometimes, murderers did exactly that. But they were the 'wrong 'uns', the 'headcases', the 'nutters', the 'weirdos' – the men who took such pleasure in killing that taunting and sometimes engaging with the police was all part of their sick inner life. Dorothy Russell simply didn't fit the bill.

'This whisper network. Is it all encrypted chats online and phone calls, or do you ever get together?'

'Mostly the former. But, assuming today went the way we wanted, some of us were going to meet at mine tonight.'

'And did it go the way you wanted?'

Dorothy finished her coffee.

'Here's my address,' she said, sliding a card across the table to Kat. 'We start at eight sharp.'

Then she got up and thanked Kat for her coffee before leaving.

Kat stayed in her seat, furiously grappling with what she'd just been told. She didn't think any of the women in Dorothy's network were guilty. But would one of them hold the clue to the identity of Mark Swift's killer?

She got up to leave. Something was telling her she'd already met the murderer.

Chapter Forty-One

Kat worked through lunch and was updating her policy book when her phone rang.

'I've got a Sir Anthony Bone down here to see you, DS Ballantyne,' Polly, from reception, said in the starchy tone she used when the brass from Welwyn Garden City were over. Then she dropped her voice to a conspiratorial murmur. 'He may be a knight of the realm, but he's an arrogant little tosser all the same.'

'Thanks for the warning. Let's have him cool his heels for a bit, eh? Tell him someone will be down to fetch him in a minute or two.'

Polly turned the volume back up and her prim tone reappeared. 'Of course, DS Ballantyne. I'll ask Sir Anthony to wait.'

Kat called across to Fez. 'Can you set a timer for five minutes and then go and fetch Mark Swift's lawyer up from reception, please?'

Fez grinned. 'Not a fan, then?'

'Just want to remind him he's in our house now.'

While Fez went about his business – which, in job-speak, was to 'hurry up and wait' – Kat went to check if an interview room was free. Normally, for an informal chat like this one, she'd head for the 'friendly' interview room. The one with the comfy, if coffee-stained, sofa, the straggly pot plants and the window admitting natural light.

She'd just returned to her desk when Fez walked through the double doors of MCU. At first, Kat thought Sir Anthony must have bailed, since Fez was alone. Then Fez sidestepped a colleague's desk and the lawyer came into view. He was short. Shorter than Kat. His diminutive frame was clad in a three-piece, navy pinstriped suit. A gold watch chain looped over his stomach. She'd checked the temperature in her walk back from the cafe. Thirty-one. Yet the little lawyer appeared perfectly cool and unruffled. She walked over to greet him.

'You must be Sir Anthony,' she said, extending her hand, which he ignored. 'I'm DS Kathryn Ballantyne. Would you like to follow me.'

'Lead on,' he said, his pale grey eyes alert behind gold-rimmed spectacles.

He wrinkled his nose as she opened the door to interview room 3. She smelled it, too. BO, sweat, farts, disinfectant. Tough. She took the chair with the padded seat with its back to the door. He had to settle his bony behind into the harder number opposite her, across the scratched table.

Before sitting, he drew a snowy white handkerchief from the display pocket of his suit jacket and snapped it across the seat. He replaced it, then twitched up the knees of his trousers and sat down.

'I see we're dispensing with the niceties, DS Ballantyne,' he said drily. 'Rather a cheap trick.'

'Like not shaking hands, Sir Anthony?' she responded. 'I'm assuming you're here to offer me and my team some help with our investigation into Mark Swift's murder?'

'In point of fact, I am here to inform you that I will not allow my late client's name to be dragged through the mud. As far as I have been able to ascertain, all you and your *team* have done since

Mark was killed is concoct an extremely unpleasant and defamatory narrative about him.'

How did he know? That was the question spinning through Kat's brain. Yes, she'd written up her suspicions about the killer's motive in her policy book, but surely he hadn't found a way to gain access to it? Had he planted someone at her press conference? Or been spying on her meeting with Dorothy? Lawyers had investigators they used, ex-cops quite often, but they'd been discreet, and Kat hadn't seen anyone acting suspiciously while she and Dorothy had talked. Carve-up? Always a possibility.

She didn't like being patronised by the sharp-eyed lawyer. Time to push back a little.

'As I imagine you know, the dead can't be defamed, so I'm not sure I understand what you're talking about. But in any case, we are investigating every single line of enquiry as we attempt to identify and arrest Mark's killer. *Do* you have some useful information to share, or do you just have time on your hands?'

'Mark was brutally murdered. Solve it. That's your job.' He leaned across the table. 'Nothing else.'

In that moment, Kat knew she was facing Mark Swift's damage-controller. The person who'd kept his crimes out of the public eye. Her stomach churned. How was this happening? How was she fighting against a murder victim's lawyer when they ought to be working together?

The answer, when she wrestled it out of her subconscious, was unexpectedly simple. Sir Anthony Bone wasn't interested in finding Mark's killer at all. He simply wanted his late client's reputation safeguarded. What would happen to a lawyer, a knighted lawyer, if it became known he'd been involved in covering up his client's crimes? It wouldn't just be Mark Swift's reputation left in tatters, would it?

A further disconcerting thought occurred to her. That somebody like Bone, or even the man himself, might be safeguarding her father's reputation, too. The need to know grew stronger.

'How long had you worked for Mark?' she asked.

He pursed his lips before answering, and she could see him weighing the pros and cons of responding. 'Since his first book deal. Why?'

'Can you tell me what sort of services you provided?'

'Legal services, what else?'

'Yes, but what kind?'

'Advice on contracts, mainly. But as his success increased, and interest from media companies grew, his needs grew with it.'

'I see. Did he ever ask you to help him avoid bad publicity?'

The clock on the wall ticked loudly. If there had been a thermometer beside it, she imagined the mercury would have been plummeting towards zero.

He lowered his chin and spoke very quietly. She caught his words, but any covert recording device, not that she'd been clumsy enough to install one, would pick up nothing.

'Listen to me, DS Ballantyne. I know all about you. You're an ambitious police officer with the beginnings of a glittering career ahead of you. Don't sacrifice it on the altar of some sort of woke crusade. One might not be able to libel the dead, but I assure you there are other legal avenues I can pursue that would be extremely detrimental to your further progress as a detective. Do I make myself clear?'

Did Bone know all about her? If so, who had helped him? A name sprang into view, rendered in ten-foot-tall neon letters in the bold red and blue of Morton Land's logo. Now she *really* wanted to know if her father was one of Bone's clients.

She sat back and raised her eyebrows. Spoke plainly and clearly, as if there actually were a mic sitting on the table between them.

'That wasn't a *threat*, was it, Sir Anthony? Because that would be a very serious offence. I'd have no option but to take all kinds of measures I imagine would put a pretty big dent in *your* career. I mean, I'm not an *expert* in these things, but that knighthood might look a bit shaky.'

Her pulse was holding steady, but it was fast, bumping in her throat and making it hard to swallow. She'd read a book the previous year, about a boy trapped on a lifeboat with a tiger. She knew which space she'd rather be inhabiting right now. It smelled of the sea.

He grinned crookedly, his mouth stretching wide, revealing the ground-down edges of his incisors and the points of his canines. 'Perhaps we got off on the wrong foot,' he said. 'And I apologise for my earlier lapse in manners. Traffic was murder, forgive the pun, and my Rolls-Royce really isn't suited to the narrow roads in this town. What can I do to help you, DS Ballantyne?'

Well, that was better. Although she was under no illusion about the arrogant little tosser's change of heart. Bullying and threats hadn't worked, so now he was trying charm. *Well, have at it*, she thought. She'd bested much more manipulative characters than Sir Anthony Bone in this interview room.

'Did you handle Mark's personal affairs? His will, for example?'

'I did, yes.'

'I'd like to see it.'

'I'm sure a lot of people would like to see it. Mark was an extremely wealthy man.'

'But I'm not anyone, I'm the detective investigating his murder. The murder you say you want to help me solve.'

The predatory smile was back, just. But she could see she was getting to him. 'Of course you can see it, DS Ballantyne.' A beat. 'Just present a warrant and I will gladly furnish you with a copy.'

'I will do that – if you insist. My DCI is hot to trot on clearing this one and I am fairly certain she'll approve my request. But all I actually want to know is the name of the main beneficiary.'

He nodded, steepling his fingers under his chin. 'I see. *Cui bono*, is that it? Find the legatee, find the murderer?'

'It's an obvious line of enquiry. If he was rich, then someone stands to benefit financially from his death. That's a hell of a motive.'

'It's also legally privileged information, DS Ballantyne. From which I must regretfully exclude you, unless and until you procure a properly executed warrant.'

Kat had had enough. Banging her head against a pinstripe-clad brick wall was not her idea of fun. And she had plenty of other lines of enquiry to pursue.

'Thank you, Sir Anthony, for clarifying the legal position. I have a meeting to go to, so we'll end this one now. I'll see you again, with a warrant. Please wait here. I'll have someone show you out.'

Kat got to her feet and closed the door behind her, heart hammering in her chest.

She was convinced the lawyer was hiding something. Was it the identity of the murderer? The motive? The solution to the locked room?

And if he was, why? What did he have to gain?

The obvious question screamed out from between her ears.

Did he *kill Mark?*

She turned to go back in. Ready to ask Bone for an alibi. Then thought better of it. The lawyer would clam up, and any help – however caveated – he might be willing to offer would vanish.

But she resolved to keep him in mind if she ran out of more promising leads.

Chapter Forty-Two

Annie was away from her desk. Linda's door was open. Kat knocked and entered, trying to wipe the scowl from her face that lingered as she thought of the arrogant lawyer.

Linda looked up. 'Blimey, what happened to you? Some lowlife criticised your interviewing technique?'

Kat groaned. 'Pretty much.' She explained about her profitless interview with Sir Anthony, concluding, 'So, basically, I need a warrant for the will.'

Linda nodded. 'Write up the application. I'll sort it out. How's the investigation going otherwise, Kat? I'm getting flak from all over. Even the mayor's waded in. Apparently, his wife was accosted by a true crime podcaster in Sainsbury's yesterday. I think it's fair to say the Lady Mayoress was not best pleased.'

Kat tugged at her right earlobe. 'Honestly, Ma-Linda? It's a bugger. Mark wasn't exactly short of enemies, but every time we find another one, they have an alibi. Half of them were schmoozing in the beer tent outside the Guildhall when it happened, so in theory it could have been one of them. But without any forensics from the scene, we're really struggling.'

'Have you figured out how the killer did it yet?'

Kat explained her theory about the champagne bottle and the beer cooler.

'How did they get away unobserved?' Linda asked.

'No idea. I've been focusing on reducing our list of potential suspects.'

'There's no secret passageway? Or a trapdoor under the carpet?'

Kat opened her mouth to reply in the negative, when she realised she'd only checked one of those options. Ernie had confirmed there was no secret passageway but she'd not thought to ask about the floor.

'I'm going to go back there now and do another search. I must have missed something. Sorry.'

'No shame in it, Kat. We've all done it. Just hurry up and sort it, will you? I think the mayor's got me on speed dial.'

Kat nodded. She left Linda's office determined to figure out how the killer had managed to commit murder in a locked room and then simply vanish.

That meant another visit to the Guildhall.

Chapter Forty-Three

Kat pulled on plastic booties and gloves, then ducked under the criss-crossed crime scene tape and entered the green room.

She closed the door behind her and switched on the lights. She turned slowly through a whole circle. Where had the murderer hidden until they'd got the chance to escape?

It *had* to be the chest. There was no other answer. She crossed the expanse of carpet and knelt before it. Maybe she just hadn't tried hard enough last time. Gripping the lid with both hands, she gave it an almighty yank. Her back protested and she winced as pain lanced down her left leg.

'Shit!' she said feelingly.

Rubbing her lower back, she went off to find Ernie. She was determined to get into the chest. He might not have a key, but she reckoned he'd have a sturdy screwdriver or, with a bit of luck, a crowbar.

But when she knocked on his cubby's door there was no reply. She was about to leave when a voice behind her made her turn. A young man – actually, now she looked closer, more of an older teenaged boy – was coming towards her, down the corridor. He was smiling and holding his hands wide.

'If you're looking for Ernie, it's his day off. I'm Dom, his assistant. It's a summer job before I go to uni.'

'I'm DS Ballantyne,' she said, holding up her warrant card. 'I need some help with a couple of tools. I don't suppose you've got a big screwdriver, have you?'

He nodded and led her inside.

'Phillips or flat-head?' he asked.

'It's not for screws. I just need something with a flat edge to get into a wooden box.'

'OK,' he said, apparently unbothered by the notion of a police officer about to bust her way into an antique wooden chest. 'How about this?'

He was holding up a foot-long prybar with a slim flat edge.

'Perfect,' she said, taking it from him and returning to the green room.

Kat set to work on the chest. It took three tries but eventually she found a place where she could slide the tip of the prybar between the lid and the side of the chest, near to the lock. Praying the chest wasn't valuable, that if it was, it was insured and that, either way, she'd find something to justify the act of vandalism she was about to perpetrate, she shoved down hard on the prybar.

With a loud crack, the lock gave way. Thankfully, the wood stayed intact. No flying splinters or split panel, although she'd put a sizeable dent in the top edge.

The chest was completely empty. No sliding drawers, half-shelves or compartments. It was easily big enough for someone to climb into, bend their knees and close the lid after them.

She knelt beside it and turned her phone torch on. When she angled the beam into the corners, a wide smile broke out across her face. In the dust in one corner was a footprint. Not complete, but it looked like part of the sole of a running shoe or sneaker of some kind.

'Got you,' she murmured.

She could see the killer now – a hunched figure, head bent up against one end, feet at the other. Mark's body cooling just a few feet away as first Bella, then Kat, crouched beside it. After they'd left, the killer had emerged, locked the chest and made their escape.

She turned the torch off and straightened up. The remaining question was, had they gone out through the window? Kat had cleared the jagged teeth of broken glass Bella had left, so it would have taken a matter of moments to climb out, but that would have carried a huge risk. Even though the window gave on to a side passage, someone could still have seen the killer walking away.

Kat called Darcy. 'I need you, Darce. I'm at the green room in the Guildhall. I think I've found the killer's footprint.'

She turned her attention to the remaining piece of the puzzle. If not the window, then how had the killer left unseen? Linda had asked about a trapdoor.

Five minutes later, Kat had dragged or carried everything clear of the carpet. She got on to her hands and knees to begin rolling it up. The dust made her sneeze, but eventually, sweating heavily in the hot, un-air-conditioned room, she'd pushed the fat sausage all the way to one wall. The floor beneath was parquet. She paced the surface, staring hard at every seam, every crack between the wooden blocks. It was absolutely devoid of trapdoors, secret or otherwise.

Once more she got to her knees and laboriously rolled the carpet back into place. She sat cross-legged in the centre, roughly where the armchair had been. Idly she prodded the circular depression in the pile where its round wooden leg had flattened the fibres. She shuffled along on her bottom until she was sitting in the centre of the square of four identical marks.

She looked around, trying to see the room as Mark would have done. About five feet in front of her were four smaller impressions. Little circles about two centimetres in diameter revealed in the light slanting across the carpet from a wall-mounted lamp. She got down on to her belly and peered across the surface of the carpet, stifling a sneeze as more dust puffed up her nostrils.

What had caused these extra depressions? She pulled her phone out and scrolled back to the initial photos she'd taken. The armchair was there, with the side table in front of it. But nothing else. Which was odd, wasn't it? What had Di said about her five-minute audience with Mark? *I had to sit on a silly little side chair.*

Kat twisted round and saw an upholstered side chair standing on the parquet floor beyond the edge of the carpet. Its legs looked about the right distance apart. They tapered, too. She brought it over, knowing as she inspected the ends of the legs that her hunch was right.

Kat placed it down on to the carpet, and sighed. The legs wouldn't square up with the depressions in the carpet.

No. This *had* to be the answer. Then she saw it. She spun the chair a quarter-turn and tried again.

The legs slotted home, millimetre perfect. The chair faced the armchair. But then why had the killer moved it from the middle of the carpet to the room's edge?

She pictured Van at home, pulling a kitchen chair over to change one of the halogen downlighters. She walked over to the spot to which the side chair had been moved. Craned her neck to look up at the ceiling. Was there a hatch up there? Was that how the killer had escaped?

Kat climbed on to the seat and looked up. Her heart sank. Where was the handle? The wire? The cabin hook or button? It was just a square panel of white plaster, smooth like wedding cake icing, complete with ornate moulding.

She continued to peer up, trying to discern even the suggestion of an outline. But there was nothing. She stretched up, but her fingers were short of the ceiling by a good four or five inches.

She climbed down and went to find Dom, swapping the prybar for a stepladder. Back in the green room, she moved the chair out of the way before standing the ladder up in the centre of the carpet and climbing until her face was just inches from the ceiling.

She switched on her phone torch a second time and shone it up at the white plasterwork. This close, she could see it wasn't white at all. It was more of a greyish cream.

Except . . .

Along one join, between the flat central square of the panel and a ridge of moulding, was a thin line of fresh white paint, smeared with greyish dust. She followed it along until the corner, where it turned through ninety degrees and carried on. The remaining four sides of the square panel were similarly treated. Someone had recently painted along the edges of the square.

Mouth dry, Kat knocked her knuckles against the centre of the panel. It emitted a hollow, wooden sound. It might mean nothing. Presumably there was just a small gap and then the floorboards above it.

Raising her arms above her head and bracing her legs against the stepladder, she thrust the heels of her hands against the centre of the panel. Nothing. She tried again, harder. The wood emitted a light crack. A third time, accompanied by a grunt of effort and a cry of 'Come *on*!'

The panel flew upwards, dust sifted down over her upturned face, and tiny flakes of white paint spiralled to the carpet. Kat stretched up, sliding the panel to one side. She put some gloves on and climbed through the hatch, into a crawlspace. Taking the route the killer must have.

Somewhere up here, Darcy would find more footprints, maybe fingerprints and, if the forensic gods were feeling well disposed to the smiling DS below them, DNA.

Kat descended the ladder and walked the room again while she waited for Darcy and the CSIs to arrive. She'd found the killer's hiding place and their escape route. But one thing they couldn't have done was heave themselves up through that hatchway carrying a slopping plastic bin of water.

So where had they dumped it? The answer, when it came to her, was breathtakingly simple, and she cursed herself for not seeing it earlier. The ficus. Keeping her gloves on, she carefully brushed a couple of handfuls of pinkish clay spheres to one side. The potting compost beneath was a dark brown, almost black. She stuck her index finger in and scooped up a clod. She squeezed it between her fingers. It was soggy.

'We'll make a CSI of you yet!' came Darcy's voice from the doorway. 'Or a gardener at least.'

Elated at her discoveries, which she shared with Darcy, Kat left the CSIs to their work and headed back to Jubilee Place. Solving the riddle of the MO was satisfying, but the killer was still in the wind. She intended to rectify that.

Maybe the meeting at Dorothy Russell's house that evening would be the first step.

Chapter Forty-Four

After dinner, Kat went upstairs to change.

Normally she'd wear her usual cop outfit: black trousers and a jacket, plus low heels. But given what Dorothy had said about trust in the police, maybe that would be the wrong call.

She opted for navy trousers and a plain white T-shirt instead.

Her stomach flittered and she suddenly needed to pee. She popped into the bathroom and then came back and sat on the bed to regroup mentally. Why was she feeling so nervous?

It wasn't hard to find the answer. It was contained in a short but devastating phrase Dorothy had used when they'd chatted in the cafe. *The police were no better.*

Kat *was* the police. The women she was only a couple of hours from meeting didn't trust her. Maybe even hated her. After all, she was trying to bring Mark's killer to justice, whereas they felt they were the ones denied justice. And that led directly to the most uncomfortable thought of all.

As a woman, Kat felt an affinity with Dorothy and the members of her whisper network. There had been times, even as an adult, when she'd crossed to the better-lit side of the street at night. Or gripped her keys so they poked out from between her knuckles. She doubted there was a woman alive today who hadn't. And that made her angry. Why should half the population have to walk around ready to defend themselves against an attack?

But as a police officer, specifically a homicide detective, she had a job to do. If she thought Mark's killer was a member of Dorothy's group, she'd arrest them and see the case through to its conclusion.

However sick it made her feel.

Chapter Forty-Five

Kat parked outside Dorothy's house in Finsbury Park. Dorothy met her at the front door and handed her a little scratchcard.

'Put that on your dashboard. The parking wardens round here are on a bonus scheme,' she said with a smile.

Trying to quell the butterflies fluttering around in her belly, Kat locked the car and followed Dorothy inside.

'We're in the kitchen,' she said.

The kitchen turned out to be a vast open-plan space in which Kat's own, far more modest space could disappear twice over with room to spare.

Ranged in a loose group on a pair of cotton-upholstered sofas either side of a low wooden coffee table were seven or eight women. Kat smiled nervously and said, 'Hi,' as she tried to make eye contact with each woman.

Clearly Mark Swift hadn't had a type. Here were women with different body shapes, skin colours, hairstyles. Their ages ranged from early twenties to forties and fifties. But what did unite them was a wary expression, visible in the looks they bestowed on Kat. A couple offered the briefest of social smiles, but most mouths were set in grim lines. One of the younger women, painfully thin, kept picking at her lips. Her chin was trembling. An older woman to her right clutched a cushion, twisting a tassel between her fingers.

Dorothy motioned for Kat to take a seat before perching on the arm of the sofa with its back to the garden and slinging a loose arm around the shoulders of the young woman holding back tears.

'Everyone, this is DS Ballantyne,' Dorothy said. 'I spoke to her in Middlehampton. I think we can trust her.'

Kat had been wondering how to begin, trying various approaches on the drive up. Before she could open her mouth, one of the older women, fortyish, with a guarded expression, spoke up.

'*Why* can we trust you?'

Such a simple question. But framing an honest answer was harder than Kat had expected. There was a time, although possibly not within her lifetime, when the answer would have been simple. *Because I'm a police officer.* She didn't need these women to tell her that wouldn't wash now.

'First of all, I just want to say thank you to Dorothy for inviting me here, and to you all for agreeing to meet me. My rank and my official title is DS Ballantyne, but I'd like you to call me Kat, please.'

She inhaled. Looked at each of them in turn. Registered the pain behind their eyes. And told the truth.

'I joined the police because my best friend had been murdered. He was a serial killer, preying on young girls. And just over a year ago, he came back to my town and started doing it again. I caught him and he's in prison now. He'll die in prison, and I'm glad.

'But now I'm investigating another murder. And it looks like the victim wasn't as popular as his book sales would lead people to believe. But I'm working just as hard to catch Mark Swift's killer as I did my friend's.

'My point is, I'm not a police officer because I want to please people or do what's popular. If I wanted to do that, I could give vigilante groups the addresses of paedophiles. I try, and I mean, I *really* try, to do what's right. I can't do anything about what Mark

Swift' – the word 'allegedly' skittered across her tongue, but she swallowed it down, this was no time for legal niceties – 'did to you. But perhaps once the case is closed there will be opportunities for you to tell your stories.'

The room was silent for a few seconds. Kat swallowed. Her nerves hadn't quietened. If anything she felt worse than before. It was like giving evidence in the Crown Court. You answered the defence barrister's questions and then waited for them to pounce.

The woman with the severe silver-grey hair spoke first. 'That's a nice speech. Did you rehearse it before coming here? Because the man you're talking about was worse than a murderer. He left his victims alive, to suffer for the rest of their lives. My name is Marion Bright. I was twenty-nine when he raped me. I was recording an audiobook. He came into the booth, locked the door and attacked me. He told me if I said anything about it he'd make sure I never worked in publishing again.'

A woman in her late twenties or maybe early thirties leaned forwards and fixed Kat with a pair of wide-set eyes. 'I'm Milly. He assaulted me in my own home. He was dropping off a manuscript for me to proofread. I did go to the police,' she said, looking around the room, getting supportive nods in return, 'and they treated me like I was the criminal. I had a scalding hot shower after he left. I tried to burn him out of me. They said that was stupid because now there was no evidence. Then I got a visit from this weird short little man who said he was Swift's lawyer. He gave me money and told me to take it. If I said anything in public I'd be sued for libel. He said I'd lose my flat, my career, everything.' She shrugged. 'What could I do?'

As the next young woman began to speak, Kat looked up from her notebook in surprise. She recognised the voice. It was the volunteer steward at *Criminal Herts* who'd discovered the body in the green room.

'My name is Bella Gabbard,' she said, glaring at Kat. 'Hello again. I'm a bit unusual here. Unlike my friends, I wasn't raped by Mark Swift. But my wife was. We'd only been married for a year and half. She used to be outgoing, a real party girl. Now she has panic attacks and agoraphobia. And you know what? I'm glad he's dead. I'd like to meet the person who killed him and shake their hand.'

A murmur of agreement coursed round the room like the distant rumble of water in old pipes. Kat looked at Bella closely. Had she done more than simply discover Mark's prostrate body? Had she killed him first? Was Kat going to have to arrest her, when a big part of her wanted to say *you did the right thing*?

After Bella spoke, every single woman there told Kat her own story. They differed in the details, the where and the when. But the picture that emerged was of a relentless and voracious sexual predator who had used his fame, money and power both to mount his attacks and to cover them up afterwards.

As Dorothy added in details she'd researched about the police response, which had been universally ineffective and, in some cases, downright offensive, Kat felt guilty by association. Was she really serving justice, or only the law?

How was this possible in the era of Me Too? When high-profile paedophiles like Jeffrey Epstein were arrested and charged? When powerful men, from news anchors to corporate executives, rappers to retailers, were hauled before the courts almost daily?

Dorothy answered the question for her.

'I know what you're thinking,' she said. 'How come we never went public, given that women are more likely to be believed nowadays? Well, we already told you about his slimy lawyer. But the fact is, Kat, the odds are stacked against us. The system's rigged.'

'But then why am I here?' Kat blurted.

'Simple. Because if you're right, and he was killed in revenge for his crimes, that's all going to come out after the trial. It'll send a message to all the predators out there that they will not get away with it. And believe me, we have some rich and powerful friends of our own, Kat. If it turns out one of his victims did it, she will get the best lawyers money can buy.'

'But that sounds almost like you're talking about vigilante justice. A rapist's victim has the right to murder him.'

'Well, she does, doesn't she?' a tearful young woman said. 'In self-defence. This is no different.'

Kat was so torn. The last thing she wanted to do was get into a legal argument about defences against murder charges. But she couldn't sit back and say nothing. She had to find something to say that would allow her to keep believing she was doing the right thing, without falling back on creaky legal arguments.

'If it happened in the moment? Yes, absolutely. Self-defence would be a workable justification. But Mark was murdered while he was alone, waiting to go onstage at a book festival. I'm sorry, but no jury, let alone a lawyer, would accept that he was killed in self-defence.'

'You're just the same as all the others,' the young woman cried out.

'No, she's not,' Marion said, dragging fingers through her steel-grey hair. 'She came here, and she listened respectfully. And she's right. We're not about ranging around the streets lynching men accused of rape. Or even ones convicted of it.'

'Thank you, Marion,' Kat said. 'Look, I get it, I promise you, I do. But I have a sworn duty to carry out, and in my current role that means bringing murderers to justice, whoever they kill. But there is something I'm interested in hearing more about, and that's Mark Swift's lawyer, Sir Anthony Bone. A couple of you mentioned that he threatened you or offered money. Can you give me any more details?'

'I can,' said a woman who'd been sitting quietly at the far end of the kitchen. She'd given her name as Rae.

'Go on.'

'After Swift left my flat, I called him – I had his number because I was a freelance editor at the time – and told him I was going to report him to the police. I was so angry, I said he ought to get ready for a media shitstorm because I was going to take this all the way. I didn't shower, I just sat there, physically in pain, feeling dirty and ashamed, crying, and I waited for the police to come and do their rape kit.

'Anyway, a couple of days later, I was on the phone to a mate and the doorbell rang. I opened the front door and Bone was standing there, asking if he could come in. I didn't know what to do, so I let him in. He sat on my sofa, doing that ridiculous thing with the knees of his trousers, and then he told me.

'He said that he had a hundred thousand pounds in his briefcase and he strongly advised me to take it in return for dropping the case. I said the police were the only ones who could drop it. Then he said I could refuse to testify, or say I'd been mistaken and it was just rough sex after all. So I stood up and told him to get out of my flat. And that's when he threatened me.'

'Threatened you how?' Kat asked.

'He said' – she closed her eyes – '"Listen to me, you little slut. A woman in your precarious financial position would do well to accept this generous offer. If you don't, I will call someone I know and he will hurt you very badly indeed. It will make what Mark did to you feel like a lover's embrace."'

She opened her eyes. They were wet with tears. Sobs filled the room. Dorothy drew her into a hug. Kat was filled with hot fury. At that precise moment, if Anthony Bone – she couldn't bring herself to use his title – had been in the room, she would have tasered him without a moment's thought.

'What happened?' Kat asked softly.

'What do you think? I paid off a big chunk of my mortgage and I was able to go out at night with only the usual amount of fear.'

'Look, Rae, I am so sorry you had to relive that just now. But this could be incredibly important. Would you be prepared to testify in court about Bone's visit?'

'I can do better than that. You know I said I couldn't think what to do when he rocked up at my front door?'

Kat nodded. 'It's totally understandable.'

'Yes, it is. But I did think of one thing. I turned on my voice memo app. I recorded our conversation. Now his cash-cow client's dead, I think we can finally take the fight to him.'

'Can I have a copy of the recording, please?'

'Hold on.'

Kat watched as Rae transferred the audio file.

'Thank you. I promise you, we will act on this. At the bare minimum, he's broken his professional code of conduct, so he'll be disbarred. But as he also tried to bribe you and made threats of violence, he'll also be facing criminal charges.'

After a few more minutes, Kat thanked them again. It was time to go.

On the drive back to Middlehampton, she reflected on everything she'd learned in the previous two hours. Mark Swift had been a serial rapist. His crimes stretched back over decades. At the time he'd attacked them, his victims had been young, vulnerable women working in publishing and the media. One word from him or his well-paid adviser and the career of that young reporter, publishing assistant or freelancer would be over. And then Rae's story flared bright as a blue light in her brain. They'd actually threatened violence against his victims to intimidate them into silence.

'You bastard!' she shouted in the Golf's silent cabin, as the lights of the M1 flickered across her face.

She jammed her foot down, and the jolt from the engine pushed her back into the seat. The speedometer crept up past 80 to 90 and then 100. A car ahead was obeying the limit. She signalled right, and as the car crossed the white line into the outside lane, she pictured Mark Swift lying dead in the green room. And for the first time in her career, she gave headspace to the one thought she'd always managed to suppress. That maybe, just maybe, a murder victim had got what was coming to him.

She shook her head, trying to physically dispel the sensation that justice had already been served. She couldn't go down that road. It ended up with her in the company of men like Frank Strutt and Stuart Carver. Men like her dad, too, who regarded everything, up to and including people's lives, as tradable commodities.

But the testimony of Dorothy and her friends had scorched Kat down to her soul. The road was quiet, and for a moment she considered finding Anthony Bone's address and racing over there to play him the recording on her phone.

No. No, Kat! She had to be careful. With a grunt of effort she let her foot ride up off the throttle and decelerated into the inside lane.

Twenty minutes later she was home, climbing into bed beside Van, who greeted her with a mumbled 'love you' and an off-centre kiss that grazed the corner of her mouth.

For a long time, she lay there beside him, still furious at Bone for his collusion in his client's crimes. Quietly at first, then louder, like a distant siren approaching at speed, another thought forced its way upwards.

Bella Gabbard had been at the whisper network meeting. She'd had motive to kill Mark Swift. She'd said she was glad he was dead. And she'd been the one to find the body.

Kat's heart sank at the thought of arresting the traumatised young woman for murder. But, ultimately, she knew she would do her sworn duty. Her mouth tasted metallic. She got out of bed to wash away the bad taste.

DAY EIGHT – FRIDAY

Chapter Forty-Six

The clock on the MCU wall said 7.45 a.m. Squared up on Kat's desk was a slim brown envelope. In Linda's unmistakeable handwriting, it was labelled, simply, *Kat. Warrant. AB.*

Kat allowed herself a swift moment of pleasurable anticipation. After checking the papers inside were all present and correct, she went back downstairs to her car.

Exactly seventy-one minutes later, she was parking on a meter in Golden Square. In the centre of Soho, the leafy space was bordered by office blocks housing advertising agencies, media companies and – the service sector that interested Kat this morning – law firms.

One firm in particular.

Anthony Bone & Partners.

To reach the grand front door, Kat had to climb a flight of five steps, tiled in black and white diamonds. A highly polished brass plaque to the right of the door gave the firm's name and a couple of legal details. Shards of sunlight so bright they hurt bounced back off its surface.

She pushed the bell. While she waited, she patted the left side of her jacket where the warrant nestled. It was uncomfortable, but she'd never carried a warrant in her bag ever since hearing via the grapevine of a hapless DC who'd lost a warrant when their briefcase was snatched on the street.

The sun was beating down on her back and, not for the first time that summer, she wished detectives could rock white rather than black suits. Or maybe just a spaghetti-strap top and a pair of shorts. Yeah, right, because that would definitely strike the right tone with the nominals. The thought of confronting some of Middlehampton's crime figures – Frank Strutt, perhaps, or the feared armed robber Peter 'Bad' Luck – dressed for a club in Ibiza made her smile.

The door opened, and a young, immaculately groomed woman stood there. She smiled back, then lifted one quizzical eyebrow, the asymmetry the only jarring note in a face that might otherwise have been created by AI.

Kat held up her warrant card. 'I'm DS Kathryn Ballantyne, Hertfordshire Police. I'd like to see Sir Anthony Bone, if he's available.'

The woman frowned, a second discordant note in the pleasant melody of her face. 'I'm afraid Sir Anthony doesn't see' – she scanned Kat from head to toe – 'callers without an appointment. Perhaps you could send an email?'

She made to close the door, but Kat stepped closer and placed her palm on the door. Firmed up her tone a notch. Eyeballed the beautiful gatekeeper. Just like her mentor Molly Steadman had taught her.

'I have a warrant for certain documents that Sir Anthony' – oh, how that title stuck in her throat – 'has in his possession. I'll come in and take them now. You can inform him I'll wait in your reception area.'

Without waiting any longer, and eager to get the sun off her back, Kat walked past the open-mouthed young woman. She took up a standing position in a room furnished with buttercup-yellow brocade armchairs.

The woman hurried to catch up with her. Her cool demeanour had deserted her and her flawless complexion had reddened.

'Can I ask which documents you need?' she asked. 'It might save some time.'

'Just call Sir Anthony for me, please. I'll explain to him in person.'

Biting her lower lip, the receptionist picked up a desk phone and poked the '1' key. She looked at Kat and offered a half-hearted smile. Then she straightened.

'Er, I have a lady – well, actually she's a detective – in reception, Sir Anthony. A DS Ballantyne. She says she has a warrant for some documents. Could you come and talk to her, please?'

She paused, inspected her nails, then looked back at Kat, the smile faltering seriously now, her expression mostly guilt overlaid with a thin scrim of social anxiety.

Then her blush deepened. Her eyes flicked nervously to Kat.

'I'm not really sure that would be a good idea, Sir Anthony. She seems rather determined.'

She listened some more, and now even Kat could hear the tinny voice that was emitting from the earpiece at sufficient volume to have the young woman flinching.

'Yes, Sir Anthony. I'm sorry. Of course.'

She replaced the receiver in the cradle and turned to Kat. She looked on the point of tears.

'I'm afraid Sir Anthony is in conference at the moment. And he'll be in meetings for the rest of the day. He asks that you come back tomorrow.' She gulped. 'If you'd like to make an appointment?'

Kat had been expecting something of this sort. Men like Bone thought they could bully and bluster, threaten and cajole their way out of whatever sort of trouble they found themselves in. Well, it was time for a little legal education.

'I see,' she said with a smile. 'OK, so . . . Sorry, I didn't catch your name.'

'It's Alice.'

'Well, Alice, this is my warrant,' Kat said, taking the envelope from her pocket and withdrawing the folded sheaf of papers. 'It's been properly drawn up and approved, which grants me certain powers. To put it in a nutshell, I *am* going to take the documents away with me this morning. I'm *not* going to come back tomorrow. And I am *definitely* not going to make an appointment. I know you're only doing what he's telling you, so this isn't on you. But I have to tell you, Alice, I have met men like him before. They do not scare me, they do not worry me and they do not intimidate me. OK?'

Kat thought her words had struck a chord with the young woman, who smiled, hesitantly, and pulled her shoulders back.

'Shall I call him again?'

'If you wouldn't mind.' Then, just as Alice picked up the phone, Kat reached out her hand. 'Let me do it.'

She took the receiver and punched in the first speed-dial number. It was answered before the other phone's ring had registered.

'Have you got rid of the jumped-up little c—'

The force of the derogatory little word hit Kat like a punch to the stomach. She inhaled sharply.

'Actually, *Mr* Bone, she is about to serve you with a warrant. See you shortly.'

She put the phone down.

'Where's his office?'

Alice extended her arm and pointed to a door in the corner of the room. 'Down the hall. Last office on the left.'

Kat strode down the hall, grabbed the shiny brass doorknob and twisted it hard before marching into Bone's office.

The walls were festooned with framed photographs of Bone with various celebrities – clients, presumably. She recognised a couple of people off the TV. One a regular on panel games, the other a judge on talent shows.

Bone was on his feet, his face red. 'How dare you barge in here! Do you know who I am? Who I could call?'

Kat held the warrant in her right hand. It felt good, possibly because she was holding all the cards in her other.

'This is a warrant for certain documents you have in your possession. Specifically, Mark Swift's will, including any codicils, and all papers relating to both his two divorces and his third marriage. Please hand them over now.'

He folded his arms. 'You're overstepping your authority, DS Ballantyne. You have no legal cause to take those documents. They are privileged.'

She took another step closer. 'I am leaving with those documents. You can either give them to me or I will seize them. By force if necessary.'

He snorted. 'Force? What are you going to do, swing your handbag at me?'

She slammed the warrant down on the desk, then reached into her shoulder bag and withdrew an ASP extendible baton. She gave the 'Extendo' a deft flick and it shot out with a very satisfying crack.

'Are you resisting my request?' she barked.

He blanched. Very slowly, not taking his eyes off her, he reached for the warrant. He took a pair of half-moon spectacles from his pocket and placed them fastidiously on the end of his nose, and began reading.

If it was a ploy, it was a poor one. Kat simply waited him out.

Finally, he flung the warrant back down and pocketed his glasses. He rounded his desk and walked across a few feet of deep-piled white carpet to a filing cabinet. He unlocked it with a key attached to his gold watch-chain, and after riffling through some green suspension files for a few seconds, withdrew a fat folder labelled, *Swift, M.* He placed it on his desk, opened it and then rapidly, as if he had been expecting this moment, extracted a sheaf of papers.

He held them out to her, not making eye contact.

Kat took them and slid them into her bag. She thumped the tip of her Extendo down on his desk to close it.

'Thank you for your cooperation,' she said.

Now he did look at her, anger etched into his cadaverous features. 'You like making enemies, DS Ballantyne. That's what I've heard. Well, you've just made another one.'

She reached into her pocket for her phone. Had half a mind to play him the recording of him threatening a rape victim with violence.

He sneered. 'What's that? Pepper spray?'

She withdrew her hand. No. She'd save it.

For now.

Chapter Forty-Seven

Back at Jubilee Place, Kat switched off the engine then checked her phone. It had pinged with a text as she was driving down the M1 from London. It was from Darcy.

Come and see me ASAP

Pulse tripping in anticipation, Kat made her way to the forensics department. It had to be the findings from the chest in the green room.

In the quiet, ordered confines of the space where the CSIs worked, Kat found Darcy perched on a high stool before a raised desk, under bright halogen lighting.

She turned as Kat approached.

'Hi, Kat. We struck gold this time. I've all sorts of goodies for you.'

'Go on, then, don't keep a girl in suspense.'

Darcy held up a glassine evidence bag. Kat took it from her and peered inside. A few black and red fibres, twisted into a little tuft.

'It's nylon,' Darcy said. 'It matches the colours from the festival lanyard.'

'So whoever was hiding in there had an official lanyard. Trouble is that's pretty much everyone – the ticket holders, the staff, the speakers, the volunteers.' *Like Bella Gabbard*, a quiet little voice whispered. 'How about the footprint?'

'I think it's a trainer, or a sneaker of some kind. I've got someone working on that. The pattern was super-clear so we should be able to get a match.'

'Thanks, mate. Keep me posted, eh?'

'Naturally,' Darcy said.

'Any DNA?'

Darcy dropped her glasses down her nose a fraction then regarded Kat over the top. 'Don't want much, do you?'

'Which is a yes?'

'Sadly not. But if you arrest somebody and they own a pair of sneakers that match the footprint, that would be good, no?'

Kat thanked Darcy and left for MCU. She handed the documents she'd seized from Bone to Leah and asked her and Fez to start working on them, looking for anything that might point to motive.

'Where are you going, boss?' Fez asked.

'To see Bella Gabbard, the girl who found the body. I'm going to ask her to come in for an interview under caution.'

'You like her for it?'

'She has a historic connection to Mark Swift. She says he raped her wife. She also has a current connection: she was volunteering at the festival.'

'And she found the body. You don't think she was trying to con us, do you?'

Leah nodded. 'Didn't I say? "The one who found it, drowned it"?'

'I just want to hear a bit more about her movements on the morning he was killed,' Kat said. 'She's way off being a suspect.'

With Fez and Leah poring over the legal documents, Kat drove over to Bella Gabbard's house. She answered the door in shorts and a T-shirt. Bare feet. Her face was red and shiny. A smear of white cream lay across her cheek. Kat smelled coconut.

'Hi, Bella, sorry to interrupt your sunbathing. I need to ask you a few questions and I wondered whether you'd come down to Jubilee Place with me. This would be an interview under caution, but it's voluntary and you'd be free to leave at any time. You'd also be entitled to legal representation.'

A woman's voice floated down the dark hallway behind Bella. 'Who is it, Bel?'

She turned her head. 'It's nothing, love. Go back into the garden. I won't be long.'

'You better not be.'

'Your wife?' Kat asked.

Bella nodded. 'TJ. Look, what are these questions about? I already gave a statement about how I found him.'

'It would be best to talk at the station. If you're OK with that?'

'Yeah, well, I'm not, am I? I told Dorothy it was a mistake inviting you last night,' she hissed, before glancing back over her shoulder again.

'There are a couple of things I just need to clear up with you,' Kat said. 'So, are you coming with me or not?'

Bella folded her arms. 'Not.'

'Bella, please. Don't make me arrest you,' Kat said, desperately hoping she could keep Bella out of a cell.

'You'll have to. Otherwise I'm not going anywhere.'

Kat nodded. She felt bad about what was coming next. Guilt and duty fought inside her. No time to be a spectator now.

'Bella Gabbard, I am arresting you on suspicion of the murder of Mark Swift—'

'This is bullshit! You're just like the rest of them. You don't care about people like TJ. Like all his other victims. You're just an arm of the state.'

Kat struggled to stay focused, professional, as she finished the official caution. She couldn't let Bella's impassioned plea start working on her.

Bella maintained total silence all the way from her house to Jubilee Place. Kat escorted her to the custody suite, where Sergeant Julia Myles was on duty.

'Who do we have here?' she inquired.

'Bella Ruth Gabbard.'

'Charge?'

'Murder.'

Bella choked out a sob. 'I didn't do it!'

Julia informed her of her rights while in custody then summoned an officer to take her to a cell.

'Right. Well I *do* want a lawyer. And I haven't got any money, so you'll have to get me one. A woman. And I hope she gets here quickly.'

Kat drove back to Bella's house, and over the protests of her wife, began a search of the property.

Most women she knew – herself included – kept their shoes in the master bedroom. In the wardrobe. So that was where she started.

Gloves on, she swung open the left-hand wardrobe door. A rail of dresses, skirts and tops. She pushed them first to one side, then the other. But the floor was bare. Not even a dust bunny marred the smooth wooden surface. The other side, then. Trousers hanging on a half-rail and a set of shelves holding plastic boxes packed with T-shirts, socks and knickers, bras, tights, and a crazy tangle of scrunchies, belts and odd bits of gear that wouldn't comfortably fit into any other category. Kat smiled. She had something similar at home.

Where did Bella and TJ keep their shoes, then?

She turned and got to her hands and knees, peering under the bed. Yes. On the side closest to the wardrobe, a long row of neatly paired shoes. Mostly flats, a couple of pairs of boots and, at the head end, several pairs of trainers. She pulled them out and bagged them.

From the doorway, TJ watched her every move, arms folded across her chest.

'You can't take those. You need a warrant.'

'Not when the subject has been arrested, TJ. I'm sorry. That's the law.'

'Well, the law's a joke!'

Kat tried to block out TJ's increasingly loud protests as she moved around the room, opening drawers, checking inside jewellery boxes, and flipping through books on bedside tables.

When she was finished, she checked the other bedroom, a small space dominated by a sewing machine on a stand and an adjustable mannequin draped in a half-finished dress. Hanging from a hook in the wall were a bunch of different-coloured lanyards. Each held a badge for *Criminal Herts*. Kat inspected them. They ranged back four years. She lifted the current year's badge off the hook and bagged it.

It was far from what Carve-up, in his more triumphalist moments, liked to call a 'slam dunk', but Kat hoped it might be the evidence she needed to close the case.

Chapter Forty-Eight

Kat dropped Bella's trainers and lanyard off with Darcy, then took the stairs two at a time up to MCU, finally feeling she might be near to closing the case. But her elation was tamped down by the thought of having to charge Bella with Mark Swift's murder. It just didn't sit right, deep down in her soul where she held her most-cherished beliefs about justice.

Carve-up was wandering between the desks as she entered, clapping the male detectives on the shoulders, laughing over-loudly at their jokes. He leaned over the women, or ignored them altogether. This was what he called 'managing by walking about'. She thought he'd be better off replacing the third word with 'dicking'.

He spotted her. His eyebrows shot up. 'There she is! Middlehampton's very own Miss Marple. Come on, people, round of applause for DS Ballantyne. She's only gone and caught the green room killer, hasn't she?'

A few handclaps followed Carve-up's mocking applause. Kat scowled but kept her head down as she made her way to her desk. But Carve-up wasn't done. He swooped in on her, bringing with him a choking cloud of Aramis.

Great, so he'd even started buying the same aftershave as her father. On Colin Morton, the fragrance, though still too strong, suggested a man comfortable enough to smell the way he always had. On Carve-up it brought to mind open-neck shirts and gold medallions cruising nightclub dancefloors.

'Not bad, not bad, DS Ballantyne,' he said. 'Hope you didn't mind the banter. I mean, it's not every week we get our very own celebrity murder case, is it? She say why she offed him yet? You know, woman to woman? A bit of girl talk in your little VW? Did she suggest a quickie in the green room and he knocked her back?' He leaned closer and dropped his voice to a murmur. 'I heard she's not great-looking.'

Trying to avoid inhaling his aftershave, she answered briefly.

'She's gay, Stu, and unlike some of us, happily married. She also told me he raped her wife, so I'm fairly sure a quickie was the last thing on her mind.'

'There you are then!' he said, putting his hands on his hips. 'You've got a vengeful dyke. Motive. She probably took the champagne in and the beer cooler. Means. And she was alone with him in the green room. Opportunity. You're welcome.'

At various times since coming to work in MCU, Kat had given serious consideration to punching Carve-up. (In one shameful episode, she'd given in, although given he'd grabbed her by the arms first, Linda had settled the matter out of court.) Once again, she found herself picking her spot. Maybe the mouth this time, surrounded by that disgusting fringe of gingery whiskers.

'Excuse me, Stu,' she said, breathing steadily if deeply through her nose. 'I have work to do.'

'Fine by me, DS Ballantyne. Just don't screw up the interview. This month's metrics are looking a bit iffy, so we could do with the win.'

Once Carve-up had left, and his miasma had dispersed, Kat reflected on what he'd said. A decent rule of thumb was that if Carve-up believed something, it was a safe bet to believe the opposite. He thought Bella was guilty, ergo she was probably innocent.

Her phone rang. Darcy. With news on the footprint.

'I'll be right down,' Kat answered.

Darcy was holding up a white sneaker, her hands protected by nitrile gloves.

'Exhibit A, Bella Gabbard's right sneaker. It's a Converse Chuck Taylor All Star. Rather nice, actually. All white, nearly new.'

She turned it round to show Kat the sole pattern. Nested diamonds with three longitudinal lines running through them, and horizontal ridges at toe and heel. Next, she picked up an A4 sheet of paper with a life-size photograph of the partial shoe print from the inside of the Jacobean chest in the green room. They were a match.

'Are they the same size shoe?' Kat asked.

'I can't say for sure, Kat, I'm sorry. If we had the whole thing, yes, we could take accurate measurements and compare them to a new one.'

Kat frowned. It was good, but it wasn't conclusive.

'Not what you were hoping for?'

'Oh, it's not that, Darce. It's just I've got a pair just like them at home. I bet half my netball team do, too. We were even joking about it the other week. You know, how we all go out in town in the same outfit. Print dress, denim jacket and white sneakers.'

Darcy nodded. 'I've got some myself. Though I'd probably go for a biker jacket.'

'In this heat? You'd melt.'

'You think it'll ever break? I actually thought about sleeping in the garden last night.'

'I don't know, mate. I just hope the case breaks first. What about the lanyard?'

'We're still working on it. It's under the scanner as we speak.'

Kat's phone rang. It was Leah: Bella Gabbard's lawyer had arrived.

With the small group convened in the interview room, Kat recited the official caution a second time and then asked, 'Can you tell me exactly what happened last Friday morning, from the moment you started work until you found Mark's body and came into the ballroom to shout that he was dead?'

Bella looked at her lawyer, a woman in her forties with darting eyes that danced between Kat, her client and her notepad. The lawyer offered a minute nod to her client.

'I was on crowd duty. That means walking around, helping people find their way around, you know, get to talks at the various venues, answer general queries. At about 10.55 a.m. Maria called me and asked if I could go and check on Swift as he was due on stage at 11.00 a.m. I went into the Guildhall and knocked on the door of the green room. There was no answer. I tried the handle, but the door was locked. I didn't know what to do, then I remembered the window overlooking the side passage. I went outside and round past the beer tent to the passage. I climbed on a big old flowerpot and I looked in through the window. I saw him lying on the floor on his back. I broke the window and climbed in and I checked for a pulse. But he was dead. I climbed back out the window and raced around to the ballroom and that's when I raised the alarm.'

'So at no time were you in the green room with Mark while he was still alive?'

'No. Why would I be?'

'I don't know. Maybe he'd asked for champagne to be brought in and you were deputised to do it.'

'No, that would have been someone from the catering company. Anyway, I just said I wasn't there with him.'

'Let's talk about your relationship with Mark.'

Bella scowled. 'I didn't have a *relationship* with him.'

'Sorry, poor choice of words. What did you think about Mark?'

'I thought he was a sexual predator. A criminal. A man who did what he wanted and used his lawyer and his money to get away with it.'

'So, given that, Bella, I'm struggling to see why you bothered breaking in and checking on him. If you disliked him that much, and I understand why, how come you didn't just leave him there? Why go in at all? I mean, you got a nasty gash on your arm when you climbed back out the window.'

Bella shrugged. 'I don't know. Not really. I've asked myself the same question a hundred times. Maybe I'm just a normal human being, unlike him. I saw a dead body and I panicked.'

'There's an old wooden chest in the green room. Do you remember seeing it?'

'No. It's all a blur. I close my eyes and I see his body, nothing else.'

'You didn't climb inside the chest at any point?'

Bella drew her head back, looking genuinely surprised by the question. 'No. Why on earth would I do that?'

Kat took from the folder in front of her the A4 photo of the shoe print.

'For the recording, I am showing Ms Gabbard a photograph of a shoe print found inside the Jacobean wood chest inside the green room.' Kat passed the print across the table to Bella. Her lawyer leaned over to have a look. 'That shoe print was found inside the wooden chest. The sole pattern is quite distinctive. The tread pattern is an exact match for one of the sneakers we recovered from your house, Bella.'

The lawyer held up a finger. 'One moment, DS Ballantyne. What make of shoe is that?'

Here it was. The question Kat had, perhaps optimistically, hoped wouldn't come up.

'It's a Converse Chuck Taylor All Star.'

The lawyer laid a hand on Bella's arm, forestalling her client's answer.

'Do you know the size?'

'At this point, no.'

The lawyer made a note. 'That's a very popular shoe. How many women were wearing them at the festival, I wonder? How many men? I've got a pair in my bag for the walk to the station. Are you going to arrest me, too?'

Kat stifled a sigh that threatened to burst free. The shoeprint had been knocked back. That only left the scrap of fibre from the lanyard. Which Darcy hadn't formed a conclusion about yet. All she could do now was bluff. And Kat felt very uncomfortable doing that to a young woman who had so little faith in the police. But she reminded herself she was investigating a murder. That had to come first.

'We also found fibres from a festival lanyard in the chest. Right now our forensics team are examining your lanyard. Are they going to find a patch of damage corresponding to the fibres?'

Bella looked to her lawyer, who raised her hand and whispered behind it.

'No comment.'

Fair enough. It was hardly a smoking gun, was it? Or in this case, a dripping bucket.

'One more thing, Bella. Can you tell me why you climbed back out of the window? Why didn't you simply unlock the door and leave that way? Was it important to you that we find the key still in the lock?'

'I don't remember. I was panicking, like I said. I'd never seen a dead body before.'

That was all the direct crime scene questions dealt with. All Kat had left was Bella's vengeful feelings towards Mark Swift. And although she'd already told Kat at the whisper network meeting at Dorothy Russell's house, she needed it on the record.

'I want to ask you a personal question, Bella. It might be difficult to answer and I am sorry if you find it upsetting or traumatising in any way. You've said you were glad Mark was dead, even though you acted like a normal human being and tried to help. Can you tell me *why* you harboured these hostile thoughts towards him?'

It was a huge gamble. Bella might lose it completely, start screaming and admit to the murder. Or at least contradict her earlier statements. Kat felt sick to her stomach for having to put the young woman through it all again.

Bella glared at Kat, eyes burning with rage. 'I hated Mark Swift because he raped my wife. He and his disgusting lawyer terrified her into not making a complaint against him. So forgive me for harbouring hostile thoughts towards him. I didn't murder that evil slug, but you know what? I'm glad he's dead, and if you were any kind of ally you'd be glad, too.' She took a ragged breath. 'But there's a difference between wishing someone was dead and actually doing it. I'm a hundred per cent guilty of the first one. And a hundred per cent innocent of the second. Are we done now, because I'd really like to get back to TJ? She'll be going out of her mind with worry.'

The lawyer closed her pad. Clicked her ballpoint pen.

'It seems to me, DS Ballantyne, that you have no grounds for holding my client any longer.'

Kat believed the young woman sitting opposite her. If her wife's rape were to be taken as motive? Well, that only placed her in the company of a great many other women who'd suffered directly. The feelings of doubt – was she really working on the side of the angels? – came roaring back.

Yes, reporting a dead body was a classic distraction technique. Psychopaths used it all the time. But with nothing more than these scant facts, Kat knew she had no option. She ended the interview and de-arrested Bella Gabbard. The murderer was still out there somewhere.

Back at her desk, she sighed and opened the first of the statements from Mark Swift's colleagues, rivals and enemies in the publishing world.

Someone must have slipped up somewhere, surely?

She read on, losing track of time as the noise of MCU faded to a background hum and then silence.

Her phone rang, making her jump. 'Kat, it's Despatch. Member of the public just reported a dead body behind the Guildhall.'

Kat jumped to her feet and grabbed her murder bag. A second murder at the Guildhall, a week after the first? Chance of a coincidence: zero per cent.

She looked around. Leah was at her desk, head in hands. The dead-eyed look coppers got when a case refused to break and the only option was more reading.

'Leah! With me, please. Bring your bag, we've got another murder.'

Chapter Forty-Nine

Kat led Leah at a trot round to the back of the Guildhall.

Standing at the head of the passageway leading down behind the kitchens was a woman wearing dirty yellow leather gloves and pads strapped round her knees. She was holding a hooked knife in one hand and she looked as though she'd been crying.

'Oh, thank God!' she said as Kat and Leah flashed their warrant cards. 'I feel sick. I was weeding the path when I saw him.' She raised her right arm and pointed. 'He's down there. Can I go now, please? I really do not feel well.'

'Right, let's get you somewhere comfortable,' Kat said. 'What's your name, my love?'

'Chioma Ofili.'

Kat turned to her bagwoman. 'Leah, could you take Chioma and find somewhere for her to sit down. Get her statement, too. And call the team in.'

Rustling along in her Tyvek suit and pale blue plastic booties, already uncomfortably warm in the unrelenting heat, Kat strode down the pathway.

She could see exactly where the gardener had been working when she came to the corpse. The gap between two flagstones was bordered by two miniature levees of crumbly dry soil and tugged-out weeds, already wilting in the heat. Chioma had been kneeling here, head down, meticulously digging out each weed. Her kneepads had left muddy scuffs on the silvery-grey flagstones. Then she'd shuffled forward, ready to resume her work. And she'd looked up.

She'd seen the outflung arm extended from behind a dustbin, the rivulet of blood seeping along another mortared crack in the stonework.

Kat reached the dustbin and looked down.

The dead man was on his back, his head twisted to the side so his face was crushed against the wall. And he'd been stabbed. Repeatedly. She counted at least five entry wounds in the blood-soaked white T-shirt. Blood had pooled beneath him and run along the gap in the flagstones before collecting around the outstretched fingers of his left arm. Flies were already buzzing loudly, settling at the edge of the congealing blood and laying their eggs. She spotted a partial shoeprint. Dark red. Also fly-blown.

Kat checked her watch. It was 1.21 p.m. She'd de-arrested Bella Gabbard at 12.30. The call had come in from Despatch at 12.57 p.m. Bella could easily have made the short journey from Jubilee Place to the Guildhall in time to murder this man and get away before Chioma discovered the body. Had Kat just made the worst mistake of her career? A mistake that had cost another man his life? She called Fez and asked him to get CCTV from Jubilee Place to the Guildhall, to see if he could track Bella's movements after she left the station.

Had she released Bella only for her to kill again? She couldn't afford to think like that. She fell back on what she'd been taught. *Secure the scene. Look for witnesses. Bring in the CSIs. Contact the pathologist. Identify the victim.*

His jacket had flapped outwards as he'd collapsed. Delicately, she felt in the inside pocket. Her gloved fingers closed on a wallet, which she slid out as carefully as she could.

She got to her feet and stepped back, positioning herself between the dustbin and the opposite wall to block the view if any curious bystanders got past Leah.

The wallet was bloodstained on the outside. She opened it and picked the credit cards out one by one. The dead man's name was Justin Davy. And he carried his driving licence on him. He lived at Lock Cottage, Eelcatch Lane, Markstead, a village along the Grand Union Canal about five miles outside Middlehampton. That address was ringing bells. But the blood-soaked corpse and the furious buzzing of the flies were interfering with her thought processes.

Kat called Fez again. 'Yes, boss?'

'Can you get me a next of kin for a Justin Davy?' She added the address.

She heard the sirens. At last, the cavalry had arrived. She rejoined Leah, who was sitting with Chioma. She'd found her a cup of tea from somewhere.

'We have an ID on the victim. His name was Justin Davy. Mean anything to you?'

'Sorry, Kat. I don't think it's come up in my interviews.'

'I'm going to see his next of kin.' Kat crouched in front of Chioma. 'Thanks for your help. I know this must have been an awful experience. Is there someone you'd like us to call for you?'

She nodded. 'My husband. He works up at the hospital. He's a porter.'

'Leah, can you sort that, please. Then liaise with Jack and Darcy when they get here. All the usual.'

Leah nodded. 'Sure. See you back at MCU?'

Kat nodded. 'I'll be back as soon as I can.'

Fez rang her back. 'Kat, I've got the next of kin. His wife. Her name's Cheryl Davy. And guess what?'

'Tell me.'

'Professionally she goes by her maiden name. Cheryl Holiday.'

'Mark Swift's first agent?'

'The very same.'

'Nice work, Fez.'

Ending the call, Kat left Leah, readying herself to deliver another death knock. It never got any easier. Her stomach was already tight with nerves and she rehearsed the stark little speech that would sharply divide somebody's life into two parts.

Before.

And after.

Chapter Fifty

Kat stood by the front door of Justin and Cheryl Davy's brick-and-flint house abutting the canal. From the looks of it, the old lock-keeper's cottage.

Behind her, the water sloshed noisily down into the lock as a man and woman on a narrowboat called up to a teenage boy operating the sluices. The smell as the jade-green water churned around the boat's long, tarry sides was equal parts mud, rotting vegetation and diesel fuel.

She turned back to face the door as it swung inwards. 'Cheryl Davy?'

The woman smiled a little. 'Can I help you?'

Kat discreetly offered her warrant card and introduced herself. 'Could I come in, please?'

'Yes, of course.'

Grateful not to have to deliver the news in front of a family of holidaymakers, Kat followed Cheryl into the cool of a tiled hallway.

The hall dog-legged through a ninety-degree angle and into a rustic kitchen. Pans hung from a steel rack above a central island, and bunches of dried herbs tied with string dangled beside a window that gave on to the canal. The boat was rising steadily, and now the heads of the parents were visible just above the lip of the lock.

'I already gave my statement to your colleague,' Cheryl said with a smile. 'Faisal?'

'It's about your husband, Mrs Davy. I'm afraid he's dead. He was murdered sometime this morning. I am most dreadfully sorry for your loss.'

Cheryl blinked. She looked out of the window at the happy family, the parents cheering the boy on as he scampered around the boat like an overexcited puppy.

Her hand fluttered up to her hair, then she brushed her fingertips over her mouth. 'You mean Justin?'

'I'm afraid so, yes. I found his wallet on the – with him.'

'But somebody could have stolen it. That's it. They stole his wallet. You found the mugger, not Justin.'

Kat's heart went out to the freshly minted widow. People reacted in so many different ways. Creating alternative scenarios was one of them.

'His face matched his driving licence. There's no doubt. I'm sorry. Do you want to sit down?'

Cheryl frowned. 'Sit down?'

'Yes. I could make you a cup of tea. Shall I do that?'

Cheryl nodded. 'Yes. You do that and I'll sit down.'

Like a newly programmed robot, Cheryl moved to a chair, pulled it out from underneath the rough-hewn table and sat gracefully, placing her hands one on top of the other on its scratched and pitted surface.

Kat filled the kettle and switched it on, started assembling mugs and teaspoons, finding tea bags and sugar.

Cheryl's sob cracked the air, a broken, jagged sound that seemed to emanate from deep inside her. Kat was already fishing out her packet of tissues, but Cheryl dragged one from her pocket. She crushed it against her eyes and sat, head in hands, her shoulders shaking in great heaving spasms.

If she'd murdered her husband, she was doing a great job of disguising it.

Kat would have to get to that, but there were other questions she could ask first.

With the tea made, and Cheryl having attained a fragile sort of composure, Kat sat adjacent to her at the table.

'Cheryl, I am working on the assumption that whoever murdered Justin also murdered Mark Swift. Can you tell me, did they know each other?'

Cheryl raised her mug to her lips and took a sip. Winced.

'Hot.' She frowned. Shook her head. 'They were best friends. From school. They went to the College. Do you know it?'

Kat nodded. 'My son goes there.'

'It's a great school. We're hoping Freddie will get in.'

'Is Freddie your son?'

Cheryl burst into fresh tears, and this time Kat was ready with the tissues. 'Oh my God, how am I going to tell him? He'll be devastated. He adores his dad.'

Kat tried not to think how Riley would react if she had to sit him down one day and tell him Van had been murdered. She focused on the grieving woman sitting with her instead.

'Do you have relatives nearby. Your parents? Or Justin's?'

Cheryl nodded, sniffing loudly. 'His mum and dad live in town. I could call them, I suppose.'

'Where's Freddie now?'

'He's at a friend's house.' Her eyes widened. 'He won't find out from social media, will he?'

'No. Not for a while anyway. We secured the scene. Nobody can get in there to see anything or take pictures, don't worry. But once I've gone, I'd talk to him as soon as you can. You were telling me about Justin's friendship with Mark?'

290

'They went to university together, stayed friends, which doesn't always happen, does it? And then afterwards too. Justin designed all Mark's covers. Even when he got so famous, he insisted on having Justin do the work. Which is great for Justin because his business hasn't been doing so well the last few years. Justin was best man at Mark's weddings. All three,' she added with a wry twist of her mouth.

'Cheryl, can you tell me the nature of *your* relationship with Mark Swift?'

'I was his agent. Until he dumped me,' she said without emotion.

'Forgive me for asking this,' Kat said, preparing for an outburst or a sharp retort at best, 'but given your own problems with Mark, how did you feel about Justin carrying on being friends with him?'

Cheryl cleared her throat. Looked down at Kat's left hand.

'You're married?'

'Yes.'

'Things are always peachy between you?'

'Not always. But we get along. We talk.'

'So did we. Justin had known Mark practically his whole life. Mark introduced us. I bounced back from when Mark shafted me. I moved on. I didn't like him and I tried to minimise my social contact with him, but that's life, isn't it? You cope. You have to or you'd go mad.'

A thought occurred to Kat, spurred by Cheryl's last remark.

'Cheryl, did Mark ever assault you? Sexually?'

'What? No! Why would you ask that?'

'You were his agent for how long?'

'Six years, give or take.'

'Did you ever hear any rumours about his having attacked young women? Raped them?'

'No! Oh my God, have you found something out about him?'

'At this stage it's just a line of enquiry. Can you think of anyone who might have wanted to hurt Justin? Maybe someone in the publishing world?'

'No. I mean he had the odd bit of argy-bargy with a client, but nothing terrible. Just disagreements over creative direction, the usual.'

'And you said his business was struggling. Had he borrowed money off anyone. Other than a bank, I mean?'

'Not as far as I know. I'm doing well, so money itself wasn't really the issue. It was his pride more than anything else.'

'I get it. I just need to ask you one more question for now, and then I'll be out of your hair. Can you tell me where you've been today, from getting up to when I arrived?'

'Ah,' Cheryl said with a long, drawn-out sigh. 'The wife's alibi. Sounds like a half-decent title for a book, don't you think? Maybe a psychological thriller? I was here all morning. On Zoom calls. I went for a walk along the towpath at about eleven, bumped into a friend, but other than that here in the cottage.'

Kat gave her a card. 'I have to go now. I'll have one of our specially trained officers come to talk to you to offer support. Could you email me details of the Zoom calls and your friend's contact details? And if you think of anything you think might help me catch Justin's killer, please call me.'

Kat left her making preparations to fetch her son home.

She wanted answers from Jack Beale.

Chapter Fifty-One

The chill of the dissection room was such a relief after the sweltering heat outside – Kat could almost forget she was mere feet away from a mortally wounded human body.

Almost.

Jack's reply to her text had been succinct, laced with a dark shaft of humour.

PM at 3.30 p.m. Be there or be []

Kat had arrived promptly. They were fifteen minutes in, and Jack had just divested Justin Davy's body of its clothes, which were waiting in evidence bags to be taken to Darcy's team at Jubilee Place. His assistant, Ashleigh, was cleaning the blood off the torso with a handheld spray unit. The rose-pink liquid gurgled into the drain.

While Jack prepared to begin the dissection, Kat looked at Justin Davy's hands and forearms. They were smooth and undamaged. Not a single cut or scrape. Normally, if people died while being attacked head-on, they raised their hands to shield their face and chest. Maybe even grappled with the assailant or grabbed the knife. Victims often sustained deep cuts to their palms or slashes across the soft skin on the insides of the forearms.

So Justin hadn't put up a fight. He hadn't been tied up or restrained in any way, which meant only one thing. He'd known his attacker, and he hadn't been expecting the attack. It would have been sudden, it would have been fast, and it would have been brutal.

'Mr Davy's chest bears five puncture wounds,' Jack said, speaking slowly and clearly. A mic on a curly black lead dangled a couple of feet above the table. He took the clear plastic rule Ashleigh was holding out and laid it along the uppermost wound. 'Wound is forty millimetres long by approximately three millimetres wide. Judging from the extremely clean edges to the cut, I would say the weapon was most likely a smooth-edged kitchen knife. The thrust was exercised with enough force to drive the blade right in, to the point the bolster bruised the skin.'

He turned to Kat and spoke through his cloth mask and clear plastic visor.

'That's a hell of a blow. Whoever did it meant business.'

He inserted a thin stainless-steel rod into the wound and read off the depth from a scale along its side.

'The wound is thirteen centimetres deep. Ashleigh, can I have a protractor please?'

Ashleigh nodded and popped open the lid of a little metal stationery kit. Kat recognised the brand. She'd had the same one at school. The blue and silver tin was emblazoned with the words *Helix Oxford Set of Mathematical Instruments Complete and Accurate*.

'Here you are, Dr— Jack.'

So Ashleigh was still having difficulty with her boss's first name. That would pass. It had for Kat with Ma-Linda. Although she had a feeling the girl would probably end up calling him Dr Jack.

Jack laid the flat edge of the protractor on the chest and slid it behind the steel rod. He tilted his head.

'Wound track is sixty degrees to the horizontal: a steep downward trajectory. The blade entered the chest just below the left clavicle, sliding cleanly between the second and third ribs. Mr Davy was five foot nine. I'd estimate we are looking for an assailant of six foot or more. Either that or his murderer stood on a chair.'

Kat flashed on Danny Elliott opening the door to her. He was well over six foot. And big with it.

After recording the measurements of the other four wounds, which matched the first, Jack asked for a PM40 scalpel and opened up the chest.

'All five strikes inflicted significant damage to the chest wall, intercostal muscles, ribs and lungs. The fatal blow punctured the left atrium just above the mitral valve. Unconsciousness would have followed within a few seconds, death would have occurred in a very short space of time after that, no longer than a minute.'

He peered at the mess of organs and blood and asked once more for the ruler. 'From the morphology of the fatal wound, I'd be happy to confirm my initial hypothesis that the weapon used was a large-bladed kitchen knife. Something used for meat, with a substantial bolster.'

'Sorry, Dr— Jack, what's a bolster?' Ashleigh asked.

'It's the reinforced bit at the handle end of a chef's knife. They help balance the blade but they also act as a finger guard. Stops your hand sliding down on to the edge.'

'Would there have been a lot of blood, Jack?' Kat asked. 'Apart from the pool we found, I mean.'

'It's hard to say. The aorta and the pulmonary arteries are undamaged apart from this superficial cut to the outer wall here. You see?' he said, pointing at an elliptical incision in the reddish-purple blood vessel.

'So no spurting?'

'Probably not. There's a lot of blood in the chest cavity, as you can see, and a fair amount would have left the body via the incisions in the chest wall, but not under pressure. His clothing would have absorbed most of the force anyway. If you're hoping CCTV will pick up a blood-soaked man leaving the Guildhall precincts, you're probably going to be disappointed.'

She sighed. Because that would make her job a lot easier, wouldn't it?

After asking – unnecessarily, she knew – for his report as soon as possible, she left for Jubilee Place, and an urgent meeting with Linda.

Kat had rung ahead, so when she arrived in the outer office for the DCI, Annie waved her through. 'She's expecting you, Kat.'

Linda dispensed with the pleasantries. 'Talk to me, Kat.'

'Dead white male, found behind the kitchen at the Guildhall by a member of staff. The body was less than twenty feet from where we found Mark. His name is Justin Davy, he was Mark's best friend and cover designer, and someone stabbed him five times with a chef's knife. He was married to Mark's former agent, who he – Mark, I mean – cheated out of a hefty commission.'

Linda puffed her cheeks out. 'Bloody hell! I thought our job was incestuous but this is ridiculous. You've been to see the wife, I take it?'

'I have.'

'Like her for it?'

'No.'

'So, what's your working theory?'

'The chances of two best friends being murdered that close together in time and space are zero for all practical purposes. It's the same killer.'

'It could have been her, then. Maybe the husband didn't show enough sympathy when his bestie double-crossed his wife, so she resolved to do them both in. Just took longer than expected to get the chance.'

'She has a solid alibi for her husband. Unchecked as yet, but it will pan out, I'm sure of it.'

'Well, come on, then, Kat. Tell me a story.'

Kat had been grinding away at the problem since halfway through the post-mortem. And the solution she'd come up with fitted the events.

'Somehow, Justin found out the identity of Mark's killer. But instead of coming to us, he saw an opportunity to make some money. His wife told me his business wasn't doing so well. He goes to the killer, maybe he even knows them, and he says, "I know what you did. You can pay me to keep quiet or I go to the cops."'

'And then what? The killer whips out a bloody great butcher knife and does him there and then?'

'No. I don't think they would have met for the first time behind the Guildhall kitchen. I think Justin probably called them. Either insisted on a meet or maybe told them he wanted however much cash and then agreed the location for the handover.'

'And the killer goes, "OK, fair enough," then turns up with a holdall stuffed with old copies of the *Echo*?' Linda said. 'He says, "It's all in there." Justin bends to check it out and he stabs him?'

'Almost. Except he was stabbed in the chest. Which means they were face to face.'

'Could it have been this woman you arrested, Bella somebody?'

'Gabbard. The timings are OK. She had plenty of time to get to the Guildhall from here.'

'So rearrest her.'

'It can't have been her, Ma-Linda. She's too short. She can't be more than five-two, five-three tops? Jack said that from the angle of the wound track, the killer must have been around about six foot tall.'

'But not if the victim was kneeling. Maybe he looks up at her and is all like, "This isn't money it's old newspapers," and then she stabs him.'

Kat wrinkled her nose. 'It works, but I just don't see it. She's petite, and Jack said the killer would have had to have been super-determined and very powerful. The blade was driven in up to the hilt.'

'But you were happy to arrest her for Swift's murder?'

'I had to – she wouldn't come in voluntarily. But in any case, there's a hell of a difference between hitting someone on the back of the head with a champagne bottle and then holding their head underwater while they're unconscious, and viciously stabbing them to death.'

Linda sighed and pushed her fingers through her hair. 'You're the lead investigator, but I need results soon. Just when the media circus was calming down a bit and some of those true crime vultures had flapped off to other towns, this happens. Now they'll all be flocking back and giving their bloody podcasts names like *The Book Butcher* or *Middlehampton Manuscript Murders.*'

'Not bad,' Kat said. 'If you ever get tired of the metrics you could always pitch those to a publisher. I could probably put you in touch with a couple.'

Linda narrowed her eyes to slits. 'Right, you. Out! Out, out, out, and catch me a killer.'

Kat headed back to MCU. And a surprise.

Chapter Fifty-Two

'Tomski!'

Tom turned and smiled at her from his desk, where he was sitting with Leah and Fez.

'Boss.'

'Is this a social call or what?' Kat asked, wheeling over a chair to join the three DCs.

'They discharged me this morning,' Tom said, grinning widely. 'I've got daily phone check-ups with my neurologist, and I have to go back if I experience any unusual headaches or mental disturbances, but other than that, I'm good.'

'That's amazing, Tomski. Have you been to see occie health?'

He nodded.

'They say I have to be on desk duties for the moment. Probably three months minimum. I guess they don't want me hallucinating or having a seizure in the middle of the street or something.'

'Yeah, our kid,' Fez said with a smile. 'Not good for the image of the service if you're lying there foaming at the mouth and shouting about angels.'

'Wow, Fez, that's a bit dark even for a copshop,' Leah said, her eyes wide with mock-horror.

'It's fine,' Tom said. 'It gets a bit tiring having all those medical students treating you like you're made of glass. I quite like getting back to the banter. And sorry I didn't call first, Kat. It's been a bit of a whirlwind, getting home and back to my old life.'

'Have you called Eleanor?'

'Yep. She's coming round to cook for me tonight.'

'"Cook",' Fez said, rolling his eyes at Leah. 'Something nice and spicy, I bet.'

'Bloody hell, Fez, I think I preferred it when I didn't like you. Kat, can you please take me away from these two? I feel like a third wheel in their blossoming bromance.'

'Actually I can. Fez, can you talk to the POLSA and get over to the Guildhall? We're looking for a bloody shoe.'

'A Converse, yes? Diamonds and whatnot?'

'That would be too much to hope for. But somewhere in this town there's a shoe with Justin Davy's blood on the sole and the murderer's DNA on the inside. Find the shoe, we find the killer.'

'What are we doing, Kat?' Leah asked.

'We're going to see Maria Sheriff again.'

'Any special reason?'

'I think she was wearing Chuck Taylors the day Mark Swift was murdered. And she's tall. Jack said Justin Davy's killer was at least six foot.'

Once Kat, Leah and Maria Sheriff were seated in the back garden, surrounded by a new flush of spiky-petalled orange blooms, Kat got straight to it.

'Maria, do you own a pair of Converse Chuck Taylor All Stars?'

Maria wrinkled her forehead. 'No. They're a bit, well, everywhere, aren't they?'

'It's just, the first time we met, I thought you were wearing some.'

Maria smiled.

'Boden flatforms.' She stuck a foot out to reveal the shoe in question. 'I suppose if you weren't looking closely, you could have mistaken them.' She looked at Leah for confirmation. 'All these white trainers look the same, don't they?'

Leah smiled. Said nothing.

Maria frowned. 'What's this about, Kat? Asking about my trainers?'

'Can you account for your whereabouts this morning? Between nine and when we arrived?'

Another frown. Deeper this time. 'Am I being watched or something? Am I *suspected* of something?'

'Please, Maria, just answer the question.'

'I got up, had a shower, all the usual. Had some breakfast. Then I went into my study and I started work on my novel. I came downstairs at about five past eleven to make myself a coffee. Took it back upstairs. And I was there when you rang the doorbell.'

'Can anyone confirm any of that?'

Maria shrugged. 'My agent called at 11.30 a.m. We spoke for about half an hour. I remember because I was anxious to get back to the book. I'd just solved a tricky little plot point, you see, and I wanted to work through it. But other than that . . .' She bit her lip. Then her eyes brightened. 'Oh! The postman – well, postwoman really – called at 10.45 a.m. or thereabouts to drop off a parcel. Why are you asking? What's happened?'

No harm in telling her, Kat reasoned. *It might be interesting to get her reaction.*

'At some point this morning, Justin Davy was murdered.'

Maria's eyes widened. 'I can't believe this. You're saying Justin has been murdered? How? When?'

'We don't have the precise time yet, but we believe it's the same person who murdered Mark.'

Maria pulled her head back. 'Wait. You're not . . . I mean, you don't think *I* killed Mark, do you? Is *that* what you're saying?'

'We're just following up every lead we have. You used to be married to Mark. You had a professional connection to him. You were in the vicinity of the place where he was murdered.'

Maria's eyes widened. 'Yes, but so were hundreds of other people.'

'Did you know Justin well?'

'He and Mark were best friends from way back and he did Mark's covers. We used to meet Justin and Cheryl for dinner from time to time. Go over to each other's houses, that sort of thing. Oh my God! Poor Cheryl. Have you told her yet? Maybe I could do it for you. It would be better coming from me.'

'I spoke to her earlier. So, Maria, can you think of anyone who might have wanted to harm Justin? Maybe not to murder him necessarily, but someone who had an axe to grind. Professionally, maybe?'

'No, not really. Justin was just, you know' – she sighed heavily – 'I don't mean this in a rude way, but Justin was Mr Average, you know? A nice guy.'

'Cheryl said his business wasn't doing so well. Are you aware of him owing money to anyone?'

'No. They have plenty of money. Cheryl's really successful. He had his pride, what man doesn't? But he was doing OK, I think.'

'Thanks, Maria. Sorry to have to be the bearer of such sad news. Cheryl could probably do with some support, so if you do have time to give her a call . . .'

'I'll do it right now. I can go over. Make tea. That's what everyone always says, isn't it. God, we British are so predictable.'

Kat got to her feet. 'Just one more thing. Would it be all right if we had a quick look around inside? Just to satisfy ourselves you don't have an old pair of Converse at the back of a wardrobe. Maybe you forgot you had them.'

Maria sat bolt upright. Her mouth dropped open. 'I *beg* your pardon. You just rock up on my doorstep and tell me a friend of mine's been murdered, and now you want to search my house when I already told you I don't have a pair of the bloody things? No you can't have "a quick look around". I've got a friend who's grieving for her husband, so if you'll excuse me I'm going to call her. I need you to leave now, please.'

Back on the street, which was bouncing sunlight and heat back at them from every hard surface, Kat turned to Leah, puffing out her cheeks. 'Well, that went well. Did you pick up anything?'

Leah shook her head. 'She appeared genuinely shocked. Alibi's paper-thin, but that goes for probably ninety per cent of them, doesn't it? You reckon Linda'd authorise a search warrant?'

Kat put on a wicked impersonation of Linda's voice. '"Christ, Kat, if we're going to start searching the home of every six-footer with a pair of Converse, that's going to include my cousin Julie."'

Leah snorted. 'Not bad. So, what next?'

Kat squinted up at the sun, which was pounding the top of her head like a mallet. 'I can't think straight in this heat. Let's find somewhere cool to talk. I need to try and put some sort of shape to all this, Leah. I'm a hundred per cent sure we've already interviewed the killer.'

'Sounds good to me. Where?'

Kat smiled as an idea formed in her head. 'You might not like it.'

Chapter Fifty-Three

Kat turned in the breeze wafting down from the overhead vents, and sighed with relief as the stream of chilled air dried the sweat on the back of her neck.

Behind her, a body lay under a green sheet. Jack was sitting in a corner writing a report. His shirtsleeves were rolled up and she tried to avoid glancing over at his tanned forearms.

Leah caught her looking. Raised her eyebrows. Then grinned mischievously. 'You all right, Kat? Shall I get Dr Beale to take a look at you?'

Kat shot her a warning look, full of *don't you dare* vibes.

'So, Leah,' Kat said, breaking the spell, 'where are we on the Mark Swift murder?'

All business now, Leah frowned. 'Plenty of people really didn't like Mark. No alibis worth their salt. They were all at *Criminal Herts* at the time he was murdered. And given he had his head bashed in and was then drowned in his own rider, means wasn't a problem.'

'Out of the people you and Fez interviewed, did anyone not consent to a DNA sample?'

'Amy Swales. Told us she'd written enough crime novels to know we had to arrest her if we wanted one.'

Kat sighed. Maybe she should have arrested Amy when she had the chance.

'What about the other one? The one who said Mark stole his idea?'

'Richard Bannister? Yeah, he was fine with it.'

'Right. So if we can find some evidence from either crime with DNA on it, we might be able to get somewhere that way. Which reminds me. Danny Elliott's DNA will be on file.'

Leah frowned. 'The thing I'm not getting is the difference between the two murders. Mark's looks like it happened in the moment. The killer used whatever was to hand.'

'Whereas whoever killed Justin took a carving knife with them.'

'Exactly. It's like they decided in advance to kill him. Why?'

Kat changed her position slightly to catch the chilled air on her face as she tried her theory out on Leah.

'What if Justin was blackmailing them and they couldn't or wouldn't pay.'

Leah nodded. 'Makes sense. At this point they're too far in. They're not a professional, clearly, so we can assume they're panicking, probably not thinking straight. They've killed once, and now they're going to be exposed and go to prison or have to fork over the kind of cash they either don't have or can't raise without really being noticed. Like remortgaging their house or something.'

Something Leah said sparked a new line of thinking in Kat's brain. Had they been approaching this all wrong from the very beginning, seduced by the sheer number of Mark Swift's enemies?

'Leah, you just said Mark's killer wasn't a professional, right?'

'Yeah. I mean, if it was any kind of professional hit, the killer would have taken a weapon with them.'

'So we're looking for an amateur. But what if they weren't just an amateur?'

'What do you mean?'

'I mean, what if they never meant to kill him?'

Leah's brows drew together. 'Not being funny, Kat, but if you lamp someone on the back of the head with a bottle and then shove their head down into a bucket of water, that kind of is deliberate.'

'Sorry, let me try again. What I'm saying is, look at other "amateur" murders. Back when I was in uniform, the first three murders I attended. One was a bloke who punched his best friend in an argument over who was going to call an Uber. One was a man who murdered his wife in a drunken rage and then called it in himself to confess. And the last was a woman who found out her sister-in-law was cheating on her brother. She wanted her sister-in-law to tell her brother and she refused, and as she put it, "things just got out of hand".'

'What's your point, Kat?'

'My point is, what if Mark's killer murdered him the same way? Things just got out of hand. They had an argument but they never meant it to go that far. In fact, what if it wasn't an enemy at all? What if it was like those murders I just told you about? A friend, a husband, a sister-in-law.'

Leah had begun shaking her head as Kat was speaking. 'That works fine for Mark. But you just said yourself, whoever killed Justin went there intending to do it. Although it can't have been Bella.'

'Why?'

'Even if she had reason to kill Mark because he raped her wife, she's not tall enough to have stabbed Justin at the required angle. What did Jack say, sixty per cent?'

At the mention of his name, Jack swivelled his head round.

'Sorry, Detectives, I couldn't help listening in a bit. Would you like my input?'

'Sure, Jack,' Kat said. 'Seeing as we keep running into brick walls, if you can find the hole we can aim for that would be great.'

Jack sauntered over to them. 'Leah's right. The fatal wound track was at sixty degrees to the horizontal. Assuming, and I don't think it's too much of a stretch, that Justin was standing when he was stabbed, at least for the first time, the killer would have to be around six foot tall. Maybe more. But it's not just about their height. Now, they got lucky, if that's the right word, and the blade slid cleanly between the victim's ribs. No cuts to the bone and the blade entered on a straight, unvarying trajectory until it stopped when the bolster hit the chest. Next time you're cooking a roast chicken, try it when it's raw. Sticking a knife into a dead, unresisting piece of meat to a depth of thirteen centimetres in one clean blow takes a lot of force and commitment. Now imagine it's a *live* piece of meat. A *person*. You're looking for someone tall, muscular and with sufficient motive – hatred, I should say – to do it and not make a mess of it.'

'Looked quite messy from when I saw it, Doc,' Leah deadpanned.

'If you have any suspects who fit the bill physically, I'd start with them.'

'Thanks, Jack, that's really helpful,' Kat said.

'Any time, Kat,' he said with a smile before returning to his desk. Kat turned back from observing Jack to find Leah grinning at her, head to one side.

'Richard Bannister's well over six feet,' Leah said. 'He's solid, too. Told me he used to play rugby.'

'So is Danny Elliott. Let's get back to Jubilee Place and see if we can dig up a bit more on them. Maybe Richard volunteered DNA because he thought he'd been careful. And Danny was job. He's probably got a tattoo reading "Forensically Aware".'

Outside, in the hospital car park, the heat radiating off the tarmac and bringing a sheen of sweat to Kat's forehead, she sensed Leah looking at her. She turned. Smiled.

'What?'

Leah waggled her eyebrows. 'Any time, Kat,' she said in a gruff voice. 'Maybe I could share my latest findings with you over a chilled glass of Chardonnay.'

Kat punched her on the shoulder. She'd dealt with her feelings towards Jack Beale ages ago. Or thought she had.

And besides, thanks to his insight they had something solid to investigate. Three options, in fact. Either Richard Bannister or Danny Elliott had killed Mark in a fast-accelerating row, or it wasn't one of Mark's many enemies at all.

And, as the sun began cooking her already overheated brain all over again, she saw it. The alternative.

Two people they'd interviewed hadn't had any beef with Mark. His second wife, Maria Sheriff, who also happened to be tall, and his current wife, Saskia, who wasn't. What if one of them had found out about the allegations against Mark? Maybe from Dorothy Russell?

She tossed the Golf's keys to Leah. 'Can you wait for me? I need to ask Jack one more question.'

Ignoring Leah's amused look, Kat ran back towards the mortuary suite.

Jack looked up as Kat banged through the double doors. 'Everything all right?'

'Yes, sorry for making you jump. Look, I'm not questioning your PM report or conclusions, but is it possible Justin Davy's killer wasn't a six-footer?'

He nodded. 'Of course it is. Off the top of my head? Maybe Justin was kneeling when they stabbed him. Maybe they were standing above him. On a wall, a chair or even an upturned box. Maybe they jumped. Maybe they just used some weirdly unusual striking technique from right overhead. Maybe he was running towards them, head down.'

'Wow. Quite the imagination, there, Doc.'

'I aim to please.' But then his smile dropped away and he sighed. 'The truth is, Kat, all I have to work with is the body before me. Wounds, debris, trauma, historic injuries, signs of disease. I can offer you an informed opinion based on what I see, but at the end of the day, that's all it is. An opinion. I won't lie to you, I've been wrong before. I probably will be again. I wish I could give you a definitive answer. But there are too many cautionary tales of celebrity forensic pathologists getting it wrong and messing up big cases.'

Kat felt a sudden warmth towards Jack. He wasn't usually one to share any signs of vulnerability. She'd always thought of him as one of those arrogant members of the medical profession who looked down their noses at mere detectives. Yet here Jack was, admitting to being fallible. She was about to rib him about it then swerved: *No. Not fair.*

'So could it have been, for example' – she pictured Saskia Swift – 'a woman of around five foot six?'

'It could. But the rest of what I said still holds, and I'm a lot surer about that. If it was a woman, and a shortish one at that, she would have had to be extremely focused and determined to plunge a knife all the way in to the hilt.'

'Thanks, Jack, that's really helpful.' She turned to go but then curiosity got the better of her. 'How was the jazz festival?'

He smiled. 'Fantastic. Gina and I try to catch a festival once a year.'

She swallowed.

'Gina?'

'Yeah. It was her choice this year.'

'Cool,' she said. *Cool? Really?* She sounded like a youthful vicar going for a down-with-the-kids vibe. So, Jack had a jazz-loving girlfriend. Disappointment and jealousy curdled in her chest. She

309

chided herself. *She* had a lovely husband who shared her love of nineties pop.

She hurried back to rejoin Leah, anxious to get back to the station. She had some legal work in mind.

Because what if Saskia had got a look at her husband's will, and found out she wasn't in it after all?

Chapter Fifty-Four

Kat gathered her team around her desk. Everyone looked hot and sweaty. The windows were open, but all they let in were the screech of concrete saws from a building site across the street and more hot, humid air.

'Tom, what have you got on Richard Bannister's socials. Anything particularly inflammatory?'

He nodded, consulted his screen, fingers flying over the keyboard.

'Yes. Here we go. From a few years ago. "Shame it wasn't @ Mark_Swift_Author lying dead in a pool of blood on p1 of *Sentence of Murder*." He added two hashtags. PoeticJustice and PlotThief.' Tom looked up from his screen. '*Sentence of Murder* was the one Richard Bannister accused Mark of stealing his idea for. Incidentally, the plot is all about a serial killer murdering famous authors.'

'Yeah, but Justin Davy wasn't famous or an author, was he?' Fez said. 'He was a cover designer.'

Tom's lips tightened into a line. 'All right, no need to shoot me down in flames. I was just answering the boss's question.'

Fez held his hands up. 'Sorry, our kid. I didn't mean nothing by it.'

'Yeah? Well, maybe do some detective work of your own before criticising everyone else's, yes?'

Kat stepped in. She chose to put Tom's out-of-character bickering down to the unrelenting heat and the new noise from the building site, a skull-pounding metallic thump once every three or four seconds. Although that niggling worry she'd had about his behaviour since coming round from his coma resurfaced.

'That's enough, boys. Tom, that's great, thank you. Can you find out whether Mark ever took any legal action in response to Richard's tweet, please? Fez, what have you got?'

Still shooting puzzled looks at Tom, Fez said, 'I've been working through the legal documents you seized off Sir Anthony Bone. I started with his third marriage. There's a pre-nup. Loads and loads of really complicated stuff about intellectual property rights. But the bit that jumps out so far is that Saskia didn't have any claim on royalties from his books if they got divorced.'

'So maybe she did if he died while they were married. What about the will?'

'Sorry, Kat, I've been so busy with witness statements and' – he shrugged – 'everything, I haven't got to it.'

'Well, could you, please? I really want to know what she stands to gain.'

He nodded quickly. 'Of course. I'm on it.'

'I know this contradicts what I just said, but I want you to reinterview Richard Bannister. Jack says it's not definitive that Justin's murderer was a well-built six-footer, but it's still the most likely explanation.'

The team dispersed. Kat stared at the murder wall. Three people were tall enough to have stabbed Justin. Maria Sheriff, Danny Elliott and Richard Bannister. The two men had motive. Maria only benefited by Mark being alive. He'd given her money in the divorce and continued speaking at the festival to help keep it viable.

As she stared at Maria's smiling face in the publicity shot, she frowned. '*Was* it amicable, though?' she asked aloud.

Maria had said it was. But now they had the paperwork from Sir Anthony Bone, Kat could check. She kicked herself for not having done it sooner.

She had just sat down at Fez's desk, intending to reread the fat file of legal paperwork when her phone rang. It was the POLSA, the police search adviser.

'Please say you found something,' she said.

'How would you like a pair of Converse Chuck Taylor All Stars, bloody soles and blood spatter on the tops, wrapped in an M&S carrier bag.'

'You're a legend! Where were they?'

'Where do amateurs always dump their stuff?'

'You're joking. Not a rubbish bin?'

'One of the ones round the back of Tesco near the river. It's a quiet enough spot and it's about three hundred metres from the Guildhall. What I'm thinking is, the killer stabs Justin Davy, then rushes away from the scene. They're in shock. They get somewhere quiet and look down and that's when they notice their trainers.'

'What size were they?'

'Nine and a half.'

Heart pounding with excitement, Kat punched the air. 'Tell whoever found them I'll buy them a coffee and a cake in Hati.'

Kat couldn't believe her luck. Finally, they had the kind of evidence that would send somebody to prison. The shoes would have Justin Davy's DNA on the outside, and, in all probability, his murderer's DNA on the inside, and maybe fingerprints, too.

All they needed now was to identify the owner and they were home. And any one of their three people of interest could have feet that size. They'd need to re-interview Danny Elliott, too.

Later that evening – after a snatched Chinese takeaway at her desk – Kat pulled the team into a huddle. The main news was that Richard Bannister was out of the frame for Justin Davy's murder.

'He was playing cricket all morning,' Fez said, with what Kat thought was an unseemly note of admiration. 'He's captain of his village team. Roughly a hundred witnesses. It wasn't him, boss. Sorry.'

Kat sighed as she crossed to the whiteboard and erased the purple line connecting Richard Bannister to Justin Davy. But at least she wouldn't have to pay for a DNA run.

'He could still have done Mark Swift, though,' Tom said.

Kat wrinkled her nose. 'You mean "murdered", Tomski?'

'Yeah, that's what I said. Jesus,' he hissed, half under his breath. 'Get the PC police in here pronto.'

Frowning, she carried on. 'He could have, but I'm not giving the two-killer theory any credence. Two best friends killed within a week and twenty feet of each other. No. It's one person. Which, people, sadly means we're still looking for our killer.' She checked her watch. 'It's after nine. Go home, get something nice to eat and a good night's sleep, and we'll start again first thing.' She clapped her hands. 'Off! Go home. I'll see you tomorrow.'

With the place to herself, she sat at her desk and started rereading witness statements from the moment Bella Gabbard had appeared in the ballroom at the Guildhall. She paused long enough to text Van to tell him she'd be late and then went back to it. Finally, as another yawn threatened to unhinge her jaw, she realised she had to call it a day.

Outside, the sky was still clinging on to daylight. But huge thunderheads the colour of fresh bruises were massed directly over Middlehampton like some unearthly mountain range.

Her car was parked right on the other side of the car park, about as far from the back doors of the station as you could get and still be inside the chain-link fencing.

Lightning crackled, and Kat smelled the seaside tang of ozone as the thunder boomed and rolled. She ducked reflexively and ran for the car. Rain sheeted down, drenching her in seconds, the shock of the cold water startling after the heat of a few minutes earlier.

She was almost at the Golf and fumbling for her keys. Already practising lines in her head to describe to Van the weirdness of the cloudburst.

And then a dark figure stepped out from behind the passenger side of her car.

Chapter Fifty-Five

Kat's pulse jacked up, and she instinctively pushed her keys out between her knuckles.

Then the figure emerged into the light cast by an overhead lamp. She swiped the rainwater out of her eyes and squinted as another gigantic flash of lightning lit up the car park like the floodlights at the Eels' London Road ground.

As the thunder slammed against her eardrums, Ethan Metcalfe smiled crookedly at her, his arms hanging loosely by his sides. He stood between Kat and her car door.

Lightning flashed again, reflecting off the lenses of his glasses and turning them pure white for a second. Thunder exploded close by, a hard, percussive noise like the flash-bangs the firearms team used to disorientate people.

Should she approach, or maintain a distance? No time for rational thought. She kept back, gripping her keys tighter still.

'What do you want, Ethan?' she shouted.

He held his hands wide, rain streaming off his fingertips.

'What do I *ever* want, Kat? To help.'

'I don't want your help, Ethan. I don't *need* your help.'

'But you haven't *caught* him yet, Kat. Of *course* you need my help! You can't keep on ignoring me. I have over two hundred thousand subscribers now. It's gone stratospheric. Ever since I was on Sky News. People all over the world are listening. I have *reach*!'

She thought what Ethan had was a borderline personality disorder. And an unhealthy interest in her cases. In *her*, full stop. Liv had been on at her for months, even playing her a clip from one of his shows where he'd actually said he loved her.

'Get away from my car, Ethan.'

'But, Kat,' he pleaded, his tone whiny, high-pitched. 'I know who it was.'

She swiped her hand across her eyes, which were stinging from so much rain pouring off her forehead. She was wet through and could feel the cold water soaking all the way through her trousers and into her knickers. Shivering violently, she folded her arms across her chest.

Could she afford to ignore Ethan when he'd just claimed to have solved it? It was a million-to-one chance, but she had to hear it.

Lightning flashed, and he looked up and grinned as the thunder cracked overhead.

'Who is it, Ethan?' she shouted, against her better judgement. 'Who killed Mark Swift and Justin Davy?'

He smiled – a sly, knowing expression. 'I can't tell you, can I? You'll just take all the credit.'

She shook her head. She was cold, she was drenched, and she was face to face with a man she realised she ought to have been calling her stalker for months.

'Three seconds, Ethan. Then I'm getting in my car. And if you make a move to stop me, I'll arrest you. One, two, th—'

'OK, OK!' he yelled as the rain lashed down, the fat drops bouncing back up off the tarmac with a crackling sound all of their own. 'But you have to give me an exclusive interview. Credit my help in solving it.'

'Tell me! Now!'

He smiled. 'It's Saskia. He's having an affair. She finds out. Speaks to motive. She confronts him in the green room. He denies it. They fight. She kills him. Justin was their best man. She suspects him of helping Mark cover up the affair. She lures him to the Guildhall and stabs him.' He held his arms wide and then, in a creepily accurate imitation of a meerkat from a TV ad campaign, said, 'Simples!'

'And you've got evidence for all this, have you?'

He shrugged. 'It's obvious.'

In that moment, she saw him as he really was. A sad, lonely man who'd somehow parlayed a local podcast show and his own obsessive personality into an international reputation as a true crime investigator. But it was all fantasy. Riley could have done as much after spending an hour or two online.

She strode right up to him. Looked into his face. 'I'm going home. Leave this car park and don't come back. If I see you here again, I'll arrest you. Now, step aside!'

He complied and she unlocked the door and slid down into the seat, pulling the door closed behind her and locking it for good measure.

Heart pounding, she slid the key into the ignition, started the engine and pulled away.

Behind her, Ethan remained still, outlined in the spray bouncing off his head and shoulders as the rain pelted him. She tried to ignore him, focusing on navigating the treacherous roads now running with free water as the drains struggled to cope.

If it was only Ethan, she thought she could probably cope, but it was just like Linda said: the town was overrun with true crime podcasters and amateur sleuths, piling in on social media with wild and unsubstantiated theories. Posting TikToks and badgering her for comment if they saw her in the street or outside Jubilee Place.

She merged into traffic on the main road leading to Stocks Green, peering ahead as the wipers struggled against the downpour. The only point where she thought Ethan might have been right was Justin Davy's role. Had he been covering for Mark somehow? They'd known each other since school. Like her and Liv. Those friendships ran deep. Look how far she'd gone to protect Liv from a charge of perverting the course of justice.

Still turning the idea over in her head, she arrived home and dashed from the kerb to her front door. She was inside seconds later, shaking her hair like Smokey after a bath.

Van was in the sitting room, watching TV.

'Hi, love,' he called out. 'You all right?'

She poked her head round the door, to give Van a good look at her bedraggled hair, which was dripping water on to the carpet.

'Got a bit damp, actually. I'm going up for a bath.'

'Want me to . . . join you?' he said, leering comically.

'Give me five then yes. I'll be naked, hot and wet, so' – she lowered her eyelashes and bit her lower lip – 'I'll need you to put my clothes in the washing machine.'

Leaving Van groaning good-naturedly, Kat went upstairs and ran a bath. Van was as good as his word, and after appearing in the bathroom, scooping up her sodden clothes and taking them downstairs, he was back with a glass of wine for her and a beer for himself.

'Here,' he said, handing her the wine. 'Cheers.'

'Cheers.'

She took a sip of the wine, then put the glass down on the corner of the bath, nerves making her stomach squirm.

'Van, there's something I need to tell you. Ought to have told you ages ago.'

He looked worried. 'Is everything OK? It's not about Liv, is it? Oh, Christ, what's she done now?'

Kat bridled. Why was *that* Van's reaction?

'No. It's not Liv. She's fine. *We're* fine.' She swallowed some more wine. 'You know that guy I was at school with? The one with the podcast Riley's always on about?'

Van frowned. 'Ethan Metcalfe. *Home Counties Homicide.*'

'Yep. Well, I think – actually I know – he's . . . well, he's stalking me.'

Van clonked his beer down on the floor and slid off the closed loo seat to kneel by the bath. He cupped her face in his hands and stared into her eyes.

'You're serious? I mean, this isn't a wind-up? I know how much you and Liv love taking the piss out of him.'

He gave her a searching look. She just waited, unable to say more until he saw it. That tonight's encounter had genuinely scared her.

'You *are* serious!' he said. 'Oh, Kat, why didn't you say something before?'

'I thought he was just some loser! Liv calls him an incel, but he was in the car park tonight, Van. I thought I was going to have to defend myself. I had my car keys ready in my hand and everything. I mean, Christ, as a girl you learn that trick the day you get your own front door key, but I never felt I'd really have to do it before tonight.'

'But what can you do? Can you report him? Is there, I don't know, an anti-stalking team?'

'There is. Abby's on it.'

'Abby?'

'Greene. She's a mate. I'll see if she's on shift tomorrow.'

'Good.' He shuffled closer, his knees cracking as he leaned over the edge of the bath to hug her bare shoulders. 'If he even *tries* to hurt you, I'll kill him.'

Kat pulled her head back so she could look at him, although this close up she couldn't bring him into focus. It was like having two worried Vans looking at her, not one. She went for a smile. Lightened her tone.

'Well, that wouldn't be any good, would it? Then I'd have to arrest you for murder.'

'Don't joke about it, love. These people can be dangerous.'

'I know, I know. I don't think Ethan's like that, but I will sort it out. I promise.'

'OK. I promise I won't worry, then.'

He sat back on the loo, drank some beer.

Kat climbed out of the bath and dried herself. She peered out the window. The rain had stopped.

'Fancy a dog walk? I really need to clear my head.'

Five minutes later, they were strolling arm in arm around the village. Smokey trotted contentedly at Kat's side, jerking her arm every ten yards as he found a new road sign or patch of weeds to sniff.

Kat drew in a deep breath. The smell of hot wet pavement flooded her nostrils. There was a word for it. She couldn't think of it. Didn't matter. She was out with Van and Smokes, she'd unburdened herself about Ethan. Maybe tomorrow would bring a break in the case.

She'd start with Justin Davy. There was more digging to be done there. Especially his friendship with Mark Swift. That was the link between the two cases.

It had to be.

DAY NINE – SATURDAY

Chapter Fifty-Six

On a Saturday morning when she had no active cases, Kat would enjoy a lie-in. Maybe start something under the covers with Van after their second cup of tea in bed.

No such luxury today. She was in work by 8.01 a.m. She found Abby in the canteen.

The PC's eyes brightened when Kat sat beside her.

'Hey! Don't tell me you're here to tell me my MCU rotation's come through?'

'Sorry, mate. Everything's gummed up at the moment. I haven't forgotten, though.'

'Thanks, Kat. It'll be so good to get the chance to learn off of you.'

'You won't be saying that when you see how much paperwork I have to complete,' Kat said. 'Anyway, look, can I talk to you professionally?'

'Of course!' Abby swung her chair round to face Kat. 'What is it?'

'Have you heard of Ethan Metcalfe?'

Abby's mouth twisted, like she'd bitten into a lemon. 'That sad little man. The crap he comes out with!'

'Yeah, well, I think he's—' Kat stopped.

She felt vulnerable all of a sudden, and a little ashamed she'd not been able to handle Mutt-calf on her own.

'He's what, Kat?' Abby asked. 'Oh, God, are you crying? Whatever it is, you'd better just tell me.'

Kat wiped her eyes on one of the tissues she reserved for victims of crime.

'He's stalking me, Abs. I've warned him and warned him but he won't stop.'

Abby became all business.

'Right, Kat. First of all, I want you to know that you've done nothing wrong. Whatever he's told you, whatever he's *suggested* to you, this is not on you,' she said, pulling her notebook from a pocket. 'You didn't send him signals or give him any kind of permission. You are not to blame. He is.'

Kat sniffed. 'Ah, thanks, Abs. I feel such an idiot for letting it get to this point.'

'No! You are a smart, clever, professional woman. He, on the other hand, is a sad loser committing a criminal offence. Now, I'm going to need you to write me up a report of everything he's done that you feel contributes to this complaint of stalking, yes? Dates, times, places. As much detail as you can remember. Once I have that, we'll arrange an interview for you, with me and one of the psychology team. After that, I'll pay him a visit and offer words of advice. If he does it again – doesn't matter how insignificant or explainable it seems – you report it to me. Then I will issue him with a police caution. If there's a repeat then it's out with the PAVA spray and the cuffs. How does that sound to you, Kat?'

'It sounds amazing, Abs. And thank you. I'm in the middle of a case right now, but I'll do it as soon as we're finished.'

Abby frowned. 'And you'll be all right until then?'

'Yeah.' Kat patted her shoulder bag. 'I've started carrying an Extendo all the time.'

'Good.' Abby raised her voice and spoke in a clear, authoritative tone of voice. 'Please remember, DS Ballantyne, that you may only use reasonable force in self-defence.' She dropped her voice to a conspiratorial murmur. 'But if he tries anything, smash the little bastard in the balls.'

◆ ◆ ◆

Feeling better, and safer, since her conversation with Abby, Kat made her way to MCU. Heading into the kitchen to make herself a coffee, she jumped as Fez came the other way.

'Morning, boss. Early start for you, too, eh?'

'Morning, Fez. Let's have a quick chat about the case, decide on tasks for the day.' She frowned. 'But before that, what do you think's going on with Tom? I'm not asking you to tell tales out of school. Just what you make of him.'

She wanted to say *and his weird behaviour*, but that might be considered prejudicial to the jury.

Fez took a sip of coffee as they walked back to his desk.

'Well,' he said finally, 'he's a nice bloke. A *really* nice bloke. And obviously what he went through on that last collar – well, that was bound to have an effect.'

'But?' she prompted.

'But sometimes he just comes out with something a bit, you know, off. Like yesterday. That business about the "PC police". He's fast-track, isn't he? That lot are much more right-on than your average jack, aren't they? Can't go through three years of uni without picking up some modern manners, can you?'

She smiled. She liked his sense of humour. And he'd zeroed in on the issue she wanted to talk about.

'He used to be, I don't know, a bit of an innocent. Peachy-keen, always sitting up straight whenever I asked him a question. Now, he's . . .'

'Cynical?'

'Yeah.'

'I can understand it, though, Kat. Guy gets attacked, and by a fellow officer at that, goes into a coma – well, it's not what we sign up for, is it? I mean, yeah, you expect to take a few knocks. But from villains, not another copper. Kind of shakes your faith a bit. It's like Naz, right? Patients can kick off sometimes. I'm not saying it's all right, but it happens. But if a junior doctor or a nurse gave her a mouthful, she'd really take it hard.'

'Look, this isn't your job, Fez, but could you keep an eye on him for me? He never used to drink and now he's started. I'm just a bit worried.'

'Sure.' He looked away. 'I can't, you know . . .'

'Be my spy? Don't worry. I don't want to hear all his secrets, and if he calls me a stroppy cow, I definitely don't need to hear that. But anything where you feel maybe he could use a little extra help with his recovery? Maybe then let me know. In strict confidence.'

'I can do that.'

'Thanks. Now. Murders. We need to solve this case before Linda's blood pressure puts *her* in hospital.'

'Right. Where do we start? Go back and look at all the persons of interest again?'

'I want to look at Mark, actually. He was a serial rapist. He was using his lawyer to silence his victims. I was wondering if he kept trophies. Locks of hair, underwear, Polaroids. But, when we looked round his office, it was all just squeaky-clean work stuff.'

Fez nodded, pursed his lips. 'He compartmentalises his life, right? Men like that, they have to lead double lives, you might

328

say. They can be married, professional men. Nobody knows. Not colleagues, not wives, not family.'

'Until it all comes out and everybody's horrified.'

'I've been wondering if he had a little bolthole somewhere. Where he decamped to when he needed to finish a book and he was blocked or whatever. A flat or a favourite hotel, or a cottage somewhere in the country.'

'And maybe that's where he kept his trophies.'

Fez nodded.

'I'm going to go over and talk to Saskia,' Kat said.

'What do you want me to do?'

'I want you to keep on at the legal documents we took from his lawyer. I'm sure we're going to find what we need in there. I also want you to go home for a couple of hours at lunchtime and spend some time with your family.'

'But—'

'That's an order, DC Mohammed.'

He grinned. 'Yes, Ma'am.'

Kat met Leah coming in as she was leaving.

'Morning, Kat. Off out?'

'Going to see Saskia Swift.'

'Need company?'

'I'm good. But Fez is in. I want you digging into Justin Davy's past. I want to know just how close his friendship was with Mark.'

'Sure. You back in later?'

'Try and keep me away.'

On the drive over to Bower Heath, Kat prayed Fez was right about Mark Swift having a bolthole somewhere, and that this wouldn't be another wasted morning chasing a dead end.

Chapter Fifty-Seven

By the time Kat parked on the gravel outside Saskia and Mark Swift's house in Bower Heath, it was as if the previous night's storm had been a figment of her imagination. The sky was a clear blue. The heat as she stepped outside nearly knocked her off her feet. And the air was so soupy it reminded her of Thailand.

When she rang the bell, Saskia appeared in the doorway properly dressed, with fresh makeup and her hair recently done. Altogether a different woman from the drunken wreck in stained pyjamas Kat and Fez had interviewed last time.

'Hi, Saskia,' Kat said. 'Can I come in?'

'Of course. Have you got some news?'

Kat followed her down the hallway, past the framed book covers and into the grand, airy and mercifully cool kitchen.

'Not precisely. But we are looking at a new line of enquiry that may lead us to the killer's motive.'

'Tea? Water?'

'Water, please.'

Saskia poured two tall glasses of water from a fancy tap that appeared to deliver at least three different kinds, and lifted her chin towards the table. They sat opposite each other.

'So what's this line of enquiry?'

'We wondered whether Mark had somewhere in addition to his study here where he did his writing. My DC called it a bolthole.'

'And this was your nice Muslim colleague who guessed, was it?'

Kat didn't know if she was being over-sensitive on Fez's behalf, but there was something in Saskia's tone that set her nerves jangling.

'Is he right? *Did* Mark have a place of his own?'

'He did, as a matter of fact. Gold star to DC Mohammed. It's an apartment in the Triton Building on Brock Street near Euston. He picked it because it's perfect for the trains from Middlehampton,' she said, as Kat made a note. 'I'm sorry if I didn't mention it before. I was in shock. Still am, I think, but my GP has given me some tablets and I feel pretty good now. Numb, but good. Like wearing a sort of emotional veil. I know I'll have to deal with it all, Kat, but not yet. I can't yet. Not until it's solved and I get some sort of closure.'

'I know, and I'm sorry. I want you to know, we're working flat out to find Mark's killer.'

'And Justin's.'

'His, too.'

'They're linked, right? That's your working assumption. They have to be.'

Kat nodded. 'That's my theory, yes. It's how I'm running the investigation.'

'But then who would want to kill them both? Mark made his fair share of enemies, but these literary disputes, Kat, they're not as out of control as they seem. It's all Twitter spats and outraged letters to the *London Review of Books*. Catty reviews of each other's novels. Snotty gossip at the Groucho Club or Soho House. People don't actually murder each other.'

Except, Kat wanted to say, they did. Maybe writers did it less than drug dealers, or gangsters. But they didn't get some exemption from the squalid mess of human emotions that led people to kill each other in depressingly large numbers.

If Fez were here he'd probably be able to name some famous writer who'd murdered their spouse or their drinking buddy, but she was on her own. And grappling with a huge problem. Just when, if at all, should she open up to Saskia about Mark's past as a serial rapist?

'Kat? I said why would anyone want to kill them?'

Kat felt terrible for what she was about to do to Saskia. It was time to tell her the truth about her husband.

Chapter Fifty-Eight

Kat took a quick breath.

'Saskia, did you know there's a group of women who all claim Mark raped them?'

Then she waited.

Chapter Fifty-Nine

Saskia straightened in her chair then leapt to her feet, her eyes wide and her lips drawn back from her teeth in a rictus. She dropped her glass, which shattered on the stone-flagged floor with a loud pop. Water splashed up, some hitting Kat in the face.

'*What* did you just say?'

Kat stayed sitting, even though her every instinct was to match Saskia's stance. She desperately needed her to calm down and stay a friendly witness. A complaint from a grieving widow to Linda or, Kat swallowed hard, the media – *And then she accused my murdered husband of being a multiple rapist!* – would cause the kind of waves that could capsize her career, however much evidence she could produce.

'Saskia, please sit down and let me explain.'

Saskia remained on her feet, but as Kat waited, the woman's lower lip trembled and she glanced upwards then out of the bifold doors, as if trying to avoid making eye contact.

'Please, Saskia,' Kat said in a soft voice, into which she injected as much quiet authority as she could muster.

Finally, Saskia pulled her chair out and sat, her slippered feet crunching on the shards of broken glass.

'You aren't serious,' Saskia said in a low voice. 'You can't be. Mark would never . . . I mean, our sex life was fine. He loved me. He was always telling me.'

Kat had experienced this sort of reaction before. Witnesses – especially family and friends – unwilling, or unable, to register the enormity of what they'd been told. It had happened to her when she was eighteen. Hearing from a female PC that Liv had been murdered. Denial, the psychologists called it. She just called it 'the wall'.

She tried to reach Saskia by taking the emotion out of it altogether. 'At this point, it's just a line of enquiry. I met these women and listened to their stories. Now, I don't have any evidence beyond their testimony, but at the very least it's something I'm duty-bound to follow up.'

'But, that's it, isn't it?' Saskia hissed. 'Testimony. It's how you catch them, isn't it? Historic sexual abuse. There never *is* any evidence.' Her eyes widened. 'Oh my God. That's why you wanted to know about Mark's flat. That's where he did it, isn't it?'

She was wringing her hands compulsively, turning her knuckles bone white as her long tapered fingers intertwined and rubbed over each other. 'This can't be happening, this can't be happening,' she mumbled. '*Mark* is the victim.'

Kat reached across the table and gently laid a hand on Saskia's. The other woman's fingers kept twisting, the knuckles rubbing unpleasantly against Kat's palm. She felt Saskia's pain as if it were her own. To have built a life with a man only to find out the foundations were sand, not rock. Swallowing down her revulsion at Swift's crimes, she focused on the tear-streaked face of the woman right in front of her.

'Saskia? Saskia! You're right. Mark *is* a victim. He was murdered. I am hunting his murderer. And Justin's. Now, *why* he was murdered may be something so awful we can't bear to think about it. But the truth is, whether or not he was guilty of the crimes these women are accusing him of, he is beyond the reach of the law now. All I can do is bring his murderer to justice.'

Saskia nodded. Her face had lost all the animation of earlier when she'd opened the door as a just-coping widow. With a single question, Kat had wrought the kind of havoc on her mind, and her memories of her husband, that might never heal.

Saskia pulled her hands free, placed them flat on the table and pushed herself to her feet with a groan. 'I'll get you the keys. And the address.'

She returned a few minutes later and handed Kat a leather key ring in the shape of a handful of books. It bore two keys. An Ingersoll and a Chubb. Then she scribbled an address on a piece of paper and handed it over wordlessly.

Kat thanked her and left, pointing the Golf towards London – and, she hoped, the identity of the murderer.

Chapter Sixty

After donning gloves, Kat opened the door to the penthouse. It swung closed behind her with a muffled click.

The wide, wood-floored hallway smelled faintly of polish.

With a feeling akin to the one she always experienced before a press conference, Kat pushed through a door. It opened into a large sitting room with picture windows looking out over the London skyline.

She tried another. A bedroom. Bed the size of a football pitch. Green and grey cushions covered in nubbly fabrics. Sun streaming in through more large windows.

No framed book covers here. What looked like expensive works of art. The subject matter made Kat's flesh crawl. Every painting depicted a nude or semi-nude woman, usually young-looking and pale-skinned. One read a book on a sofa in a sun-striped room. Another stood on a geranium-bedecked balcony looking down at the street. A third lay back on a bed – green and grey cushions – her fingers trailing between her legs. Kat squinted at the daubed signature in the bottom right corner of the nearest one. *J. Davy.*

The graphic designer had had a side line painting what he no doubt called 'erotic art'.

Swallowing down her disgust, she tried another door. A kitchen, bristling with high-end appliances, a sleek knife block and the kind of artfully placed utensil pots Kat saw when she occasionally picked up a cooking magazine in WHSmith.

And another door.

A wide, pale wooden desk faced a floor-to-ceiling window. From this one, she could just make out the London Eye in the hazy distance. Bookshelves lined one wall, mostly stacked with multiple copies of each of Mark Swift's books.

She sat in the sprung office chair behind the desk and tried the topmost drawer beneath it. It opened. Even though there was a lock. The pride of the man! So sure his little London eyrie, far away from Middlehampton, was secret that he'd not taken the most basic precautions. Not that, at this point, a lock would have stopped her.

Lying on top of a pile of pristine white paper was a black A5 notebook, held closed with a black elastic ribbon bound into the spine.

She opened it. The flyleaf was headed, in neat black capitals, *VOLUME 5*. With a trembling finger, she turned over the page.

The heading read, *Louise Murphy, 21, Bermondsey, London. Jan 7, 2024.*

What followed, as she read, nausea roiling in her gut, was a handwritten story in which a young woman was taken out for dinner by an older writer, who took her back to his penthouse and raped her. At the end was a string of letters and numbers Kat couldn't immediately understand: some sort of private code.

She turned the page. Another heading. *Ziporah Cohen, 24, Finchley, London. Feb 19, 2024.*

Barely able to read, she forced herself to skim the words, which were doubling in her misting vision, feeling as though she might throw up at any moment. With trembling fingers she scanned the rest of the book. There were more than a dozen entries before she finally came to a blank page.

Each entry concluded with one of those codes. Only they weren't random at all. As her emotions steadied, the characters stopped dancing in front of her.

The first read:

lm21BL010724

The young woman's initials, age, location and the date from the top of the page. Was it simply a code? Why, when the story was right there? But it had to stand for something. She assumed these were accounts of rapes Swift had carried out right here in this flat. But was she right? He had been a writer, after all. They could just be stories. Deeply unpleasant, disturbing stories, but stories all the same. She imagined a smooth-talking barrister making just such a suggestion to a jury.

She went back into the sun-filled bedroom. Looked around, scanning the ceiling, the walls, the headboard of the bed, the window frame. The pictures. But everything looked normal. Then, from the centre of a painting, a brief flash caught her eye. And she saw it in a patch of deep shadow beneath the girl's hip. A tiny lens reflecting the sun.

She gripped the frame on each side and carefully lifted it up and away from the wall. The lens stayed where it was, revealing a neat hole cut or drilled through the canvas.

She placed the picture on the bed and turned back to the wall. And there, sitting squarely in a cuboid niche, was a small digital camera, linked by a thin black lead to the lens.

He'd filmed himself. Now she had evidence, her gut steadied. She fell back on her training. And as her mind cleared, the meaning of the book codes jumped out at her. Not codes; file names. Of course. Swift had written up and recorded the rapes for his own twisted pleasure and transferred the videos on to his computer.

She strode back into the office and shuffled the mouse to wake up the computer.

It demanded a password.

Her fingers hovered over the keyboard. And then she looked down at the still-open desk drawer. Swift couldn't even be bothered to lock it. Would he take any more care over his computer password?

She pulled the keyboard closer and entered the eight-character password everyone in digital forensics joked about.

Password

The screen went black. Kat swore. Then it brightened.

Hello Mark!

She opened a file search window and typed in the first code from the notebook. A video file popped up immediately. Kat braced herself mentally and double-clicked.

A video player opened and then, in agonisingly clear detail, the event depicted in the notebook unspooled before her. She forced herself to watch to the end, by which time tears were flowing down her cheeks and plopping on to the clean, polished wooden desktop.

The folder that contained the video was subdivided into years and months. She opened each folder and began counting the videos. She reached twenty-seven before she stopped, rushed to the toilet and threw up.

Nose stinging, throat burning, eyes wet from tears, she splashed cold water on to her face, dried it, and then went back to the office.

She was sure, now. Mark Swift had been murdered in revenge for a rape he'd carried out. No other explanation made sense. But who had done it? Who had finally snapped? One of the victims? A mother? A father? A brother or sister? Her thoughts returned to Bella Gabbard. A wife? Everyone they'd spoken to had a solid motive.

The only two people who didn't were Saskia Swift, wife number three, and Maria Sheriff, wife number two.

Depending on who she asked, Maria's divorce had been either amicable or akin to the post-mating ritual of praying mantises. Mark had agreed to a generous settlement when they'd divorced, and she'd kept inviting him to the festival.

But what if Maria had discovered his crimes?

Saskia had seemed genuinely oblivious to them. As shocked in her own way when Kat had asked the question as Kat had been just now, watching that repellent video. But Kat hadn't asked Maria the same question.

If Maria had found out what Mark had been doing, she could have confronted him in the green room. He'd have been dismissive. Kat could almost hear him saying, *Do your worst. I'll sic Sir Anthony Bone on you. You'll be ruined and this won't even make it to court. Anthony will see to that.*

Perhaps she'd lost it. Murdered him in a fit of rage. Then hid in the Jacobean chest before fleeing via the hatch in the ceiling.

And what about Justin's murder? He must have seen her and put two and two together. Tried to blackmail her over Mark's murder. Cheryl had said his business was struggling, after all. Maria had agreed to meet him and then stabbed him. She'd run from the scene in her bloody Converse before dumping them. The knife would be down a drain somewhere, or at the bottom of the river. They might find it, they might not.

She called Leah. 'I need you to go and see Maria Sheriff, urgently. I want her fingerprints and a DNA sample.'

'You think it's her?'

'I'm not sure. Can you do it for me?'

'Of course. If she refuses do you want me to arrest her?'

'No. Not for now. I'm in Mark Swift's flat in London. He *was* a rapist, Leah. A *serial*. I've got evidence: at least twenty-seven videos. God knows what else we're going to find.'

'That's the motive, then. Those women in the whisper network must all be in the frame, too, surely?'

'I can't see it, I really can't. We know how rape affects women. It's only in films where they turn into vigilantes, carving up their attackers,' she said. 'Dorothy talked about how she wanted men to face justice for their crimes, not death.'

'Yeah, but that doesn't mean they all thought that way. Or even that she did.'

'I know, I know. But just for now, let's focus on Maria, yes?'

'Sorry, Kat. I was just, I mean, this is just . . .'

'I know. So just focus on your job, gather evidence, and we'll go where it takes us.'

She ended the call and left the flat, double-locking the door behind her. Before leaving, she called her Met contact and informed her what was happening. The Met officer agreed to send a team over to secure the scene. As the rapes had occurred in their jurisdiction it would fall to them to investigate those crimes, even though the perpetrator was dead.

Back on the street again, Kat headed towards her car.

At the corner of the street, she turned back and squinted up at the tower where Mark Swift had committed his crimes.

He had already met one form of justice. Now it was Kat's duty to bring his murderer in to face another.

And yet, as the sickening memory of the video set her stomach churning again, she resisted. Mark Swift, by any sane person's definition, had been a psychopath. A serial rapist who could easily have escalated to murder. Was she really going to ignore that, and arrest his killer? A person who was likely morally justified in what they had done?

Or could she run the clock, and the budget, down? Take the flak from the brass before the heat went out of the case as it surely must out of the weather? Wait for the inevitable new case, with its own victim clamouring for justice from the grave?

She stood there for a full minute, barely aware of the people flowing past her, some gazing at her curiously before moving on and chalking it down to 'just a London thing'.

Finally, with a heavy heart, she moved. She'd made her decision. She just prayed she could live with it.

Chapter Sixty-One

Kat re-entered MCU. She'd spent the drive back from London planning the endgame in her hunt for Mark and Justin's killer.

In that long moment outside the Triton Building, she'd realised that if her life was to have any meaning, she had to choose the law, not natural justice. She was no vigilante. Not even a renegade. She was a cop. A detective. She'd do her duty and deal with the consequences.

Leah came over to Kat's desk with an A4 image flapping in her hand.

'Kat! You have to see this. I called the *Echo*. I thought maybe they'd had a photographer at *Criminal Herts*. They didn't. Budget cuts apparently. But they bought some photos off a freelancer. Look at this one.'

Kat accepted the printout and switched on the bright desk lamp she'd brought in from home. Essential for those late-night reading sessions.

The photo had captured two young women with their heads thrown back, laughing. One wore a red-and-white polka-dotted headscarf, the other had a full sleeve of tattoos on her right arm. They both carried *Criminal Herts* totes bulging with books.

Kat squinted. The tattooed woman was holding a beer bottle. Her friend had a glass of wine. 'What am I looking at, Leah?'

'Not the girls,' Leah said, crouching beside Kat and stabbing a finger at a dark corner of the photo. 'Who does that look like?'

Kat peered at the blurry part of the image. A tall, well-built man stood with his face half turned towards the camera. He was standing at the entrance to the herringbone-brick passage that led to the back of the green room. His biceps were encircled with tattoos. He was smoking a cigarette. And he bore an uncanny resemblance to Danny Elliott.

'He has to be worth another visit, don't you think?' Leah asked.

'I do. But not solo, this time. You up for it?'

'Absolutely.'

'But wear something loose. Something that'll cover a Taser.'

Chapter Sixty-Two

When Danny opened the door of his flat and took in Kat and Leah standing there, his welcoming smile vanished.

'Two of you?'

'Danny, something's come up and I'd really like you to come down to Jubilee Place to discuss it,' Kat began. She knew her next proposition would be met with a rebuff, but she had to suggest it anyway. 'I'd like to invite you to come in for a voluntary interview under caution.'

'Not going to happen,' he said, folding his arms. 'You want me in your nick, you're going to have to arrest me. And I doubt you've got sufficient evidence. Nice try but it's a no from me.'

Kat disagreed with Danny. She had evidence. Circumstantial, but enough for an arrest. She had one last try for a voluntary interview.

'I really can't persuade you?'

'Nope.'

He gripped the door and made to close it.

Kat stuck her hand out and stopped him. Beside her, Leah took a step back and did something subtle with her hand in the region of her right hip.

'Danny Elliott, I am arresting you on suspicion of the murder of Mark Swift.'

For once, Danny didn't interrupt her. He listened, open-mouthed, as she recited the caution and then asked him to turn around while she cuffed him.

She and Leah led him back to the car.

'You're making a big mistake,' he growled from the back seat as she passed the halfway point to Jubilee Place.

She ignored him.

'I'll have your badge.'

She ignored this as well.

'Fucking plonks.'

Pulse throbbing in her neck, she checked her mirror, indicated, and pulled over smoothly at the side of the road. Turned around in her seat and eyeballed him.

'I'd rather be a plonk than a prick, Danny. Now have you finished or do you have more to say?'

She held his gaze – dark, hostile eyes boring into hers. The attack by Will Paxton had been shocking at the time, but it had tempered Kat's always-rebellious spirit into something far harder and stronger. No way was another violent cop, current or ex, going to intimidate her.

Danny broke eye contact first. Stared out the window and mumbled, 'Come on then. Let's get it over with.'

Twenty minutes later, Danny was booked in and calling his lawyer. Kat left him in the cells to stew for a while.

Danny Elliott sat beside his solicitor. Kat knew Ben Short – he'd helped her out when she'd been facing the corruption charge, but now here he was on the other side of the table. They exchanged the briefest of nods.

The preliminaries out of the way, Kat pushed the photo across the table to Danny.

'For the record, I am showing Danny Elliott a photograph taken at 10.43 a.m. on Friday, July 19th, 2024. Danny, can you take a close look at the man in the background? That's you, isn't it?'

Danny pulled a pair of reading glasses from his jacket pocket and placed them on his nose. He peered at the photo. Wrinkled his nose. 'Could be anybody.'

'Come on, Danny. That's clearly you. You're standing less than twenty metres from where Mark Swift was murdered at or around the time it happened.'

'You've already had an answer, Detective Sergeant,' Ben said.

'You've shown up in one photo, Danny,' Kat said, readying a bluff. 'You'll turn up in others. Clearer, too. We're going through them all at the moment. It's a long job, but you remember what detective work is like, don't you? Long hours poring over screens, CCTV, all that. But if it's there, we find it, don't we?'

He looked sideways at Ben, then at Kat. Most of the hostility had gone, replaced with a tired expression. Was he about to break? Had the pressure of concealing his crime finally got to him? Was it going to be that simple?

She kept her breathing slow and steady.

'I remember now,' Danny said. 'I popped in for a bit on the Friday morning. But everyone was too busy gossiping to talk to me so I decided to leave. I'd just lit up when that photo was taken. I left a few minutes later. You won't find me in any more photos.'

It sounded like the truth. But she wasn't satisfied. Not yet.

'You told me you didn't attend *Criminal Herts*. Why did you lie to me, Danny?'

'Why do you think?' he said loudly. 'I knew you'd find out about my dispute with Swift. And my record. A violent ex-cop with a big-money grudge against the deceased? If I gave you opportunity as well, I knew what would happen.'

'Do you own a pair of Converse Chuck Taylor All Stars?'

He frowned. Looked genuinely surprised by the question. 'I'm a bit old for baseball boots.'

'Is that a yes or a no, Danny?'

'No.'

The interview was going nowhere. She was grasping at straws. Maybe one last lunge, then. See if she could poke a sore point. Get him to lose it.

'Did you kill Mark Swift, Danny? Did it get too much, being there, knowing he'd be on stage in a few minutes, crowing about his success? Success he'd built on screwing you out of your rightful fee?'

Danny didn't even wait for Ben to admonish Kat for badgering his client. He favoured her with a level gaze. And, in her opinion, told her the truth.

'No. I did not.'

That was that. She'd hardly expected him to give her a confession based on such flimsy evidence. And with nothing else in her bag, she had no option.

She de-arrested him. Another suspect eliminated. Her list of possibles was shrinking.

Chapter Sixty-Three

Leah called over to Kat as soon as she entered the busy confines of MCU.

'Maria refused to give her prints or her DNA. She cited her human rights and claimed we were trying to set her up,' she said. 'She went off on this long rant about being suspicious of the police given the recent convictions of Couzens and Carrick.'

Kat frowned. 'That's not what she said when I spoke to her the first time.'

'So what do we do now?'

'If I'm right, and it's a big "if", Maria found out about Mark's crimes. But I can't see her getting access to his London flat. So how would she have known?'

'How about the whisper network?'

'I'll talk to Dorothy Russell again.'

Back at her desk, Kat called Dorothy.

'Hey, Kat. Any progress?'

'I think so, yes. Can I ask you whether Maria Sheriff is a member of your network?'

Dorothy made a noise halfway between a cough and a snort of derision. 'Her? I personally called her and told her what her husband was doing. She acted all horrified. Or maybe she actually *was*, I don't know. But she denied her husband had a bad bone in his body and refused to have anything to do with me. She even threatened me with legal action if I went public.'

'And can I ask, when was this?'

'Seven years ago. That's when I set up the network.'

Kat thanked Dorothy, then ended the call.

Dorothy had supplied an important piece of evidence. Maria Sheriff had known about Mark's crimes well before his murder. But also a question. If she'd known for seven years, why had she only decided to act now? Kat checked the various witness statements. Maria and Mark had divorced six years ago. Was that why? It would explain the nature of the settlement. She'd confronted him. He'd denied it. She'd told him about Dorothy's call. He'd doubled down. Finally, he'd resorted to his usual MO. Money and threats. Which brought Kat straight back to Sir Anthony Bone.

She looked around for Fez. He was emerging from the kitchen, two mugs in his right hand. He put one down in front of Leah, then carried on to his own desk.

Kat hurried over. 'Fez. Did you finish up with those legal papers?'

He nodded. 'Oh, did I ever. I was just about to come and find you. It's all there in black and white.'

'Give me the headlines.'

'Number one, Mark Swift's will. Everything goes to Saskia. The money, the royalties, the copyrights. She's a rich woman. Or she will be shortly.'

'I thought you said she *didn't* get the royalties?'

'Nah, that's only if she divorced him. The pre-nup, remember?'

'Right, so now she gets everything,' Kat said, frantically recalibrating her suspicions about Mark's third wife. 'If he'd tired of her, or she him, she'd have got something, but not the whole kit and caboodle.'

'You think that's the motive after all?'

'I don't know. She gave me alibis for both murders. Can you double-check them both, please?'

'Sure. You want the other headline? It's a killer. Pun intended.'

'Go on.'

'I went through Mark and Maria's divorce settlement. It's not a pre-nup. More of a post-nup-slash-NDA. Basically, she got a decent whack of money and his ongoing support for the festival, and she had to keep quiet about him and the accusations made against him. Anything outside his books or writing process was verboten.'

Tom came over. 'Morning, Kat. Anything for me to do?'

'Yes. I'm almost certain Maria Sheriff murdered Mark and Justin. But the one piece of evidence I can't find is the container she used to drown Mark in. There's nothing in the green room big enough. So whatever it was, she must have taken it with her when she left. Which she did via a hatch in the ceiling.'

'You know I can't leave the station. I mean, I'd love to, believe me, but occie health are one step away from fitting me with an ankle tag as it is.'

'No. I don't want you to go over there. I want a photo. Sometime between 11.00 a.m. and let's say 6.00 p.m., she must have come out somewhere. Now, maybe she left the bucket or whatever it was behind, but I need to be sure. People under stress like she would have been, they're not thinking straight, so maybe she held on to it.'

'But there's no CCTV at the Guildhall.'

'I know, Tomski. So I need you to get creative. Find a list of delegates or visitors or whatever they're called and call round. See if you can get their selfies. Maybe Maria's in the background.'

'There's hundreds of them! It'll take forever.'

This wasn't like Tom. Arguing, pushing back on a task. Where was her eager-beaver rookie DC? She wondered whether occie health had dropped the ball letting him come back to work, even on desk duties.

'Look, we're investigating two linked murders, and believe me, after what I discovered this morning, at least twenty-seven rapes. So make a start, yes?'

'Fine.'

He slouched off, shoulders down, and slumped into his chair with a huge sigh. It could have been Riley that Kat was watching, not a grown man. In fact, now she came to think about it, some of his changed behaviour was more like a teenager's. Kat looked at Fez. He shrugged.

Making a mental note to talk to a neurologist about Tom, she returned to her own desk. All she needed was a single piece of evidence to arrest Maria, and then she'd be able to get her prints and a DNA sample – whether she trusted the police or not.

One piece of evidence.

Kat stood in the centre of the team's group of desks.

'Change of plan. Without evidence, we can't arrest Maria Sheriff. Without an arrest, we can't get any evidence. We can't search her house without a warrant and there's no way I'll get one of those either. And Maria's not going to throw her front door open wide and let us have a "little look around".' She scanned their faces. 'Thoughts?'

'You searched Swift's place, but we haven't done Davy's yet,' Tom said. 'Maybe you'll find a connection to Maria.'

'Yes, good idea, Tomski. All right, Fez, with me. Tomski, you and Leah split the photo search.'

She took the stairs at a brisk clip down to the ground floor, Fez clattering along behind her.

Chapter Sixty-Four

The canal gurgling and sloshing through the gates behind them, Kat rang the doorbell of Lock Cottage.

She hoped Cheryl would be more accommodating about a search than Maria Sheriff. The door opened.

'Hi, Cheryl,' Kat said, 'can we come in?'

Cheryl stood aside as the two detectives squeezed past her and walked down the tiled hallway.

'I know it's no consolation,' Fez said, when they reached the kitchen, 'but I'm a massive fan of your husband's cover artwork. Really evocative.'

Cheryl dipped her head. 'Thank you. He was very talented. He wanted to be a proper artist when he was at university but' – she shrugged listlessly – 'you know, bills don't pay themselves, so he put his dreams aside.'

Kat shuddered as an image of one of the paintings in Mark Swift's flat swam queasily before her eyes.

'We were wondering whether we could have a look round Justin's studio. Did he work from home or did he rent somewhere?'

Cheryl nodded towards the second door leading out of the kitchen.

'It's through there. Help yourselves.'

'Thank you. Come on, Fez. Gloves on.'

She led Fez out of the kitchen.

Behind her, Cheryl turned the tap on.

'I'll make tea.'

Where Mark Swift's writing room had been pristine, Justin's studio was cluttered. A drawing board occupied one corner facing the window. A smaller desk with an iMac was squeezed into a space between two filing cabinets. Paper proofs of book covers were taped to every vertical surface, some clearly marked 'draft' by hand in coloured pen.

Fez seemed transfixed, staring at each one in turn. 'Classic psychological thriller,' he muttered, pointing to a cover depicting a suburban semi at night, one upper window lit, the title blazing out in fluorescent yellow below the author's name.

Others showed rough-looking men holding improbably large pistols, occult symbols, cute cartoon couples embracing outside sweetshops, women in 1940s outfits staring at steam trains and, most disturbingly of all, a small pink shoe lying on its side on a road glistening with rain, a dark silhouetted figure in the background.

'You take the filing cabinets,' Kat said. 'I'll make a start on the desk. I struck lucky once today, maybe I will again.'

'Two's the charm, eh, our kid? Ooh, this is interesting.'

'What?'

'It must be the last Mark Swift. It's not out yet.'

'Yeah, they'll probably want to hold off on the big publicity campaign for that one.'

Kat sat at the desk and began pulling open drawers. Nothing but stationery items in the uppermost. She took out the plastic tray. Beneath it were a few punched-out circles of coloured paper and a scattering of single staples.

The next drawer down held a tangle of cables, chargers, old remote controls, desk mics and power leads. Van had one just like it at home. She gave it a desultory poke then shut the drawer. No, wait. What was that at the back?

She pulled it open again. What she'd taken for a TV remote was a blocky old phone. Tiny screen and proper clickable buttons. She thumbed the power button and the green screen immediately flashed and flickered into life.

'I've got something here, Fez,' she muttered as she worked through the various menus.

'Me, too. You're going to want to see this, Kat.'

She turned away from the phone. Fez was holding out an A4 printout of a book cover.

'*The Guilty Party*,' Kat read aloud. 'So this was his final book.'

'I'm not so sure it was. Look at the quote at the bottom.'

The yellow text was on a grey background. Kat started reading.

'His best yet.' G.D. Evans

'Swift has done it again.' Rob Kershaw

'If I'm dead, talk to Maria Sheriff.' Justin Davy

Kat looked at Fez. 'It's not a book at all. It's a dead man's declaration.'

He nodded. 'Looks like it. What have you got?'

'Looks like a burner. Hold on.'

She clicked through to the phone book. It contained a single mobile number. Pulse tripping along, Kat pressed the Call button.

While it rang, she looked up from her chair at Fez. He returned her gaze. Two cops on the point of a breakthrough.

The line clicked. Kat jerked upright in the chair as the phone's owner answered.

'Hello, this is Maria. Who is this?'

Kat clicked the red phone button and got to her feet.

It was almost over.

Chapter Sixty-Five

Fez thunked his door closed as Kat started the engine.

'Right. Let's get over there and put the cuffs on her.'

'Hold on. If we go in all hot and heavy, I'm worried she'll just clam up and call her lawyer.'

His eyebrows drew together.

'Boss, you've got clear evidence that she murdered one man, and the cover text makes that possibly two. We have to go now and arrest her.'

'No, Fez. I can see how this will go, believe me. Give me the cover printout. I'm going to drop you off at Jubilee Place. Get the arrest warrant sorted. Talk to Tom and Leah. See if they've had any joy finding a picture of Maria coming out of the Guildhall after Mark was discovered.'

'What are you going to do?'

'I'm going to go and talk to Maria on my own. And hopefully, when she's told me what I want to know, I'll arrest her.'

Fez argued virtually the whole way back to the station, only desisting when she ushered him out of the car.

'Warrant!' she called after him.

She turned the car round and set off for Maria's house in Mortimer Grove. If, as seemed increasingly likely, this entire case had been leading back to Mark Swift's crimes, a woman-to-woman approach might reap richer rewards than the bite of a pair of handcuffs.

◆　◆　◆

Kat had barely taken her finger off the doorbell when Maria appeared. She looked flustered, red-faced, a film of sweat on her forehead.

Kat took a step forwards. 'Can I come in, please? There's something I need to talk to you about. It concerns Mark.'

Maria frowned. 'Can't it wait? I've just got going on my novel.'

'I'm afraid not. May I come in?'

'Well, yes, I suppose so. Will it take long?' Maria asked, turning to lead Kat into the kitchen.

'Not too long, I hope.'

'Coffee?'

'No thanks.'

They sat facing each other across the table. Kat could see a silver laptop open on the table in the garden, shaded by a banana palm. She tried to keep her breathing slow and steady, but inside, butterflies screeched round her belly like wall-of-death riders.

'What's your book about?' Kat asked. 'More murder and mayhem?'

Maria stared out of the window. 'Actually, I ditched that story. I've decided to move away from crime. It's so depressing, don't you think? I'm shifting into romance. This is called – well, provisionally, of course – *Previously Loved*. It's set in a vintage fashion shop.'

'Sounds like more my kind of book. My husband's the crime fan. He loved Mark's books.'

'Mark would have hated it. He called romance "clit lit". Said it was just masturbatory fantasies for middle-aged women.' Maria flicked a crumb off the table. Sniffed. 'Anyway, he's dead now, isn't he, so his opinion doesn't count anymore. What did you want to ask me about?'

Kat took out the printout of the cover for *The Guilty Party* and handed it to Maria.

'I want you to look at this.'

Maria glanced at it. 'And?'

'Read the review on the bottom edge. It's a bit cropped but you can still make it out.'

Kat watched as Maria returned her gaze to the printout. The top edge of the sheet started trembling as her eyes flicked left and right. Slowly she handed the paper back to Kat. She smiled resignedly. 'Was that you calling me earlier?'

'Yes. From a pay-as-you-go phone I found in Justin Davy's home studio. I think he saw you just before or just after you killed Mark. He was blackmailing you, wasn't he?'

Maria sighed heavily. Her body seemed to collapse in on itself. She hung her head for a few seconds before lifting her gaze back to Kat.

'Seven years ago, I got a call from a journalist called Dorothy Russell. She told me Mark was a rapist.' She coughed. Took a sip of her water. 'Correction – a *serial* rapist. I was in shock. I denied it. Told her never to contact me again, or words to that effect. But I did some discreet enquiring of my own and I found it was all true, if not something of an open secret in certain quarters. I told Mark I was disgusted. That he was a criminal. I said he had to stop and turn himself in. You know what he did, Kat?'

'What?'

'He laughed in my face. Literally stood in front of me and laughed. He said I didn't have evidence that would stand up in a pub, let alone a court of law. So I asked for a divorce.'

'It wasn't amicable at all, was it?'

Maria laughed bitterly. 'Amicable? Have you met Sir Anthony Bone? The man doesn't know the meaning of the word. He more or less coerced me into signing the agreement. It stipulated a large financial settlement, which I needed to be able to carry on writing and running the festival. We were having terrible trouble, and this was even before Covid.' She wiped her forehead with her hand, then frowned and ran her palm across the table. 'I had to stay silent about Mark's crimes but continue inviting him to speak at *Criminal Herts*. Plus, if I ever went public, I'd forfeit the money and Bone would hit me with other legal penalties including an immediate multimillion-pound libel suit. My only, *tiny* measure of revenge was to boot Mark off any of the top spots. I'm not proud of what I did, Kat. Not at all. Staying silent like that? It was a betrayal of all those poor women.'

'So why did you change your mind after all that time?'

'Because there's just been so much stuff in the press this year, and I realised I couldn't carry on. I wasn't prepared to keep his disgusting secret any longer. Even if it meant legal sanctions from Sir Anthony Bone. I'd been complicit in his crimes. Knowing he was about to give yet another smug interview at my festival, all the while probably covering up even more rapes, I just felt sick. I had to make it all stop. That day, I went to see Mark in the green room and I told him it was over. Either he handed himself into the police literally right then or I would expose him onstage at the festival.

'Well, guess what? Mark laughed at me. Again. He told me I was being emotional, a typical woman. And in case I didn't remember, I'd signed a legally binding document. He turned his back on me, Kat, and he told me to get out. Then he laughed again and he said – and I'll remember these words for the rest of my life – "Actually, no, open my champagne and then get out. Go back to your clit lit."

'And a red mist descended over me. I literally could see my own blood pulsing in my eyes. I didn't think, I just picked up the bottle and smashed it down on his head. He slumped sideways and then I dragged the beer bucket over, took the bottles out and pushed his head down into it. When I was sure he was dead, I lifted him out and dragged him on to the floor. I walkie-talkied Bella to check on him then climbed into the chest. I thought she'd leave via the door, unlocking it, so I could leave shortly afterwards. But the silly girl went back out the way she'd come in.'

That sounded a bit too slick to Kat's trained ear.

'How did you get into the chest? It was locked when I checked it.'

Maria frowned. Hesitated. A tell.

'I had a key. I locked the chest after I left the green room.'

'So it wasn't a red mist thing at all,' Kat said. 'If you took a key with you, you must have been intending to hide in the chest. It was premeditated.'

'No! I got muddled. I was in shock. I remember now. The chest was unlocked in the first place.'

'So how did it end up locked after you'd left?'

Maria's eyes were flicking left and right, and up at the ceiling, as if she thought another providential hatch would appear in her own ceiling.

'I think there was a key on the windowsill. Yes! I tried it on the off-chance and it fitted the lock.'

Kat was sure now that Maria was lying, trying to stay one step ahead of her own story.

'Where is it now?'

'Where is what now?'

'The key, Maria,' Kat said patiently.

'Oh. I . . . I dropped it down a drain. I don't remember where.'

'How did you know about the ceiling hatch? That was pretty convenient for you when your first plan didn't pan out. And why didn't you go out that way in the first place, rather than hiding in the chest where you might be discovered?'

Maria paused. Her eyes drifted away. A tell. Kat was sure what came out of her mouth next would be a lie.

'It was on the plans. I found them once when I was looking for a spot to do an escape room. But it was much harder to get out that way, with the water bucket. My original plan was much easier.'

'What did you do with the water?'

'I tipped it into the ficus,' she answered immediately.

Back to the truth.

'And the beer bucket?'

'I took it up into the ceiling space with me. I waited for fifteen minutes, then came down into another empty room and took it out to the beer tent.'

'Why did you kill Justin?'

'You're right. He *was* blackmailing me. He saw me going into the green room and he waited because he wanted a drink with Mark. But when I didn't come out, he got suspicious. Once the news broke that Mark was dead, Justin came to see me. Told me he wanted half a million pounds or he'd go to the police. I agreed to meet him and I took a knife from my kitchen and I stabbed him.'

'Where's the knife?'

'Gone. You'll never find it.'

Kat tilted her head. 'You never know. We might get lucky.'

'I doubt it.'

'I do have one more question,' Kat said. 'Why did you push the little table with the champagne bucket against the armchair? If you'd put it to one side, I might never have realised he'd been murdered.'

Maria shrugged. 'Have you ever killed someone, Kat?'

'No.'

'I freaked out. I was hyperventilating. I felt sick. I was in a blind panic. Maybe I just tried to tidy up after myself. I don't know. I felt like I was losing my mind.'

So that was it. The random action a woman barely able to think straight, unable to comprehend the horror of what she'd just done. And maybe just the hint of a possible defence strategy? It might work for the first murder, but the second? No. That had been premeditated. No jury would buy a temporary insanity plea from a woman who'd stabbed a man to death with a kitchen knife she'd brought with her to a prearranged meeting.

'Is there anything else you want to tell me, Maria?'

'No. I think that pretty much covers it.'

'So, just to confirm, you're telling me that you murdered Mark Swift and Justin Davy.'

'I am.'

'OK, thank you for your honesty. Could you just wait there while I make a quick call?'

Kat called Fez and learned the warrant was ready.

Then she stood and arrested Maria.

Chapter Sixty-Six

Maria insisted on a lawyer as soon as she was read her rights by Julia Myles, the custody sergeant.

'And it won't be a legal aid one, either,' she called over her shoulder before striding off to the cells.

'Lady's got balls,' Julia said.

Kat nodded. Fearing the worst.

As she entered MCU, everyone burst into applause. Usually, Kat was happy to accept her colleagues' congratulations. But today felt different. She wasn't proud of having arrested Maria. She didn't feel like she'd taken a dangerous individual off the streets. She'd done her job and that was all. The triumph was bittersweet at best. And why, given Maria had made a full confession, had she lied about how she'd escaped from the green room? Had someone helped her?

No time for that now. The PACE clock was ticking.

She sat at her desk and began the laborious job of completing the first in a mountain of required documents. Her eyes glazing immediately, she changed her mind. There was another task that would give her immense pleasure.

She called her contact at the Met.

'Kat. You all right? We got your crime scene secured. Bloody hell, we're going to be busy for weeks on this, but you came through for us. What can I do to help?'

'There's a solicitor, name of Sir Anthony Bone. His offices are in Golden Square in Soho.'

'OK. And . . .'

'He acted for Mark Swift. I have a phone recording of him offering a bribe to a rape victim—'

'One of Swift's?'

'Yes. And on the recording he makes a threat of violence against her.'

'Right, send everything you have across to me. I'll run it past my guv'nor. We'll give him a tug for bribery and possibly perverting the course of justice. Whatever else we can come up with. Maybe even conspiracy to rape. I owe you, Kat. Next time you're in town, give me a bell. I'll buy you a drink and a meal out.'

'Thanks, I will.'

She put her phone away and allowed herself a brief smile of satisfaction. Did Sirs get to keep their knighthoods if they were banged up?

'Kat who got the cream, eh?'

She looked up as Carve-up's mocking tone spoiled her brief good mood. He was sporting a new suit in a soft grey and a bright pink tie.

'I suppose congratulations are in order, DS Ballantyne,' he said. 'Another one I can move to the solved column. I tell you, those bloody spreadsheets will be the death of me.'

Was Carve-up going for some matey banter? Unbelievable. With a shudder of disgust, she found she could trace a direct line between Mark Swift and the man in front of her. The one-time member of a group of bent coppers calling themselves 'the

Three Musketeers', who years ago used to extort sex workers in Middlehampton.

She forced herself to meet his half-mocking gaze. 'Swift was a serial rapist, Stu. I hate them as much as I hate murderers. In fact, you know what? Sometimes I can understand murderers. But rapists?' She glared up at him. Hard. 'They're just evil.'

Either he missed the reference to his own sex crimes or he didn't care. He smirked.

'Someone's halo appears to be slipping. I thought you were all about justice for all and nobody deserves to be murdered?'

'I do think that,' she said, breathing hard. 'I think *all* criminals should face justice for their crimes.'

Did he understand her this time? He looked away, just for a moment. And she caught it. A flash of guilt that sparked behind his eyes and disappeared just as quickly.

'Yes, well, finish up your paperwork. And don't screw it up.'

She bent her head to avoid swearing at him.

'Hey, Kat?'

She looked up again. It was Tom. He was smiling. 'Tomski! You look happy. What have you got for me?'

'You won't believe this. I found a picture of Maria Sheriff carrying a plastic bucket into the beer tent at 11.23 a.m. branded with the festival caterer's logo. *Bread and Circuses*.'

'Amazing, Tomski! I knew you could do it. How, though? You can't have struck lucky with a punter so quickly.'

He shook his head. 'The festival had an official photographer. I called her. She said she was there the entire time. All day, every day. She reckoned she'd taken close to five thousand pictures. And one of them had Maria in the background. Twenty-seven minutes after Bella reported Mark dead.'

'But how the hell did you find it if there were so many?'

'Fez has a mate in Birmingham who's got access to their facial recognition software. I put in the faces of all our persons of interest as reference images and uploaded the pictures the photographer took. The longest bit was waiting for them all to load. After that it took eight minutes.'

Kat sighed. 'Brilliant work, Tomski. Honestly. It's so good to have you back.'

'Boss?'

Kat turned, still smiling. It was Leah.

'Maria Sheriff's lawyer's here. Guess who?'

Kat barely needed time to think before answering. 'Beth Sharpe?'

'In one. They're ready to go. Interview room two.'

'Thanks, Leah. We'll do this together. Make it an all-woman affair, eh?'

Kat gathered her papers and headed towards the interview room. What would Middlehampton's best and most expensive criminal defence solicitor have advised her client?

Chapter Sixty-Seven

Beth Sharpe had represented rapists. Kat and Leah had arrested them. Maria Sheriff had protected one, then murdered him. Four women linked by a disgusting, monstrous crime, but facing off against each other.

It felt wrong to Kat. Why weren't they all on the same side of the table? She pushed the thought away. Maybe Dorothy Russell would have the answer. Right now she had a job to do. And Maria had already confessed to the two murders. Now to make it official.

Kat nodded to Leah. Leah switched on the recorder. Once its nails-down-a-blackboard screech petered out, Kat began the official caution.

'Maria Sheriff, you have been arrested on suspicion of the murders of Mark Swift and Justin Davy.'

When she'd finished and everybody had identified themselves, she took a moment to compose herself and then looked at Maria. Not smiling, but not hostile either. Even with the worst scumbags, which Maria most certainly wasn't, she tried to keep her face neutral. Sometimes people were just so relieved it was all finally over, they took the smallest sign of friendship as an on-switch to start pouring out their confession.

'Maria, did you kill Mark Swift?'

Maria picked a speck of lint off the sleeve of her grey police-issue sweatshirt. Looked up at Kat.

'No.'

Kat felt a pang of disappointment. But she wasn't surprised. What else would an expensive and experienced criminal defence solicitor like Beth Sharpe do but advise her client to deny everything?

'And did you kill Justin Davy.'

The briefest of pauses.

'No.'

'At your house you told me you murdered both men. Why are you denying it now?'

'On the advice of my legal representative, I decline to answer that question.'

'We found a pair of Converse trainers in a rubbish bin. The right one has Justin Davy's blood on the sole, and once they come back from the lab we will find your DNA on the inside. Can you explain that?'

Maria maintained her level stare. Not even a blink. God, she was a cool one.

'On the advice of my legal representative, I decline to answer that question.'

'Why was your number on a pay-as-you-go phone we found in Justin Davy's studio?'

'On the advice of my legal representative, I decline to answer that question.'

With a sinking feeling, Kat saw how the interview was going to go. But she had to persevere. Perhaps she'd be able to pierce Maria's defences.

'How would you react, Maria, if I told you we found a printed-out mock-up of a book cover in Justin Davy's studio that contained the words "If I'm dead, talk to Maria Sheriff"?'

Once again, Maria recited the stock answer Beth had prescribed.

Kat continued. 'We have a photograph of you carrying a large bucket towards the beer tent shortly after Mark Swift was murdered by drowning. Can you explain that?'

The same answer.

'How did you know to hide in the chest inside the green room?'

Again.

'Or escape through the hatch in the ceiling?'

Again.

Kat exhaled quietly through her nose. Didn't want to give Maria the satisfaction of hearing her sigh.

'Did you snap? Is that why you murdered Mark? Did he insult you one too many times? I could understand it if you did. You knew about his crimes. He'd forced you to stay silent through a mixture of financial inducements and threats by his lawyer. If you're worried about Sir Anthony Bone, please don't be. He will shortly be facing criminal charges of his own.'

Nothing beyond the sterile legal non-answer.

'Was Justin Davy blackmailing you? Profiting from his friendship with Mark? That must have made you sick. I watched a video of one of the rapes, Maria. It made me want to cry.'

And there, for the first time, Kat saw it. The briefest flicker of Maria's right eyelid. A tightening of her nostrils. She pressed her lips together as if trying to force whatever words were about to tumble from her lips back down her throat.

Maria huffed in a shallow breath. Opened her mouth. And recited the standard answer.

Kat stared at her notes. Back up at Maria. Then Leah. At Beth. Then Maria again, whose eyes were welling with tears.

As she watched Maria's composure crumble, Kat thought back to her conversation with Venetia Shelby-Hales. Realisation dawned. As clear as a lightning flash.

'Maria, did Mark ever rape you?' she asked softly.

The room was utterly silent. Seconds ticked by. Kat made eye contact with Beth. She stared back. Not hostile, not friendly. A steady professional gaze, shorn of emotion, free of significance. She was there to do her job, just as Kat was, and she was doing it right now.

Maria swallowed. And very slowly, a tear overspilled her left eyelid and tracked slowly down her cheek.

'On the . . .' Her breath hitched. She swallowed. Snatched a thready breath. 'On the advice of my legal representative, I . . . I decline to answer that question.'

Then she bent her head and sobbed silently. Her shoulders heaving, jerking, her hands grasping each other, tears plopping down on to the scratched surface of the little table separating them.

Kat knew. Leah knew. Beth knew. Maria hadn't just murdered *a* rapist. She'd murdered *her* rapist. She'd kept quiet for all those years. Borne the feelings of shame, disgust and self-loathing. Until one day, his endless provocations and her knowledge of his continuing crimes – and her own complicity – had become too much to bear. Was it revenge after all? Or had she been telling the truth when she'd confessed to Kat in her kitchen? It didn't matter now. Kat had achieved what she'd set out to do. She'd broken through the other woman's defences. But faced with what she'd uncovered, she felt no pleasure.

'Interview terminated.'

Kat stood. Let the CPS have their way with it. She was done. She led Leah out of the interview room.

'I'm going home. I feel dirty, you know? Sullied. I need a shower and I need to see my family.'

Leah nodded. She looked close to tears.

'How come we're charging her and not him, Kat? It's not right. And please don't tell me it's because he's already dead.'

Kat sighed now. A deep, drawn-out exhalation in which she felt some of the cloying, depressing weight of the previous twenty minutes leave her body.

'It's simple, mate. Maria committed two murders. It's our duty. I don't always like it, but nobody said policing was about doing what we like.'

'Yeah, but look at what Swift did.' Leah leaned closer and dropped her voice to a whisper. 'She should get a medal.'

Kat shook her head sadly. 'Finish up then go home to Emily. Cook something nice or go to the pub. Have a few drinks. Or a lot. Take tomorrow off. I'll see you on Monday.'

Leah nodded. 'OK. Thanks, Kat.'

Kat smiled. Reached out and held Leah by the shoulders.

'It'll be fine.'

Then she patted her pocket to check on her car keys and headed home.

Chapter Sixty-Eight

Kat opened her front door. Riley's newly deep voice blared down the hallway. 'Hi, Mum! You hungry? I'm making macaroni cheese.'

'Hi, lovely. Just let me get my shoes off and dump my stuff.'

Smiling for the first time in what felt like days, Kat pulled her boots off, hooked her bag over the newel post and went to find Riley and Van.

'Hey, love,' Van said, rising from his chair to give her a kiss.

'Hug, please,' she said, folding herself inside his arms. 'You smell nice.'

'Why, thank you. You do, too.'

She pulled back, eyed him sceptically. 'I smell like a copshop interview room.'

'Yeah . . . but in a nice way.'

'Hey, Mum, come and have a taste,' Riley said, holding out a wooden spoon coated in a creamy yellow sauce.

She joined him at the cooker and tasted the sauce. Rich, peppery, and tangy with sharp Cheddar.

'Wow, that is amazing. I can't wait.' Then she pulled him in for a kiss, planting a smacker on his cheek, which had been sprouting soft bristles for a while now. 'I love you, Riley.'

'I love you too, Mum,' he said, wriggling in her arms. 'But why are you acting all weird?'

She sighed.

'Work.'

'Is the case dragging on? What do you call them? A runner?'

'No. As a matter of fact I arrested the murderer today. She's in a cell at Jubilee Place.'

'She?'

'Mm-hmm. Look, I do want to talk to you about it' – she turned to Van – 'to both of you. But I really need a shower. I'll be down in a little while.'

Kat took her time. She turned the temperature up, scrubbed her body with a wash mitt until her skin tingled. Washed her hair, used conditioner, rinsed it, and then just stood there under the burning water, head back.

Alone with her feelings, she returned to the interview with Maria, and the conversation at her house before her arrest. Maria had lied twice about how she'd managed to escape from the green room. She must have had help. The hatch was painted along the cracks, after all. She couldn't have done that after she'd left, could she? But who?

The answer presented itself immediately: Ernie, the caretaker.

Why, though? Had he stumbled in on her? But he was an ex-cop. Why had he helped her instead of reporting her? Kat remained under the water, turning those questions over and over in her head, until the water started to cool.

She used her favourite body lotion, applied moisturiser, combed her hair out and fixed it in a claw clip. And then dressed in a loose white broderie anglaise dress.

Downstairs again, she gratefully accepted the glass of white wine Van handed her. He gave her an appreciative look.

'Wow. You should have long days in the office on a Saturday more often.'

She drank some of the wine. Felt the cold hit and then the relaxing warmth as the alcohol found its way to her brain.

Riley served up bowls of macaroni cheese, and as they ate, Kat felt some of the tension start to leave her. She looked at her son. He had been talking about girls a lot recently. She wasn't sure if he had a girlfriend. His friendships sounded more like the kind of intense relationships she'd had at his age. Maybe he had a boyfriend, then? She gave a mental shrug. It didn't matter. What *was* important was that he was a good and loving person for whoever he went out with.

She looked at each of them in turn.

'I need to tell you about the case,' she said. 'It was awful. I can't say certain things now but you'll learn soon enough. But it turns out things were a lot more complicated than I first thought. Someone involved was a very evil man. The worst kind, really. And I . . . I just hope, Riley, that you never think of women and girls like they're just things. You remember those photos your friend put into your group chat? What was his name, Luke Tockley?'

Riley's eyebrows shot up and he opened his mouth to protest. 'Mum, what the actual? We talked about that. I would never!'

Kat stretched out a hand and grabbed his. Squeezed it hard.

'Sorry, sorry, my lovely boy, I know you don't. But sometimes boys go through phases and it's all "ho" this and "sket" that, isn't it?'

He narrowed his eyes. 'This is about Swift, isn't it? I *told* you! I *said*, didn't I? Well, I *am* glad he's dead. Maybe some boys do say stuff like that – girls, too, actually. But *I* don't, and nor do my mates.'

'I know, honey. I'm sorry. I just needed to get it off my chest. There's probably going to be a lot about this in the media, social especially. Just try to stay out of it. For me?'

'OK.' He forked another huge mouthful of macaroni cheese in. Spoke around it. 'Don't let it get to you, Mum. You were just doing your job.'

Kat swallowed hard against the lump that had formed in her throat. Tried to clear it with the rest of her wine.

After loading the dishwasher, she clipped Smokey on to his lead and took him out. The shower, and the air-clearing conversation over dinner, had helped. She thought a bracing hour in the fields around Stocks Green would disperse the last of her sadness. And maybe a chat with Barrie.

They reached The Gallops as the sun was just starting its dip behind the distant hills. She let Smokey off and he bounded away, yelping with joy, heading like a bullet into the golden-headed wheat.

A black and white lurcher emerged from a gap in the hedge fifty yards further down the track. Lois lifted her long nose and sniffed the air, then loped into the wheat to join Smokey.

Kat's friend, Barrie, appeared a few moments later, his thistledown hair a golden corona in the slanting sunlight. He waved and she held a hand high in greeting. When he reached her, he nodded towards the centre of the field.

'They'll be a while yet. Liquorice Allsort, Skip?'

He held out a crumpled white paper bag. She spread the mouth wide and peered in. Spotted her favourite, a pink aniseed jelly coated in tiny, crunchy bobbles.

'How are you, Barrie?'

'Good. Good. The old arthritis is a pain, literally, but my tablets do a pretty good job. How about you?'

'Closed the case today.'

He nodded. 'Good for you. Who was it then?'

'His ex-wife. Well, one of them.'

He nodded again. 'Ninety-nine times out of a hundred, that's it, isn't it, Skip?'

'Yes, but he was a serial rapist, Barrie. She found out and he forced her into keeping quiet about it.' She swallowed the sweet. 'One thing's bothering me, though. I figured out almost everything about it except how she knew what to do to escape unseen. And the only thing I can think of is she had help.'

'An accomplice, you mean?'

'I'm not sure. Look, I know you're friends, so please don't take this the wrong way, but do you think there's any way Ernie could have helped her? I know he was job, but humour me.'

She'd been expecting Barrie to bridle at the insinuation that his friend might be an accessory to murder. Maybe reply stiffly that he'd expected better of her. But his response surprised her.

He reached into the bag and extracted another sweet. Put it into his mouth and chewed, his brow furrowing with deep grooves that reminded Kat of The Gallops when the field was newly ploughed.

'Ernie is a lovely man. Something happened. A family tragedy. It changed his whole life. I can't say more but you should go and talk to him, Skip. If you really want to know.'

He lifted his chin and emitted a piercing whistle. Lois came bounding out of the field and hurtled up to him. He scratched her behind the ears before putting her lead back on.

'I'll see you next time, Skip.'

Kat watched him go. Smokey ran after Lois for twenty yards or so then trotted back. He sat, and looked up at Kat with that winky eye, as if to say, *Was it something I said?*

But it wasn't.

It was something Barrie had said.

Chapter Sixty-Nine

Kat knocked on Ernie's front door, gleaming white uPVC with two stained-glass panels. Roses and ivy.

As she waited, she realised the heat had disappeared. It was cool. She shivered. A shadow appeared behind the glass.

The door opened.

'Hello, Ernie. Can I come in, please?'

He smiled. 'Of course. Nice to see you, Kat. I was just making tea. Want a cup?'

'Yes, please.'

He led her into a neat sitting room.

A young woman sat watching a gameshow on TV. Her hands were occupied with a piece of crochet, mechanically adding stitches while her gaze never left the TV screen.

Ernie gestured towards her. 'This is Heather.'

'Hi, Heather,' Kat said.

'Hi,' the woman answered, not looking away from the shrieking contestants and gurning host.

'Let's go into the kitchen,' Ernie said. 'Heather gets a little agitated if people talk over her programmes.'

He made a pot of tea, keeping up a flow of inconsequential chatter about the weather, his friendship with Barrie, the Eels' new manager. Innocuous subjects Kat recognised for what they were.

An attempt to stave off something more consequential. It happened with villains. Witnesses, too. And victims. If they could just keep talking, they wouldn't have to face the truth.

Tea poured, they sat facing each other across the table.

Ernie blew across the surface of his tea and sipped cautiously. 'So, what brings you to my humble abode?'

'We arrested Maria Sheriff today. She denied her guilt, then went no comment, but there's forensic evidence that'll convict her for sure.'

'Well, that's a surprise . . . but well done, you. Can't have been easy.'

'No, it wasn't. But there's something I wanted to ask you about.'

He smiled easily. Drank some more tea.

'Ask away, then.'

'I know how she did it, Ernie. She hid in the Jacobean chest and escaped through a hatch in the ceiling.'

He frowned. It was a good act, she'd give him that.

'Hatch? I've been the caretaker there for years and I never knew about a hatch. And I told you, I always thought the chest was locked.'

'She must have had help, Ernie. It's the only way it makes sense. And I'm wondering whether it was you.'

'Me? Why would I help a murderer escape justice?'

'That's what I've been wondering, too.' Kat thought about Barrie's words from earlier. *A family tragedy*. And the man Maria Sheriff had murdered. 'Ernie, did something happen to Heather?'

Ernie had been on the point of drinking some more tea. But his hand stilled in mid-air. Slowly he replaced the cup in the saucer with a tiny clink.

'Barrie called me,' he said. 'Said you were a smart young woman. That you'd figured it out. He said you were sound, too.

High praise coming from him. So I want to tell you a story, if you'll listen?'

'Of course I'll listen.'

He straightened in his chair, put his hands flat on the table.

'Once, there was a clever, ambitious, outgoing, beautiful young girl. She'd just graduated from university, York, with a degree in English. She temped for a while before she landed her dream job at a publishing company. Her job was author relations, and she loved meeting all these famous writers. Then, one day, she met a man who was the most famous writer of all. Only he was a truly evil man. And he' – Ernie dropped his gaze to his hands, before returning his gaze to Kat – 'he raped the young woman. She was too scared, too ashamed to report it. Even though her dad pleaded with her, she wouldn't be moved. She said she'd rather kill herself. She had to leave her job. Then she stopped going out. Kept having panic attacks. He had to leave his job for one with easier hours so he could care for her. And every day, when he looked at her, all he could see was that monster.

'The dad harboured thoughts of revenge, and even found a way to get close to the monster, but there was no way he could risk going to prison when his daughter needed him. Even though she loved her daughter, his wife eventually tired of his obsession and divorced him. Then, one day, at work, a woman rushed out of a room and said *she* had killed the monster. She wanted to confess to the police, but he persuaded her not to. He told her how she could make it so difficult to solve the crime that she would get away with it. To go back into the room and lock the door again from the inside. Then lock the chest she'd hidden in with a key he gave her and leave through a trapdoor in the ceiling, which he'd cover up later. And then the woman killed another man. And the dad started to wonder if he'd done the right thing after all, but by then it was too late.'

He swallowed the last of his tea. Set it back down.

Kat let out a breath. She knuckled a tear out of her eye.

'Ernie, I'm so sorry. For you and for Heather.'

'Why?' he said, quirking his mouth to one side. 'That was just a story, Kat. Heather and I are fine.'

She said nothing for a very long time. Then she stood up.

'Thanks for telling me the story, Ernie. I'll see myself out.'

Back on the street again, she looked up into the cloudless sky. Had she just crossed a line? Ernie had as good as admitted he'd helped Maria Sheriff escape the green room. He was an accessory to murder. Or had he only done what he'd said he'd done? Told her a story? A very sad story, in which a father cared for his daughter after a terrible crime, before making an error of judgement?

She could look for evidence. She might even find some. Then she could go back and arrest him. He might get convicted and sent down. And then who would care for Heather? She'd be a victim twice over.

Kat shook her head. She'd already made her decision. She'd live with it. Life was life. Stories were stories.

She turned away from the front door with its pretty, stained-glass panels. Thought maybe she was still on the side of the angels.

Just.

Epilogue

Kat woke to the sun streaming in through a gap in the curtains. Beside her, Van was snoring lightly.

She dressed silently and slipped out of the bedroom, closing the door softly behind her. She ate a quick breakfast, walked Smokey, then drove up to Middlehampton General.

It took twenty minutes and a repeated story about her concern for a colleague, but eventually she found herself sitting opposite a consultant neurologist in her office.

'You're enquiring about one of our patients, is that right?' the doctor asked.

'He's a colleague of mine. My bagman, actually. Tom Gray?'

'Oh, yes,' the doctor said, her stern face breaking into a wide smile. 'A real success story. He's making such fantastic progress.'

Kat nodded. Tried to shape her mouth into a smile. Fell somewhat short.

'Yeah, it is great. Only, I've noticed he's been showing some—' She looked down at her intertwined fingers, carefully unknotted them. 'Well, I don't know how to put this in the correct terms . . .'

The doctor smiled again. 'Just tell me plainly. What's going on?'

'He's being stroppy, argumentative. Making sarcastic remarks.'

'Was he like this before?'

Kat cast her mind back to before Will Paxton's murderous attack. 'Maybe. But much more jokingly, you know? And he's started drinking.'

'Well, he was probably missing it after spending all that time in this place. I need a big gin and tonic after a single shift.'

'No, that's the point! He gave up while he was still a student.'

'I see. Is he drinking heavily? At inappropriate times? Is it affecting his behaviour or his performance?'

'Not really. I mean – no.'

The doctor nodded. 'Perhaps he just decided life's too short. It happens.'

'Maybe. Look, I just wondered, is there any way he could have, I don't know, been changed by the coma?'

'You must know, I can't discuss individual patients. But here's what I *can* tell you. A coma is a brain injury. Whether it's the result of trauma or medically induced, it's a significant neurological event. People who have suffered brain injuries can experience or exhibit all kinds of symptoms, from anxiety or depression to changes in their behaviour. Increased risk-taking, for example.'

'Is that what's happening to Tom?'

'It varies hugely from patient to patient. Just look after Tom as you would any of your subordinates – I get the sense you're a good manager. And if you're genuinely worried, come and talk to me again. Or, better yet, get Tom to come in. But try not to worry too much. Tom's still very early into his recovery. Things may well feel strange for him, too, for a while. But I'm sure they'll settle down eventually.'

Kat sighed out a breath. It was reassuring, just to get it off her chest. She thanked the doctor and made her way back through the maze of corridors to her car.

She had another visit to make.

◆ ◆ ◆

Kat stuck the key in the ignition. Then her phone rang. Glancing at the screen her pulse doubled.

'Hi, Iris. I'd almost given up hope.'

'Oh, you should never do that, Kat. Aristotle said, "Patience is bitter, but its fruit is sweet."'

Kat smiled. Was this it? 'Does that mean you have something sweet for me, Iris?'

'Yes! I do. You remember my private investigator?'

'Enrique? Of course. How's his whiplash?'

'Better, I assume, although he's likely to be stiff for a while. These injuries can be stubborn. So his doctor told me. I'm paying for him to go private. The healthcare system in the Bahamas struggles and I want the best for him.'

'That's very you, Iris.'

'Anyway, you were right. The person who arranged the transfer of the fifty thousand pounds *was* Suzanne Watkins. Is that helpful?'

Kat looked down at her right hand, clenched into a fist on her thigh. Her father's dog-loyal PA, who'd once offered the young Kathryn Morton sweets from a big glass jar on her desk, was hers.

'Oh, Iris, you have no idea. Thank you so much.'

After saying goodbye to Iris, Kat immediately called another number.

'Hello, who is this please?'

'Hi, Suzy, it's Kat.'

Kat's pulse was racing.

Kat caught the slight hesitation before Suzy spoke again.

'Oh! Kat! Hi. How are you? Is this a social call?'

'I'm afraid not. I just found out the identity of the person who authorised the bank transfer from the Swiss account.' She heard the

386

click as Suzy's lips parted with the start of a lie. 'It wasn't my dad, it was you. Please don't bother denying it. I know, Suzy. I bloody *know*! Out of your bonkers sense of loyalty, you helped him fit me up on a corruption charge to stop me looking into his affairs.'

Kat listened to Suzy's breath catch. The line was so clear, she could have been sitting in the passenger seat.

'What do you want?' Suzy asked in a quiet little voice.

Kat readied herself to spring the trap.

'I thought I wanted my dad to fire you. I could have insisted on it, as my price for not turning you both over to the anti-bribery team.'

'No, you can't. I love my job! Please don't, Kat. I'll do anything.'

Kat nodded with quiet satisfaction. Suzy had sprung the trap for her.

'I said I *thought* that's what I wanted, Suzy. But I've changed my mind. What I actually want is information. A little bit now, maybe more later on. Tell me, does my father use a London lawyer called Sir Anthony Bone?'

'I . . . I can't, Kat. Colin would kill me if he found out I'd told you.'

'And I'll arrest you if you don't. Does he?'

Suzy said nothing. Kat waited her out. She checked the dashboard display. The temperature was dropping. Suzy cleared her throat.

'Sometimes,' she whispered. 'Not always. But for the really important stuff.'

'Thanks. We'll speak again.'

She ended the call. The first with her new confidential informant. But not the last.

Traffic was light as Kat drove to the cemetery in Hampton Hill.

She indicated left and pulled into the access road. Once she'd parked, she consulted her handwritten notes and set off towards a distant corner.

Five minutes later, she stood in front of a simple black granite gravestone.

The text read:

Jo Morris

1990–2024

Beloved wife and daughter.

Taken too soon.

'He will wipe away every tear from their eyes, and
death shall be no more, neither shall there be mourning,
nor crying, nor pain anymore, for the former things
have passed away.'

Revelation 21:4

Kat knelt. Rested her palms on her thighs. Took the bunch of white carnations she was carrying and laid them in front of the headstone.

'Hey, Jo. I'm Kat, your half-sister. We never got to talk when you were alive and now it's too late. You can't have been all bad. But that poor girl killed herself because of what you did, and I wish I knew why you hurt her so much at school. Anyway, I just wanted to come to see you. I might come again. I've been working this really bad case, but it's over now.'

She got up, pushing off the springy grass – burnt, like every other patch in Middlehampton, to a dry, beige crisp.

Back in her car, she sat for a moment, the door open. Thinking.

She pulled out her phone and called Reuben Starling. As well as being Middlehampton's MP, Reuben was Jo's uncle.

'Kat? Hello. What can I do for you?'

'I was wondering whether you had any information about the crash that killed your brother and his wife.'

There was a long pause.

'I do, yes. Do you want to come by the house and collect it? There's quite a lot, I'm afraid.'

'Yes, please. I'll take whatever you have.'

'OK. Good. Yes, good. I'll put it all together for you. See you shortly.'

Kat detoured to Reuben's house to collect the material – four file boxes stuffed with documents – and then headed home.

She was already planning how to reorganise her little home office.

Those walls would soon be covered again.

AUTHOR'S NOTE

There comes a point in every crime writer's career when they consider that classic genre convention – or trope, if you prefer – the locked room mystery. It's a rite of passage, I guess. Just as horror writers write a 'buried alive' story.

This particular form of murder mystery has its roots in the Golden Age of crime fiction, at the heart of which stands a kind-faced colossus with a penchant for poison, Agatha Christie. It's been updated time and again, changing and twisting, much like the plots of the books we all, as writers and readers, enjoy.

The appeal of this particular mechanic, to use Amy Swales's word, lies in its flummoxing nature. Yes, every murder story presents the reader, and the fictional detective investigating it, with a puzzle. Who did it? Why did they do it? But the locked room mystery – or perhaps we should create a suitably police-y acronym and call it the LRM – adds a third, frustrating, question. *How* did they do it? Or even, how the *hell* did they do it?

Back in the day, LRM writers invented all kinds of methods to separate the murderer from their victim by a locked door. My favourite is a cuckoo clock to whose occupant's beak the murderer had glued a poisoned needle. It sprang out at noon and did for the victim, who liked to stand in the exact same spot every day to enjoy a cup of tea. I doubt the modern reader would be content with anything quite so rococo. Instead, the contemporary author – or, to be more exact, the author of a contemporary crime thriller – must perforce engineer something the reader can't simply roll their eyes at, muttering, 'well that would never happen'.

I had the idea for this book as I strolled around the garden of the Old Swan Hotel, venue for the crime-writing festival everybody refers to, simply, as 'Harrogate'. Wouldn't it be cool, I thought, to set a murder story at a crime-writing festival? Cooler, still, a story that paid homage to Agatha Christie herself, who in 1926 disappeared for eleven days to the Old Swan?

So, the idea for *my* LRM was born. But then I had the problem I would be setting my readers. How on earth *do* you murder somebody and leave the corpse inside a locked room while you escape, unseen and undetected?

I decided I wanted the murderer to commit their crime in person. To be there, inside the green room with Mark Swift. It felt more real, and also more challenging. As a working solution, I settled on an idea that, even as I was writing the first draft, I decided fell woefully short of the standard readers would expect. A secret passageway. Really? In the end it became a dead end, pun intended, for Kat. She, like I, had to think harder.

I hope you enjoyed the solution I created. I don't think Kat did. Though it led to Ernie the caretaker's involvement, a last-minute development I honestly did not see coming until I was typing out that final conversation between him and Kat.

When I first pitched the LRM to my editor, Victoria Pepe, she frowned, just a little (she's very kind), and said, 'It sounds a little cosy.' Which is definitely not Kat-land. That sent me off into more thinking, not about the mechanic, but the victim and the way I'd tell the story.

Initially, I pictured Mark Swift as the traditional 'innocent' victim. Wrong place, wrong time. But as I set about constructing the plot, the horrific truth about him emerged. Anything less cosy I couldn't imagine. From there, the story really came into its own, pushing Kat hard to consider the relative weight she ought to place on upholding the law versus delivering justice. I felt it, then – a story that would live up to the comment of a nice reviewer on Amazon who said, of an earlier book in the series, 'A traditional whodunnit with a moral dilemma thrown in.'

As to style, and how far to acknowledge what was happening on the page, I had to walk a fine line between a nudge-nudge, 'look what I'm doing' approach and treating the case just like any other. For example, Kat voicing the thought that it was almost as if she and her team were in the middle of one of Mark's own books would have been a step too far. Wouldn't it?

In the end, with gentle prompting from Victoria and my developmental editor, Russel McLean, I did lean in to the craziness of the situation Kat finds herself in and have a couple of colleagues ribbing her about it. I also included a few little Easter eggs for the keen-eyed to spot.

But overall, the mood of the book darkened beyond the initial puzzle of the locked room. A big issue I had to grapple with was public trust in the police. Specifically, the trust of the female half of the population. There have been too many recent cases, which people mention in the book, of police officers being convicted of rape for a story dealing with sexual violence to ignore. I tried to balance the criticisms with the fact that Kat herself and most of her colleagues are decent, honest people, trying against enormous odds to catch criminals.

Finally, people have asked me if I based Mark Swift on a real author. Let me just say this. Me Too wasn't a flash in the pan. It's still relevant. Frighteningly so. Rappers, record producers, billionaires, TV 'personalities', members of royal households, news anchors, cops, retail bosses: these men are everywhere, along with their enablers in the PR, security and legal 'professions'. Still committing their crimes and still, frighteningly, believing they are above the law, or beyond its reach. It would be naive to imagine that publishing is immune to the problem. I don't.

Thankfully, and despite the crimes of men like Wayne Couzens and David Carrick, we do, still, have dedicated police officers, some of whom I'm proud to call my friends, who chase these men down, arrest and charge them.

Good.

Andy Maslen,
Salisbury, October 2024

ACKNOWLEDGEMENTS

I want to thank you for buying this book. I hope you enjoyed it.

As an author is only part of the team of people who make a book the best it can be, this is my chance to thank the people on my team.

For their patience, professionalism and support, the fabulous publishing team at Thomas & Mercer, led by Eoin Purcell and Sammia Hamer. I want to thank Sammia specifically for her help in developing Fez Mohammed as a three-dimensional character (and for coming up with his nickname). Also, my editor, Victoria Pepe, who, as well as having a sure literary touch and the sort of commercial vision that turns books into bestsellers, I count as a friend. My developmental editor, Russel McLean, is a fiction eagle, able to see an entire plot from his vantage point, but with the visual acuity to spot a clunky phrase from half a mile up. He outdid himself this time with a suggested cut in the first bloody sentence! And lastly (but not leastly), my copyeditor, Jill Sawyer, and proofreader, Gemma Wain, without whom I am sure many of my authorial glitches would have escaped on to the finished page.

Plus the wonderful marketing team including Rebecca Hills and Nicole Wagner. And Dominic Forbes, who, once again, really smashed the brief with another awesome cover design.

For sharing their knowledge and experience of The Job, former and current police officers Andy Booth, Ross Coombs, Jen Gibbons, Neil Lancaster, Sean Memory, Trevor Morgan, Olly Royston, Chris Saunby, Ty Tapper, Sarah Warner and Sam Yeo.

The members of my Facebook Group, The Wolfe Pack, are an incredibly supportive and also helpful bunch of people. Thank you to them, also.

And for being an inspiration and source of love and laughter, and making it all worthwhile, my family: Jo, Rory and Jacob.

Lastly, I want to remember and thank Merlin, our family whippet, who went for his final sleep on the sofa this year after giving us nearly fourteen years of loyalty, friendship and love.

Andy Maslen
Salisbury, 2024

BOOK GROUP QUESTIONS

1. At multiple points throughout *The Lying Man*, Kat finds herself wondering, even agonising over, whether she is doing the right thing by pursuing Mark Swift's killer. After all, as she says herself, he was the real monster.

Do you think she got it right? Did the advent of Justin Davy's death change anything for you?

2. When Kat introduces Fez to Leah, she reacts badly, giving him the cold shoulder.

How did the confrontation between Leah and Fez make you feel? Was she in any way justified, do you think, given what we learn about the reasons for her initial animosity?

3. As this series has progressed, we have learned more and more about DI Stuart 'Carve-up' Carver. He began as an almost comedic character, over-fond of designer suits and his bright red 'penis substitute' in the staff car park. By the end of *The Silent*

Wife, he deliberately sends Kat and Tom into a potentially lethal confrontation with a murder suspect.

Do you think Kat is dealing with him in the best way? She wants to take him down. Should she do it herself, with covert help from her team, or simply report him to the anti-corruption team he sent after her?

4. Kat and Liv seem to have repaired the deep fracture in their relationship caused by Liv deciding to fake her own death and disappear to Bryn Glas farm in Wales. Van still worries about Kat, though – specifically the impact her renewed friendship with Liv could have on her mental health.

Should Kat be worried for herself as well? Is Liv a true friend?

5. Right at the end of the book, Kat discovers that Ernie, the retired cop and Guildhall caretaker, helped Maria to escape unseen. He was the architect of the locked room mystery Kat had to solve. After listening to his heartbreaking story about his daughter, Heather, Kat leaves him, resolving not to take any further action against him.

How did Kat's decision make you feel? Ernie was an accessory to murder, after all.

ABOUT THE AUTHOR

Photo © 2021, Kin Ho

Andy Maslen was born in Nottingham, England. After leaving university with a degree in psychology, he worked in business for thirty years as a copywriter, while also continuing to write poetry and short fiction. In his spare time, he plays blues and jazz guitar. He lives in Wiltshire.

Follow the Author on Amazon

If you enjoyed this book, follow Andy Maslen on Amazon to be notified when the author releases a new book!

To do this, please follow these instructions:

Desktop:

1) Search for the author's name on Amazon or in the Amazon App.
2) Click on the author's name to arrive on their Amazon page.
3) Click the 'Follow' button.

Mobile and Tablet:

1) Search for the author's name on Amazon or in the Amazon App.
2) Click on one of the author's books.
3) Click on the author's name to arrive on their Amazon page.
4) Click the 'Follow' button.

Kindle eReader and Kindle App:

If you enjoyed this book on a Kindle eReader or in the Kindle App, you will find the author 'Follow' button after the last page.

Printed in Great Britain
by Amazon

61509175R00234